Mysteries of Eleusis

MARGARET DOODY

Mysteries of Eleusis

Ἀριστοτέλης καὶ Στέφανος
An Aristotle and Stephanos Novel

arrow books

Published by Arrow in 2006

1 3 5 7 9 10 8 6 4 2

Frist published in the United Kingdom in 2005 by Century
The Random House Group Limited
20 Vauxhall Bridge Road, London, SW1V 2SA

Random House Australia (Pty) Limited
20 Alfred Street, Milsons Point, Sydney,
New South Wales 2061, Australia

Random House New Zealand Limited
18 Poland Road, Glenfield
Auckland 10, New Zealand

Random House South Africa (Pty) Limited
Isle of Houghton, Corner of Boundary Road & Carse O'Gowrie,
Houghton 2198, South Africa

The Random House Group Limited Reg. No. 954009

www.randomhouse.co.uk

A CIP catalogue record for this book is available from the British Library

Papers used by Random House are natural, recyclable products made
from wood grown in sustainable forests. The manufacturing processes
conform to the environmental regulations of the country of origin

ISBN 0-994-46834-4

Typeset by SX Composing DTP, Rayleigh, Essex
Printed and bound in Great Britain by
Bookmarque Ltd, Croydon, Surrey

To
JOANN and JASON BRADLEY
and to their son
AIDAN

who arrived 7 August 2004, while this story was being written, this book is dedicated.

Love and best wishes, now and always.

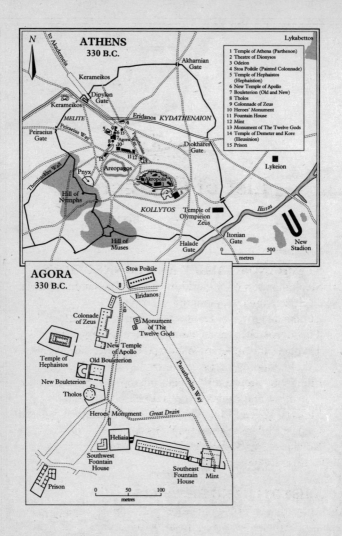

ATHENS
330 B.C.

N

To Akademia

Lykabettos

Akharnian Gate

Kerameikos

Dipylon Gate

Kerameikos

MELITE

Eridanos KYDATHENAION

Peiraeus Gate

Peiraeus Way

Diokhares Gate

Pnyx

Areopagos

Lykeion

Hill of Nymphs

Akropolis

Themistokles Wall

KOLLYTOS

Temple of Olympieion Zeus

Ilissos

Itonian Gate

New Stadion

Halade Gate

Hill of Muses

0   500
metres

1 Temple of Athena (Parthenon)
2 Theatre of Dionysos
3 Odeion
4 Stoa Poikile (Painted Colonnade)
5 Temple of Hephaistos
   (Hephaistion)
6 New Temple of Apollo
7 Bouleterion (Old and New)
8 Tholos
9 Colonnade of Zeus
10 Heroes' Monument
11 Fountain House
12 Mint
13 Monument of The Twelve Gods
14 Temple of Demeter and Kore
   (Eleusinion)
15 Prison

AGORA
330 B.C.

Stoa Poikile

Eridanos

Colonade of Zeus

Monument of The Twelve Gods

Temple of Hephaistos

New Temple of Apollo

Old Boulerion

Panathenian Way

New Boulerion

Tholos

Heroes' Monument   Great Drain

Heliaia

Southwest Fountain House

Southeast Fountain House   Mint

Prison

0   50   100
metres

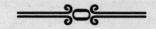

List of Characters

STEPHANOS' FAMILY AND CONNECTIONS

Stephanos son of Nikiarkhos of Kydathenaion: Athenian citizen aged 26; planning marriage

Eunike daughter of Diogeiton: Stephanos' mother

Theodoros: Stephanos' younger brother, age 10

Tryphos: incompetent male slave of Stephanos' household, missing part of a finger

Philemon: Stephanos' jovial cousin, son of Nikiarkhos' brother and Eudoxia (both deceased); age 26

Melissa: Wife of Philemon, blonde and beautiful, age 20

Lykias; Philemon's son by Melissa, age 4

Nousia: slave, Melissa's old nurse, attendant on her and little Lykias

ARISTOTLE AND HIS CIRCLE

Aristotle son of Nikomakhos: philosopher, alien resident of Athens (*metoikos*); head of the Lykeion in Athens, age 56

Pythias daughter of Aristotle, age 6½: philospher's only child by his wife Pythias recently deceased

Herpyllis: handsome female slave who looks after little

Pythias, and takes care of Aristotle, age 23

Phokon: Aristotle's senior male slave

Theophrastos: Aristotle's right-hand man in the Lykeion, adherent of Pythagorean religious philosophy and a devoted scholar of plants; age 40

Demetrios of Phaleron: strikingly beautiful young man, scholar and researcher at the Lykeion, age 20

Hipparkhos of Argos: conscientious researcher in his late 20s who looks somewhat like a horse

Eudemos of Rhodos: suave and good-humoured senior scholar at Lykeion, near Theophrastos' age

DENIZENS OF ELEUSIS

Smikrenes son of Thariades: farmer of land near Eleusis, short-tempered father of Philomela

Philomena: daughter of Smikrenes: Stephanos' intended bride, age 15

Geta: Smikrenes' slave, Philomela's old nurse

Diognetos of Eleusis: citizen, friend of Hieron; citizen, member of clan of Kerykes; acts as Stephanos' *mystagogos* (guide to initiation)

Thymades of Eleusis: citizen, owner of modest apartment building in Eleusis, becomes *mystagogos* of Aristotle

Oulias: owner of a shop making images of Demeter

Lampos: Oulias' assistant, freedman from Tanagra in Boiotia

Melanthios: marble-seller of Eleusis: maker of grave monuments

Sophilos: little man with twisted feet, occasional beggar

Strabax: Sophilos' nephew, age 15

Strabax's mother: sister of Sophilos

Demarkh of Eleusis: official in charge of the deme, first to be informed of murder

The Hierophant: high priest of Temple of Demeter and Persephone

The Daidoukhos: personal name Hanias, holds high religious office in Eleusinian worship of Demeter and the Maiden as Torch-bearer

The Priestess of the Two Goddesses: chief celebrant of Demeter and her daughter

Servants and slaves of Sanctuary of Eleusis

HYMETTOS FAMILY AND THEIR NEIGHBOURS

Philonike: Smikrenes' estranged wife, mother of Philomela; a bee-keeper living on her family's farm on Mount Hymettos

Philokleia: mother of Philonike, grandmother of Philomela, manager of family farm in Hymettos

Dropides; Philokleia's second husband, a confirmed invalid

Philokles: legal owner of farm, absent son of Philokleia and uncle of Philomela; now in Kos with mistress Nanno

Mika: Elderly slave woman of the household at Hymettos

Lykon: neighbour who brings a civil suit against Philokles' family and against Stephanos for property encroachment and flood damage

Smikythos: neighbour of Lykon, widower, looking for suitable wife with dowry

Asimos: neighbour who creates prickly hedges; keeps sheep and pigs

Zobia; Asimos' red-haired daughter, with unusual habits

Pantakles: white-haired man with farm further up Hymettos slope, lives with nephew

NEIGHBOURS AND ACQUAINTANCES IN ATHENS AND ENVIRONS

Hieron: citizen, owner of house in Kydathenaion, not far from Stephanos

Hippobatos of Thorikos: citizen, Hieron's brother-in-law

Halirrhothios: citizen, neighbour of Hieron and Stephanos

Eurynome: slave child, daughter of Halirrhothios by a slave, age 8

Euphranor: best friend of Theodoros, nephew of sculptor Euphranor, age 9

Gorgias: wealthy citizen, son of rich silversmith, age 24

Nikeratos: well-born young citizen, old school friend of Stephanos

Philokedes: well-born and privileged friend of Nikeratos

Lysiphon of Kholargos: arkhon; a magistrate whose dinner is interrupted

Thratta: freedwoman, prostitute from Thrace who plies her trade not far from Stephanos' dwelling

Theophon: rosy-faced wealthy citizen with mercantile interests; inhabitant of deme of Kydathenaion, friend and neighbour of Halirrhothios

Lamas: middle-aged citizen with long brown beard, serious historian of Kydathenaion, supporter of Halirrhothios

Mendandros son of Diopeithes of Kephisia: witty boy who wants to be a scholar in the Lykeion, age 11

Kallimakhos of Kollytos: middle-aged citizen; his daughter Karmia once considered as a marriage prospect for Stephanos

Euthykritos of Phaleron: rich shipper and merchant with dealings in Byzantion, associate of Kallimakhos

Antigone: beautiful courtesan, freedwoman, friend of Philotas

Glykera: Antigone's sweet daughter, already beautiful at age 11

Epimeletes of Emporion: one of the supervisors of the harbour port at Peiraieus

Bread-seller in Agora: old female with portable oven

The Mageiros: the cook with blustering ways and a short temper

Tile-master: owner of tile-making shop, also an expert roofer

Two slave assistants to tile-master in roofing Stephanos' house; one of them very frightened of something

Assistant cooks, tile-makers, etc.

PERSONS FROM ABROAD

Antigonos the One-Eyed: Makedonian officer, returned from the East

Arkhias: Actor from Greek cities in southern Italia, also acts as a spy for Antipater

Abdelmelkart: merchant of Phoenicia who deals in costly gems

Phoinician female slave: old woman who keeps Abdelmelkart's accounts

CONTENTS

Prologue

O Demeter, bright-haired goddess, giver of grain and life, be gracious to myself and my children and to all mankind. And lovely Maiden, the daughter taken from the field of flowers to Hades' house of darkness, rejoice our eyes with perpetual return in Spring. Hear, O Two Goddesses, and let food abound upon the kindly earth. We give thanks for the glorious vision offered to your initiates in holy Eleusis. Blessed is every mortal who has beheld your holy things in the great Mysteries.

O Divine Mother and Daughter, let my narration redound to your praise. I have to tell of bold robbery and intrepid theft, of tearless shedding of blood. But the Goddesses did not permit such wickedness to go unpunished. You, O Holy Two, have delivered us, with the help of Aristotle, whose departed wife was a faithful servant of Demeter. I pray you, deliver all of us from dark prisons, both now and hereafter.

I

The Hole in the Wall

I was still in darkness that morning. Aroused by dim cries, I sat up in bed, glancing towards the window, but the shuttered aperture was only a dark patch in the wall. The dim cries, however, came nearer. A shouting in the street. Certainly someone has had too much wine, I thought crossly. I myself had drunk of the wine the previous evening, as I was entertaining Aristotle. 'You won't be able to sit up drinking with me once you are a married man,' he had teased. Doubtless the slaves were determined to sleep through this insistent noise. The male house slave, Tryphos, a man of all work who did all work badly and whose chief feature was the loss of a finger to an axe, was a stalwart sleeper. Inwardly grumbling, I rose, intending to tell these revellers to take their party somewhere else. Endeavouring to cast my cloak about my naked body as I went, I proceeded more slowly than I would have done before I was wounded in the East. Not wishing to awaken my guest, I lit no lamp.

This was a useless precaution as matters fell out, for someone was banging at our house door, and yelling, 'Is Aristotle within? Help – we seek Aristotle of Stageira!'

Aristotle must have awakened already, for he was suddenly just behind me, like myself trying to put on his himation. 'Be careful!' I said. 'It might be a trap.'

'Unlikely,' he said mildly. 'These people sound anxious rather than angry.' I advanced to the threshold, motioning Aristotle to stand back, and unlatched the door, pulling it open, but not fully.

Though the street itself was dark, I could suddenly see. One of the party of three men at my door carried a torch – not a large one, a small brand with a flickering light. Still, the torchbearer had long arms and held the light bravely aloft, so it almost dazzled my sleepy eyes. 'What do you want?' I enquired harshly. 'Why do you come to a man's house before it is day?'

'Please, Stephanos,' said the stoutest of the men, not the torchbearer. 'It's your neighbour Hieron. I live nearby.'

'I do know you,' I acknowledged with a nod. Indeed, I knew my neighbour Hieron well enough, though he now appeared somewhat dishevelled. At least he had the advantage of me in being fully clothed. My himation, so hastily thrown on, was about to slip off entirely.

'I ran with my friends here – Diognetos of Eleusis, and Halirrhothios – to ask for help!' Hieron's eyes were bulging, and he was breathing too hard to make speech easy. His breath was laden with wine-fumes. He certainly seemed more upset than the other two men. One of these was unfamiliar, but I was slightly acquainted with the man holding the torch, Hieron's neighbour and mine, Halirrhothios.

'We ask,' explained the man I didn't know, who must be Diognetos, 'because we heard that you had the great philosopher staying at your house, and we wish him to help us find who did it.'

'Did *what*?' I demanded, but Diognetos was in midsentence.

'. . . I who suggested we come here first – when Hieron first spied the hole in his wall—'

'It was Hieron's idea to find Aristotle,' interposed the third man, Halirrhothios. This neighbour, slightly taller than the other two, acted as the torchbearer; his sinewy arm held the torch high and steadily. Muscular but wiry, Halirrhothios was not breathing hard from the run.

Hieron had caught his breath by now. 'My house – it's certainly been broken into,' he amplified. 'Night burglary! Any help you can give – *any* light the philosopher can throw . . .' he continued. 'Oh, where *is* Aristotle?'

'Here,' said my elder friend, quietly. He was by now neatly wrapped in his cloak and looked awake.

'Come,' said heavy-breathing Hieron. My neighbour stretched his hand towards us in physical entreaty. '*Please* – at once! We haven't gone in – the burglars may still be there! We could catch them.'

His urgent fumbling hand caught Aristotle's cloak and he pulled the philosopher into the street. As the distraught householder began to run, Aristotle was ridiculously compelled to follow, unless he wished to lose his cloak and go naked in the cool air of an early autumn night. Surprised, I followed quickly and barefoot, sliding as I went on a slippery patch on my front doorstep; fortunately I regained my balance. Pride insisted I maintain a brisk pace, despite residual weakness.

The streets were quiet. Some nocturnal birds could still be heard, Athena's owls crying about the Akropolis. It was by no means day. My shoulder ached from the spear-wound, not quite healed. Yet I was able almost to keep up with Hieron and Aristotle, the other two galloping along behind me as best they might. This blundering run through dark streets was not for any great distance. Hieron stopped short at his house, and the rest of us did likewise.

'Come!' gasped Hieron with an elaborate pantomime of secrecy, leading us suddenly tip-toe to the side of his dwelling (the left side if you looked at his house from the street). He pointed to the wall. 'You see!' he said in a jerky whisper. 'There! I spied this as I was coming home – I'd been out all night.' Halirrhothios shone his now dwindling torch at the side of the house. What we saw removed my hope that Hieron's agitation resulted from a delusion born of midnight wine-drinking.

The wall definitely had a hole in it. A ragged good-sized hole, not large enough to endanger the wall, but large enough to let a grown man, if he were slender and agile, into the house. A visible gap, yawning like a rent in fabric. A number of mud bricks had been efficiently removed.

'Ah!' said Aristotle in a low tone. 'The time-honoured method of house-breaking. Why attempt a door when a wall is more permeable? Am I to take it you haven't yet been inside?'

Hieron nodded. 'Come,' he beckoned. 'The thieves might still be there,' he added in his nervous mutter. I was glad he did not propose that any of us should launch ourselves into that dark gap in the wall. We went bravely to his front door, following him, an entourage of guardians. I wished we had more light.

The owner of the broken dwelling flung open the door, and we trooped inside. We didn't speak, but any burglars still in the house would be fully alerted to our trampling presence. I stumbled into something warm and, to my darkened eyes, shapeless, in the entryway. 'Oh!' I said aloud. 'I've stepped on someone!' There was a moan at my feet. Halirrhothios shone the light in the direction of the sound. Somebody was prostrate in a heap, somebody who was now stirring, and emitting gentle groans.

'My house slave!' said Hieron, in great agitation. 'Someone has attacked my man! He is supposed to attend to the door. Oh, what has happened?'

Aristotle knelt by the prostrate shape, and touched it. Then he put his ear to the man's chest. Aristotle, a descendant of Asklepios and the son of a physician, had a physician's skill.

'He'll do,' Aristotle said, rising. 'Blow to the head. He's only stunned. Let him rest a while; he should come to naturally—'

'Hush!' commanded Hieron. '*They* are perhaps here still. Let us go on to the *andron.*'

We tiptoed quietly (as quietly as five men can) into the main room, the room for the males of the family and their male visitors. The *andron*, the best room in a house, usually a large front room, would naturally be the place where a burglar would go. Customarily this chamber contains the best furniture and ornaments, often the money-box of the master of the house. Hieron's *andron*, on the left side of the short entryway, was the part of the dwelling into whose outer wall someone had punched a great hole.

Beside the doorway was a bracket holding unlit torches, and Hieron was able to take a fresh stick of pine, lighting it at the inadequate twinkling light of Halirrhothios' brand. At last we could see our surroundings as well as each other. The owner of this small mansion glanced around his room and gave a sudden cry.

'The golden crown! It's gone! Stolen! My grandfather's golden crown—'

'Hush,' said Halirrhothios. '*They* may be still here – if we catch them you will get it back.'

'Oh, I cannot believe it – this is such a safe room!'

'So 'tis,' said Halirrhothios. 'Only one little window high up – nearly in the ceiling.'

'Right,' said Diognetos. 'Let's keep looking – you can tell us what else is missing.' And he began moving into the back of the room, where an irregularity in the wall had created a sort of alcove not fully visible from where we had been standing. Halirrhothios, taking a fresh torch for himself, followed Diognetos.

'My money, still here,' murmured Hieron, waving his torch about. The flame blew like a banner in the breeze from the gap in the wall. A chilly wind sighed about the defenceless room. 'But my best antique cup! I don't see it—'

'Zeus!' exclaimed Diognetos. 'Great Hera help us!' cried Halirrhothios at almost the exact same moment. The rest of us rushed into the alcove, stumbling into each other.

'*Ai! Iou!*' cried Hieron. 'Blood pollution – a man is killed!'

In the flickering torchlight I was looking – as we all were looking – at the man face down on the floor. A slave, I thought at first, as the man was wearing nothing but a tunic. But then Hieron rolled him over; the inert head made a strange noise as he did so. The man was bearded. This was the face of a free citizen. Or rather – it had been a proper face until recently. A citizen no longer.

'Oh no!' Hieron cried. 'I think it's Hippobatos, my wife's brother! Aristotle – is he really gone? Can you be sure?'

Aristotle had slipped down by the side of the man on the floor, and touched him. He did not spend much time on this exercise.

'Dead, certainly,' he pronounced. 'Not very long, look how a little blood still oozes, and the body is slightly warm. But this man is certainly dead. Curious,' he added. 'I wonder – more light here!'

Aristotle stood up. Hieron went to a high table against

the wall, on which stood several lamps. Using his torch, he tried to light one of the lamps, but his hand was shaking and he nearly dropped the first one he tried. He was more successful in lighting other lamps, though soot fluttered from the torch and sent dark flakes here and there. Oil ran about under the lamp-shelf and soaked into the floor. Like most of the floors in my own deme, this was of packed earth so refined and closely tamped down that it had a good surface or skin upon it. Now it was greasily stained. Hieron, so I thought, must have splashed a quantity of oil out of the lamp he had almost dropped.

The room emerged in a softer, more constant glow, a relief from the lightning-like swoops and the shadows cast by the torches. Aristotle took a lamp in his steady hand and thoughtfully went to and fro, bent over, looking sometimes at the corpse but more often at the floor.

'I wonder how . . . But it's becoming clear. This poor fellow was hit once on the front of the head. Bad enough, but not instantly fatal. That happened, I think, in the centre of the *andron* itself. Then as he tried to run – or perhaps just crawl away? Yes, yes, I think he crawled. Look at the dirt on his knees.' Aristotle was busy with his examination. '*Then* he was hit on the back of the head. With considerable force, by some heavy object. Look at that trail of blood. He was killed here, but someone moved him a little – perhaps to make the corpse less visible to a casual visitor to the room. Though he survived the first attack, this poor fellow must have died at once from that second massive blow to the back of the head. You can see that his head is like a cracked eggshell, spilling its contents.'

One of the men gagged. I tried to look cool and indifferent. I was assisted in this endeavour by the fact that this wasn't the first dead citizen in a good house that

I had beheld in my lifetime. But the body in Hieron's broken house was a strange sight enough, and unpleasing. I had never before seen the result of a heavy blow to the head. It certainly did look like an eggshell, once you started to think of it. A runny mess. The olive oil from the lamp had begun in a disagreeably intimate domestic way to mingle with the trail of blood and a sort of whey-like egg-white that came out of the dead man's skull.

'The brain has got out with the blood,' said Aristotle thoughtfully, again examining that red and watery liquor. The blows had made dents, reforming the very shape of the original head and somehow moving the position of the face; it had slipped, like melted wax. When Aristotle held the head gently there was again a strange grinding sound.

'Hark!' said Aristotle. 'You can even hear the crepitation of the bones of his skull. There could be no chance of saving anybody with a wound like that. A *very* heavy blow. Instant death.'

'Oh-h!' Hieron staggered and leaned on Halirrhothios. 'Alas for Hippobatos! My brother-in-law, gentlemen – Hippobatos of Thorikos. I didn't know he would be here tonight. My wife's away visiting her parents – she's taken the children. I expected Hippobatos tomorrow – not until tomorrow . . .'

'Maybe you misunderstood each other,' suggested Diognetos. 'Sunset begins the new day, so he may have meant he was arriving this evening.'

'But I expected him in the proper day – in daylight. Who travels at night? Oh dear! What shall I tell my wife – her favourite brother! Hippobatos must have chosen to come early, and found that I had gone out. I just joined a little celebration at a tavern for the birth of a friend's son. Maybe Hippobatos went to bed and then got up to see what the noise was – and the villains found him!'

'Alas for your brother-in-law,' said Halirrhothios gravely, 'that he did not go out also. Too bad he did not postpone his visit. For had this wretched Hippobatos not been here, you would have suffered only the loss of things and no loss of life at all.'

'Nor,' said Diognetos with a shudder, 'would your rooms be painted in this horrible way!'

Now that we had leisure to examine, I could see that the room was discoloured. The white-plastered wall was now enriched with spatterings of blood, and there was a slimy trail along the floor, a red that had got upon the legs of one of the finely carved wood chairs. Unaware of this new decoration, Hieron, overcome, sat down in the chair.

'*Ai! Ai!* This is terrible! And I have lost my great-grandfather's cup! I don't know how much the robbers have taken from me, besides depriving me of the life of my wife's dearest brother! And the golden crown that my grandfather won – it was a family treasure—'

'Yes, yes,' said Aristotle. 'But what else? Anything else removed? Out of place? I wonder what was the murderous weapon they used.'

'I know nothing,' Hieron said dully. 'Nothing that would do the work. For a pot would shatter if it hit a man's head; it could hardly strike *that* hard. Perhaps a brick from the wall.'

'No,' said Aristotle. 'Bricks of mud crumble. There's no dirt in the wound itself. A stone would do it, a very clean—'

'Stone!' screamed Hieron suddenly, in an ecstasy of mental pain. 'Stone – Ai! Ai! *Marble!* Oh, my wife's brother – her older brother, a man of Thorikos, as I have said – was going to bring us a little piece of statuary. Just the marble head of a child. In memory of their little brother who died.'

'Ah well,' said Diognetos wisely. 'There you are. The brother-in-law might have set the statue head out in your room when he arrived. And probably the robbers took it.'

'But then,' I proffered, 'the men might have come armed with house-breaking implements – a hammer and crowbar or something of the sort.'

'That could be,' said Aristotle. 'But I would expect a different shape of wound. He was hit with something bigger than the average hammer, and certainly not long and narrow like a crowbar.' The philosopher bent and looked again along the floor. 'There! Do you see? Here in the earth of the floor there is a slight dent – as of a round thing that sat there for a while. If they hit him with the stone, they might have laid the weapon down for a short while.'

'You mean,' said Diognetos, 'while they made sure he was dead, and then moved the corpse a little.'

'Yes,' Aristotle agreed, straightening up. 'The scene could have gone thus: the man heard the intruders in the middle of the night and came into the *andron*. He had already brought the statue and left it in here, on a table or somewhere where it was visible to the thieves. Then they hit him on the head with the statue he himself had brought.'

'Would that explain the wounds, Aristotle?' asked Halirrhothios.

'A round piece of marble could certainly hit hard. It could break a head,' I mused aloud. 'But Hieron must ask Hippobatos' household if he brought any such piece with him.'

'That is of the first importance,' Aristotle agreed. 'It is only a hypothesis that the marble was used as a weapon. An interesting hypothesis. How rapidly would the thieves have to clean off a piece of marble so no stain was left? Would the thieves – *murderers* we should rather call them – try to sell the piece of statuary? Might they not, more prudently, throw it away?'

'The murder could not remain a secret,' I argued. 'It would be better not to carry the weapon with them. Yet – if they threw a statue head away, it could readily attract attention and be easily identified. Not like a pebble from the beach.'

'I agree,' said Aristotle. 'Hieron, if it turns out that your brother-in-law Hippobatos did indeed bring this small piece of statuary with him to Athens and it now cannot be found, that piece of round stone is the most likely weapon. If found, it might yield some more information as to who used it.'

'If the marble head you speak of actually was the weapon,' observed Halirrhothios, 'then the intruders obviously did not *intend* to commit murder. Otherwise they would have come armed.'

'Possibly so,' said Aristotle. 'The argument will scarcely help the villain – or villains – in a court of law. Those who commit theft of any kind *at night* are subject to the severest penalty. As are those who steal – as these thieves appear to have done – goods worth more than fifty drakhmai.'

'That's right!' I exclaimed. 'Though theft by day of something worth less than fifty drakhmai can be atoned for by giving the victim money or goods to twice the value.'

'Inapplicable here. The penalty for a midnight burglary such as this – with or without murder – is plainly death.'

'Poor Hippobatos!' Hieron rocked to and fro in the bloodstained chair. 'I must send for the women – we must plan for his funeral. Oh, could I have prevented this? Do you think . . .' Hieron asked tremulously, 'do you think that had we gone into my house earlier, instead of coming for you, it might have made a difference?'

'No,' said Aristotle. 'I think not. How long had you been away from home?'

'Oh, it's hard to say. I was out with some friends, celebrating, as I said, and then at some point I met with my friend Diognetos of Eleusis here. He invited me to come on to a little drinking-party – no grand affair. It seemed no harm – my wife is away. And then – I don't know – Halirrhothios came, and I forget . . .'

'I had been at the party with you,' Halirrhothios reminded him patiently, 'and I said I would walk home with you, as we are neighbours. But you reminded me that Diognetos needed somewhere to stay overnight, since his home is in Eleusis . . .'

'That's right,' said Hieron. 'So there you are. Now I remember – I offered to give everyone a drink when we got to my house. And then when we got here, we saw the hole in the wall, and knew there were robbers. So without entering the house, we hurried to find you. And I do hope you help us to discover who did this, so they can be properly punished.'

'Yes,' said Halirrhothios, 'and your grandfather's gold crown recovered too.'

'A family treasure,' said Hieron. 'Given to my grandfather for his services to Athens.' He rubbed his face with his hands. 'Oh, my going out to see friends this evening – it has cost poor Hippobatos his life.'

'Do not distress yourself unduly,' said Aristotle in kindly tones. 'How could one predict such a horrid event? Let us consider the question of time. Once you saw the breach in the wall, it could not have taken you three long at all to come and fetch us, and Stephanos and I wasted no time but promptly returned with you. Now, is it true that none of you heard any noise within the house, nor saw any lights?'

'Nothing at all,' said Halirrhothios, and Diognetos

added, 'Silent as the tomb,' and then seemed startled at his own expression.

'The intruders had probably already departed some time before you arrived. I cannot tell you exactly when your poor brother-in-law was killed, but the body was cooling when I touched it – he would have been dead for some little while. Certainly longer than it took you to run to my house and back. Once the second great blow was struck, Hieron, nothing on earth could have saved this man.'

'Terrible,' said Halirrhothios. 'Nothing like this has happened in our neighbourhood before. Boutades got himself killed some years ago, but that was in a very wealthy deme, of noble families. *We* are good respectable people in Kydathenaion. Why don't you keep a dog?'

'We do,' said Hieron. 'I haven't heard him – I wonder . . .' He arose, took a lamp and went out to the courtyard; we followed him. The sky, heavily clouded, was beginning to be streaked with grey. It was easy to see, even by a small lamp, that the house dog had breathed his last. There was froth on his muzzle.

'Poisoned,' said Aristotle. 'The thieves probably tossed some meat over into the courtyard, and then waited.'

'Shocking!' exclaimed Halirrhothios. 'We in this neighbourhood shall have to think of ways of preventing any such thing happening again.'

A small group of female servants had begun to assemble at the door on the other side of the courtyard, peering timidly at us.

'I must tell them,' said Hieron. 'They will have to give the body the first attentions. And our poor house is polluted now. Yet, I must send at once for my wife – and of course I must send a messenger to prepare poor Hippobatos' wife as well.'

'The body will have to be taken to Thorikos for the funeral,' suggested Diognetos.

'Yes – yes of course. Oh, but how to get him to Thorikos in this condition? The women will have to wash him and bind him tight.'

It was really not our place to be here when Hieron broke the news to the family and set about the preparations for a family funeral. We needed to get away and find ritual cleansing from this blood pollution.

'We should leave you, friend Hieron,' said Aristotle. 'You and your household will have much to do. But first I ought to have another look at the slave who was knocked down.'

We trooped back inside, avoiding the sepulchral room where life had disappeared. When we got to the front entryway, the slave who had been stunned was sitting up, stretching and yawning. Aristotle looked him over and felt his head.

'The skull is sound,' Aristotle the physician pronounced. 'But he has a good-sized lump on the head. Are you able to speak, fellow? What happened?'

'Don' know.' The slave spoke in a slurred voice, but what he said was comprehensible. 'Someone . . . Noticed someone . . . Dark. Went to look.'

'Did you see anybody?'

'I lit . . . lamp. Night person. All covered up. Cloak . . . very dark. No face. I had a lamp, but he reached out and put out the light. I don't remember anything else. Must have hit me then.'

'I suppose the lamp that the thief extinguished was cast down upon the floor,' said Aristotle, searching. 'No, the only one is this.' And he pointed to a large unornamented lamp on a table in a corner, such a shadowy corner it had been invisible to us until now. The slave, dutiful but uninterested turned to look, then groaned from the ill effects of moving his head too rapidly.

'Give him a drink of water by and by, but sparingly,'

said Aristotle. 'Put cold water and vinegar on the bump on his head. I believe he will recover fully.'

'If this fellow has to give his evidence in court,' Halirrhothios commented, 'you know the rule. Slaves cannot give evidence in a legal case without being tortured first. So you'd better get him strong enough to bear the torture when he is questioned.'

The slave fainted.

It really seemed a good time to leave. 'Our condolences,' I said hastily.

More practical, Halirrhothios said to Hieron, 'I can offer one of my slaves to act as messenger for you to Thorikos. He can prepare Hippobatos' household for the arrival of the body. Meanwhile, I know you wish to thank Aristotle for his kind assistance – as kind as it was unavailing.'

'Perhaps, Halirrhothios, as it's so dark and cloudy, with dawn not fully here yet, you could give Stephanos and Aristotle a light to guide their steps home,' Diognetos suggested. Poor Hieron, stunned and taken aback by all that confronted him, acquiesced dejectedly in these suggestions.

'Yes, yes, thank you very much, Aristotle of Stageira. I appreciate your promptness. And thanks to Stephanos son of Nikiarkhos too. Though you didn't do us any good, you might have done. Here . . .' Hieron fumbled on the low table, 'take this lamp, why don't you? Halirrhothios can go with you, as Diognetos suggests, and bring the lamp back again.' He popped the wick from the lamp he carried into the larger one found in the entryway, and lit it. Aristotle took it.

'My condolences for all that has happened here,' the Master of the Lykeion said to the dejected householder. 'You have my deepest sympathy. I cannot think your brother-in-law suffered long at all, if that is any consolation. Please let me know if I can be of any further service.'

'To be sure,' said Halirrhothios. 'I speak for poor Hieron, of course – you see how difficult things are for him at the moment.'

We turned to the door, secretly happy to remove ourselves from the scene. I was already thinking about how quickly we could become cleansed of blood and corpse-presence. As the door opened, some dull light entered from the slowly lifting sky, casting a tentative illumination upon the lamp itself. Fortunately Aristotle was looking at the lamp just as he was about to cross the threshold.

'By Herakles!' he cried. 'This is a precious lamp indeed – for, though dull clay without, it gleams of gold within.'

He snatched out the wick, and turned the lamp upside down. A little – remarkably little – oil spilled out, but there was a light tinkling sound, and a few gold leaves fell on the floor.

'I believe,' he said, 'that we have here the golden crown of your grandfather, O Hieron. But it has been broken up, I fear.' And he twisted a finger inside the clay container and soon had the gold leaves out, along with a neat circle of golden wire. There were admiring exclamations of 'Wonderful!' and 'How amazing!' from Diognetos and Halirrhothios.

'So,' said Hieron, his eyes wide, 'so the thieves had torn the crown into small bits and packed it up, ready to take away?'

'You can reassemble it,' Aristotle said. 'I count here thirteen gold leaves. How many were there?'

'Fourteen,' said the amazed Hieron. 'No, one got lost before. Thirteen leaves.'

'The crown at least you have not lost,' said Aristotle. 'You can circulate a description of your great-grandfather's cup. And get someone to give an account of the marble head. Stephanos and I will strip, and shake out our cloaks . . .' here he suited action to the word, and I did likewise. 'To assure all men – including ourselves – that no object has accidentally found its way into our clothing.'

'No need,' protested Hieron feebly.

'You should keep the lamp as evidence.' And Aristotle thrust it into the hands of the stunned householder.

Hieron looked at it blankly. 'But that – that clumsy thing isn't one of ours!' he protested. '*We* don't use anything like this, even the slaves.'

'You're sure,' asked Diognetos, 'absolutely *sure* it isn't one of yours?'

'It isn't ours,' insisted Hieron. 'Ours are good ones, and they all look the same. This is large and clumsy.'

'Well then,' said Aristotle drily, 'you are the better for a new lamp, and the worse for an antique cup and a brother-in-law. There is enough daylight by now, I think, for us to require no lighting home. Farewell.'

And we walked off, out of the broken house and down the street. The grey dawn was gathering. Somewhere an early cock crowed to encourage the light.

'What a dreadful thing!' I said. 'A crime like that, almost on my own street! I suppose the theft was intended, and the killing unplanned.'

'So it would seem,' said Aristotle. 'Stunning the slave would have been part of the plan – killing the brother-in-law came later, I dare say. When did they run away, forgetting some of the products of their industry?' The Master appeared less serene than he had been when looking at the corpse of hapless Hippobatos. 'Our kind fortune appears to have held good, Stephanos. For if I had crossed the threshold, lamp in hand, I might have been accused of the theft of a gold crown – and you perhaps with me.'

II

A Public Betrothal, and Offerings at Eleusis

The funeral of the wretched Hippobatos took place with sad decorum in Thorikos; his wife (now widowed) asserted that the dead man had carried with him to Athens that evening the marble head of a boy. That object was not found. Even while the unfortunate Hieron was helping to bury his brother-in-law, we heard of another robbery. It could not exactly be called a house-breaking, as the door had been open, and someone had got in and taken away all the money in the house. This took place in daylight, and only forty drakhmai were taken, so the offence would not have warranted the strictest procedures against the criminal if he – or they – were caught. But no thief *was* caught. Then there was the theft of some wealthy men's clothing at the baths, which caused a great outcry. Of course, the most immediate outcry was from the bathers, who suddenly found they might have to go naked into the street. As most of these men were of middle age, it would not have been a pretty sight for the observers either. (Fortunately they were rich enough to send home for fresh garments.) A popular gymnasium for youths was likewise robbed, though in that case people did not much object to seeing unclothed *kouroi* wandering through the city. Both of these offences were of a serious nature. Stealers of clothes from baths and other such places were by law to be treated as evil-doers of the worst sort, subject to the severest punishment.

'It puzzles me,' I said to Aristotle, 'why the Athenian law should treat it as worse to steal clothes from the baths or a gymnasium than to go into someone else's house and take all his coins.'

'A good question,' admitted Aristotle, 'but there is a rational principle at work here. It is relatively hard to get into someone else's house unobserved. To enter and steal is a very definite and risky step. Whereas it is extremely easy to steal clothes from a bathhouse, where all men come and go. If the law were to deal leniently with this action we should soon have no baths or gymnasia. The Lykeion is glad of such protection. Only the well-to-do are likely to be the target of house robbers, but a poor man at the bath might have the only clothes he possesses taken from him.'

'I just wish,' said my young brother Theodoros, 'that *I* could catch the thief stealing the things. I would take him to the Eleven and make him own up. Then people could get their things back.'

Theodoros, at the great age of nearly ten years, was imagining himself publicly praised, glorified, a hero among his playmates. The procedure of *apagoge* he outlined was proper, arresting the accused and taking him before one of the Justices, but an adult would be needed to compel a stout thief to submit to law.

'Mind you don't do anything of the sort,' I said sternly. 'It's too dangerous. If the thief were a murderer he might take your life. You should tell a grown-up person, and then *he* could lay hands on the thief. Better, you could go to the Eleven and ask them to arrest the person, explaining why. This would be safer every way. Because if you personally arrest the wrong person, you are in for a fine of one thousand drakhmai.'

'O Stepho!' Theodoros was annoyed. 'You are always spoiling my fun. I am not a little boy now. I am strong – I do exercises at the gymnasium. If I took the thief by surprise when he actually was carrying the goods away I could not possibly be fined. And maybe the one who is stealing from the baths is not at all the same person who killed our neighbour's brother-in-law.'

'There is something in what you say,' Aristotle admitted. 'We have no way of knowing that it *is* the same.'

Although the question of the bathhouse thefts remained open, other incidents followed. Some were still relatively trivial – people (both slave and free) finding at a shop that their change had been stolen before they picked it up, or their purchases had been filched. But other thefts were more serious, indicating a dedicated pursuit of objects of real value. Another gold crown was stolen, likewise (from a different house) some precious silver pots and pans. Valuable and historic pieces of pottery disappeared. The home of a most distinguished hetaira was ransacked when she and her 'sister' were entertaining guests. The thieves took a good horde of coins, according to the ladies' account, and also some bracelets and costly earrings with gemstones. Some virtuous citizens might sniff and say these 'ladies' asked for such treatment. But then one of the sniffers himself was deeply chagrined when his own wife's jewellery was suddenly missing.

'Bad, very bad,' said Aristotle. 'It makes us all suspicious of each other. There is something very low and nasty about stealing. Murder is patently worse. Yet there can be an heroic element in murder – for instance, an intense desire for revenge. Strength of soul is absent from such low cases of theft.'

'Certainly,' I said. 'But surely, sometimes pure need drives men to theft.'

'Were theft committed only by the extremely poor, there might be some excuse for it,' Aristotle responded. 'But in general that is by no means the case. The greatest crimes are not committed for want of basic necessities. History tells of great frauds, enormous peculations – these were not committed because a man had no winter cloak!'

'How do we prevent theft, then?' I said.

'We cannot *prevent* it entirely. But we should do everything we can – not just by making laws, but also by changing people's minds. Education. The safest man is the one who does not want to steal, who finds the idea loathsome and melancholy. Theft is a cutting of the bond between man and man, damaging a basic kind of human friendship that makes society possible.'

I had reason to think of the bond that binds man to man. I was assuming a very serious tie in undertaking a betrothal. Two days after the terrible events at the house of Hieron, I went through the formal ceremony of *engye* as my future father-in-law, Smikrenes of Eleusis, and I had planned it earlier. Although it was not necessary to undertake it in so public a place, we chose to create this bond while standing at the heart of the *polis*, in the centre of the Athenian Agora. We wanted our contract to be public. Never should any doubt be cast on the legality of our wedding. I was the more anxious for this as my cousin Philemon's marriage was (to say the least) somewhat obscure. I had also heard Aristotle's story of his own marriage to his beloved wife Pythias (recently deceased), and it had struck me as hideously unorthodox and unsatisfactory. My wedding should be plain as day to all, my children would always be known as legitimate Athenians.

Smikrenes and I had come to amicable (on the whole) arrangements about dowry and the use of the property. Smikrenes, at the end of our wrangling, had actually given me a share during his lifetime in the Eleusis property, contingent of course on the marriage being carried out. Smikrenes proved wealthier than I had suspected; the dowry was more than I had dared to hope.

Thus we met, Smikrenes and I, as arranged on the fourth day of the month of Pyanepsion. I had a fleeting wish that Smikrenes had looked cleaner and not quite so rustic, and that he had worn neat sandals and not those stout boots with nails in them that he seemed to favour. But there he was, and there I was, both of us blown about by the wind as we stood by the Statues of the Heroes. I had asked some friends to come so there would be witnesses. Passers-by swelled our group into a small crowd, gazing on us curiously. My cheeks burned. But there was not much to the business after all.

'I Stephanos of Athens son of Nikiarkhos, desire, O Smikrenes of Eleusis, to take in marriage your daughter Philomela by name, on the understanding that she is a true Athenian and a virgin, daughter of yourself by Philonike daughter of Philokles of Hymettos.'

'If that is your wish and desire, then I will make known to all present and to the whole city that I, Smikrenes son of Thariades of Eleusis, freely and without constraint give to you my virgin daughter Philomela by name, sole daughter of myself, citizen, and Philonike daughter of Philokles of Hymettos, citizen.'

We shook hands. There was a little burst of applause. This broke out again after Smikrenes named the amount of dowry he would offer us, handsomer than anyone could expect from his rustic appearance. 'I give this in consideration of *apotimema*,' he added formally. I in turn agreed to offer a piece of land as security in *apotimema*, 'So that in case of divorce or death the bride's father would have compensation for the value of the dowry,' as Smikrenes had explained to me.

'Divorce! Horrible word – wicked idea!' I had exclaimed. 'I am sure your daughter is all she ought to be, and I certainly shall never wish to put an end to a good marriage.'

'The wedding is to take place in Gamelion,' I now announced. 'Let us publicly exchange the documents of our agreement.'

This was an extra flourish, but we both had good reason to want our complex affairs regarding money and property to be clearly put into writing – and known to be so recorded. The documents dealt not only with the land I offered in *apotimema*, but also with other arrangements concerning his land in Eleusis, my farm in the country, and the house in Athens. I had also added some separate information concerning the claim I had made to Philomela's uncle for a share in the proceeds of the Hymettos property. Smikrenes and I arranged to deposit a copy of our documents in the Temple of Zeus.

That was all there was to it. It seemed strange that I should have done such a big thing in such a short period of time. For now I was really bound to Smikrenes. Only something very untoward indeed – like the death of myself or of Philomela, the gods forbid! – could stop my marriage now.

'It is a pity, old fellow, that you are going to jump into this trap just as your life has taken some turns for the better,' grumbled Nikeratos, my old school friend. Nikeratos hadn't stuck by me when affairs were at their worst, but among my contemporaries he was one of those who had been least uncivil to me during the bad time. I had asked him to come, and was now free to talk with him for a moment, as my father-in-law-to-be was speaking to a couple of men as old and nearly as gnarled as himself. Nikeratos, who was my age and not yet thinking of marrying, was not very encouraging.

'You know what my father says. Marriage has no survivors. Even if your wife dies a month after the wedding, you still will have been a husband – and a husband you will remain. Poor Stephanos! You may say "Farewell, my youth!"'

'Well, none of us would be here if someone hadn't got married before us,' said Gorgias pacifically. Gorgias usually looked on the melancholy side of things, so this remark was unusually optimistic for him. This wealthy son of a silversmith was an acquaintance rather than a friend, but I had asked him in order to make sure I had a sufficient number of Athenians as auditors and witnesses. I had not wanted Aristotle and his troop to be there. Many of Aristotle's associates, like himself, were foreign. Today was an Athenian occasion, an important day in my life as a citizen of Athens.

'Tell you something,' said Nikeratos. 'You ought to have a party – a real symposium – before you tie yourself down to that charming rustic with hobnail boots who is to be your papa. After all, you are well-born, as was your father Nikiarkhos, who started out moderately rich. His father Lykias gave parties. And your mother's grand-father, your great-grandfather Theodoros, was famous for dinner parties, so they say. It would be good for you to remind everyone that you have some claim to position, and good blood – not like the manufacturers and so on.' Nikeratos looked pointedly at Gorgias. This was rude. But Nikeratos was an aristocrat of a truly famous family, descended from a celebrated general, and could be allowed to say almost anything he wished. I was struck by a certain truth at the core of his suggestion.

I had promised my future father-in-law to accompany him back to Eleusis and stay overnight, so we set off without further delay. 'Nothing to do in Athens' Agora save gossip and spend your money,' Smikrenes grumbled. 'I trouble Athens – the town within the walls, I mean – as little as possible.'

'But you must come for the Ekklesia,' I pointed out. Every citizen is supposed to attend the meetings to discuss affairs, policy and expenditure. 'Most of us don't go to *every* meeting,' I admitted. 'But you do need to go fairly regularly.'

My companion took this in bad part. '"Come for the Ekklesia," says the boy! It's all very well for *you*, with the Pnyx next door to your own deme. But I'm supposed to walk this great distance and wear out shoe leather every ten days? To hear a lot of fine townsmen gabbling? And me with a farm! Real work to do. And I'm no speaker to prose away – let alone an orator like Hypereides and Demades and their sort.'

I was unwilling to let the argument drop entirely. After all, one of the advantages of marrying Smikrenes was that he was an Athenian, so I felt he ought to cut a good figure. 'But,' I responded, 'the Ekklesia is the core of democratic rule! A man sustains his position as one of the Athenian citizens if he turns up at the Ekklesia, even if he isn't a speaker.'

Smikrenes snorted. 'As if I need to be taught about Athens at my time of life! You just be glad you're tying in with a good solid Athenian family, and not some of these flashy foreigners that you go about with. Your sons'll have the right to vote well enough.'

I did my best to mollify him as we tramped steadily along on the way to Eleusis deme, and had succeeded before we crossed the bridge over the river Kephisos, by the marshes and the streams in which the Eleusinian priests preserve fish for their own use. Smikrenes went to buy something for supper, and I went off on my own to stare at the outside of the great Sanctuary of Demeter and Kore. This place is not like an ordinary temple, which any man can easily enter and gaze at. It is forbidden to all but those initiated into the Mysteries, or those who seek initiation. The area is sacred, surrounded by high walls; one can see that the buildings go up a gentle hill. Peering over the wall, I could make out little of the gleaming Telesterion, the great Hall of Mysteries where the final rites take place. Within that edifice, I knew, was the ancient Palace of Demeter, the Anaktoron: a temple within a temple, hidden like a child within the womb. The whole place was both repellent in its proud and fortified aloofness, and compelling.

'You want a guide? I show you Eleusis.' As I turned to go back to the market, I found myself accosted by a little man with a wispy beard; rather an unpleasant little man he struck me, and very shabbily dressed.

'No,' I said, annoyed.'I know Eleusis very well, I am visiting a friend here.'

'I show you,' he said, undeterred. 'I can show you the Agora of Eleusis. Many fine shops.'

And the little fellow shuffled along with me, in his irritating way. There was something wrong with his feet. I gave him one of those little coins that come short of half an obol, once we came to the little agora, and so shook him off, joining Smikrenes, who had bought some fish (rather stale) in my honour.

It was a relief, after a long day, to arrive at Smikrenes' rural abode. Not that Smikrenes' abode was ever luxurious at the best of times. This time it was less pleasant than usual; the scrupulous father had seen fit to pack Philomela and her old nurse out of the house at this juncture, in order to observe the utmost in propriety at the time of our betrothal. In the spring I had actually once met and talked with the girl who was now my intended bride – though of course I did not intend to let that immodest fact slip into public ears. Since our marriage had been mooted, Philomela and I had neither met nor spoken. Yet I had occasionally had a glimpse of her, the girl with the big green eyes and hair the colour of a ripe acorn, and heard her voice in the kitchen, and taken heed of her graceful step about the house. Not only was Smikrenes' house this day the duller for her absence, the meal was decidedly below the usual standard set by the adept if nearly invisible Philomela when in residence.

Next day I went with Smikrenes to the centre of Eleusis town, in order to repeat the statement of *engye*. Although such repetition was not strictly necessary, Smikrenes strongly wished it and I agreed. It was as well that men of Eleusis should hear how matters stood. The announcement would warn off any would-be local suitors looking for an alliance with Smikrenes' daughter and her inheritance of his acres. I had heard of at least one of these, a fellow named Biton, the son of a neighbour. But Smikrenes before I knew him had quarrelled with the neighbour. An irreparable quarrel, the argument ending with Smikrenes' boot on the neighbour's backside, thus putting an end, so it seemed, to any possibility of a match.

I hadn't really seen much of what might be called Eleusis proper, which is why I had lingered to look at the Sanctuary the previous evening. Customarily, I took a short cut to the north in order to see Smikrenes at his inland farm; on the one occasion on which I had travelled to the place I had been in haste, accompanying Aristotle on the way to Delphi on the track of a stolen heiress. Now, with nothing else to do, I could saunter and take a good look. In the company of Smikrenes I was in little danger of being harassed by local beggars and self-styled guides. True, Smikrenes was not the kind of leisurely companion given to sauntering and staring, and he had dustier boots than I could wish, and was carrying a large leather bag. But the walk was enjoyable enough. The entire area is very agreeable, being a flat plain stretching towards the gentle curve of the bay, the sea quite placid at this part of the coast. Eleusis' land is fertile, and good for grain-growing.

'Best in Attika,' said Smikrenes proudly. 'The first land in the world that was ever sown and bore crops. Our city is as ancient as Athens.'

'Or nearly,' I said.

'Nay, it's ancienter. For it was here that grain-growing was discovered, so they say. The worship of Demeter and Persephone belongs properly to Eleusis. But later Athens came meddling in, and pretended an equal share. So they made the procession to the goddess at Eleusis start from Athens, and added in all those extra bits. Likely at the start there was just the Priestess.'

'You think so?' It seemed an odd idea.

'The Priestess is all right. They asked one of 'em — Theano her name was — to curse Alkibiades for his impiety, but she said she wasn't in the cursing business. Now we have a Hierophant and a Daidoukhos — all sorts of priests. Some of them living in Athens.' He spat on the roadway. 'Eleusis owes nothing to Athens. Better if the religion had just stayed here.'

I hadn't thought Smikrenes capable of so much civic pride. True, Eleusis is ancient. Eleusis and Athens formerly fought. Subdued by Theseus, Eleusis was attached to Athens in Solon's time, though it had tried to break away after that. But now it was part of Athens, one of its demes. A war between little Eleusis and Athens would be ridiculous. Yet Eleusis is very famous in its own right, for the worship of the goddess of the grain, and because of the magnificent shrine of Demeter and Persephone, which we were approaching.

'Have you been initiated, then?' I asked, surprised at hearing Smikrenes so warm in the cause of Demeter.

'Me? Catch me! Not me, nor Philomela either. Fripperies and crowds! Too many priests. Besides, it's expensive. Religion costs money.'

We were approaching the great and holy place, but naturally we did not go into the forecourt or through the Great Gate, which is like the Propylaia of the Parthenon in Athens but smaller. The outer gate of the complex is part of the wall of the city itself. Within the precinct through the open gate we could get a better glimpse of the shining Telesterion with its many columns. But we could not go very far, being uninitiated, and forbidden to enter on pain of death. I wondered a little what it would be like to be an initiate. It seemed odd that a born Eleusinian like Smikrenes was so determined against initiation. But then, Smikrenes was no great friend to religious observance, his life being perpetually soured by the presence of shrines to Pan and the Nymphs on his land.

Yet the presence of the holy shrine of Demeter and the Kore had wrought great good for Eleusis. The Mysteries had become famous throughout Greece and beyond. To undergo the experience is said to change a person, although those who have been initiated into the Mysteries of Eleusis are sworn – on pain of death – not to reveal what they have seen in the rites and revelations of the Telesterion. The numbers of those seeking initiation increases annually – by now, two thousand or more come every year. The Two Goddesses are unusually generous. Anyone, man or woman, can become an initiate if he or she can speak Greek, is over fifteen years of age, and has never committed murder. Slaves can come just the same as free people. Each would-be initiate must have an Eleusinian of the right family tree as sponsor and guide. The best are of the tribe of Eumolpos; these mostly have beautiful voices, as the name of their founder, the first Hierophant of Eleusis, indicates. They sing hymns well, and are good at explaining meanings. The Eumolpidai can do rather well out of this service.

This day was visibly a special one. There was a bustle about the Propylaia and a little crowd of watchers, whom we joined. In a short time the gate opened, and there were the priests dressed in their regalia. The chief priest, the Hierophant, he who shows the Sacred Things, was not there. Of course, I remembered, the Hierophant and the Chief Herald would be in Athens today – for I realised what the occasion must be. The remnant of the priestly company were looking quite magnificent in the sunshine. Their robes fluttered about them in the wind. A secondary herald advanced and spoke to the little crowd.

'Today, the fifth day of the month Pyanepsion, we declare the feast of the Proerosia. Thanks be to the gods, we have lived to see the day for the first ploughing of the land. In thanks to Demeter and Kore, and in prayer for success in the new harvest, all Athenians offer a preliminary sacrifice. All are invited to the sacrifice, and those of the lands beyond the seas who count themselves Athenian are free to participate and gain the favour of the corn goddess.'

This same proclamation would have been made this morning at the Temple of Demeter in Athens, by the Herald himself in full regalia.

'There you are!' said Smikrenes. 'Always something!

Today the ploughing offertory. Then at the first harvest in summer, when we have to offer the first-fruits – a tenth or so – you'll see men bringing grain by the waggonload. If you live in Eleusis itself, there's no getting out of it.'

'I know,' I said. 'We send something from the farm every year to the Eleusinion in Athens. Though with us it's vegetables – we're not much at grain-growing. Something at the Proerosia and more at harvest. And it all comes here. Where do they put all the wheat and barley?'

'In the towers and more in the granary pits. You see them granaries over there.' Against the hill of the Eleusinian Akropolis I now spied some businesslike storage buildings in a row, covering the underground grain pits.

'Isn't tomorrow the day of Sacred Ploughing? When the priests plough the Rarian Field that belongs to Demeter? I've never seen that,' I remarked.

'I've seen it more than enough. Ploughing!' Smikrenes snorted. 'They don't really do what I'd call ploughing! Imagine the Hierophant in his purple robe and pretty buskins ankle-deep in soil pushing a plough? Nowadays them priests don't cultivate nothing theirselves.'

'They get enough grain from the offerings.'

'The priests and such take other stuff too,' Smikrenes pointed out. 'Oxen or other useful beasts. And all sorts of jewellery and rich adornments for the goddesses. Gold and silver *coins*.' He spat contemptuously. 'Coins is what fancy folk spend now, think they're too good to give cabbages or wheat.'

A little trickle of people – some citizens, some obviously slaves – were making their offerings. Many carried small bags, presumably containing coins rather than produce. A few drove waggons or carts, although the Proerosia offering was slight compared to the big offering that would follow in the warmth of summer and the first-fruits of the new stalks of ripened grain. Just before the elections in Athens and the official beginning of the New Year, in summer's full heat when harvest is done and people have time for politics again.

I had missed the collections and the harvest summer during my strange journey to the eastern islands. My return from Asia, recovery from my wound, and my efforts to cement the engagement to Smikrenes and his daughter – all my affairs, I realised, had let the farm tithes slip my memory. This Proerosia, I would wait until the third day and pay at the Eleusinion in Athens, so as not to offend Smikrenes by the sight of my coins.

My father-in-law-to-be with much ceremony handed over the contents of his bulky bag and took a receipt. Alliance with a citizen of the deme of Eleusis, it suddenly struck me, might well make me much more visible to the priests of Demeter. I could hardly hope to avoid fresh assessment.

Within the precincts junior priests and temple slaves were hauling the offerings away in their own waggons, towards the long low buildings constructed for storage. The slaves in the sanctuary had to be initiates too.

'So there's something thrown away,' growled Smikrenes as we left the threshold of the sacred precinct to make our way into the town. –'I am grateful to Demeter, she's always treated me right, there's no denying. But hereabouts there are too many priests with their hands out!'

As we walked along to the west of the Sacred Precinct, we found that the area around the council house at the present time was unpleasantly noisy and dusty from all the building work going on. Ox-carts full of stones pushed us off the roadway, and a number of dust-covered workers were making a great hammering.

'Repairing the wall,' explained Smikrenes. 'That's how Lykourgos spends our taxes! They love to spend money on the buildings of Eleusis; at least Lykourgos is giving us a road too. All the priests can think of is making things pretty and making 'em big. Them priests is always craving money to look good with.'

The town of Eleusis, which starts in an organised way with its Bouleuterion and then straggles off towards the sea, boasts (as I had realised the night before) a large gymnasium and baths, and several streets. In the narrow streets we passed some shops of tinkers and sandal-makers and so on, and also of vendors of images. The marketplace of Eleusis is nothing very much to anyone used to Athens' great Agora – just a little space near the ruins of an ancient shrine to some local hero. Here was the place to make a public announcement to all of Eleusis of our *engye*. We addressed only a few uninterested passers-by and the captive audience of the shop men and the toothless women selling bread. Luckily, there was no sign of the possibly disconsolate Biton, or other discontented young men. The real crowd was at the entrance to the Sanctuary, paying its portion, or gaping at those who did.

At Smikrenes' insistence we returned to his farm for something to eat. (My father-in-law-to-be did not share my enjoyment of food bought and consumed in market-places, regarding that as scandalous waste.) When we went into his house he set down his empty leather bag on the table in the main room. But now this table supported a square box – this had surely not been there in the morning when we left.

'By the piss of Herakles! What's this?'

III

❧⊂❍⊃❧

A Cedar Box, a Dinner of Beans, and a Woolly Branch

Smikrenes picked up the box and examined it cautiously from the outside. A neat pretty box, of cedar wood with some ornamentation upon it.

'Ho, Geta! What's this? Who's been messing with my table?'

The elderly slavewoman, formerly Philomela's nurse, peered round the door.

'Someone has left this for you,' she said. 'But more pertikler, for young Master Stephanos here. They said you was to have it 'gainst the wedding.'

Smikrenes opened the box and peered in. 'Ho!' he said. He sat down heavily. 'Women's foolishness. I know well who *this* trumpery must be from.'

He thrust the open box towards me. This *pyxis* of cedar wood, carefully lined with fine-woven woollen fabric, contained two sets of beautiful earrings, and an elegant necklace of gold filigree. A small piece of bark paper bore the words 'For Philomela'. There could be no mistake. Though I had not seen that writing before, nor these earrings, I knew who the donor must be.

'Philomela's mother has sent these,' I affirmed.

'Takes no Persian *magos* to figure out as much,' said Smikrenes. 'She – my wife Philonike – done it to plague me. Her and her own mother! They waited until our backs was turned – they knew that I'd be in Eleusis saying the tithe pledge, as well as for the *engye*. Then they ran in like weasels! Cunning they are – as goblins.'

'They probably sent a slave,' I said soothingly.

'My own wife! Philonike – who should be in this here house, doing her spinning and taking her sup with me. And when it comes time for her own daughter's wedding, she ups and sends a secret box. But she'd not put herself within a bow-shot of me, her own husband! Oh no. I tell you, I won't have it!' Smikrenes jumped up; he was working himself up to a rage. 'I have a mind to throw this trash into the road itself – or stay! I'll send it down the well! Turning my own daughter against me with her trinkets!'

'No, no,' I said. 'Just a kindly thought – it means they have heard of the marriage plans and betrothal, and approve.' I took hold of the box, in what I hoped was neither too violent nor too greedy a manner.

'It would be a shame to destroy it. Let your child, O Smikrenes, your *only* child, have the pleasure of these things. If you wish, I will take them away to our house in Athens, but I shall promise not to give them to Philomela until the wedding.'

Smikrenes let go of his end of the box, and sat down again.

'All right, if you must have it! I am too kind a parent, that's my fault. I can never cross my girl in the least little thing, though her mother played me a shrewd trick when she upped and offed. I tell you, I don't want to see them things lying about. I remember when my Philonike herself used to wear that there pair of earrings with the red and blue little stones and the fine gold work and everything. So take them out of my sight, that's all.'

I was glad enough to do so, when I left early the next morning. As Philomela was keeping herself out of sight with great propriety at this important juncture, and as Smikrenes at the best of times was not given to entertainment, it seemed best to be gone. And I had no great interest in seeing the ritual first ploughing by the priests in Eleusis' Rarian Field. My departure was, however, delayed by another unexpected gift – a pastry bird, made by Philomela herself, as Smikrenes remarked when Geta presented it to me.

'For your autumn branch,' Geta insisted. It was a pretty thought of my bride-to-be, to present a gift for the good-luck branch decorated at the time of the first seeds and first ploughing. The pastry bird was attractive and delicately made, but how to convey it was a puzzle. We put it in a piece of cloth, and I laid it on top of the jewellery in the cedar box, to be carried carefully back to Athens.

There was a risk in taking charge of real jewellery on the open road. As Philomela and I were not yet married, these valuables didn't truly belong to me. I didn't intend to tell anyone about the new ornaments. But then I met Gorgias, wealthy son of the eminent silversmith's family, on the road towards my house.

'What are you carrying?' he demanded. 'Ornaments for some lady friend?' Perhaps as a silversmith he recognised a container of jewellery, or even smelt out the baubles in some way. So I felt obliged to explain, and then Gorgias wanted to see. I cautiously opened the box a little, and he pushed the pastry bird aside to get a look.

When I got home I couldn't decide whether to tell my mother, Eunike daughter of Diogeiton, about the jewellery or not. It would mean explaining in more detail the unorthodox marriage of Smikrenes of Eleusis and his wife – who lived in Hymettos. Of course, Mother really knew this, in broad outline anyway, as she had spent the summer in an enforced visit (in order to escape danger) to the women's quarters of Smikrenes' home. There she had become acquainted with the girl I had already decided to marry. I knew, however, that she found it easier most of the time to think of Philomela as a half-orphan. Philonike had left her husband not for another man but for a chaste life in her paternal home, but that was almost immaterial to Mother. Upon my production of the cedar box of jewellery I would be treated to her full opinion of females who had run off from their husband's house. So, without bothering my mother with this fact, I left the cedar box in the *andron*, where I could see it every day, though I hid it by placing it behind the largest ornamental pot.

Philomela's pastry bird had one wingtip broken off – whether through the bumping of the journey or the intervention of Gorgias I did not know. The women mended it with flour paste, and it still looked pretty. Since it was slightly damaged, Mother said we should keep it and not send it out with our branch. I was pleased not to let go of Philomela's bird, in our own celebration of the autumn festival.

Pyanepsia is one of my favourite festivals, with no slaughter of animals or long rituals or big speeches. This day is happy and light, celebrating the time of seeds, in which the land is ploughed and the seeds put in the ground. I was glad to be home for the Pyanepsia supper, the dinner of boiled beans and of all sorts of seeds, a *panspermia*, though this is a frugal feast, and some of it has to be offered to Apollo, just as Theseus and his companions when they had safely arrived home made offerings of their frugal stew of legumes.

'There are lots of parties up and down the street,' remarked Theodoros. To gain a better vantage than his height allowed him, he stood upon a heap of broken tiles and brick rubble, the detritus from the house repair of a neighbour. Our house is a corner house; on one side it shares a wall with the next house, on the other is the street. The unsightly huddle of broken tiles and old wall was not at our front entrance, but at the side, around the corner. I ought to have remonstrated with the neighbour who lived behind me on the side street about clearing this nuisance away, but Theodoros certainly enjoyed the outlook from his little hill. 'I just saw one of the arkhons go into the neighbours' three houses away,' he announced.

'Even arkhons must eat,' I replied with philosophic calm. It was nothing to me if my neighbour entertained one of the governing magistrates of Athens. Though it occurred to me that I didn't know any arkhons well enough to invite them to dinner.

'Maybe he came because of another theft,' Theodoros suggested hopefully. 'Two doors away they lost a silver beaker. *Solid* silver – very valuable, the man said. And you remember the lady from the house over the way – the kind of lady Mother doesn't want us to talk about – who lost a big gold bracelet, like dolphins. One of a pair, she says.'

'Humph,' snorted Mother. 'That kind of "lady" has a lot of ways to lose and find gold bracelets. I shouldn't worry about *her*. And the arkhon is going to a little bean party, like everybody else.'

'Aristotle is coming to our house,' said Theodoros. 'He's a philosopher, I know – is he a Pythagorean? If he's a Pythagorean, he can't eat beans. Did you know that? I knew you cannot eat meat or fish if you are a Pythagorean. But it's odd you cannot even eat beans. There'd have to be a special gruel made up, just little seeds.'

'Aristotle isn't a Pythagorean,' I said. 'Aristotle eats everything. Theophrastos is a Pythagorean, I think, but he's not coming.' I was happy that Aristotle's second-in-command, the earnest Theophrastos, had refused my lukewarm invitation.

'Eat your beans and be thankful,' said my mother. 'And it's best,' she added, 'not to eat up too many seeds. I didn't put in a lot of grain, since Athens may need more for the planting. Last year's harvest was not very large. We need a good crop next summer.'

'I'm not going to eat at home,' Theodoros said proudly. 'I've got to be off, Mother, I shall have my bean feast at another house. I'm carrying our *eiresione*. Look! Haven't I made a beautiful one?'

He ran out and fetched it, so that he could display his handiwork to us. It was indeed a very fine *eiresione*, a straight bough from one of our olive trees at the farm, wound about carefully and in patterns with wool that Mother had given him. Woollen fillets fluttered from the bough. I had offered a little jar of Hymettos honey, and the boy had also attached figs and some late grapes and a couple of ripe apples. Mother had obviously humoured him, for the branch also bore, dangling by threads among the olive leaves and the woolly fillets, little pastry piglets, looking quite charming.

'I am the *eiresione*-bringer – I bear good luck throughout the year!' Theodoros chanted. He took his bough outside and carried it gaily, looking the walking image of autumn fruitfulness and good cheer. His dog, Molossos-Molossou, went capering off with him. It was always hard for Moloss-Molou (his usual nickname) to allow Theodoros out of his sight. I let the dog run off. He would protect Theodoros against the older youths who tried to bully little boys and grab the branch, or strip the good things from it.

I watched as Theodoros met a boy from a neighbouring house, and the two of them together started the old song:

The *eiresione*, the good *eiresione*, best tree of the year!
Honey and grapes it bears, figs and oil so fine,
Eat, drink and fall asleep with a cup of good wine –
But give us something, so your luck will be near.

Theodoros and his companion were soon part of a
little throng of boys. Each carrying his family's woolly
branch, the youthful luck-bearers went weaving about
and among the houses, singing as they went. My little
brother would stop when he was tired – and when offered
a gift sufficient to buy the *eiresione* and its good luck.

Aristotle arrived (at which Mother modestly and
properly retired), and he and I stood in our doorway,
laughing at the frisks and flourishes of the little boys who
came our way, and the fine things they had put on their
various branches. We did not bribe any of these for an
eiresione, since I had promised Theodoros that I would
wait for his best friend Euphranor, and make an offer for
his branch. Aristotle, I was pleased to see, had apparently
recovered from the sorrows and vicissitudes of our
summer and its journeys, and was his usual cheerful self.
We went over my news (the *engye*) and his news, which
partly explained his good humour.

'I have heard from Alexander,' he said. 'Letters take a
long time to come from the desolate mountain region
where he is now – still pursuing the rascal Bessus, who is
now wearing the imperial diadem and calling himself
King of the Persians. But Alexander has sent me a letter.
A note rather. And some new specimens of animals.'

'For your great treatise on all the animals,' I said,
amused. It seemed funny that Aristotle, instead of
following Plato and thinking all the time about the Good
and the Beautiful, should spend so much of his time
deciding how to describe and categorise animals. 'What
did he say about your adventures among the pirates?'

'He still knew nothing of that, I think, when he wrote. Nor does he mention Harpalos.'

'Just as well.' With Aristotle in Asia, I had met Harpalos, treasurer to Alexander, a puzzling man, cause of a good deal of trouble to ourselves.

'And Theophrastos too – Alexander sent him some plants. You know how ambitious he is to understand and categorise all plants. The King of Makedon tells me also that his distinguished officer Antigonos has lost an eye, and is coming to Athens temporarily to seek medical treatment among the doctors here. So I have that to look forward to. And I have also heard from my good friend the general Parmenion, who is in fine health despite the wearing journey he has been engaged upon, escorting the treasure of Persepolis, with a train of five hundred camels. Here . . .' He brought out some battered tablets. 'I was meaning to show you this epistle, as it partly concerns you.'

The wax had been rather softened and chipped in transport, but the letter was still legible, in a precise hand:

Parmenion to Aristotle, Greeting

I trust you are in good health, as I am. Hearty thanks to you and to your friend that my grandson is safe and well likewise. Of course I shall acknowledge him; funds will be sent to Kos for his education. Eventually he can join either myself or Philotas, who does well. I could wish he were not recently attached to a Greek female who calls herself Antigone, and leads him into loud talk and drunken riots. Still, Philotas is young yet. I write from Ekbatana of the Medes, whither I have come with a great camel train, proving the truth of the common saying that wealth makes trouble. For the treasure of Persepolis has been no great joy to me, though I cannot sign myself a philosopher. Still I sign myself your good friend,

Parmenion

I was pleased that Aristotle had let me see a communication from someone so important – a letter that had come all the way from Ekbatana.

'The general, you see, will not only acknowledge but support young Parmenion, despite his grandson's being born out of wedlock. So all that should turn out well.'

'Good indeed,' I pronounced, and added hesitantly, 'What about the . . . you know, the rumour or whatever it was we heard last summer, on several sides, that Alexander had fallen out with Parmenion and Philotas?'

'That must have been a temporary difficulty. Nothing serious. Certainly, the venerable Parmenion, if old, is still wonderfully able. As for Philotas, he is a jewel! A great warrior with strong judgement. A loyal companion of Alexander since his youth. As Alexander ventures further into foreign regions, he may appreciate the more the staunch friends of his past. Anyway, Philotas is evidently well. Even if Parmenion does not like his son's new woman, Philotas' interest in her indicates robust health, does it not?'

'Many officers abroad,' I reflected, 'amuse themselves with Greek women, if they can. Harpalos the Treasurer did as much. I wonder if this Athenian woman could be the prostitute Antigone? The freedwoman that we met last summer, with the sandals like green tendrils.' I remembered those sandals, and the neat feet in them, very well.

'The woman associated with that cheating merchant of perfumes? But Antigone is not an uncommon name, Stephanos. Philotas' woman may be merely a prisoner of war. In any event, I am glad to hear of him. And relieved to be in regular correspondence with Alexander again.'

Aristotle put away his letter as Euphranor arrived, waving his branch, which was undeniably fine. He had been given by Theodoros (with my permission) another

bough from one of our olive trees, and had decorated it
beautifully in coloured wools and broad white ribands,
with little pots of honey dangling from it. To cap it all,
there were pastry figures so surprising, like complete
little statues of youths and maidens, of Theseus and
Athena's owl, that I thought the boy's uncle, the sculptor
Euphranor, must have taken a personal hand in the
business.

'Your *eiresione* is worth waiting for,' I remarked – and,
in accordance with his secret pact with Theodoros, paid
him obols enough to make him stop.

'Let us set it here, by the front door,' said Euphranor
eagerly. 'You have the bracket – throw the old one away.'
He took the wizened brown vegetable matter that was
the remains of last year's good-luck branch out of the
iron staple by the door and cast it aside. Quickly he
inserted his creation. '*Now*,' the boy said proudly, 'you
have your new one, the best! It will look so handsome!
And you will know it is bringing you good luck the whole
year.'

The branch, as the boy predicted, did look handsome.
We took Euphranor inside with us for the modest feast of
beans and seeds. Just as we were about to begin, I
suddenly remembered that I hadn't put Philomela's bird
on the branch, and I wanted to be able to tell Smikrenes
I had done so. So I retrieved the pastry figure, and went
out to the front door. Our *eiresione* was waving its fillets
gaily in the breeze, and showing off its ornaments. As I
attached the pastry bird, my fingers touched something
cold. Something hard. Not pastry nor fig. Metal. I pulled
the foreign object out from among the leaves and
ribbons. A heavy gold bracelet with ends like dolphins'
heads. A large bracelet. Not ours – and now attached to
the branch and our house.

I yelled to Euphranor, who had followed me. 'Go to

the arkhon – he's nearby, at that house.' And I pointed it out to him. 'Say "Theft!"' I commanded. 'Someone has left a stolen object – has attached a stolen object to our branch!'

Euphranor stared at it, horrified. 'There was nothing like that there – this afternoon. I know *everything* that is on the bough!' he protested.

'Of course you do! It wasn't on the *eiresione* before. It has just come!'

Euphranor ran off. I stood at the doorway and waited, while the rest of the household, catching my excitement, stood as close to the entry as they felt right, in order to peer at the *eiresione*. The lad was soon back with the arkhon and the arkhon's host.

'Theft!' I cried. 'A stolen object has been attached to our *eiresione*!' The arkhon took the gold bracelet and examined it. Now that I saw him, I recognised this magistrate as Lysiphon of the deme Kholargos. He was impressed with the weight of the gold, I could see. His host, my neighbour, looked over Lysiphon's shoulder. Other neighbours, Hieron among them, came up the street to find out what was going on.

'Well, interesting. Very interesting,' the arkhon murmured, in an officially neutral tone. I suddenly guessed that he was wondering if one of us had stolen it, had become upset by the danger and was trying to get rid of it in this ridiculous way. Aristotle saw the same thing.

'The object of this absurd exercise,' he said mildly, 'would seem to be to cause discomfort to Stephanos son of Nikiarkhos. Who comes from an old and upright Athenian family.'

'Well, maybe.' Lysiphon the arkhon was hesitant, turning the bracelet over and over and then frowning at the decorated olive bough.

'As soon as it was discovered, Stephanos notified you,'

Aristotle continued. 'Although it would have been easier to throw the bracelet into the street or on to some dung-heap nearby. Stephanos son of Nikiarkhos always does the honest thing.'

'But what about my silver beaker?' one of my other neighbours cried. 'That wasn't stolen for no joke, I'll be bound. Pretty sort of jesting when there are thieves and robbers about!'

The crowd murmured its agreement. The group around my threshold had grown, with the arrival of other dwellers in the deme, including, by now, Halirrhothios.

'At least,' said the arkhon, 'we can certainly return the bracelet to the woman who lost it. And *you* may need to come along to explain,' he told me sternly.

'Perhaps,' suggested Hieron, 'the bracelet was stolen in order to offer Stephanos an insult, by giving him a whore's bracelet – if you will forgive the phrase.'

'A serious business, meddling with someone else's valuables,' Lysiphon announced sternly. 'Let us hope, Stephanos, that this bauble is not worth fifty drakhmai. Then you will get off with returning twice the value to the person from whom you stole it. That's the law.'

Though the arkhon was correct as to the law, some of my neighbours registered disgust. 'Paying a whore for returning her bracelet to her,' one exclaimed. 'That's your idea of justice?'

'*I* have had nothing to do with this bracelet being here,' I affirmed. 'I am willing to come to the house of the woman concerned and make sure the object is restored to her. But it is not my fault. Wait just a little,' I added. 'I must make sure everything is safe at home, and give instructions to the servants . . .'

I hastened indoors, not proposing to waste time with further propitiation of the official. I wanted to make sure that my own valuables were safe before I left the house, for what would probably be a long, prosy session with this magistrate. Once I saw the cedar box again I would give strict instructions that someone was to sit beside it.

I hurried into the *andron*. Looked in the place beside the ornamental pot. Not there. Looked behind the ornamental pot – and saw what I had forgotten, that the room's one window was in the wall behind that 'safe' place. High above it, but still . . . Anxiety increasing with every heartbeat, I looked about the room – and then had to call Mother. This meant quick explanations, but she swore she had not seen the box, as she hadn't been in the *andron*. No servant of ours would have taken it. I rushed back out again. It now seemed fortunate that the arkhon was still there.

'Theft!' I cried. 'I have just been the victim of a burglar! While we were all talking out here, a thief has made away with a box of valuables from within my house.'

'Amazing impudence!' said Halirrhothios. 'Who would have thought *you*, Stephanos, had such valuables! Do you want us to shake out our cloaks?'

'Are you sure it happened just now?' asked Lysiphon the arkhon.

'It might have been earlier, when we were all looking at the *eiresione*,' I admitted. 'But the theft is very recent – this evening. He – the burglar – probably came in by the back of the house, or the side . . .'

'No, stay,' said Aristotle. 'Let us look.' He led the way round the corner of the house, to the hillock of rubble upon which Theodoros had stood earlier that evening.

'You see,' the philosopher began, pointing to the heap. 'There is the old *eiresione*, thrown away at the top of the rubbish. There you see little Theodoros' prints, where he stood earlier before he went off with his new *eiresione*. And on top of those, and pressing into the old branch, we see the later prints of a big foot, the foot of a grown man.'

'That's it!' I exclaimed, much excited at this discovery. 'Exactly – the philosopher is quite right. There are the marks of little brother's childish feet. And the even more recent print of a grown man. Perhaps he just stood on one foot, and reached through the window. That proves it!' I straightened my back and turned away from the fascinating text of rubble, the better to explain to the arkhon.

'The thief reached quickly through a window – the work of a moment. If we search immediately, we might find the things on the thief, or in his house.'

'True,' said the arkhon, '*if* we knew who the thief was. I am sorry for your loss, Stephanos. But this is only talk. General surmise. *Anybody* might walk on that rubbish – it's in the way of all foot-travellers. You need to make a specific charge. If you want a search, you must name the suspected thief!'

IV

A Naked Search

'You must name the suspected thief!' Lysiphon repeated impatiently. We all stood about him as if turned to stone. What the arkhon said was true. But how hazardous it would be to name someone!

'As for what you claim to have lost,' he added. 'Trinkets, you say – of what value?'

'Truly valuable,' I asserted defiantly. 'There is a gold necklace, and earrings with real gems. Blue stones and reddish, in drops, and gold.'

'Why don't you keep a house-dog, if you have all these valuables to protect?'

'There is a dog. But Moloss-Molou – the dog – is out with my little brother, going about with the *eiresione*. Someone else may have realised the house would be free of that guardian.'

'Who else knows of these alleged objects? Can anyone else give an account of them?' My neighbours were naturally silent. 'And your own household – who among them knows of the ornaments?' He turned impatiently to me.

'Nobody,' I had to admit. 'I have told nobody yet that

I had them – for safety's sake. But my promised father-in-law Smikrenes, from whom I had them, will be able to speak about them.'

At least I think he will, I added mentally. Smikrenes, I knew, was not fond of public speaking.

'Where does this Smikrenes live?'

'In Eleusis.'

'Oh? All that way?' The magistrate shrugged. 'Difficult. You ask us to believe in unknown valuables, and then to send for a witness at a distance.'

'Too bad!' said one of the neighbours. 'Shall we send for the – er – lady with the dolphin bracelet to claim *her* property?'

'Well, Stephanos,' said the magistrate to me, 'if you have nothing more to allege, we really had better wait for this female to identify her bracelet. Then she can lay a complaint against *you*, as the thief – or not, as she thinks best.' The pompous Lysiphon turned to one of the slaves who accompanied him.

'Run to the dwelling of Thratta, where she plies her trade, not many streets from this place, and ask her to come and identify her bracelet.'

'She may be away from home, eating her *panspermia* elsewhere,' someone suggested.

'Ah, it will be other seeds that she has on her lips,' an obscener wit retorted. The arkhon scowled at the ensuing hilarity. After silencing the ribald ones by severity of countenance, he turned back to me.

'Regarding the loss you yourself claim, Stephanos, how can you expect me to act? Nobody here, by your own admission, knows of these baubles. And you can name no one as thief—'

'But I can!' I burst out. 'I *do* name a man. I name Halirrhothios. And I demand to be able to conduct an immediate search of his house.'

Gasps and cries followed this announcement, which was something of a surprise even to myself. 'Nonsense!' Halirrhothios exclaimed indignantly. He turned a little pale under the shock of the accusation, however, and did not tumble into profuse speech, as I half expected.

'Really, Stephanos,' said the arkhon, with anxious severity, 'do you know what you say? Remember, this is by no means a game. You risk at very least your own good name if you make a light accusation.'

'It is not made lightly,' I retorted. A hard, determined anger filled me. The arkhon seemed to me a fool who was standing in the way of my doing myself justice. I was going to get back those things – Philomela's things.

'Let us be clear about this,' said Lysiphon's host, the man who had been quietly entertaining his arkhon friend at dinner when our problem dragged them from their table. 'You, Stephanos, allege that you have lost certain property. How many ornaments? What precisely is their value?'

'We didn't know – we could scarcely guess,' said Halirrhothios, 'that you had *any* valuables, Stephanos son of Nikiarkhos.'

'Quite so,' said Theophon, Halirrhothios' immediate neighbour. A tall, square man with a rosy face, still relatively young, Theophon commanded attention. He was much richer than Halirrhothios or indeed than most of us. A bud on a lesser branch of a truly ancient family, he had inherited from his father an interest in trade. Theophon had ships that regularly went to Byzantion and Egypt, and he had made money from the cargoes. He was also well-born, well-educated, and very talkative. So everyone in our neighbourhood listened patiently whenever Theophon spoke.

'I am truly sorry to see this, Stephanos,' he said in his usual loud tone. 'It's hard to believe you would raise such a serious charge against your old neighbour Halirrhothios here – my good friend. I am a man of some repute hereabout – I think I can be said to know my own neighbourhood. How can you claim to have suffered the robbery of valuables when – sorry to mention it – a couple of years ago your family was so much in debt that you sold one thing after another!'

'Barely a pot left to piss in!' interjected Halirrhothios. The man had looked dumbfounded at my first accusation, but was quickly plucking up a spirit. It was rational for him to hope that his supporters would suppress my charge.

'Indeed,' said the arkhon. '*How* exactly did you come by these alleged valuables, Stephanos?'

'They were a gift to my future wife, on the occasion of the *engye*. I brought them from my future father-in-law's house in Eleusis just yesterday,' I protested, truthfully enough. Though I elided the part played by the Hymettos family and my bride's mother, estranged wife of my future father-in-law. No sense in dragging everybody into it, I told myself.

'Tush,' said Halirrhothios. '*Anybody* could claim that he had pretty objects that suddenly disappeared.'

'Quite,' said Theophon. '*I* could claim that I had a cup made of pure gold that someone had taken! Pretty jewels, Stephanos son of Nikiarkhos, but perhaps imaginary?'

'We ought to send for the intended father-in-law, who can vouch for them,' insisted my own next-door neighbour, defending me. 'Even if we have to wait for him to come from Eleusis.'

'If we have to send to Eleusis for a witness,' the arkhon pronounced, 'that will give us a couple of days for everyone to cool down and consider.'

'If I wait two days, or even one,' I protested, 'I may as well wait ten days! The things would certainly be gone from their hiding-place in that time. Fortunately, there is one man in Athens who has seen these jewels and can describe them. Gorgias, son of the silversmith Lysippos. Let Gorgias at once be sent for! If he is not at home, his servants will know where he is. Meanwhile, let us go to Halirrhothios' house together.'

My firmness in this matter established a certain respect for me in the crowd, and there was a murmur of assent as the arkhon sent for Gorgias.

'I should go to my house first, while you wait, in order to prepare my household for this invasion,' said Halirrhothios.

'No, I think not,' said the arkhon, pursing his lips judiciously. 'I have just dispatched a slave – a good messenger – to fetch Gorgias and bring him to your house, Halirrhothios. It is best for us all to go there in a body. Then no unfair and suspicious things can be said of you.' And he tucked Halirrhothios' arm under his own and walked off. I was pleased at this point with the man's caution.

'Bring the branch – it may be evidence,' he called over his shoulder. So we followed decorously, myself and Aristotle, with little Euphranor carrying our unhappy *eiresione*, and after us a crowd of neighbours.

When we arrived at Halirrhothios' house, Lysiphon was determined that we should still wait for Gorgias. Such a doubt of my word! Such delay! Gorgias might be celebrating the day by taking his seed-dinner in some distant deme. So I was relieved to see him coming along at a good pace. The messenger must have impressed upon him the need for haste.

'I understand,' Gorgias said, 'that you, Stephanos, have lost the valuables you showed to me. I am sorry to hear it! You need me to describe them?'

'Yes,' I assented. I hoped Gorgias would remember

how much he owed to Aristotle and myself. We had supported him and his sister during a time of difficulty, keeping their family's name sweet when it might have gone rancid. I somewhat distrusted Gorgias, who seemed too self-concerned and poetical to make a practical friend. But he performed well on this occasion.

'I can describe exactly what I saw in Stephanos' possession,' he said, turning to the arkhon. 'There were two sets of earrings. One was large gold loops, with intricate lace-work in wire at the top. And the other pair had delicate stones of lapis and cornelian, in finely wrought gold, four drops to a side. Each drop a string of little balls, in graded order. The necklace has a central drop of cornelian, and is gold filigree, light in weight but finely wrought and pure. Such ornaments might be – probably are – family heirlooms, though not of the oldest kind. Undoubtedly valuable.'

'Well, well,' said the arkhon. 'Did you see anything else?'

'The box they came in – a good cedar-wood box lined with a woollen fabric. And a pastry in the shape of a bird, with one wing torn.'

There was a shout of laughter, and I could feel myself flushing with vexation.

'Well,' declared Halirrhothios. 'Now I am made responsible for a pastry bird!'

'So,' said Halirrhothios' rosy-cheeked neighbour Theophon, enjoying an excursion into satire, 'I hope we are not all going to have our houses turned upside down while someone looks for this stray pastry? And perhaps accuses us of tearing the wing!'

'No,' I said calmly. 'For the bird is not lost – it is on our *eiresione*. But the box with the jewellery was put in our *andron*, with no one's knowledge but my own. Yet the table on which the box reposed was under a window, which may be how the thief got it.'

'All speculation!' Theophon waved his hand airily, but I could see a delicate film of sweat coming over Halirrhothios' features. Perhaps because he saw who was approaching.

'Here comes the woman!'

'It's Thratta, right enough!'

The crowd parted to admit this personage into the group, welcoming the diversion.

'Good evening, Thratta,' one of my neighbours murmured in a familiar manner.

The woman who bustled through the crowd was well-clad, with a long-fringed stole or shawl wrapped round her tunic. Though she was somewhat heavy-set, she carried herself well. Not quite in her first youth, it was easy to guess, though one could not clearly make out her lightly veiled face. She made a low bow to the arkhon.

'Woman,' he said to her, 'though formerly a slave, and living now in a house purchased by your owner, you appear as a freedwoman. Before today you have claimed that you had lost—'

'Lost! I never lost anything!' She was loud and indignant. 'The first bracelet of a pair was *stolen* – and by Herakles, if the mate to it wasn't stolen this very day! I had just discovered the theft, and was setting out to find a magistrate when your messenger—'

'Look here,' commanded Lysiphon the arkhon. 'You say you lost a bracelet from your house. Do you identify it as this one?' He showed her in his own hand the bracelet I had found lurking in the pretty branch.

'Oh yes, that's mine. Indeed it is,' she responded. That she was the Thracian her name indicated was audible in her accent. 'It's one of a pair. Where did you find it?'

'It was found on this *eiresione*. Have you seen this before?' The magistrate beckoned to Euphranor, who brought over his waving good-luck branch. Thratta and some of the others peered at it as if they hoped to find more jewels perching among the olive leaves in company with the pastry shapes.

'No, I have never seen that *eiresione*. I am puzzled how my bracelet got there. I am very glad to have it back.'

The woman reached out for the golden ornament, but the arkhon drew it back.

'Not yet,' he said. 'This bracelet may be evidence. Do you, Thratta the prostitute, now a freedwoman, know the man who found it? This gentleman is Stephanos son of Nikiarkhos, citizen of Athens.'

'Oh, the messenger explained,' the woman said to me. 'I am so very grateful.' Thratta gazed at me through her light veiling, and blushed becomingly. Her breasts had begun to point to the earth, but were not without their attractions as a delicate red spread over their creamy expanse, not entirely hidden from beholders.

'Does the bracelet belong to you outright, or was it from your former owner? Do you or your former owner wish to lay any charge against Stephanos son of Nikiarkhos?'

'The gold bracelet's all mine – my owner has nothing to do with it. As for Stephanos here, who found my lovely bracelet in a branch and restored it? By Persephone, no! And I don't see how he'd be a thief. *He's* no customer of mine. Not likely he'd know about my fine things, is it?'

'Well then,' remarked the arkhon's host, rather disappointed, 'it seems that Stephanos is clear on the subject of the bracelet. And we will have to go back to this other charge.'

'As we have begun the process,' said Aristotle, 'which is a claim of theft, by public statement, had we not better continue? The laws of Athens allow the person on whom the theft was perpetrated – Stephanos in this instance – to demand to search the house of the alleged thief. An accusation has been made in public, and in the presence of the arkhon. The accusation can be withdrawn. Or else the accuser – in this instance Stephanos – if persisting in the charge, should be allowed access at once to the house of Halirrhothios, the man who he claims has wronged him.'

'Yes,' said one of my own supporters. 'And the goods taken are obviously worth a lot of money, too! A serious business.'

'The law,' said Aristotle, 'offers this course of action as an *immediate* remedy only. The search should be undertaken as soon as may be.'

'Right!' exclaimed Thratta, who showed no disposition to depart from this scene. 'So let us get on with it, as the philosopher advises.'

'I agree,' said the arkhon. 'We must proceed now, and the sooner we get it over with the better. Unless you withdraw, Stephanos? There's still time.'

'No,' I said.

'Men of Athens,' the arkhon said in a formal tone, 'the law is very clear about what is to be done in such a case, and makes specific demands. The search must be a *naked* search. That is, the searcher should be undressed, so that he cannot secrete the articles in question – or any others – in his clothing or about his person and plant them in the dwelling of the person whom he accuses. Stephanos, you must strip in my sight.'

'Don't embarrass yourself,' urged Theophon, but I stood firm.

Turning to his slave, the arkhon commanded, 'Fetch a couple of strips of plain linen, boy!' He then explained to us: 'I shall allow you to wear a loincloth while searching the house, but nothing of your own or made of cloth from your household. Only a loincloth – not even sandals. Aristotle, if you wish to accompany him in the search, you must go similarly naked.'

'And I too volunteer to conduct this search,' said Thratta, 'even if I have to go naked myself.' There was open and raucous laughter throughout the crowd.

'Woman,' said the magistrate, 'you have nothing to do with this case!'

'Well, but I *do*,' said the persistent prostitute. 'I lost a necklace as well as the first gold bracelet of the pair. If the second bracelet turned up in this part of Kydathenaion, likely the thief lives hereabouts. Friends of mine have lost goods too. The thefts should be put an end to. Bad for business. The women lose their rewards – which are their savings – while the men get suspicious of us and each other. Now, these two gentlemen . . .' nodding at myself and Aristotle, 'may be all the law requires, but they have one big weakness atween them. You know, *they*, being citizen men, can't go a-searching of the women's quarters. If *I* was a man, I'd secrete any goods I stole in my women's quarters, and then say they was out of bounds and forbidden to any searchers, let the searchers be the Basileus and the priestly Hierophant together!'

The arkhon had much to do to quell the hubbub and the laughter. But Thratta persisted.

'I've had things stolen from me,' she insisted. 'There was a necklace, as I say, and the other bracelet. A silver mug with my name scratched on it – like this other gentleman here lost a silver beaker. My girlfriends have lost several things, too. Anyway, you are making a big mistake if you try to search a house without being able to enter the women's quarters.'

'There is a certain logic in her argument,' Aristotle said dispassionately.

The arkhon reluctantly agreed. Permission was given to all three of us to conduct the naked search. The messenger, returned with the strips of linen borrowed from a nearby householder, handed me my new and scanty loincloth. Theophon was right, I found it oddly embarrassing to take off one's clothes in such a case: I did it with what aplomb I could, turned about to show the unimpressed crowd I was completely naked, and then humbly took the proffered strip and wound it about my privates. Aristotle went through the same performance. After that, Thratta, undaunted by a rapt and increasingly raucous audience of well-wishers, did the same thing in her own style. Her admirers whistled, shouted, and sang snatches of melody. Theophon seemed greatly taken with her, and moved closer to gaze upon her charms. Naked Thratta gave her robe and stole to the care of a female slave among the watchers, while Aristotle and I made young Euphranor the guardian of our own garments. Having undergone this ceremony, we proceeded into the house, in the company of the fully clad and indignant Halirrhothios.

I had not imagined how difficult and embarrassing such a search would be. How rude it seems to irrupt into a man's house against his will! And how dreamlike to enter for the first time an unknown house – a house belonging to a man of good breeding and decent fortune – clad in so airy a manner. The house seemed alien to me and strange. As soon as I entered I could hardly wait to leave. The search I was to undertake seemed a crack-brained idea, futile and self-willed. I forced myself not to rush through the rooms but to go slowly, looking carefully at walls and tables. Halirrhothios' *andron* was, like my own, a trifle dusty, but reasonably well furnished. I noted that he had the walls painted in the new fashion, in a line of oblongs of different colours, like imaginary bricks of celestial hues. Or rather, someone had started to paint the wall, but it was unfinished, a patch of bright oblongs left to gather dust and dullness with the rest. There was a wooden chest by one chair, and I looked into that, finding nothing but tally sticks and figures scribbled on rough tablets, as one sometimes does with important accounts. Near this chest was a handsome pot with lively pictures of Apollo and Artemis; I ruthlessly turned it upside down, but nothing came out save a dead spider.

We continued relentlessly on, moving in a phalanx of three into the kitchen area, where one tremulous slave watched us as we pawed over pots and ewers, and overset the cooking stove. We stirred the water in the great water-pot with a long wooden stick, to hear if anything clanked at the bottom of this *hydria*. Behind the kitchen, as in my own house, there was a small room for washing, and a used commode. I grimly promised myself that we would have to come back and search this unpleasant receptacle if nothing else offered. The small tub was innocent of contents. Back in the kitchen, Thratta made for the stores, and with a metal rod pierced without compunction into the depths of the stored-up wheat, and barley, and dried beans. We read the entrails of the lentils, and shook again at the cooking utensils as if they were able to reveal the Mysteries.

Ceasing to be entertained by the kitchen, like rude guests we departed, leaving things in a mess, and made for the stairs. Now there was shrieking overhead, as the women protested against our advent.

'Don't worry, dearies,' shrieked Thratta in turn as she ascended. 'It is only I as will come to your room! Rest easy, I shan't let the men in at all!'

This assurance did not seem greatly to ease their minds. Renewed shrieking was followed by sobbing. I could hear Halirrhothios' wife protesting to her husband, 'How could you!'

The women crowded into one upstairs room, a bedroom it must have been, and we were free to search the room vacated. This was a well-lighted weaving room, with a nicely set-up loom. We inspected the loom weights, and looked behind the fabric. We found a round wooden box, such as women keep treasures in, but it was empty. Thratta emptied the large box full of blankets and shook each one carefully. At first nothing rolled into view. But then something did. With a sharp crack a pottery thing fell out of one of the folds of a blanket.

'A doll,' said Aristotle picking it up. 'A fairly large one. It is a jointed doll—'

'A child's toy only. Now you've probably broken it!' said Halirrhothios sharply.

The door opened and a little girl came rushing in, a child in a blur one might say from her haste.

'That's *mine*!' she said, grabbing the doll. 'I've been looking for her *everywhere*! You mustn't hurt my Atalanta!'

'Go back, child!' Halirrhothios ordered. 'Leave her alone!' he commanded us.

'Nobody's going to hurt a little girl, nobody thinks of any harm,' cooed Thratta, as gently as a sucking dove to her young. 'What is your name, child?'

'Eurynome,' was the answer, almost whispered. The child so bold on her entrance was suddenly shy with the strangers, especially Thratta who knelt beside her. Eurynome, who might have been seven or eight years old, looked with affright and curiosity at this strange sight, a woman with finely bound hair but without any clothes on except a curious strip about her plump middle. I inspected the child through the dusty motes our activity had stirred up in the weaving room. Little Eurynome must be the child of this mansion, surely, to speak with such assurance and to claim her possession. She wore earrings, too, I noticed, not very pretty ones, rather ugly boxes of bone, each dangling at the end of a wire chain.

Yet she was simply dressed, in a tunic, though not unbleached. Her hair was cut short, like that of a slave.

'And whose might you be, my pretty child?' cooed Thratta again, coming closer and taking the child's chin in her hand.

'Let her be!' ordered Halirrhothios. 'She has nothing to do with the likes of you. Get back, child – back to the other women!'

'That's all right,' said Thratta soothingly. 'Of course you will go back, child, but no need to take such earrings – such *ugly* earrings – with you. And you will leave us the doll, for a while.'

'We will return Atalanta,' I assured the girl. But I was watching in surprise as Thratta deftly removed the boxy earrings from the child's burdened head.

'Wonderfully made, some of these things are,' she mused. 'What jewellers put these together, I wonder?' And she cracked open one of the bone boxes – and there nestling within it was one of the precious earrings of lapis and carnelian that were to go to Philomela.

'There it is!' I exclaimed, while Aristotle added, 'It fits well with the silversmith's description.'

'Nice,' said Thratta with approbation. 'Now, let's see if we can find its twin. One-two-three, child – and look at this!' She produced with a flourish the mate to the first earring.

'There – those are mine!' I exclaimed. 'Halirrhothios, I declare you *are* a thief!'

'We must look for the rest,' said Aristotle. 'I think this toy may—'

'Give *me* that doll!' I ordered him. Taking the object, I twisted off its head, while the little girl screamed, though she had not cried out when Thratta took her earrings. My necklace came tumbling out of the doll's body, accompanied by a silver chain that I did not recognise.

'Oho!' said Thratta. 'That belongs to a girl I know! She'll swear to it before all the arkhons as ever lived.'

'I am still missing a pair of plain gold earrings,' I declared. 'I suggest, Thratta, that you lead the search in the other room.'

'And I'm missing my other bracelet! And a silver cup. So let's flutter these chickens!' Stout-hearted Thratta led the way to the room where the women were pent up. They emerged shrieking and clucking, like a flock of fowl disturbed by a fox. As the little crowd of women were making for the weaving room, Thratta waylaid them, trying to subject each individually to her search. There was a good deal of argument. Aristotle and I were thus free to make our way into the empty bedroom the women had just occupied. Unlike the weaving room it was not well lighted. Even on this temperate evening it was hot, as there was no window, only a small slit near the ceiling. I could hear Thratta ordering the women to hand over any boxes and to lend their jewellery for inspection. The slaves gave in meekly enough, but Halirrhothios' wife put up a spirited defence. Eventually Thratta was able to bring to us the jewellery the women had been wearing that day, which we were at leisure to inspect closely, as well as slippers and belts. Nothing untoward was found. I was determined, however, to search this second room thoroughly. What Thratta said was true. The woman's quarters offered perhaps the best hiding-place in a citizen's house.

'Let's look to see where else this magpie might have put his store,' I said. 'Thieves!' I yelled out of a window, to keep the crowd below posted. My blood was up and I was eager to pursue the hunt. Standing on a stool, I looked around the rough ceiling. Behind one of the slats of rafter I found a silver cup, which Thratta loudly claimed. Then a silver beaker, somewhat tarnished –

probably that of my neighbour. I rummaged about the dried reeds, the *kalameia* that lined the ceiling under the rafters of this upstairs room, and soon found a plain round *pyxis* hidden behind the musty reeds. It contained a little hoard of pretty objects, including the other set of missing earrings given to my keeping by Smikrenes.

'Here!' I said, jumping down from my chair and losing my modest loincloth. 'Here is a box of thievery!'

'But no marble head, nor valuable cup,' mused Aristotle, who had taken the box from me while I tied on my cloth again.

Halirrhothios was shaking and pale. The arkhon came in at the sound of our cries, and I displayed to him what we had found. The arkhon turned pale himself.

'I command you below,' he shouted through a window slit, 'detain this Halirrhothios! Don't let him go!'

A clamour could be heard without doors. We started off towards the stairs, the arkhon holding Halirrhothios by the arm.

'This child can probably tell you how it was,' said Thratta, who had paused at the door of the weaving room. She spied her quarry among the grieving women and grabbed Eurynome by the wrist, forcing her to join in our excited procession.

'He is caught!' I proclaimed when we reached the street. 'The thief is taken red-handed with all these stolen goods within his house!' Before a wondering audience, the magistrate's servant began to lay out the found objects upon a red cloth in the middle of the street. It looked like a Peiraieus sale.

'What more proof do you need!' I cried. My anger was in full spate. 'Halirrhothios is a thief! A terrible robber – a housebreaker – and a thief.'

'This child can tell us about it,' said Thratta, with a little shake. 'Where's my other bracelet, girl? She was wearing the stolen earrings! Perhaps she is a thief also. She is a slave, I'll be bound, so she can be tortured – let her be put to the question!'

The child Eurynome put her hands to her eyes as if by shutting out the sight of all of us she could obliterate what was happening.

'No!' cried Halirrhothios. 'Let her go! The child has nothing to do with it – *nothing*.' His face registered real anguish.

'This child is yours, then? Is that the case?' the arkhon asked sharply. 'By one of your slaves – is that right? She's not registered to this deme as a citizen's daughter.'

'She's mine, as you say,' answered the wretched Halirrhothios. He appealed to the little crowd. 'This child, my Eurynome – a mere infant, men of Athens – had nothing to do with it. *She* didn't know the other earrings were in her own. She knows *nothing* – I did it all.' He turned again to the arkhon. 'There is no need of torture. I confess – I confess to stealing all these things. I admit all.'

'But – why?' asked Aristotle. '*Why?*'

Halirrhothios shrugged. 'Who knows? I suppose just because I have always been fond of things that sparkle and shine. "Magpie", Stephanos said. Perhaps that was it, just a desire to have some good shiny things.'

'But . . .' sputtered the arkhon, 'this is a gross number of valuables, man, things that cost much money! Why, you have stolen enough to condemn you. This is no light theft of a few obols – I'll be bound, you have stolen goods to the value of fifty drakhmai, or rather, much more!'

Halirrhothios shrugged. 'I scarcely know.'

'Well,' snapped Lysiphon. 'You *ought* to have known. It was worth your notice. For you have been found in the act, with the goods secreted in your own home, and of a value over fifty drakhmai! You see what that means?'

'And this man has confessed his guilt,' I observed. 'He has just made an open confession before a magistrate!'

The crowd gave one long gasp or sigh, as if everyone simultaneously had come to the realisation of what was happening.

'Yes,' said the arkhon Lysiphon, gravely. 'O Halirrhothios, you have confessed openly in front of these witnesses and before me, an arkhon of Athens, to an atrocious theft – or rather, a number of thefts. Stolen goods found in your house in the deme of Kydathenaion you have declared to have been taken by you, including goods taken out of houses forced open, to the value of over fifty drakhmai. This crime is capital. And, since you have confessed in front of not only myself but a sufficient number of Athenian citizens, no further trial is required. Out of your own mouth, you are condemned to death!'

V

Sentence of Death

It was with a most peculiar sense of triumph that I saw Halirrhothios' face turn ashen at this pronouncement. He made no attempt to run or fight – just stood there, pale and sweating with his jaw hanging slightly open.

'Bind his hands,' Lysiphon curtly commanded. Halirrhothios meekly allowed his hands to be tied with rope behind him. The tendons on his long scrawny arms showed the strain. 'Take him to the gaol,' the arkhon continued. 'I can send for the Skythian archers, if need be, but I expect no trouble. If some of the man's neighbours will give surety that they won't abet his escape, they may escort him to his destination. I shall accompany him, to prevent disturbance and to explain to the gaoler.'

'Well now, *here's* justice,' crowed Thratta, who was busy putting her clothes back on in full view of her audience. She dared to ask the question which almost everyone must have wished to ask. 'It's death – so *when*? How long before the sentence is carried out?'

'No need for undue haste,' said the arkhon. 'We can certainly allow this man, a citizen, three days, perhaps a trifle more. I must speak to the Basileus. All will be done properly.'

In the full bloom of his authority Lysiphon took command. As the evening was advancing rapidly, he ordered torches and torchbearer for his party. Then he took charge of his detachment, which now included at its centre the unhappy Halirrhothios. Quite a little procession formed: first the arkhon with a torchbearer, then Halirrhothios, led along by the first of the arkhon's slaves, with the other slave walking closely behind him, followed by the host of Lysiphon's abortive supper, and one of this man's slaves as another torchbearer. A few of my neighbours joined the party, though not many. Everyone else watched in silence as the group, only partially visible under the long flames of the torches, wound its way down the street and disappeared.

'Death!' said one. 'At least there is some justice left. No one could expect to get away with such enormous thefts. A lot of things haven't turned up yet, though that Thracian whore's got hers back.'

'I hope,' said another, 'that they continue to search the house. My family lost two tunics and some coins.'

'Hardly the same as a whore's silver cup, or gold jewellery with gems,' said another drily. 'Stephanos is a rich man, so it seems. He must look after his property.'

'It concerns everybody!' another exclaimed heatedly. 'Terrible, all this thieving and the suspicion. No one can be easy, even at home. I for one will be glad to see it put to rest.'

'Halirrhothios always had a sneaking way with him that I did not quite like,' another citizen interjected.

'Ah,' said another, one of Halirrhothios' near neighbours. 'Death, though – that is hard. One cannot like it for a citizen.'

'And,' said another with some relish, 'you know what

it means. He'll be led out of the city and there by the wayside his hands and feet will be stapled to a board – or nailed to it, to be quicker. And there he will be left, writhing and turning black until he's crows' meat.'

Aristotle winced. I remembered that he had once had a very good friend who had died in this fashion. I did not care for the picture myself.

'Maybe not,' proffered another. 'Halirrhothios is well-born enough to take the better way. He can buy a more genteel death – by drinking hemlock. He can scrape up enough funds to pay for a good ending.'

'Maybe and maybe not!' this pessimist snorted. 'He can have but little money – that's why he stole, belike. If he has to pay a fine and restore all the stolen goods, it's hard to know where the extra drakhmai for that hemlock will come from.'

'His friends will club together,' suggested another. 'Better in the long run for Athens. A private ending. It does not expose a citizen to the gaze of the highway, disgracing his family and bringing the whole deme into disrepute. The body is not destroyed or debased – not beyond the repair of washing. And the relatives can still have a good funeral.'

I had had enough of this conversation, and I could see that Aristotle was not enjoying it at all. This talk touched nearly upon the death of two people important in his thought and life: Sokrates, the spiritual father of all modern philosophy in Athens, and Hermias of Atarneos, Aristotle's friend, father or guardian of the Master's beloved wife Pythias.

We walked off, through what was no longer evening air, but had thickened into night. I encouraged him to stop in at home so we could finish our uneaten *panspermia*, and enjoy some wine. We neither of us had any remaining hunger, but the wine was welcome, and I had no wish to qualify it with too much water.

'You have surprised me today, Stephanos,' said Aristotle once we were settled. 'I must admit, I thought you would be posed when the arkhon asked you to name a name. Yet you seemed so confident. What made you so sure that Halirrhothios was the thief?'

'I'm not quite sure,' I mused. 'Rationally I could not be absolutely certain. Yet I was suddenly convinced that I *knew* Halirrhothios was the thief. And yet – I really had a reason.'

'Indeed? What were the rational grounds for your accusation?'

'A simple thing. On that night when Hieron came to seek us, and grasped you and sped away, I followed and slipped on a greasy patch on my own doorsill. It was where Halirrhothios had been standing. Later, inside Hieron's house, we found somebody had spilled oil from a lamp, near the corpse. At first I presumed that it was Hieron himself, trying to light the lamp with shaky hands. But then – the lamp in which the crown of gold leaves was discovered must have been emptied in order to make way for its new contents. If somebody had spilled oil in Hieron's house during the incursion, and not Hieron himself later, then that person was a thief – or one of the thieves – and a murderer. And Halirrhothios had oil on his foot.'

'So you decided that Halirrhothios is connected with not only a robbery but the murder of Hippobatos?'

'Yes. I haven't really thought it through. But then, it was something in his voice when he talked to me among the crowd after I found the jewellery had gone missing. He could have known the dog wasn't there. And he has long scrawny arms with a good reach – I suddenly felt *sure* that he was the thief.'

'You were fortunate, Stephanos,' said Aristotle. 'I

drink to your intrepidity. The deduction you offer seems ingenious – I did not know about the oil on your threshold. I had not come to your conclusion. Yet I will admit, once we were in Halirrhothios' house, I started looking for the things stolen from Hieron – including that missing marble head of a boy.'

'They probably threw it into a ditch somewhere. Though it might not stay hidden.'

'Imprudent to cast it away too quickly, anywhere where it would attract attention. Certainly it would not be rational to keep the statue in the house. You do realise, Stephanos, that you took a great risk! Suppose nothing had come of your search? Were Halirrhothios ever so great a thief, he might have had an external resort, a place outside his house, in which to deposit his goods. Indeed, if he is a proper thief, he must have such a depository. We did not find Thratta's first bracelet, only the one newly stolen.'

'Once the search began,' I admitted, 'I realised that he might have hidden the things somewhere else. After all, I now think that he put the newly stolen bracelet in my *eiresione* intending to hide it there only momentarily rather than keep it on his person.'

'I suppose,' said Aristotle, 'that he dropped the bracelet into your branch so as to have free hands for the window theft. After that, someone was too near the branch – perhaps Euphranor – for him to recover the object quickly, and he needed at once to dispose of Philomela's jewellery.'

'I hadn't done so much thinking,' I said. 'My blood was up. I simply wanted the things – Philomela's things – back. The gifts come from her mother and grandmother. What would her family all think of me had I lost them the first day! It is a most wretched husband who cannot keep his goods in store.'

Aristotle laughed. 'Surely other would-be thieves will

think three times before meddling with you, Stephanos. A very Herakles in tracking down missing objects!' Aristotle laughed and then the laughter died upon his lips and he looked soberly at me.

'Your thinking leads to the conclusion – is this correct? – that Halirrhothios is not only the thief of your goods, and the goods of others, but also the murderer of Hippobatos.'

'Yes,' I agreed. 'But what does it matter? Halirrhothios will pay the price of his crime now. He ought to have thought of the consequences of his actions. Caught with his great guilt upon him, he will be executed in any case, whether judged a murderer or not.'

'Ah, Stephanos!' Aristotle shook his head. 'You might now begin to wonder whether this – what shall we call it? This festival of crime – could be the work of one man. A mere Halirrhothios. A man whose chief talent lies in his long and scrawny arms – and in his impudence. Useful to be sure, but Halirrhothios is otherwise unremarkable, of middling intelligence and status. He has the advantage of living in a central deme in the city and is of sufficiently good birth never to be taken for a ruffian. But surely we must doubt whether he can be the chief actor, the leading spirit, in whatever is going on.'

'I *do* think so,' I replied firmly. 'He was the leader and I have caught him. He will not trouble Athens any more, and there will be a cessation of all these thefts.'

I was annoyed at Aristotle's suggestion. Certainly, if Halirrhothios were not the leading criminal, that made my own part in the day's work less glorious. Surely Athenians would admire me now. I had acted with steadfastness and decision. I had Philomela's ornaments safe. And I had been so angry, so very angry! How deeply satisfactory it had been to act through the anger and obtain revenge. Revenge, a thirst quenched.

Of course I had to explain to my household, which meant chiefly Mother, about the loss of the lovely ornaments and their recovery. Another box was found for the precious things, and we all swore to keep an eye on them until the wedding day. Euphranor chimed in impressively to assure Theodoros that my conduct had been heroic. The boy burst into giggles, however, when he described myself, Aristotle and Thratta getting naked and then entering the house with white cloths tied about our middles and wearing nothing else, not even our sandals. The little boys were curious to know precisely when Halirrhothios would be executed. I was curious too, though I did not wish to seem to think much upon the matter.

I went about the next two days in a state of satisfaction mingled with relief. I imagined that all my friends and neighbours felt as I did – but this proved not to be the case. The first hint that I had that my satisfaction was not shared came from my old schoolfriend Nikeratos.

'Oh, you're a hot-tempered one, I hear,' he teased. 'Everyone's frightened of you. You fix people with your basilisk eye and they will say anything!'

'Nonsense,' I retorted. 'That man's guilt was clearly upon him, apparent to all.'

'The fellow had an unlucky day, apparently,' said a young citizen whom Nikeratos had just introduced, a well-born and handsome person named Philokedes. This Philokedes spoke lightly, but Nikeratos, to my surprise, went on in a graver tone.

'Seriously, Stephanos, don't you think there is something . . . ungraceful, shall we say? . . . in con-demning a neighbour like that? *You* are certainly brave – for you are going to have to live the rest of your life with his friends and relations around you. My father says he's glad I am not in your position. Halirrhothios' relatives will remember this injury for fifty years to come.'

Strangely, I had not thought about this at all. Intent upon getting the jewellery back and putting an end to the thefts, I had thought of myself as some kind of impersonal force in the business. A spoke on the wheel of Necessity. An inexorable agent of Nemesis. I had said that Halirrhothios ought to have thought of the consequences of his actions. But here was I, going blindly along not looking at the consequences to myself.

Had that been all, I might have shrugged it off. I had not lived this long to take my cues from Nikeratos. But I wasn't left to think this matter over in the luxury of solitude. That very evening saw a more effective assault upon my resolution. Disturbance arrived when sounds at the threshold let me know that my house slave Tryphos the incompetent was being surprised by unexpected visitors. He backed into the room, mouth agape.

'You want to see the folks at the door?' Tryphos enquired. Names were beyond him, he didn't regard them as his province.

I wished, as frequently I had cause to do, for a superior doorkeeper of suavity and discernment who would keep track of comings and goings and announce visitors with sufficient gravity, as in the best houses. I assured my fellow with all the dignity my voice could muster that I would see whoever it was, but a little delegation of citizens was already walking into my *andron*. I recognised all three of these, as they were neighbours. One was Hieron, victim of that grisly house-breaking. Another was a middle-aged man called Lamas, with a pale, delicate face and a fine rippling brown beard. I recalled that he was a student of history. The chief spokesman appeared to be Theophon, the tall merchant with the rosy face, the man who had spoken up for Halirrhothios on the day of the search.

'A good new day to you, Stephanos son of Nikiarkhos,' Theophon said formally, in his usual loud voice. It was just after sunset, so it was indeed officially the beginning of the new day. 'We apologise for coming unexpectedly, and will not detain you long,' he continued, thus making it clear they hadn't come around for a pot of wine and some gossip. Still, I roused myself to a show of hospitality.

'Welcome. Would you like some wine?' I asked. 'Lamas, you look so pale, I am sure you must be fatigued. Is it true you are writing a history?'

'Yes,' said Lamas, looking less displeased, but not smiling. 'Just of our own deme Kydathenaion here. No wine for any of us, please.'

'A history of our deme? Our heroes and festivals? Wonderful! So it is the studying and staying indoors that makes you so pale. Do take a comfortable chair.' I bustled about in a parade of hospitable solicitude.

'It's true, I do find,' Lamas admitted, 'that all the reading and writing means I don't get out of doors as often—'

'Might as well be a weaver and have done with it,' commented Theophon. 'All good citizens should take healthy exercise in the open air. Our women of course we expect to stay within doors. Pale slender womenfolk – sign of a prosperous man. I myself am devoted to reading – I was always an excellent scholar, and came first in declamation. But you must keep up your health, Lamas.'

'Please, good Theophon, take a seat. Pray, make yourself at home in the best my poor dwelling has to offer.' I looked sharply at Theophon, indicating that I need not so soon have forgiven his remarks. If he wasn't the one who had referred to our not having a pot to piss in, he had at least incited that unjust observation. The large Theophon sighed gustily, like a man bowed down with such sorrow that he cannot attend to lighter matters.

'We are all neighbours of poor Halirrhothios,' he announced. Unnecessarily.

'I see that you are,' I acknowledged.

'And we are also his friends. O Stephanos, how wretched a condition we are all in! His poor wife! His kinfolk hide their heads, and live in fear of a wrathful and irrevocable day.'

'I am sorry for them.'

'But – Stephanos . . .' It was poor Hieron, pale and breathing heavily. 'Though I have suffered, as you know – and I thank you for your kindness on that night . . . Although I and my poor wife have suffered – terribly, as you know – from a house-breaking, I too beg you desist. This affair of Halirrhothios will only make matters worse. Much worse.'

'Exactly,' agreed Theophon. 'If even Hieron, who has suffered so much from crime, thinks clemency appropriate in this admittedly lesser instance . . . O Stephanos, son of Nikiarkhos, pray consider!'

'Consider,' Lamas repeated, running his hand down his rippling brown beard and looking at me earnestly. 'Think! What a bad reputation this gives to our deme! And what a horror to visit upon a man! Without even a trial.'

'But there's no call for a trial,' I protested. 'The law of Athens is very clear on that point. When a man confesses *in front of a magistrate* to his guilt in a plain and acknowledged crime, then there is no need for a trial. The arkhon was there. The piles of stolen things were there. And Halirrhothios confessed, and in public. *Nobody* could ever claim that he was deranged, or that there was insufficient evidence.'

'But . . . but consider,' protested Lamas. He kept

stroking his delicate brown beard with his fingers. 'Pray, think about the situation, Stephanos. We beg you, remember that day – the confusion abounding that afternoon. And the three of you – including that unspeakably vile woman, that dirty Thracian whore – rushing about his house. His children and wife in danger of insult! Halirrhothios' house contaminated by the visitation of a vile prostitute!'

'The arkhon was there,' I said doggedly. 'Had there been anything wrong, Lysiphon would not have authorised the proceeding.'

'We are not performing our difficult task well,' said Theophon. 'I apologise for our lack of clarity. You must know, Stephanos, that Halirrhothios now tells a different story.'

'A *story*? What right has Halirrhothios to tell stories? Everything was as clear as noon and as plain as a lampstand. We saw with our own eyes. The stolen goods were secreted in his house. The man was guilty. Most assuredly guilty.'

'Yes – and again – no. The goods – or some stolen objects – were in his house. We shall all, I suppose, have to admit that. But the poor man is the victim of a childish trick. *He* knew nothing of the matter.'

'Knew nothing? When he had all the things hidden away in the women's quarters, and had secreted the valuable earrings in the bone boxes he hung on the child—'

'Yes – there you are. *The child.* Exactly. You see how it was. At the moment of confusion, with all the trampling through his house, and in fear for his family, Halirrhothios was moved to protest his own guilt in order to save his hapless womenfolk. Foolish of him, but admirable. Since then, the real truth has come out.'

'The real truth? What do you mean?'

'It was the child who took the things.'

'The child? What? That little girl, Eurynome?'

'Yes. A child not endowed with great wit, nor, one might add, the finer moral sense one would find in a citizen's legitimate daughter. Moved by a base love for bright objects. Not understanding their full worth, nor even the nature of her deed. This creature is a slave child after all – what's bred in the bone, you know. Her father acknowledges her, but she is neither freeborn nor freed.'

'So he wants to blame it all on the child, does he?'

Lamas leaned forward eagerly, his large mild brown eyes fixed fully and reproachfully on my face.

'The child *is* to blame, Stephanos. But you must not fear – the law will not go hard upon her. Halirrhothios made sure to ascertain that, before he spoke out. She – the little slave girl – will not be executed. The magistrates are willing to treat her leniently, if they are able to exonerate poor Halirrhothios and free him from this terrible position.'

'It seems, then,' I said slowly, 'that this is a case for a trial after all. At the Areopagos.'

'Not at the Areopagos, Stephanos! That's for murders.'

I could feel myself beginning to flush with embarrassment at my blunder. In a slip of the mind, I had been thinking of Halirrhothios as the murderer of Hippobatos. But of course there was no proof of that, and no real possibility of bringing such a charge.

'Perhaps you remember too vividly your own trial, Stephanos,' added Theophon. 'I mean the one at which you assisted to help your cousin. The arkhon waives Halirrhothios' confession, which is now esteemed invalid. But if you did bring an accusation, our poor neighbour would be tried in front of the Eleven – for theft. That is, *if* you or others persist in bringing the accusation.'

'But if you do not,' chimed in Lamas, 'then the Justices

could proceed to release Halirrhothios and have the child flogged.'

'It seems more like true Justice to have a trial,' I persisted.

'Oh, the child will not be flogged to death, never fear,' Theophon assured me. 'Just enough punishment to make her detest bright objects for ever after, and live a humble life in her patron's family. Why, I daresay if the little creature had full understanding she would prefer to be flogged herself to seeing her papa hideously done to death!'

'Consider how grim the child's fortune will be if her owner is executed,' Lamas added earnestly. 'Instead of being a protected child in a well-to-do family, she will be sold to any man who cares to have her. The whole household will be rent asunder.'

'Think of Halirrhothios' wretched and innocent wife!' implored Hieron.

'And if there is a trial, just consider the scandal!' said Theophon. 'Even if Halirrhothios were acquitted. Kydathenaion would gain a reputation for backbiting and disquiet. A scandal in our own deme! Just as you are about to bring a wife to it, young Stephanos. Unless you are planning on retiring to the country, this is the deme in which your children will be born and grow up.'

There was more power in this argument than I cared at that moment to admit.

'Gentlemen,' I said, 'I acknowledge your trouble in coming, and regret that I cannot pursue the matter further at this time. I have appointed a meeting elsewhere.'

'We regret intruding upon your time,' said Lamas. 'We should not have done so had the matter not been distressingly urgent.'

I faced them all.

'Let me make myself clear,' I said, a little in the grand

Hektor style. 'You ought to realise that I intend – though I cannot speak for anyone else – to pursue the matter of the thefts. All it will take is intelligence, perseverance and a bit of time.' I stood up. 'I want to make sure my own deme is cleansed of robbers and house-breakers!'

'Surely, we all feel that,' said Lamas. 'Your object is most commendable.'

'But you are *wrong*,' said Theophon decidedly. 'Wrong in this instance.'

'I will consider deeply all that you have said.' I inclined my head with what I hoped was cool politeness. 'You – or rather the magistrates – will know my mind soon.'

'But when? *When?*' Theophon gave way to the extent that he reluctantly arose also. The successful merchant was evidently disappointed, but had the grace not to dispute my somewhat ungracious dismissal. 'We are sorry to seem importunate, but this is a case for quick decision. Otherwise the law will be offended. Quick execution of a self-acknowledged criminal is provided for, as you pointed out. The man's initial confession does create a problem. So generously dishonest, that so-called confession! You must take account of the *true* explanation for Halirrhothios' mad self-incrimination. I am sure you will honour him for it, when you think it over.'

'And you should know, O Stephanos,' added Lamas, 'that the Basileus himself and all the arkhons are deeply concerned. Many important people – including the Hierophant, high priest of Eleusis, and the Daidoukhos, torchbearer of Demeter and the Maiden – have interceded. They don't want to see poor Halirrhothios executed. Do you know the Hierophant? Or the Daidoukhos?'

'No,' I had to admit.

'Hanias, the goddesses' Daidoukhos, giving light in the great processions and rituals, belongs to the tribe of

the Heralds and is connected with the best families of
Eleusis and Athens. He tries to compose this turmoil. His
is likewise the judgement of Eurymedon, the exegete
who may be the next Hierophant. All of these holy men
have personally begged the Basileus to look into the
matter and settle it in a becoming way. Without putting
an admirable if unfortunate citizen to death.'

'The Hierophant is a man of peace,' said Theophon
with approbation.

'The arkhon of the case – I presume it is Lysiphon –
will hear from me soon,' I replied. 'There seems no need
for great haste. Obviously, they are *not* impatient to
execute Halirrhothios.'

With that my visitors had to be content, if not
satisfied. They departed, their farewells lacking in
warmth of affection. I was left with the problem to chew
upon. My thoughts were dismal enough. I had lied about
having an appointment that evening, though I now
thought of visiting a prostitute, but felt too tired, still
weakened as I was. Besides, the memory of Thratta was
not appetising. (In a few days' time I did indeed treat
myself to a visit to one of the better brothels, not
realising the series of problems and disasters into which
that visit was to plunge me – but that is part of another
sequence of events.)

On this particular evening, before I sought my couch
I had decided to call upon Aristotle in the morning, and
seek his response to the problem of Halirrhothios.
Accordingly, next day I went to the Lykeion, and found
the Master of it with a couple of his senior scholars or
assistants, Hipparkhos and Demetrios, in the 'book
pantry', a room finely equipped for the writing of books.
Demetrios of Phaleron should not, I suppose, be called a
senior scholar, for at the time he cannot yet have arrived
at the age of twenty-one, but he was one of Aristotle's

chosen band. Unlike the pale Lamas, young Demetrios didn't look like one's picture of a scholar, being unusually handsome, with golden hair, and the noble profile and straight nose of an old aristocratic family. Demetrios was one of the shining people whose beauty is of such a different order from the average that one thinks of the gods. At that time, however, he didn't play much upon his looks but was a devoted student of philosophy. Hipparkhos, by contrast, was more what one thinks a scholar should look like, stolid and middle-aged with a long lugubrious face like a serious horse.

The new 'book pantry', first seen the previous summer, I admired, with its clean plaster walls, and the wide shelves expensively made of imported wood. There were also neatly wrought leather buckets, sufficient to hold a number of scrolls in current use. It would have been nice to sit in the doorway and read in a leisurely way one of the many attractive papyrus scrolls.

'We are just trying to write up the birds,' Hipparkhos told me earnestly. 'We have finished with the molluscs, at least for now. It is much harder to draw pictures of the parts of birds.'

'Where is Theophrastos?' I enquired. I never really craved the sight of Aristotle's serious coadjutor, a slab-sided awkward fellow, but he was devoted to assisting Aristotle in his researches, and I had rather expected to see him with the others working in the Lykeion.

'Oh, Theophrastos has started digging more of his new garden,' said Demetrios, laughing.

'Eager to start his winter planting.'

'Yes,' said Aristotle. 'He has just begun planting – in orderly rows – the seeds of his new treatise on plants. It will be the counterpart of our present work on animal life.'

'Plants and animals are very different,' I remarked brightly.

'True, Stephanos, but they also have much in common. Consider!' Aristotle held his head on one side, as men do who are about to ask a riddle. 'Why is a plant like an acrobat?'

'Oh, I don't know – because it sends its seed through the air?'

'Very good! My answer is because both plants and acrobats go upside down.'

'How do you make that out?'

'Think of a plant. Its mouth is in the earth, in the roots where it takes in nourishment. And it waves its legs and colourful genitals in the air with giddy abandon. Whereas we men – save for acrobats – walk with our mouths up in the air at the top, and our legs and genitals nearer the earth.'

This little joke must have been familiar to the members of the Lykeion, if not to me. Ordinarily I should have been charmed to see their work, but not now.

'I have something serious to say,' I blurted out.

'Well?' Aristotle looked at me expectantly.

'It's a question of Justice, I suppose. How people should behave to each other.'

'An important question, Stephanos.' Aristotle looked at me with bright earnestness.

'I become more and more concerned about how our individual behaviour affects the whole community.'

'He is thinking of a series of lectures on Ethics,' interjected Demetrios.

'Yes. I have spoken and written much of late on Politics, but a political life does not exist without the life of individuals. A good community cannot exist without good people. How shall an individual be good? By what standards must he live? Justice is a basic virtue, as Sokrates recognised. For without Justice, other virtues are vain or lose direction.'

'So,' said Hipparkhos, 'have you brought Aristotle a nice new problem?'

'It is a problem of Justice and it is not nice at all. But it concerns you too, Aristotle, as you were in the search with me. Now Halirrhothios is saying he committed no theft.'

'No theft at all? How then does he explain the goods found at his house?'

'He blames it all on the little girl – the child Eurynome. The earrings meant for Philomela were in the child's earrings. And some other objects were found in her doll.'

'Do *you* think the girl did it? Stole your jewellery and the silver beaker and everything?' demanded Demetrios. Almost everyone in Athens must know about the case by now.

'No, of course I don't. She is only eight years old! How could she go about and take all those things? I believe Halirrhothios was right when he confessed, but then he thought of a better story, that would get him off. These people – the arkhon, and even the Hierophant and Daidoukhos of Eleusis – desire to avoid the execution of a citizen. They would rather see the little girl flogged.'

'Nasty for you,' said Demetrios. 'But the question of Justice remains.' And he looked as golden and severe as a serene image on a coin. 'Is it just to let the real thief go free?'

'No, I think not,' said Aristotle slowly. 'There are many implications to this development. I should like to talk with you privately, Stephanos. Perhaps we should consult—'

'I see someone coming,' said Hipparkhos. 'Someone in haste. It's your friend, that Makedonian they now call Antigonos the One-Eyed.'

'Antigonos? You should not make fun of his one eye –

he was wounded in honourable combat. Antigonos has come from the East! Probably he brings the latest news of Alexander's conquests – we will find where he has got to now. And perhaps I shall hear some news of my nephew Kallisthenes. We must offer Antigonos something to drink.' Aristotle sprang up with delight to welcome this newcomer.

The man Antigonos looked all sinew and bone, just as a man should look who has been in combat service. He had evidently been badly injured at one time; his face had a horrible scar running all the way down from eyebrow to chin. His beard would not grow over the scar, and one eye was seamed and permanently shut. This man strode into the book-lined apartment, grim and unsmiling. Aristotle had sprung up delightedly to greet him, but then took a step back. It was as if a killing frost had entered the room.

'I bring bad news, O Aristotle of Stageira,' the man said.

'Kallisthenes!' Aristotle turned white.

'No, not that. But Philotas. Your friend. And his father. Very bad news about Philotas.'

'Tell me.'

'Philotas is dead.' Antigonos took a deep breath. 'If only I could tell you he had fallen in battle! But he has been executed at the behest of Alexander.'

'Executed.' Aristotle sat down heavily, without excuse for not offering his guest a chair. Antigonos continued to stand.

'Run and fetch Theophrastos,' said Demetrios of Phaleron to Hipparkhos. And although Hipparkhos was the elder, he obeyed without a word.

'Philotas was accused of a conspiracy,' said Antigonos. 'Actually, there may indeed have been a conspiracy of some sort, or rumours of one. Philotas did not take it seriously. That's what he said – that he had heard a garbled tale of some sort of plot against Alexander, but didn't think it meant anything. Alexander was furious!'

'Yes, he would be,' said Aristotle.

'So, he – Alexander – conspired in a room with his officers to hide behind a tapestry hanging when they brought Philotas in and questioned him. And Philotas answered them frankly, just as I have said. Of course they then put him to the torture. He still denied any part in any plot against Alexander, while they increased the pain. At last he cried out, "I see that you are determined to kill me!"

'Then Alexander came out from behind the tapestry hanging, raging like a wild lion. He hurled curses at the man, said he had trusted him wrongly, that Philotas the false friend who visited his own tent twice a day wanted to take the breath from his body. Killing was too good for Philotas, so he said, and urged more torture, until the officers objected. After all, Philotas had been an officer too.

'Then they ran him out, Philotas with his arms tied, and bleeding – I say "ran", but they carried him upright really. He could hardly walk, and they needed to save his strength for the last ordeal. Outdoors, they lined up Makedonian soldiers, the best at shooting the javelins. And then they untied Philotas' hands and made him run – lurch and stagger, I mean – down a path. They all shot at him. It didn't last long. A number of the javelins hit him. Of course he soon fell, but they continued to throw missiles that struck him even after the breath had left his body.'

'Alas – oh, alas for Philotas! How terrible!' said Aristotle. He had turned very pale. 'What a great grief for his poor father, the great Parmenion.'

'Parmenion did not have long to grieve, as you shall

hear. Alexander swore that the father who had spawned
Philotas must have had a share in the son's wicked
design. It would be dangerous to leave Parmenion alive,
angry at the horrid death of Philotas. Two men were sent
to Parmenion with a letter from the Commander. The
two stood by while he read it – you know, as if waiting for
his reply. Parmenion read the letter, which started in a
quite ordinary way – this was one of Alexander's cunning
jokes. "Alexander to Parmenion, Greetings, and I hope
you are well." Near the end the letter told him the plot
was discovered, Philotas was dead and Parmenion too
would be dead before he had finished reading this epistle!
And that was true. For the men who brought the letter
waited only for his gasp of horror – then they stabbed
him.'

'At least,' I said consolingly to Aristotle, 'the poor
father did not have to suffer for a long time.'

'Nothing takes long with Alexander now,' said
Antigonos. 'He daily gets more suspicious. Those around
him cannot please him as they used to do. And he takes
no advice. Ever since he captured Persepolis, he believes
his own will to be good law. Now he is so far away, in the
mountainous wilds of Sogdania, not even in Persia
proper, he becomes ever rougher and wilder.'

'He now has no home, really – that makes him more
suspicious and fierce. Oh, this rage of cruelty that grows
upon him,' groaned Aristotle. 'It was in him from a child,
but it has become worse.'

'Aristotle!' Theophrastos burst into the room. 'I have
just heard – enough to guess the rest!'

Theophrastos was so peculiarly accoutred that in any
other circumstances he would have looked comical. He was
attired in an old torn leather tunic, and wore coarse gloves
too big for him; his arms were much scratched and he bore
dirt on his arms and even on his face. He looked like a

peasant, and was still carrying a little digging tool. I was oddly reminded of the farmer Laertes, Odysseus' father, when Odysseus goes to see him and finds him at work. There was something comforting about Theophrastos in this guise. He knelt down beside Aristotle's chair.

'I see it in your face. So it is true – Philotas is dead. And as I surmise, Parmenion must be dead also?'

'Even so. Antigonos will tell you all. I cannot hear it a second time.' Aristotle dabbed at his eyes, and shaded his face with his hand.

'Thankful. I must be thankful,' said Theophrastos, 'that you did not decide to try to deliver young Parmenion to his uncle or grandfather last summer.'

'The boy is in Kos, living with the good doctors,' I chimed in. 'He is safe.'

'For a time, at least. Pray he may continue so,' exclaimed Aristotle. 'Let him live a quiet life and learn to be a doctor and escape observation. I am thankful now for the boy's illegitimacy, which may make it easier for him to go unnoticed. But oh, Philotas! So handsome, so brilliant, so generous, so ill-fated! Philotas, and grey-haired Parmenion, whom I knew so well!'

'We see here,' said Theophrastos, in his unhurried, precise manner, 'the effects of blood-lust and cruelty. Anger allowed to pass beyond the bounds of reason, and selfishness which cares nothing for the pains of others. How easily these qualities blend with tyranny!'

'I see,' said Demetrios, 'the rage that loses sight of order and Justice. These Makedonian kings lack all sense of Justice towards mankind!'

'Hush!' said Theophrastos. 'That is impolite to Antigonos. You see how he, a Makedonian, suffers in telling the tale. After all, Parmenion's family are of Makedon.'

It seemed best for me to slip away, leaving Aristotle to

his grief. With a few hurried words of condolence, I slipped out of the Lykeion, and set off for home. But Antigonos' account, Aristotle's sudden sorrow and dismay, had made a deep impression. So too had Theophrastos' commentary. 'The effects of blood-lust and cruelty,' I repeated to myself. It was suddenly hard to see how I could persist in seeking the death of Halirrhothios. My satisfying state of rage seemed to have ebbed away. I did not want to become an Alexander, determined that anyone he suspected of injuring him must die a horrid death.

Yet was this decision in itself just? My heart smote me when I thought that I was delivering the child up to an undeserved public whipping. But Theophon was right: if this illegitimate slave's father and patron were to die by execution, her lot would become even worse.

That afternoon I called personally upon the arkhon Lysiphon and told him that, as far as I was concerned, if he believed Halirrhothios' new version of what had happened, I was satisfied. Thratta had already capitulated. And Halirrhothios was a free man by next day's sunset.

VI

Repairs and Recriminations

'You will have to retile the roof,' my mother announced.
This bald statement, certainly less pleasing to my ears
than music of a lyre, could hardly be denied. We both
looked at the large damp patch in the upstairs, staining
the rough beams and the underside of the roof-tiles. 'It
looks like a camel,' declared Theodoros, joining us. My
little brother liked to be in on anything going forward. 'It
has a big hump in the middle,' he elaborated. 'A very
large camel.'

'How do you know?' I rejoined. 'You've never seen a
camel.'

'Neither have you,' he retorted disrespectfully. I
pretended not to hear, but pondered on the state of our
house-top.

A heavy fall of rain had come upon us at the end of the
month of Pyanepsion when the days grow shorter and
the winds stronger. Subtle fingers of rain and wind had
found the cracks in the tiles and prised them further open,
tossing some aside while gaining admittance for the
intruding water. During most of that month my
attention had been largely taken up with the case of the

poisoning stepmother, a case that set all of Athens agog.
My own concern was not in mere gossip. I was involved
in the case as a witness, since I had – unfortunately – been
one of the discoverers of a corpse in a bawdy-house. To
my chagrin, my future father-in-law looked askance at
my appearing as a witness in a public trial recounting my
adventures in a brothel. Smikrenes even threatened to
postpone my marriage to his daughter until the long
embarrassments of the trial were over. Fortunately, with
Aristotle's intervention truth had come to light and the
case had been brought to a quick finish. Now my wedding
was on again, and I believed – in my ignorance – that
there would be no further impediments. The bubbling
pot of scandal in Athens had simmered down. The
constant nuisance of the thefts remained.

'You should have thought of it before,' Mother
pronounced. 'It's a careless householder who waits till
the winter rains come to mend his roof. Our poor old
house will be under water by Gamelion. *If* that stubborn
old man in Eleusis remains in his right mind, and *if* you
are going to bring your bride here in Gamelion' (she
sniffed), 'and *if* you are going to hold a wedding party,
then you need to turn your mind to repairing this
house. All our neighbours will notice. And your bride's
kindred – that's to say, supposing she has any worth
speaking of.'

I let this barb fall to the floor and did not pick it up.
My mother Eunike daughter of Diognetos can be very
gentle, but she has her tougher side. Her ancestors claim
direct descent from Erektheus, so she comes from a
lineage of snake-quellers.

'We haven't had a change of tiles since well before
your poor father died,' she remarked, in a softer tone.
'Poor Nikiarkhos!' she sniffed again, but this time in
dutiful and reminiscent sadness.

'That's a long time,' said Theodoros. 'No wonder the tiles are cracking up.'

'And you should think of painting the outside as well,' Mother continued. 'Dear! The penalty for having such a large house as ours, when it comes to painting or changing tiles.'

'It *is* a large house,' I said with some satisfaction. 'We have an upstairs area for bedrooms, not just downstairs. And a proper front courtyard. Some day we'll turn those square pillars into pretty columns. The little back courtyard in back is useful for a washing-ground, and we have a good well, which should please my bride. And even stable room for donkeys, and storage room.'

'Those buildings around the back courtyard need to be repaired too, Stephanos. A lot of rooms means a lot of trouble. We could certainly put up a good many slaves, if we only had them. It's an unusual house. Your father always said that the back premises were used for a tiler or a smith – something like that – in the old days. Then it was joined to another – our front house.'

'I can hardly believe it!' I didn't want my good house associated with lowly trades, mechanic occupations unsuited to men of gentle blood and education.

'I don't know, I'm sure. Long before my time. But all I'm saying is, it costs *money* to repair such a big house, and you need to paint the whole outside. Not to mention the inside. *Some* of us, you know, have nothing to look at but these four walls all day. Your bride, too, when she comes. But there, you've been too busy with your travels to Delphi and the eastern islands and the gods-know-where, as well as rushing off to law courts, to pay any attention to *this* house.'

'That is not true,' I said indignantly. 'I have had much to worry about. I am *always* working for the welfare of this household.'

'Yes,' Mother said, slowly. 'I suppose you have been, dear Stephanos – but you don't *think* enough. Spending your time with foreigners. And then sending a neighbour to prison and a dreadful death – what would that do for us?'

'Halirrhothios isn't dead at all,' said Theodoros. 'He isn't in prison either. He came home and went to the Ekklesia next day, and then on to the Agora, just as if nothing had happened. Euphranor says he puts a brave face on. That's what his uncle said. Funny, I thought it was people with masks at the theatre who put a face on.'

I knew even better than Theodoros that Halirrhothios had appeared and gone on with normal life. He performed his living with a kind of defiance in his countenance that was not very reassuring. I had encountered him in the Agora myself only the day before, when he had given me not a glare but a kind of blank stare.

'But,' Theodoros continued, 'people say that lady – you know, the one who went in naked to look for the dolphin bracelet – she has not been seen, they say, since Halirrhothios left the gaol.'

'Hush, Theodoros!' said my mother. 'You ought not to know about ladies like that – and if you do, you oughtn't to speak of them. *She's* probably off on a jaunt. Bad women travel, good ones stay at home. Or they've sent her to Peiraieus to work the port. Good riddance!'

So Thratta had disappeared. But then there were many ways of getting a prostitute out of the way. Perhaps she had merely gone off to the country as a companion to some man who paid for her services by the long term. Thratta certainly did not interest me. I felt a more anxious unwilling interest in the little girl, Eurynome, whose image would not depart from my mind. I had not really wanted to know what had befallen her, but expansive Theophon had insisted on telling me.

'She was whipped before the magistrate,' he said. 'The

enormity of her crime of theft was explained to her. Then she was stripped and tied to the post and flogged. They were going to give her thirty lashes, but they relented at twenty-five. Laid on slowly and carefully, and counted. The executioner was ordered not to be too harsh. Her father took her home. So that is that.'

At least now nobody spoke of the child, and she would be hidden from view.

'Well,' said my mother, 'no good to stand gaping at the ceiling, Stephanos. You see for yourself how really bad the roof is. We need a leather patch or something until you can get the tiler to come – which had best be soon.'

This was unarguable. I procured a large piece of leather, and left to Tryphos and Theodoros the business of adjusting it as a patch over the worst of the roof. It might protect us for a little but not for long. I could not, like the industrious country folk, make my own roof myself. Had we lived in the kind of great house that a few men have, we would have supplied our own roof; large estates furnish skilled slaves to make tiles. But our family estate in the country was a relatively small affair, though we grew good olives. I had no slaves skilled enough for such work, and would have to pay for a city tile-maker's labourers as well as for his tiles.

That very day I went to the tile-works most frequently recommended, one whose master was also a builder and repairer of roofs. As I came into the yard, I entered a cloud of dust. One brawny-armed worker was energetically and monotonously pounding the earth with a heavy mallet, to make it into fine clay; his activity was sending thousands of particles up into the air. This slave was covered with the red earth powder; in places it had combined with his sweat and hardened, so he looked almost as if he himself were made of ceramic ware. On the other side of the yard more men, each in the short tunic of slaves, were turning clay into tiles. Carefully they kneaded balls of the red clay, a stiff recalcitrant dough, pushing it into shape to fit the moulds for the bigger tiles. Nearby, one man was cutting the clay into oblong strips, while others, nearly naked, were deftly folding each oblong piece over a thigh, quickly turning out the cheapest of ordinary tiles. All of these workers kept a distance from the fiery heat of the oven, in which shaped tiles were cooked.

The tile-master loomed up at me, cheerful and red-faced, appearing through the cloud of dust like the sun in a rosy mist. He was happy to hear of my order, and promised to come later that very day to take some exact measurements.

'I know your house well, pass it often,' he remarked. 'A good place but oldish. A little bigger than most, with the back buildings. Ordinary house tiles is what you want – Lakonian, we call 'em. No need for Korinthian, which is more for temples and grand buildings.'

Once I told him about the leaks, he asked me about things I wasn't sure of.

'New rafters? You probably ought to add costs for replacement of some of the rafters,' he advised kindly. '*I* know your kind of house and what the roof does in the rain. House has been let go, there's no denying. So we must allow for replacement and repair of rafters – and wood doesn't come cheap. I expect you know that.'

'Nothing comes cheap,' I said sourly.

'And what about a nice lining? Call me old-fashioned, but I always think there's nothing like *kalameia*. We don't want reeds from salt marshes, but our good *kalamoi* are not expensive, and they act beautiful – conduct water away, don't rot, and make the place cool in summer and warm in winter. Best of 'em are sweet-smelling too. I always say, *kalamoi* for a real home.'

'Oh yes, by all means,' I said. 'That's what we have now, but the reeds are musty by this time.'

The entire enterprise seemed bigger than I had wanted it to be, and inevitably productive of dust and disturbance. The master tile-maker seemed happy at the prospect of such a good order, and was soon adding to the expense, encouraging me to purchase some fine terminal ornaments for the largest tiles, the end ones.

'Just adds a nice finishing touch with those *akroteria*,' he cajoled. 'Makes a good impression. As you're going to be married,' he urged, 'you will want to make the house look its very best. Do honour to yourself, sir, and to the bride and her family.'

'Going to be married – *what* a great event,' said another customer who had just appeared. 'We should all congratulate you, Stephanos, on this occasion.'

'Thank you,' I said, turning to find I was addressing Lamas, the man with the thoughtful brown beard. One of the men who had come to talk to me on that dull and painful evening about saving Halirrhothios. The pale scholar who was writing a history of our deme seemed even paler now in the outdoor light, especially in contrast to the ruddy tile-master. Lamas' long, elegantly combed brown beard rippled within this mechanic scene as a sign of leisure and learning. I felt I had to reciprocate his attention with neighbourly civility.

'You're coming to my wedding, I hope,' I said.

'Honoured and delighted. To be sure. Yes, and I congratulate you on everything turning out so well in that little matter we spoke of.' Lamas leaned towards me confidentially. I turned away slightly to contemplate the finial ornaments the master was holding out for my inspection. 'I quite like the sea-nymph, and also the griffin,' I said.

'Surely,' said Lamas, in mild surprise, 'the sea-nymph

is more the sort of thing one would find on the roof of a brothel?'

'Nothing of the sort. Many 'spectable people has 'em,' said the tile-maker indignantly. 'Of course,' he added broad-mindedly, 'you could have a sphinx instead.'

'Then you would be required to speak in riddles,' said Lamas. 'The palmette seems the only thing in good taste. But consider, my dear Stephanos – since we are on such a friendly footing, I hope you won't mind.' Lamas spoke in quite an avuncular manner. 'Consider. Can you afford the expenditure? I ask you, neighbours, is Stephanos here not better advised to be a trifle frugal?'

Lamas thus included in our conversation my neighbours Theophon and Hieron who had entered the tile-yard just after him. Theophon, tall, fresh-faced and well-barbered, looked slightly less rosy when put in competition with the tile-master, but his countenance was suited to the general ruddiness of things. He greeted me genially. Hieron, having buried his brother-in-law and mended his house wall, had apparently recovered from the shock of the burglary, though he seemed a little subdued.

'So here you are again, the three of you,' I said with forced geniality.

'I am so glad that painful matter was resolved,' said Theophon.

'Ah, yes,' I replied. 'But I still meant what I said at our last meeting. I *do* intend to pursue the matter of the thefts. I haven't laid the problem aside; it is a duty to cleanse my own deme, at least, of robbers and house-breakers. I believe with intelligence and time I shall succeed.'

There was a short embarrassed silence.

'I'm sure,' said Theophon stiffly, 'that we all wish a quiet deme. I hear you are repairing your house, Stephanos?'

'I was just urging young Stephanos here to prudence in the matter of expenditure on his house decoration,' Lamas explained to them. 'Your good neighbours, Stephanos, cannot help being aware of your difficulties. Of course, you have done extremely well, after the sad death of poor Nikiarkhos, an amiable man if not careful in little things. But still . . .'

'I am *not* a pauper,' I said, with some heat. I knew I should control my temper, but unwanted advice is irritating. 'And I have some new interests in Hymettos, through my wife's — I mean my intended bride's — relations. Honey. A business likely to prove quite profitable.'

'Aha! Well done! Hymettos honey, how sweet!' said Hieron.

'Appropriate, too — is not honey an image of marriage and the sweets of generation?' Theophon asked rhetorically. 'Beware,' said Lamas, smiling through his silky beard. 'Some would say a wife belongs rather to the party of vinegar.'

My visit to the tile-yard brought gratifyingly quick results. Two days later (fortunately on a fine day) the tile-master and two of his henchmen came to my abode with a load of new tiles that quickly blocked the way in the street outside, evoking comments from passers-by — or, rather, from those who were trying to pass by. The most unfair of these complainers was my neighbour who had furnished me with the nuisance hillock of rubble. The tile-master made his decision as to which tiles required replacing and which could stay. Nimbly the men ran up a rough ladder, and started dismantling large parts of our roof. Tiles were flung through the air with zeal, and landed with little crashes. The area became not only impeded but dangerous with flying missiles, despite repeated warnings (particularly from me), and Mother's little screams from within doors. Falling tiles had killed people in Athens before now. A funeral and a pretty lawsuit with damages could result. Of course a tile that killed anybody would have to have a separate trial of its own, and be formally execrated and cast from the city.

I brooded a little on these legal possibilities. The men, however, seemed to enjoy the storm of tiles, though it was happily brief. Soon most of the roof was laid bare, and one of the slaves swept up the old broken tiles into one heap. My house was laid open to the elements – very odd, like a head without a scalp. A survey of the roof area by the master himself then elicited the judgement of the number of new rafters required. Of course he had brought boards with him, made to the standard measure, though if need arose he and his men could cut them to any size wanted.

'Good you're repairing at last. Need to do most of it right now,' he advised me, "less you want the whole roof to come a-tumbling down on all of you.'

As I could not say this was desirable, I acquiesced. Strong wood was scarce, so the greater the number of new boards, the greater the expense. New rafters were cut straight away and put in place before I could wax impatient; then the business of the tiling began. Nimbly the men pranced about, walking almost on air, as they filled in the empty spaces with the agreeably new tiles, as fresh-coloured as roses. I tried to keep an eye on the action. It was my part to make sure that all the tiles used were good, and that the master and his workers were not making do with misshapen or damaged ones to eke out the good. The master, however, was effusive in his invitations to me to see the roof for myself, and when it was half done I hopped up the ladder to take a personal inspection.

The tiles were evidently good – none cracked or crumbled at the edges – and they were generously and cleverly laid, with sufficient overlap to discourage leaking. I was able not only to discern the new roof taking shape at the highest point of the house, but also to take in a good view of the layout of our residence. The front courtyard was a square, and the smaller back one a rectangle. If I peered down I could see the squat supports of the projecting roof at the back of the front courtyard, the area that provided a kind of porch, a shady work space for women and slaves. I sighed as I thought how much better the house would look if these old-fashioned square pillars were turned into elegant columns. Some day, when I had enough money, I vowed I would do that.

Then I looked outward, away from my house, enjoying the strange vision of my neighbourhood from this vantage point. I could not only see into my next-door neighbour's courtyard, but could also look along the streets winding away from me. I was surprised at how much I could see from here: courtyards and wellheads hidden behind walls, washing hung out, a pretty herb garden. In our own street, the people seemed smaller as they threaded their way through the diminishing heaps of new tiles in front of my door. When they looked up at me and my roof, their faces appeared like tilted plates. Suddenly I realised that one of these tilted plates belonged to Halirrhothios. He hadn't spoken to me the last time we encountered each other. But now he addressed me.

'O Stephanos son of Nikiarkhos,' he said, 'are you becoming a god up there? Or are you taking up a new line of work?'

I was annoyed. It is not the thing for a well-born citizen – a member of an historic deme, an educated man – to engage in low mechanic occupations. Up here in my short khiton, dusty with the ambient powder created by the tile-flinging, I must look not very different from the slave workmen. One of these workmen turned to look at the speaker who had hailed me from below. I was amazed to see this slave's face turn pale. The fellow dropped a hammer as well as a tile, and both objects went cascading over the edge and crashed near Halirrhothios' feet. The tile (though not the hammer) broke on impact. The clumsy workman turned hastily away. But I had the decided impression that he had recognised Halirrhothios, and feared him for some reason.

'Careless fellow,' observed Halirrhothios, looking at the implement and the broken tile, and then lifting his head to talk to me. 'You would pay mighty damages, Stephanos, if that hammer there or even the tile had struck somebody. But I hear you are coming into money. Sweets of Hymettos, they say. So I daresay you are too rich to care. It is best, however, not to hire inefficient workmen.'

'Nothing wrong with my workmen,' said the tile-factory owner, bristling. Though he had been about to berate the slave himself, he could ill tolerate the insult.

'Have it your own way,' said Halirrhothios, shrugging. 'At least, Stephanos, you can put a roof over your head.' He stalked off, threading his way through the heaps of discarded tiles and the little rosy piles of new ones.

Puzzled, I tried to ask the workman why he had been so startled at seeing Halirrhothios.

'Oh no, sir,' he said earnestly. 'It was my mate startled me, see, and I let the tool drop.'

I let it go at that. I had seen the incident clearly enough, however, to know this description was not the truth. Could Halirrhothios be a former owner of this slave? If so, why did the man not say as much? He certainly now belonged legally to the tile-factory – he could hardly have worked constantly in public places had it been otherwise.

When the work was done and the whole roof was tiled, the master urged me to have another look for myself. He promised to return in two days, once the tiles had had a chance to settle, to inspect them, and bring the new end tiles and ornaments. These end tiles were worth waiting for, with the ornaments I had chosen as finials. Some handsome griffins, with beautiful curly manes, guarded the corners of the roof. These domestic *akroteria* did look nice, I thought – though the gleaming red roof of new tiles made the house's need of a new coat of limewash more apparent. I was standing pondering in the street, gazing at my house where Philomela would be living in a few months, when somebody touched my elbow.

'Sorry to bother you,' said Hieron. The unfortunate man looked apologetic. 'But I thought I should tell you, since you've tried to be helpful to me, that you're going to be served with a lawsuit.'

'A lawsuit?'

'Yes. I heard it from Theophon. It is about to be declared this morning in the Agora by the Statues of the Heroes.'

'*Theophon* is bringing a lawsuit?'

'No, no. Not at all. It is a neighbour of your relatives – or somebody – in Hymettos. I don't quite understand it, but Hymettos comes into it.'

I strode to the Agora, and found it was true. A notice about the lawsuit was pinned up by the Statues. It declared that one Lykon of Hymettos was bringing a civil suit, an action against myself for causing flooding to the neighbouring property by building a wall unlawfully, the aforesaid wall not only being set upon Lykon's right of way but also encroaching directly upon his property. A separate suit was brought against Dropides, the husband of Philokleia (though it was she who actually ran the property). And of course the major suit was brought against the absent Philokles, my fiancée's uncle, legal owner of the farm at Hymettos. I could not help cursing aloud as I read the notices by the unruffled heroic Statues. 'The gods throw it all in the Styx!' I muttered. 'If it isn't one thing, it's two others!'

Could *I* really be held liable for any problems with the farm at Hymettos? It seemed clear to me that I should not, but I was not sure. Perhaps from force of habit I made my way to the Lykeion to talk with Aristotle about it. I wasn't sure whether, after the shock of the news about Philotas, he would feel up to seeing me. Fortunately for me, he did. He was in his pleasant room at home, the room with the many books, but his usually cheerful face was pensive, and there were sleepless dark smudges under his eyes.

'I have been thinking about you, Stephanos,' Aristotle said. 'It seems I shall have occasion to go to Eleusis. Since I know you often have matters to attend to there, I thought we might walk thither together soon, some fine day.'

'That would be nice,' I said, without much interest. 'But at the moment it is the affairs of Hymettos that are troubling me, not of Eleusis.' And I explained glumly about the lawsuit.

'Quite like old times,' said Aristotle.

This evening was indeed rather like the first time I had seen the room, myself in trouble because of a lawsuit and coming to Aristotle for advice. It was later in the autumn now, and a few coals of olive stones were glowing in a little brazier. There were even more books than before. Aristotle sent for wine, as on the historic occasion. This time, however, the wine was brought by the very striking slavewoman Herpyllis. She had been a favourite slave of Aristotle's first wife, Pythias; I had first laid eyes on her at Pythias' funeral, and had seen her for the second time when Aristotle, about to depart for the East, had taken leave of his household, including this slavewoman with the curling dark hair and large blue eyes. Herpyllis still took care of the little Pythias, though her duties had been extended to those of a housekeeper. I now knew they went beyond that.

'Serve our guest first, Herpyllis,' Aristotle advised, though her first impulse was obviously to serve him. She turned to me, and I noticed how gracefully she moved. Her sandals were of fine leather and the thongs curled round the finest pair of ankles any man could wish to see. Herpyllis handed me a cup and brought to her master the wine-jar and the water, arranging these neatly on a little table. 'Here is some honey,' she said to him, 'in case you wish to sweeten it.'

'I think not,' said Aristotle. 'Mix the wine, Herpyllis, and pour it out for us.'

She deftly did as he asked. As bidden, she poured the wine and water into my cup and then turned back to her master and delicately served him. She waited while we both made libation, and then poured again for her master, so he might drink from a full cup.

'You have given it sweetness,' Aristotle said, in a light, teasing voice. And he touched her hand as she gave him the wine-cup.

She smiled, saying nothing, and left the room. Her quiet exit did nothing to allay my vivid impression of the little flame that there was between them. Strange. Aristotle had professed himself so much in love with his wife. He had grieved for Pythias so heartily – nay, even dangerously. Aristotle to take up with his servant-maid, like any common man! Not every man, however, would have had a servant-maid like Herpyllis.

'In such small comforts,' Aristotle observed, staring into the coals of the little brazier, 'a man finds relief from the shocks of life.' I could see then he had not got over the death of Pythias, nor the recent shock of the killing of Philotas. 'Ah well. Distract me, Stephanos. Tell me about your case.'

'Somebody I don't even know – one Lykon, a neighbour of the family at Hymettos – is bringing a lawsuit against me. But I'm not an owner of the farm at Hymettos! He is suing Philokles, which is right as Philokles is the legal owner. And he's also laying a charge against that stupid Dropides. But this man Lykon has brought me into it too!'

'That fact,' Aristotle pronounced, 'would seem to indicate that somebody knows of the agreement you signed with Philokles in Kos last summer. Have you been talking with anybody about it?'

'Smikrenes knows about it, naturally. I may have mentioned it to some friends. And I definitely said something about it to Lamas and Hieron,' I admitted. 'Very recently.'

'It is perhaps not surprising that you are being treated as a partner in the farm,' said Aristotle. 'It may not be your fault the information has got about. The women at Hymettos, or even Dropides, may have said something as well about the arrangement. It is not a state secret! This Lykon will argue that you are a partner, intending to profit in a legal arrangement between you and the real owner, and thus must be liable for any damage done to the neighbour in Hymettos. Now, what damage does this man claim to have sustained?'

'He claims that I – that we – have built a wall illegally on a right of way and stopped a water-course. And the blockage has diverted the water so that it has flooded his property and caused damage. Not only so, but he says the wall is encroaching on his property and must be removed.'

'If the people at the Hymettos farm *have* built any new walls, it may be the harder for you,' said Aristotle. 'Arguments about water-courses and rights of way are common in Athens. Sometimes such a charge is used by a man who wants to claim the property – or a part of it – for himself. This case seems a trifle suspect. After all, Lykon could have raised his objections to the wall-builder before the structure was even finished. He might have persuaded other residents of the area to back him up.'

'That's true,' I agreed, imagining the scene. 'He should have said something like this: "Philokles (or Dropides), what are you doing? Don't you realise what will happen if you obstruct this water-course? As soon as it rains, there will be terrible flooding and the water will run the wrong way into my land!"'

'Quite so,' said Aristotle, laughing a little. 'Lykon *ought* to have spoken thus – supposing this was a genuine complaint. Find out from the people of Hymettos whether there has been any such complaint in the past, which would also tell in favour of Lykon's charge. You had probably better look for yourself at the allegedly offensive wall. Although in *any* case, you will argue that you personally have been associated with this property for only two or three months or so, and are by no means liable for anything that was done before. Refer everything to Philokles.'

'I was thinking myself I should go to Hymettos and look at the spot,' I said. 'A nuisance. The damages asked for by this Lykon are extensive. And just as we had started to do so well! I was relying on the income from Hymettos to help with house repair, maybe even buying a slave, in preparation for marriage. If this action doesn't injure me directly, it will injure me through making my wife's relatives poorer.'

'Just so,' said Aristotle. 'Indeed, that may be the whole point. To subject you to a nuisance. Lawsuits are a part of Athenian life, a way in which potentially powerful men are held in check – as the iniquitous Euphorbos, such a trouble to us last summer, is now happily tied up. Someone is perhaps trying to keep *you* in check, Stephanos. Though there may be no political malice in it at all. Merely a matter of business. Lykon may hope simply for money damages. But take care – he may intend establishing a claim to part of Philokles' land!'

I set out for Hymettos a few days later, in order to find out for myself, literally, how the land lay. I had sent word in advance. My first visit to the Hymettos farm owned by relatives of my bride-to-be had been early in the previous summer. Then I had moved through fields freshly shorn or just ripe for reaping, and on turning up the slope had found relief from the heat under the shade of the pine trees and beside the flowing Ilissos. Now the fields were dull, or ploughed in ridged furrows with damp settling between. The river was quiet and full, the weather too cool for me to require shade. Then the constant hum of bees had rendered Philokles' part of the mountain alive with cheerful energy; now they were still, and there was no mysterious female beekeeper moving among the hives.

Hymettos had already been good to me this autumn. I had last gone to the farm in need of money, after my return to Attika, still weak from my wound. Philomela's grandmother, who managed the estate and did much of the work on it in the absence of her son Philokles, had kindly advanced me two hundred and fifty drakhmai, as well as a good load of honey to sell. (The events surrounding the honey-sale had unfortunately been loosely associated with unpleasant matters.) How I had rejoiced when I left the farm with coins in my pouch, and all that honey! Financially, things had been looking up – so I had then thought. Perhaps, I reflected glumly as I plodded through the dismal countryside and up the bare slopes, perhaps I should have known that all would not go so well.

Brooding upon past and present, I had turned up the road (little better than a pathway here) that would take me to the farm itself when somebody bumped into me. Had I been less abstracted, I should certainly have noticed this person running down the path, and avoided her. For it was a woman, a young woman, without a veil or head covering. Her hair flowed in a bushy reddish mess of curls down her back. She ran with determination, but with a slight limp. The running girl was somewhat plump, not unpleasingly so, but a palpable object with which to collide. I took her by the shoulders to push her gently away; I could hear her panting.

'Zobia! Zobia, stop!' A man came round the bend, running very briskly too. An older man, running to catch her. Now he caught sight of us. 'Behave! Don't speak to strange men! Get away from that!' I had already detached myself from the heavy-breathing runner, and now stepped back further. She did not seem disconcerted, but stopped where she stood and pushed back her hair.

'Girl, you shouldn't run away like that!' The man, drawing level with us, grabbed her arm.

He was much older than she, a sunburned man with dark curly hair and a well-shaped beard, curly also. 'Child, when will you learn proper behaviour! Leaving the house – and without any veil!'

'I have to search, Papa!' she said earnestly. 'I have search for my baby! I am looking for Baby everywhere!'

Her father blushed deeply. 'Let me introduce myself,'

I said. 'Stephanos of Athens. I am betrothed to the niece of Philokles who owns the farm over there . . .'

'Yes, yes, I know Philokles. I am Asimos, his neighbour.'

'So you must know Lykon?'

'I live on the other side of Philokles from Lykon – my farm is just down that way.'

'Lykon is cross. But he has a little dog. Philokles is gone. He didn't have a baby. There is no baby at that farm,' the girl assured me. She looked me in the face in the most unnatural way for the girl child of a citizen, who ought to be utterly modest. I could see from this gaze that she was probably crazy, or an idiot of some sort.

'She imagines a baby?' I asked.

He groaned. 'No. There was a baby right enough. Poor girl, the shame! She roams, I fear. This girl roams. I have built walls about our dwelling, higher and higher, but she will get out.'

'I want my baby. Artemis gave me a baby boy, and I *want* him!'

'Please say nothing of this, sir, she's not right in her intellects, as you can see.'

'My condolences. I suppose the infant was . . .' I made the sign that people usually make when they mean 'exposed' but don't wish to speak the word.

'No,' Asimos replied, blushing. 'The gods forgive my weakness – I could deny her nothing. It was not exposed. Died of its own accord, before it lived three days. But she's still grieving for it, as a cow will for a calf.'

'I can find it,' she insisted. 'It got lost, but I can find it! I have milk, so it must come back!'

'Come now, daughter,' Asimos said coaxingly. 'Come home and have something to eat.' He tucked his arm firmly into hers, and she consented to go; they soon vanished along that path.

Life in rural Hymettos was more perturbed than one would have thought, I mused, as I went on to my destination. Even before this threatened lawsuit, there were some difficulties in doing business with the farm at Hymettos to which my new marriage was binding me. Theoretically, the man of the house was Dropides, second husband of my fiancée's grandmother. This Dropides, however, was the man in the world least likely to trouble himself about anything. I now found this indolent husband much as I had seen him on the two previous occasions, but even more intent on warming himself. He was sitting close by a brazier in a great chair well padded with fleecy sheepskins, and a sheepskin over most of his front. In autumn as in summer he held a large pottery cup of wine and water to which he gave constant attention, sipping slowly and gravely.

'The doctor advises it, for my cough and other complaints,' he explained, not moving to welcome me, and offering no refreshment. 'I'm no better, but thanks to the gods, no worse. You want to talk with Philokleia. Nuisance, but it can't be helped. Mika, fetch your mistress!'

The short and stubby maidservant, taciturn as always, ran off at this expected command.

'I have just met your neighbour Asimos,' I said, to fill in time. 'I'm not quite certain where his property is.'

'Asimos? His place touches on ours. As you come up the hill towards our place above the spring of Ilissos, his farm is to the left, but down a bit. And this troublesome Lykon's property is to the right, and a bit above. Always building walls, Asimos is. So people tell me. Builds walls and stuffs the cracks with thorn bushes. But his walls don't encroach on our land.'

Philomela's energetic grandmother entered the little chamber next to the room where we men were sitting. A curtain was hastily nailed up, so that Philokleia and I could as usual converse without my actually seeing her. I was always aware how great a wrong it would be to look upon another citizen's wife, mother or grown daughter. Had Dropides been willing to take his own part in things, I need not have conversed with women at all.

'Never meddle with business myself,' Dropides said. 'As for this lawsuit, it gives me jumps and sweats. I'm not sure it won't bring on a fever.'

'Please ask your wife,' I said, maintaining the thread-bare fiction that I was really conversing with Dropides, 'where the site is about which complaint is made, and what exactly has happened.'

'She can show you, she and Philonike,' said Dropides carelessly. I was startled at this impropriety. 'The women can go ahead of you and stand at a distance and point,' he suggested. '*I'm* not well enough to walk all that way! Can barely stir.' He sighed gustily, inviting sympathy. 'Did you buy a good servant with all that money we gave you?' he added pointedly.

'I haven't bought a slave yet,' I had to admit. 'Of necessity I have just had the roof retiled, and other work needs to be done on the house, including painting. And I have to pay for a proper wedding party at my house. So I don't expect to make a purchase very soon.'

'We can help you a little more,' said Philokleia thoughtfully. 'Now, don't protest, husband. If Lykon's suit goes against us, we might be glad to have deposited some money with Stephanos.'

'If we lose, *he* loses,' said Dropides with satisfaction.

'Never mind that now, husband. As for this lawsuit,' said the energetic Philokleia, ostensibly addressing Dropides again, 'you can tell Stephanos that I believe Lykon has had his own designs on getting some part of this estate. Now he thinks he sees a chance.'

'Was a new wall really put up?' I ventured.

As Dropides was unwilling to go to the trouble of repeating our words, his elderly wife and I were left to carry on the conversation as we chose. She replied directly to my query.

'There is *no* new wall. I just had an old one repaired at the end of the summer, but that wall has been standing for fifteen years, I tell you!'

'He claims that you have caused flooding to his property, and also cut off a right of way.'

'Bah! Lunacy! It could not have caused flooding. If it did, it would have done so fifteen years ago. And what he calls "a water-course" and "right of way" is part of *our* land. It is even planted. You will see when I show you. We have family graves up there! It is ridiculous to call any of that area a "water-course" or "right of way". The Ilissos and its streams changed their courses a long time ago. This land is ours. We have harmed nobody. I can only suppose that Lykon is trying his tricks now because he knows that Philokles is the owner, and Philokles has gone to the East.'

'Lykon has charged me – made me a party to the case. Someone has informed Lykon of my share in the farm's produce according to our agreement.'

She sighed. 'Not good for my granddaughter.'

A veiled shape loomed behind her. The younger woman, Philonike, my Philomela's mother.

'I hope it is not going to affect the marriage,' Philonike said anxiously. 'We do not want any further put-offs from Smikrenes.'

'I see no prospect of that,' I said reassuringly. 'Please show me – let me be shown – exactly what part of the property is the subject of the complaint.'

'Follow us,' demanded Philokleia. Taking charge of her daughter, she left the house. I followed at a respectful distance. We wound our way about the farm, through groves and fields, with a view of upland meadows; their bees had the whole of Hymettos' thymey mountain in which to range.

'There,' said gaunt Philokleia, pointing. 'You can see our wall. Stone foundation, mud bricks on top. You can see how it has been patched. There are a couple of new stones – there – and new bricks of course, but you can see how that bit joins the old wall on both sides. And that area there going down the slope is what he claims is a water-course and part of his right of way. Now, how could that be? Look how it is planted with trees! Old fig trees and mature almond trees! Those didn't come up overnight. And yonder there are markers for the graves of members of the family. That bit has been a burying-ground for a long time. You don't make family burying-grounds in a month or two!'

'I should draw a picture of it,' I mused. 'A sort of plan so I could make this clear to the jury.'

'*I* could do that,' offered Philonike. 'But take a look at Lykon's property. You will see his land hasn't suffered from flooding – not because of our wall, anyway.'

'He might have been flooded when the last rain came,' said Philokleia. 'The water trickles to his place down the mountain, above us, and he takes little precaution against that. If his manure heap was swept away his farmyard would turn into a bog.'

'I see.' I knew I ought to obtain real witnesses to look at the property. Women didn't count, even if these women had been neutral observers – which they certainly weren't. I walked along the wall myself and peered over it. Impatient with this indeterminate activity, I gave way to impulse, and scrambled up and over the partition, jumping down on the other side. True, the ground here was a bit soft and mushy, but that was because Lykon had created a little ditch on his side of the wall. There were no serious signs of flooding, no shelves of earth carried away downhill. As this was the flank of Hymettos, naturally everything was downhill (or uphill), more or less, though Philokles' farm, with good arable land, was on one of the flattest areas.

'No signs of water damage,' I said aloud, but even as I did so a yapping dog suddenly came at me, closely followed by a man. I realised that this must be Lykon.

'Ho! You!' He waved a stick at me, cut from some orchard tree, it seemed. The dog fussed about my shins but did not bite. It was not a giant mastiff, but only a little dog from Melite, with a curly tail. 'What do you think you're doing? Walking on another man's property, without a by-your-leave!'

I was clearly in the wrong, which didn't make me better tempered.

'I am Stephanos son of Nikiarkhos, citizen of Athens,' I announced haughtily. 'One whom you have wrongly accused of—'

'*Wrongly?* I should have you before a magistrate for your trespass at this very moment! Explain *that* to a jury, can you? Stalking boldly about on my land! What good that will do your case I don't—'

'Not *my* case,' I said, remembering (belatedly) Aristotle's advice. 'I am not an owner nor part owner. The owner of this property is Philokles.'

'Well, the owner of the property that your boots are on at this moment is myself. Lykon of Hymettos.' He treated me to an ironic nod. I had expected someone like the irascible Smikrenes, but this man was much smoother, better educated, and even somewhat younger than I expected. He did not have the grimy hands of the peasant toiler, and his black hair and beard held no grey. This well-combed citizen and man of property continued his discourse.

'I know, O Stephanos son of Nikiarkhos, that you now maintain an interest in that property – on the *other* side of the wall. From which you intend to make profit, in the absence of Philokles. I believe *you* have advised the reconstruction of this wall. Damage has been done. You have encroached on my land. I suffer losses from your creation of an artificial water-course. My own land has been rendered useless!'

'Not really. And anyway, it's not me,' I protested weakly. I was not proud of my performance, particularly when I recollected the two women could hear it all, though they had hidden themselves among the almond trees. Lykon waved my feeble objection away.

'I am in the right to demand satisfaction. So I have issued a charge for damage. I will add to it the charge of actual trespass. You are bodily on the wrong side of that detestable wall.'

'I came only to check whether there was any real damage – and there isn't. I shall readily depart,' I added, keeping an eye on the little dog.

'Do so, with speed,' advised Lykon. 'Else I shall take steps to assist your departure.' He waved his stick and I had to turn tail and scramble over the wall, with the man and dog both watching me. The dog sniffed at my departing ankles in a disparaging manner, but neither he nor his master attempted any more energetic measure.

'Well, that was a pretty encounter,' I said to the women. I felt like apologising for the rash error of going over the wall, but one doesn't apologise to women. I walked back towards the house again. The women at first kept a suitable distance, but then Philonike drew closer to me.

'This trouble truly won't affect your marriage, will it?' she pleaded, her voice clearly audible through the veil. 'I could not bear to think of your wedding to my daughter being postponed again. Or the prospect ended because of

Smikrenes' uncertain temper. Or because of lawsuits. I have been so glad to think of Philomela being safe, in a home in Athens, and with a reasonable and responsible husband.'

'The marriage will go forward in Gamelion,' I said, consenting to take part in this unorthodox conversation with a citizen woman. 'Smikrenes will stand by the *engye*. And your pretty gifts – the things sent in the cedar box – will be given to your Philomela on her wedding night. But I hope that you will come yourself to the wedding.'

'Oh no!' Philonike shook her head. 'I dare not come. I cannot set foot on Smikrenes' land. He would claim his right as a husband. He would seize me and lock me up.'

'I meant, come to the part of the wedding party that takes place at my house in Athens,' I explained. 'Then you'd know the house that Philomela will be living in, and meet her mother-in-law. Come – you must! Your only child, and you could think of not being there?'

She waved her hand, as if pushing the suggestion away from her, sadly rather than vehemently.

'It's too dangerous. I should love to come if Smikrenes were out of the question. But he isn't. He would see me there, and could claim me as his and take me away with him. I do not hate him. But I will not go back and live with him down in Eleusis.'

'You are not a good mother!' I exclaimed.

'No, I am not,' she agreed sadly. 'Yet I would give so much to see my daughter wed! I would pay almost anything – but not myself.'

'Think of it again,' I urged. 'You would only be among the women after all, no need for the men of the wedding party to see you. Stay in the women's quarters. There you can help Philomela with her bath and adorning.'

'You tempt me,' she said. 'I should love to see her – so much. But I cannot imagine it.'

VII

Lost Sausages, and a Philosophical Walk

If my strange mother-in-law-to-be were unable to imagine attending her daughter's own wedding, she seemed deficient in imaginative capacity – so I judged. I omitted to notice that I myself might be lacking in the capacity to entertain a variety of possibilities. There were contingencies I had nowise taken into account. How limited, alas, are we mortals – how little apt to measure correctly the multiple dispositions of human affairs!

The very day after my encounter with the disagreeable Lykon of Hymettos I heard more bad news, and again endured a meeting with someone whom I did not wish to see. I was passing through the Agora on my way home, carrying with me the produce of the day's shopping, chiefly two sausages and a large water-pot. My mother had reminded me that the biggest water-pot in our home was chipped, and not really the *hydria* to have on hand to welcome a new bride. So I had brought a new one, useful albeit plain.

The slave Tryphos had gone on an errand in the other direction, so I was left to take the purchases home myself. Naturally I did not wish to carry the bulky *hydria* in the ordinary way, which would mean gripping it by both large handles ('by the ears', as they say) and thus looking like a woman or slave coming from the Fountain House. Shopping in the Agora is the department of the head of the household, but drawing water is certainly not. So I decided to carry the pot horizontally, and put the sausages within it for safekeeping. Engaged in this homely task, I was not proposing to stop and chat with anyone, but I found myself greeted forcefully by someone standing right in front of me.

'O Stephanos! I must speak with you!'

Perforce I had to stop. Peering above my *hydria* I looked at the person who was in my way. Somebody I had not seen in a long time.

'Good day to you, O Kallimakhos.'

What I should really have liked to say was 'By Herakles, it's Kallimakhos! Who of all people should be ashamed even to speak to me. Be off!' I could not quite say this to such a respected citizen as Kallimakhos of Kollytos. Long ago, he and my father had talked of marrying me off to his daughter, Kharmia. This match seemed an advantageous alliance for our family, but wealthy Kallimakhos had hastily drawn off once my father's death had made clear to all that our financial fortunes were at low water, unlikely soon to rise. He had subsequently made a point of not associating with me. I had seen the man at the Ekklesia and so on, but we had rarely spoken to each other. Later, when my affairs were going a little better, he had become odiously agreeable when we met in public, but I had made no response to these overtures.

At the time when he first broke off negotiations, I did not wish to undertake marriage at all. Yet, oddly, despite my relief at the time, I had always borne this citizen a decided grudge. Though there had been no *engye*, and no substantial promise let alone betrothal. . . .

'I wonder, Stephanos, you aren't ashamed to look me in the face,' declared Kallimakhos. I thought *I* might more properly have said this. Although I was not exactly looking him straight in the face, as I was peering over the round bulk of the pot.

I did not intend to give him the satisfaction of asking how he came by his wonderment, but he kindly supplied me with his reasoning on the topic.

'When I hear,' he said dramatically, 'when *I* have to hear from others that you have pronounced an *engye* with some peasant from Eleusis without so much as consulting me!'

'I fear I do not understand you,' I said politely. 'There was no reason to consult you in such a matter.'

'How! You treat an engagement to marry — an agreement of long standing — as *nothing*!' Kallimakhos raised his hands and his voice dramatically. Idlers in the marketplace began to gather, hoping for an interesting scene.

'What?' Realising I could not proceed without an argument with this man, I set the pot down, with the two long sausages inside it. At least now I could look him in the eye. He was as he had always been, a square-built man of above middle height. He still had his handsome dark hair and beard, well combed and running only a little to grey. Kallimakhos, customarily well-dressed, today looked even better turned out than usual — as if, thought I, he had planned our encounter and wished to make a good impression on any audience that might fall to our lot.

'May I remind you,' he continued, in a tone of weary patience, 'that you were always to marry my daughter Kharmia. We thought it best,' he added virtuously, 'to put off the wedding for a while, as you were both young to marry. But the agreement was never formally

annulled. And then for a while, you were so busy
travelling—'

'It could not be broken off *formally*,' I retorted with
heat, 'because there was no formal *engye*. Whatever you
and my father may have spoken about – long, *long* ago –
there was no betrothal. That is why I felt I had no right
to complain when you moved yourself and your daughter
afar off once you found there was too little to gain!'

Laughter and applause from onlookers, most of them
the sort who are always looking for entertainment, and
will choose to gather round men in dispute when there
isn't a cock-fight to go to.

'Well, my boy, your manners have not improved, I will
say that,' announced Kallimakhos. 'And now my poor girl
in Kollytos is to go without her wedding because you
hanker after the barley-bearing lands of flat Eleusis. As if a
marriage were to be on or off merely at your whim!'

'This is not doing your daughter any good,' I
remonstrated. 'Besides, I heard you had betrothed the
girl to another.'

'Pay no heed to gossip, Stephanos son of Nikiarkhos.
My daughter is still unmarried. She waits for you. I am a
reasonable man. Let's go to a tavern in a friendly way and
discuss it. You won't find me dull in the matter of a
dowry. Come,' he said, ostensibly addressing me, but
really getting his effect up for the benefit of the
onlookers, 'come with me now, and let us talk it over in a
kapeleion with some mediating friends around. To make
up the agreement.'

'Certainly not,' I said. 'This is all nonsense—'

At this point there was an unexpected diversion. Two
dogs, little white creatures with curly tails, came chasing
each other through the Agora. The first one, a female, ran
swiftly straight into our group. Narrowly avoiding me,
the little bitch collided with my new *hydria* and sent it

toppling sidewise to the ground. This offender sped off, but her companion or suitor, smelling the sausages, momentarily gave over his amorous chase. Putting his little snout into the jar, he pulled out the sausages and went careening off. The dog soon dropped one prize, but proudly carried the other sausage drooping from his mouth so the ends dragged in the dust.

'Hi! Stop, thief! You come back – whose dog is that?' I cried, to the intense amusement of the company.

'I commiserate with you,' said Kallimakhos. 'I dare say that for your household the loss of the sausages is no small financial setback. I am willing to do the handsome thing and give you money enough to buy more . . .' and he reached for his money pouch.

'Certainly not,' I said. 'This is absurd.' And it was, like a satyr-play, the farce after the tragedies are done. The grinning men around us might as well have been a *khoros* of satyrs themselves for all the help they were to me. 'Oh ho, too bad,' they sniggered. One wit added, 'A man who's lost his sausage is surely not able to think of a wedding!'

'I have no more to discuss with you, good Kallimakhos of Kollytos,' I said as coldly and politely as I could manage. 'You are mistaken in this instance. Cast your mind back, and I am sure you will remember that you yourself broke off any and all negotiations with our family. Good day.'

And I stalked off, my dignity impeded by having to pick up my *hydria* as I went. My temper was not improved at finding there was a crack in it now. I had also lost the sausages, but in this instance at least the theft was not mysterious, nor the culprit hidden.

I found myself explaining to Mother how the *hydria* had got broken, and in the course of this explanation somehow it all came out, the dreary encounter with

Kallimakhos. Eunike daughter of Diogeiton was not at all pleased to hear of it.

'I'm sure,' she said reproachfully, 'you might have treated Kallimakhos more politely earlier, Stephanos. Poor boy, so thoughtless. Now look! Another enemy, another law case!'

'So you wanted me to marry Kallimakhos' daughter?'

'No – don't think that. Though they're a respected town family and not peasants still grubbing in the fields.' I let this pass. 'But that family was always out for what they could get. I'm sure Kallimakhos would have diddled Nikiarkhos, your father. At least he would have if my poor husband hadn't been so involved in his affairs that Kallimakhos couldn't be sure he'd get anything. That man tried to coax your father to settle good lands on yourself and his daughter. Nikiarkhos hated business – just as well in this case – so he put it off and nothing was really agreed to. Kallimakhos himself would never be clear about the dowry for his dowdy of a girl.'

'*Is* she a dowdy? I thought she was handsome. And she was supposed to be very good at her weaving, sensible and industrious.'

'Oh, I daresay she could weave,' my mother said grudgingly. 'She's not an absolute fright, but stubby, and no nose to speak of. No beauty even then, and she cannot have improved by keeping. I have a kind of notion that Kallimakhos recently tried to wed her to another man's son. Come to think of it, that seems likely. I'll see if I can find out from the other women in the street.'

'Be careful,' I said. 'I can handle this without resorting to women's gossip.' (Though I don't know what made me so certain of that.)

'Not if you don't know how to handle the men,' Mother replied.

'Oh, I can handle the men,' I assured her. 'I'm going to

do something you will approve. You always urge me to mingle with the better class of Athenians. To make friends with a man who is *kalos k'agathos* – one of the Beautiful and Good. Now, I have a plan, to restore the repute of myself and our family. I am going to give a symposium, and invite some of the Beautiful and Good to it. A symposium in this house. The beginning of the next month, I think that would be the best time.'

This was the first Mother had heard of it, and it certainly distracted her attention.

Indeed, despite the vexations of Lykon's lawsuit, I had not forgotten the suggestion of my old schoolfellow Nikeratos, that I should give a dinner party. With yet another lawsuit pending (possibly), it seemed advisable for me to proceed. I ought to take care to render myself of good repute among honourable and influential citizens. I was certainly a true Athenian citizen, of good lineage, from whose ancestral lands sprang from time immemorial the sacred olive trees of Athena. It was time to remind everyone of these facts, so I and my children would be well established. A man who has friends to back him up in court will certainly be more likely to succeed in a lawsuit than the man who does not. And the effort I was putting into cleaning and beautifying my house before my wedding should not be wasted.

This dinner-party must be an all-Athenian affair. Aristotle would not, unfortunately, be a suitable guest at such an occasion. He was not only a foreign resident, a *metoikos*, but a known friend of Alexander and of Alexander's regent, Antipater. Yet, despite my design of omitting the philosopher from my symposium, I did wish to speak with Aristotle. I had not planned to trouble him again with my problem with Lykon and the Hymettos estate – even if I had now made matters worse by tangling with Lykon myself. Hymettos was really

Philokles' affair. But now there was the new threatened lawsuit of Kallimakhos. Talking matters over with a woman doesn't count as getting advice. I really wanted Aristotle's view of the matter.

A couple of days later, I went early to the Lykeion hoping to find Aristotle and speak with him privately. I did find Aristotle, but only as he and Theophrastos were setting out for a walk – along with the scholars Eudemos of Rhodos and Demetrios of Phaleron.

'Just the man!' they said, on seeing me. 'Join us in a walk to Eleusis.'

'At least,' amended Eudemos, 'Aristotle and Theophrastos are going to Eleusis. Demetrios and I, like indolent observers following the Eleusinian Procession, will walk with them merely for a couple of stadia. Or perhaps only as far as the Agora.'

'To Eleusis? Why?'

'Oh – I have business there. One thing and another,' Aristotle said evasively. 'I had intended to ask you to come, Stephanos, as I mentioned before, but then Theophrastos agreed to walk with me.'

Swallowing a slight chagrin, I agreed, since I had promised to see Smikrenes again, and today seemed as good as any. Though we were now at the beginning of Maimakterion, the month of rain and wind, this day was clear and slightly sunny. A good day for the olive harvest, which comes just before winter; I really should have gone to our farm. We set off, Eudemos and Demetrios walking behind us and Aristotle, myself and Theophrastos in front. I always think three is an awkward number for a walk. The first part of our journey led us back into the Agora.

'I have had nothing to eat today,' announced Aristotle's right-hand man. 'And I have been cultivating my garden even before dawn. So perhaps it would be prudent for me to have a piece of bread before we set out.' Theophrastos was standing right by a bread-seller, one of the low women who haunt public places selling things. This particular female to whom Theophrastos gave his moderate custom was blind, but she used her portable oven very handily. After ordering a fresh-baked flat cake, the Pythagorean philosopher was prosing on in his usual style.

'I am no friend to excess of nutriment,' Theophrastos pondered aloud, 'but it is folly to expect inanition to support prolonged activity. Thank you, my good woman. How much?'

'Half an obol.'

'Half an obol! One should obtain three little loaves, at the least, for that sum.'

'That's the price. You can try any of the other bread-sellers, foreign gent, and they will say the same.'

Theophrastos stared.

'How did you – how could you think I was *foreign*?' he demanded.

'Knew it by the way you speak. You speak the Attika speech, but it's too perfect. Only a foreigner could talk that way.'

'Give her an obol for her wit and intelligence,' said Aristotle, laughing. The affronted Theophrastos yielded his money with a kind of snort, and we went on our way.

As the five of us departed, I heard someone in the marketplace, not too far off, say, 'There goes the Makedonian philosopher, with his train of bastards and foreigners!'

We pretended not to hear – perhaps not all of our party did hear this insult. I was embarrassed, but the incident corroborated my judgement about the dinner-invitations. Certainly, it was best not to invite anyone connected with the Lykeion, those foreigners. I was curious, however, about the term 'bastards'. I had not thought about it formerly, but Demetrios of Phaleron, no foreigner, was always called after the deme he was born in, not named as the son of a father. Was he a bastard – and were some of the others bastards as well? Who more likely to take up a life of philosophic study than the bastard son of a rich man, attached to no lands or household?

Demetrios and Eudemos parted from us at the city gate, perhaps because they trusted me to keep the two other philosophers in good spirits. As we passed beyond the city walls, Theophrastos was still mulling over the slur on his accent.

'*Pheu!* All nonsense! – I speak the Greek of Attika, *perfectly*,' he protested.

'You do, yes, Theophrastos. That was her point. The poor woman is blind, after all, so she relies on her hearing. She listens acutely. You know,' said Aristotle, turning to me, 'I told you before, I think, that Theophrastos was born and brought up in the island of Lesbos. But under my tuition he has lost his Lesbian dialect and even the accent, and has learned to speak in pure Greek of Attika. And to speak brilliantly. Do you know what his name is?'

'His name? Theophrastos, of course.'

'And who gave him that name? I did,' said Aristotle complacently. 'He was originally named Tyrtamos. But he did so well in his study of Athenian Greek style that I renamed him Theophrastos, as one who speaks divinely. He has really come on since he was encouraged by his new name. Very few people study spoken language with that intensity of application.'

'True,' I said. 'Only real Athenians speak like Athenians. Most of us learn to speak without thinking about it. It's a natural thing.'

'Language,' said Theophrastos, 'is not a *natural* thing. And if one wishes to speak purely—'

'He's very fond of the pure and clean,' Aristotle said, teasingly. It struck me that the two men must have been having some kind of private argument before I joined them. 'Another thing you don't know, Stephanos,' Aristotle added, 'and it's not generally known hereabouts, save to the senior scholars at the Lykeion, is that Theophrastos' father was in the garment-cleaning trade.'

'You mean Theophrastos takes after him in wanting things clean?'

'Yes. Papa – although only adoptive Papa but that's another secret – was a fuller, who could make one's *khiton* gleam whitely. He used certain fine earths, and some extracts of plants, to take spots out of clothes. Some hold that explains why Theophrastos is attracted to the earth and to the plants that grow out of it.'

'Need we communicate *all* the facts of my early life to the whole of Athens?' Theophrastos demanded bitterly. His pride was hurt, and Aristotle evidently felt he had gone too far.

There was some tension between the two men that I could not understand. To change the subject, I introduced the unhappy topic of my new lawsuit. The two philosophers were both amused by the account of the water-jar, the accusation, and the lost sausages.

'And I was going to ask Aristotle's advice,' I concluded. 'You know how distant Kallimakhos has been – ever since my father died and he discovered we weren't rich. I cannot see how the man can dream he could bring me to court for any kind of damages! We entered into no agreement, not even an informal betrothal.'

'It certainly seems highly unlikely that he could get anywhere in a court of law,' pronounced Theophrastos.

'But,' said Aristotle, 'as the man probably has friends of some importance, he might be able to get up a court case and vex you by it.'

'You say,' added Theophrastos, 'that this man Kallimakhos drew off earlier, when he found you weren't rich. Perhaps he has found out that you are richer now. No, that won't work. He must be aware that your current prospects of wealth all arise from your association with the family in Eleusis and Hymettos. Without that marriage, you are not much better off than you were originally.'

'That's not quite fair! I pulled our family affairs out of the bog before I ever met Smikrenes. But it really is too bad! And at the time of my marriage, which makes it worse. First comes the threat of the Hymettos suit, and now this one.'

'I wonder,' said Aristotle, 'if this is entirely a coincidence. Is somebody determined to decorate you with lawsuits like an *eiresione*?'

'It's possible, I suppose.' I pondered this. 'I cannot think of any particular enemy, though. If only people were good and would behave well! How are you getting on with your plan for a series of lectures on Ethics?'

'I have been thinking a great deal about it, Stephanos. It is now clearer to me than ever that the nature of Ethics depends on the idea of *choice*. The free person makes a voluntary choice.'

'So the free-born person is always able to make a free choice?'

'Well – not always. I discount actions under compulsion, not truly voluntary – if somebody commands you to do a bad thing or he will kill your child, for example. But in common life the real problem, the great curb on freedom, is the *character*. The character that we have is created by all our actions, all our previous choices.'

'So we are almost like puppets of our own past?'

'Strikingly put. We are what we do. Not what we say we are, or wish we were.'

'But,' I said, argumentatively, 'what would be the point of calling Tyrtamos "Theophrastos" if words and wishes don't have anything to do with it?'

Aristotle frowned slightly. 'You take me up on a chance anecdote, indeed, Stephanos. Consider. Once he is known to himself as Theophrastos, Tyrtamos is free to recognise the sum of his former acts, and move towards future ones. He manifests what he does: speak well and persuade honestly, undergo labour in researches and then give clear descriptions, attract students whom he cares for and to whom he offers truth. He is his acts, he just didn't know it.'

'I wish you wouldn't use me as an object lesson,' Theophrastos objected.

'You see, Stephanos, the character is created by a sum of former acts. Tell lies often, and lying will seem a "natural" choice. If you always get drunk at the *kapeleion*, why should tonight be any different? Similarly, if you always look for pleasure and shirk discomfort, you are extremely unlikely suddenly to be able to decide to be brave and self-denying.'

'That is almost frightening,' I exclaimed. 'So even free citizens are not truly free?'

'Only in relation to the character they are creating. We are – all of us – our deeds. A man cannot call back his previous acts, erase them like words scrawled in sand, as if they had never been. Every action is eternal, as it were. You might wish you could rescind your deed, but truly you cannot. You are powerless to make them as if they had never been. You might *wish* you can, but you cannot. Think about throwing a stone. Once the stone has left your hand it has gone! Whatever your wishes, you cannot recall it.'

I pondered this, thinking of some deeds that I could wish erased – stones that had left my hand. 'How then,' I objected, 'can we have a good city, a good state, unless there are men in it fit to govern – who have never, as it were, thrown that stone?'

'Education may be part of the answer,' interjected Theophrastos. 'Those dreadful thefts demonstrate that better education is needed. And yet – I don't know. Did not somebody try to educate Alexander once?' with a sidewise glance at Aristotle. 'Even taught him Ethics, so I hear. And look what he is capable of!'

'I did indeed try to educate the young prince,' Aristotle said gravely. 'And in some ways he responded better than one could have hoped. His love of poetry, for example! He is not – he was not – petty. He is undoubtedly brave, capable of self-denial and of undergoing great hardships. He is naturally generous and inspires loyalty, which he himself feels – or used to feel,' Aristotle added, sighing. 'Now he is too far from home! And there is one grave deficiency in my teaching: I taught the son of King Philip how to be a king of Makedon. Now that he is so far from home, trying to govern a strange people – a conquered empire – everything is unfamiliar. He is strange to himself now, I fear.'

'The rules for barbarian princes must be different in any case from standards fit for a citizen,' I observed.

'Do not forget, Stephanos, that democratic assemblies are also capable of mad acts and great cruelties,' Aristotle responded quickly. 'In some ways it is easier to bring a monarchy to reason, for you have only to work on one man, while in a democracy or oligarchy you have to work on many! What you say is true, however. Cities with free citizens require some science of moral behaviour, so that men more effectively guide their actions.'

'Simply tell people never to get angry or lustful?' I acquiesced dutifully.

'No, no. Without lust, no babies. And thus no citizens

or cities. Without anger, no justice. Someone wrongs you, you are angry. If that is with the right person it is a judgement. If someone has wronged another person, it is also fitting for you to be angry. The art is to be angry only at the right time and in the right way. Plato says one should not beat even a slave if one is carried away by wrath. If you are not angry in the right way, you may be angry with the wrong object. Some people enjoy their anger too much. I fear Alexander has reached this point.'

'Anger is frequently destructive,' said Theophrastos. 'Hasty and ungenerous anger can destroy friendships.' He looked narrowly at Aristotle as he spoke. 'Carried further, anger leads to very cruel things. Like Phaleris the tyrant who erected a great hollow image of a bull made of brass, big enough to put a man or two into its belly. He would put men alive into the brazen bull. And then had the fire kindled underneath it, so he could hear the sufferers as they broiled – roaring and bellowing out of the bull's mouth.'

'But really,' protested Aristotle, 'I am addressing normal people. I am not talking about some extra-ordinary being capable of great enormity, like Phaleris. I know of a man who killed his associate and then cut out his liver and cooked and ate it! It is useless to talk philosophically about such unnatural acts, they are so far from most human beings.'

It didn't seem a good thing for these two to be discussing anger, so I attempted a diversion.

'What most people want,' I said, 'is just a little happiness.'

'Yes, Stephanos. Yes. But what is that? Look at what people *think* they want: more money, more pleasure, more wine, more dancing girls – or more power. But all of these are only means to an end, which is imagined as "happiness".'

'But we cannot stop pursuing happiness?'

'No – but we need to think about pursuing it in the right way. Most men – and among them almost all of the vulgar, including women, slaves and children – think that the Good is Pleasure. What they pursue is a life of gratification. The Pleasure Life. Others, higher-minded, pursue activity, honour and some power – they are given to the Political Life. And a third class, higher yet, is given to the Contemplative Life, the life of thought and observation.'

'You won't persuade many human beings to become truly engaged in a Contemplative Life,' declared Theophrastos, as we marched along in the roadway between the fields. 'Most people, even well-born men in high position, are really like Sardanapallos, the Syrian king, who said, "Eat, drink and fuck – all else is not worth a snap of your fingers." A slightly more elegant form of this sentiment was put on his tombstone. The sentiment itself is appreciated by those who have never heard of the Syrian king or even of Syria.'

'Quite so,' Aristotle agreed. 'It is a pity that so many of mankind, rich and poor, prefer a life fit for beasts.' He was looking at some harmless donkeys in a field as he spoke.

'Some beasts have a hard time of it,' I mused. 'Anyway, Aristotle, why does your pursuit of happiness take you to Eleusis today?'

Aristotle looked a little self-conscious. It was Theophrastos who responded.

'Aristotle is going to Eleusis to get a Eumolpid.' He said this as calmly as if he had said, 'Aristotle is going to market to buy a mop.'

'A Eumolpid?' The Eumolpidai belonged to the sacred family of Eleusis and were all connected with the Mysteries, so of course Eleusis was full of them, but I was surprised that Aristotle should think he needed one.

'Yes,' said Aristotle, a little defiantly. 'It seems odd, perhaps, but I am doing a good turn to somebody else. Herpyllis — you know Herpyllis — ardently wishes to be an initiate in the Mysteries. There seems no good reason not to gratify her. She will need a guide, like every other person who undertakes initiation. Now, Eurymedon, a priest of Demeter highly regarded in Athens as an Eleusinian exegete, an expounder of the religious law, has been hostile to me. You remember — last summer!'

He paused and we both nodded. Indeed, it was hard not to remember that appalling scene, when Eurymedon had denied Aristotle the right to bury the body of his wife Pythias in the Kerameikos, and assisted in ordering the immediate destruction of her monument, claiming it was an impious representation of Pythias as Demeter. It seemed strange, after that episode, that Aristotle would have anything to do with the religion of Eleusis. Theophrastos gave voice to the objection.

'I say again, Aristotle, though you won't listen — it is madness to have any dealings with this religion. Leave Eleusis alone! The Mysteries as you know have been the pretext for most charges of impiety in Athens. Besides, it is not the walk of a philosopher to join the ranks of the too-religious. You start with Eleusis, and soon you're the kind of man who cannot see a weasel cross his path without taking it for an omen, and consulting a soothsayer.'

'Thus speaks the man who will eat no meat, the follower of Pythagoras and Orpheus,' teased Aristotle. 'The man who feels he is committing a misdeed in walking on a public road! Come, now. It is not as if *I* were becoming an initiate! I am unwilling to deny Herpyllis a joy on which she has set her heart. It seemed best not to work with the representatives of Eleusis in Athens, but to seek out some humbler Eumolpid in Eleusis. Qualified, of course, but without strong Athenian connections.'

'So now you see, Stephanos,' explained Theophrastos, with slightly elaborate patience, 'why we are trotting off to Eleusis. Herpyllis is a slave, but there is no bar against slaves being initiated in the Mysteries. The woman is a Greek speaker, and she is of age. Indeed, she is long past fifteen – nearly thirty—'

'Twenty-three,' said Aristotle.

'And she has, one supposes, committed no murder. Those are the only qualifications. And of course she – or rather, Aristotle for her – has to pay for the sponsor, the priest and a pig or two. The whole affair should cost about twenty drakhmai – maybe less.'

'It seems a good idea,' I said. 'At least it is the kind of gift that nobody can steal.'

'Exactly,' said Theophrastos. 'Lysias the orator gave it to his whore girlfriend, as it was the one gift he could give that her madam couldn't take from her.'

'I shall arrange it,' said Aristotle, disregarding this sally, 'so that Herpyllis can go through the preliminary initiation in spring at the time of the Anthesterion, and be perfectly ready for the Great Mysteries in Boedromion, just at the beginning of the next autumn.'

It seemed to me an important gift, offered to a woman becoming very important in Aristotle's life.

VIII

Images of Demeter

On entering Eleusis, my companions from the Lykeion and I paused, as everyone must, to admire what we could see of the great structure of the Sanctuary of Demeter and Persephone, its strong walls and handsome round towers gleaming gently in the sunlight of late autumn.

'A fortress,' said Aristotle. 'Fortified for grain and mysteries. Strange,' he added, 'that entrance into those buildings and participation in a secret ritual is believed to confer immortality. Immortality! Unknown stuff, of which not even the offspring of the gods may be sure.'

'Be careful!' said Theophrastos. 'Alleged defamation of the Mysteries of Eleusis as well as revelation of the sacred rites constitutes impiety, and the penalty is death.'

'Better men than ourselves,' I said, 'have thought well of the power of the Mysteries. Sophokles says in his *Triptolemos*:

'Thrice-blessed among all mortals doomed to death
Who look with living eyes upon these rites,
Before seeing Hades; only these have life—'

I broke off my own recitation. 'Oh, what a strange little shop! I don't recollect ever having noticed it before. Let us look.'

I had rudely cut myself off, and distracted us with this folly, because I thought I had seen a familiar shape coming towards the Eleusinian Agora. A tall young man with a very round head, slightly too large for his body. A person I did not care to meet. So I led our little party across the way to another street, displaying an exaggerated interest in the small shop. A cart stood outside, the donkey in the shafts waiting patiently while men loaded the little vehicle.

'In *this* life, at any rate,' commented Aristotle, 'the Mysteries do handsomely by the people of Eleusis. How much profit there is to be made!'

He glanced at the goods being placed in the cart – a quantity of plaques displaying the story of Demeter and the Maiden, and some statuary images. The shop was fully responsible for both. Samples of the painted earthenware plaques were fixed to the exterior wall by the door. Inside we could already see some doll-like images of Demeter; some representing the Goddess of the Grain by herself, others exhibiting her with Persephone. The Goddess-Mother as always was painted so as to suggest a mature beauty, her hair tied in a knot, golden as corn, her dress warmly painted and a kindly countenance, while her daughter was slender and had rippling reddish-gold hair, and an enigmatic expression. Belatedly I realised this shop was not the best choice. As we had just been alluding to the death of Pythias, a devotee of Demeter, and the fracas over her tombstone, it was hardly tactful to bring Aristotle to look at such images.

'Come and buy,' suggested a man from the shadows within, naturally encouraging our custom. 'Oulias of Eleusis,' the man added, emerging from his shop. He wore a well-worn and earth-spattered leather apron, protection against the clay and dust of his trade. 'At your service. You may know my wares anywhere.'

'Do you get your clay from Eleusis? I should have thought it was largely sand here,' Aristotle said prosaically. He picked up a plaque from the cart and studied it, not apparently perturbed by all these reminders of Demeter. The plaque was an oblong, with a slightly raised figure of the goddess upon it, her name spelled out beside her so there should be no mistake. He picked up another, which showed the goddess and some ears of barley, with a scrawny youth whose legs seemed somewhat mismatched.

'Who's that?' I wondered aloud. 'Oh, Triptolemos, of course. He who later became a lawgiver and a judge in Hades. The goddess gave the secret of grain-growing to him and he went off in a chariot drawn by dragons to tell the people of the earth. I heard about him when I was a child. But later,' I recollected, 'I wondered, how could it be Triptolemos the son of Akhilleus who introduced cultivation of wheat to the people? For we know that the men fighting the Trojan War ate bread already. Odysseus refers to "men who eat bread" several times.'

'Probably different stories fastened together,' suggested Aristotle. 'But you see the joke — by their own account, the Athenians are the discoverers of both wheat and laws. The wheat, at least, they use.'

'I liked the story of Triptolemos when I was at school,' I added. 'I always wanted to see a chariot drawn by dragons.'

'And now I don't suppose you ever will,' Theophrastos said drily.

'These pieces on the cart — not all of it our very best work, sir,' said Oulias, addressing Aristotle deferentially. 'I can see you have a taste in works of art. Come inside!'

And we went into his little shop, or the front part of it, an attractive place if barely big enough for the three of us in front of his display table on which figures were arranged. Many plaques were fastened to the walls. Beyond this room was another, full of rolls of clay and flat pieces set out like a pastry not cut. That workplace was reddened with the clay, and white with the paint used on the images.

'You must have a yard where you work the clay itself,' suggested Theophrastos.

'Yes, indeed. We're very careful of the quality of the earth that we use – no salt! It has to be cleansed and refined. We mix it with pure water. For of course you want the very best quality for these images! They give comfort to your family at home, after you come back from Eleusis,' Oulias expounded. 'Sometimes we send our best wares off in the cart, more often just our basic work, as you might say. There's a good deal of demand for simple plaques as votive offerings – in Etruria in the West, and now in the liberated cities of the East, and Byzantion. People put them in graves, or hang them up at their private shrine, or just on a wall in a favourite room or the courtyard.'

'The kind of thing some men like to do,' agreed Theophrastos drily. 'You see, Aristotle, some of the pieces are uneven, and not well painted.'

'I am surprised you still have so many images,' observed Aristotle to Oulias, 'after the Mysteries, when I should think you had a great run on your stock.'

'That's true enough, sir. As I said just now, some of these remaining are, frankly, *not* our best work. The greater part of our goods were sold during the Mysteries. We have the winter before us to build up our stock again. But nowadays there's a constant call to send pieces abroad.'

'This one is better,' said Aristotle with approval, looking at a tall statue of Demeter holding an ear of corn. 'Finely done – her hair and the folds in the gown very good. More like Boiotian ware than Athenian.'

'Right!' said the master of the establishment. 'I *knew* you were a man of taste, sir. Obviously you have travelled. I come from Boiotia, and the best work is done there. I have just hired a young man from Tanagra, in Boiotia, to help. Real artistic.' And he nodded to a slender young man in a light leather apron, who had just come from the courtyard behind into the inner room and hovered, undecided whether to stay or go now that strangers were here.

'This,' the merchant of images announced, 'is Lampos. My best assistant. Good at the modelling – makes the best figures. He has the hands for it.'

We all looked at the young man's hands, while he blushed. His arms were muscular – one wouldn't think that just swinging clay about could create muscle – and his hands were wide and strong, long fingers with red clay under the nails.

'We're a bit behindhand,' said Oulias. 'We should have sent the cart full of goods out to Peiraieus ten days ago, but the festival of Athena Ergane cut into our time.'

I understood. The celebration of Athena Ergane, Athena of Work, comes at the end of Pyanepsion, and provides a festival holiday for all who work with their hands, mechanical people like blacksmiths and potters.

'Pleasant as it may be to look at your wares,' said Theophrastos with stiff courtesy, 'we should not take up your time.' He turned to Aristotle. 'We should go in pursuit of your Eumolpid. Thymades, I think you said his name is.'

'Oh,' said Oulias, letting a little of his disappointment at our non-purchase escape. 'Do come back some other time. If you'd fancy a figure of Demeter, sir, I can let you have it at a good price . . .' looking at Aristotle, who hastily set the figure down.

'Demeter pursues me,' the philosopher said. 'Not I her.'

'Good reduction in price, in honour of the first time you came into my shop. Why not?' Recognising the failure of this wheedling, Oulias continued, 'As for Thymades of the tribe of Eumolpos, you will find his dwelling on the next street. On the right. He runs a *synoikos* – but I think all his chambers are let. You'll know the place – there's a statue of Apollo in the front.'

Thus advised, we set off. I was surprised to find that there was someone accompanying us, a thin little man with a wispy beard and large grey eyes. I recognised this weedy fellow – my would-be guide on the evening of the *engye*, when I was last in Eleusis.

'You were asking for Thymades?' this man asked in a thin voice. 'I can direct you, sirs – trust me!'

'We need no assistance,' said Theophrastos.

'No trouble, no trouble! Just a little way – the turning to the street is on your left, and then the house is on the right. Oulias wasn't making it clear. Do you have business in Byzantion?'

'No,' I said. I wondered if this little fellow were quite in his right mind.

'I would like to go to Byzantion. Business. Meanwhile I stay in Eleusis. You can count on me. Sophilos of Eleusis. I know Eleusis, I see where everything is.'

This peculiar personage led us along at a good enough pace, though one foot shuffled as he walked. Sophilos of Eleusis did not seem old; his wispy beard showed no grey – he might be forty. Hard to tell, I reflected, whether the fellow was a natural idiot, or one slightly afflicted in his wits by bad health or accident; he conducted himself as one little better than a beggar, not like a citizen of Eleusis. Yet his clothes were clean enough, not verminous, and he had tattered sandals on his inturned feet. Perhaps this Sophilos had a family who let him out, hoping he could coax enough money out of strangers to buy food and drink in some tavern. He scuffled along importantly as if we had put him in charge. Yet he kept close to us, too, as if he felt safer in a group of large men – for we were all taller and broader than he.

'Very fine town, Eleusis.' Sophilos' voice was like the whispering of wind through sedge. 'Good marketplace, vegetables, and also slaves. Donkeys and pots, and marbles too. Everything. Good statues. Thymades has an Apollo. Melanthios makes fine statues. But don't go into the marble shop this morning. Bad temper. Here is the *synoikos* of Thymades!'

The abode pointed at by Sophilos was, as the image-seller had indicated, an apartment house. A squat and rather ill-tempered Apollo stood scowling in marble outside the door. There were patently only four sets of apartments and Thymades, owner of all, lived in the front one on the ground floor. The man was sitting in the doorway of his little property, between his herm and his short Apollo, gazing down the street, probably in the hope of some excitement. He brightened when he saw us advancing towards him.

'Thymades. Here he is,' piped the little Sophilos.

'Good day, Thymades of Eleusis,' began Theophrastos.

'Surely that is my name, gentlemen. I am flattered that you look for me. What can I do to serve you?' The owner of the *synoikos* stood up politely to address us.

'Here,' I said in an urgent undertone to the little wispy fellow, 'buy yourself a drink of wine somewhere. Good health,' and I handed him, generously, an obol. It was one of the coins of King Philip, strangely battered and all gone about the nose; still, I grudged it slightly out of my little store. It served its purpose. Sophilos smiled with satisfaction, and shuffled off.

'I understand, Thymades of Eleusis,' said Aristotle, addressing the apartment owner formally, 'that you are of the tribe of Eumolpos, and act as a guide to individuals undertaking initiation into the Mysteries. And that your wife can act as guide to women who wish initiation.'

'Perfectly true, sir. Do come inside. Ill-done to conduct sacred business in the roadway.'

We followed the man into his dwelling, and into his *andron*. This was small and inevitably stuffy. But there were three chairs, and an abundance of stools. The walls were unusually adorned with a number of plaques displaying Demeter and Persephone. Obviously from Oulias' shop, I thought, though in slightly better style than the ones in the cart.

'Do seat yourselves,' Thymades said hospitably. He showed Aristotle to a chair but remained standing. 'I take it some or all of you have decided to be initiated into the Mysteries. I congratulate you! You have taken an important step. You know the Mysteries have been held here since Demeter first taught us, instructing Eumolpos, the first Hierophant. Only once did Athens and Eleusis declare they were not to be celebrated – when the terrible news came of Alexander's destruction of Thebes. And only once were they prevented by force of circumstances, in the year of the invasion of Xerxes, when Athens was evacuated, and the great sea-battle of Salamis was in preparation. At that time, on the day of the Mysteries, though no men and women of flesh and blood were able to participate, people heard the trampling, the singing and chanting of a great heavenly procession. A divine host celebrated within the Sacred Precinct! Lights were seen emanating from the

Telesterion, giving cheer to the hearts of the Greeks who stood against the mighty invaders.'

'Something of this sort is in the history books,' admitted Theophrastos.

'The miracle certainly came to pass. Demeter stood by us and the Persians were defeated. But our generous goddess is a goddess not of war but of peace. She gives food to all mankind. As a Eumolpid and citizen of Eleusis, whose family has been dwelling here from time immemorial, I am certainly qualified to act as guide and sponsor in your progress to enlightenment. But I can act for only one. One mystagogue to each initiate. I can find other—'

'It isn't for any of us,' Aristotle said hastily. 'I am making enquiries for a personal servant, a slave, formerly my mother's, now mine. She wishes exceedingly to become an initiate in the Mysteries, so I am offering this to her as a gift.'

'Excellent gift!' pronounced Thymades. 'None better. Cups break, jewellery is lost or stolen, clothes wear out – but this will remain ever bright. Yes, even when her body decays, she will survive. Thanks to the Goddess, the ultimate great giver, for the gift of the Mysteries.'

'Quite so,' said Theophrastos drily.

'Even though you say it is not for yourselves, gentlemen, you should hear what the step entails. Now, sir, you are taking responsibility for this slavewoman' – looking directly at Aristotle. 'Your name? Aristotle son of Nikomakhos? Master of the Lykeion? Very good. Later I shall come myself to Athens with my wife, who like myself is of the tribe of Eumolpos, an initiate and teacher; she can instruct your woman in what she needs to know. Meanwhile, please to pass on to the woman the essential information that I shall give you.' Thymades at last sat down.

'That I can do,' said Aristotle.

'I hope you have a good memory. Well,' said Thymades, leaning back in his chair, 'let me explain. The Mysteries invite all who fulfil the simplest basic requirements and are willing to follow the rituals. This woman – what is her name?'

'Herpyllis. From Euboia.'

'Herpyllis of Euboia. That she is a slave is no matter – the Goddess is generous and welcomes all, Athenian and foreign, slave and free. The woman speaks Greek?'

'She has never to my knowledge spoken anything else.'

'She is above fifteen years of age – and has done no murder?'

'She is not inclined to slaughter and will be twenty-four years of age.'

'Splendid. Well, the first stage entails a ceremony at the time of the Anthesterion, next spring. You – or the woman, rather – will be taught some simple prayers and undergo an initial purification at the Fields of Agrai by the sacred waters of Ilissos in Athens. You see why the candidate needs to be a Greek speaker? Otherwise she could not follow the prayers nor understand the story of great Demeter. Which I shall proceed to tell you, in a short form.'

'No need. We know it already,' interjected Theophrastos.

'Not as I tell it. And this narrative must be repeated to the woman. A pity she isn't here to look at the pictures.' The little apartment-house owner arose and went to his wall, standing beside the plaques, whence he addressed us:

'See and hear now, the Story of Demeter. Demeter the mother goddess, deity of the fields and grain that feed mankind, was happy in the possession of a beautiful daughter, Persephone.'

Here Thymades pointed to the plaque where the two women together were clearly represented.

'Together the women gods made the grass and flowers and grain grow, and introduced wheat and barley that give life to man. But Ploutos, God of the Underworld, loved Persephone, the Daughter, and Zeus gave him permission to take her. Ploutos spied on her and pursued her, and deliberately came upon her when she was not with her mother.'

Here Thymades drew our attention to another image, showing the god approaching Persephone when alone.

'She was with her playmates gathering spring flowers. He was prepared, in his swift chariot with his rapid night-black horses. He snatched the girl, disregarding her wails. In a rapture of darkness he forced her into his chariot and the chariot plunged – downward, downward! – into the depths of the earth. And Persephone found herself in the dark Underworld, in Hades, the place of all things dead. Oh dreadful union! Uncouth marriage! Wed perforce was the Maiden, wed to the god of darkness and death.'

After this lamentation, delivered in a wail as if he were personally grieved by what he related, Thymades moved to the next plaque, and resumed his narrative in a more tranquil tone.

'When she could not find her daughter anywhere, Demeter went lamenting through the world. Here you see the portrait of Demeter grieving. She sought her child perpetually and could not find her anywhere on earth – as the girl was not on the earth but *under* it. Some did not recognise the goddess in her searching – she appeared as an old hag to one who in pity offered her wine. When the Mother refused, she was given a gruel of grains and seeds. Here we see this in the picture. This simple drink of seeds – the *kykeion* – has an important part in the Mysteries. Don't forget to mention it.

'As she continued her fruitless search, the Sorrowing One, the Laughterless, grew so melancholy that she refused to make the shoots and the grain grow. Mankind was starving, the animals too. The gods had no food from the sacrifices! Something had to be done. Zeus told the grieving Mother where her daughter was, though even Zeus could not set the girl entirely free, for Persephone had eaten a pomegranate seed while in the Underworld, and that made Hades her home. A compromise was reached, whereby Persephone visits the world and her mother for six months of the year, and the kindly goddess gives the growing grain, on which mankind relies for sustenance.'

'We all know this story,' said Aristotle gently. 'With different variations and additions, but the same story.'

'Exactly so. The initiated know much more about the end of the story than I can tell now. But you will note that in the Mysteries we do more than hear a story, or say the Goddess is good, or pity her unhappiness. In the Mysteries we accompany Demeter and moreover become one with her. We march in the great procession from Athens to Eleusis.'

'*Everybody* knows that,' I said.

'There are several important stops along the road. At the boundary of Eleusis, the wrists and ankles of the would-be initiates are bound with yellow thread, representing submission to King Krokos, whose realm this once was. But the crocuses are also flowers of Persephone, among those she was gathering when snatched away. Each *mystes* is to be known by the yellow sign.'

'I shall remember,' said Aristotle gently.

'At the bridge we shall be confronted by Iambe, the only creature who could make cheerless Demeter laugh.

There will be a joke-telling. Do not despise the bridge-jests, but seek to hear and comprehend their whole meaning.'

'Rather like a riddle,' said Theophrastos. 'Aristotle likes enigmas. I don't know about the capacity of a slave-girl to see deeper meanings.'

'In the Mysteries,' said Thymades, 'we all — all of us who seek — have the divine privilege of *sharing* the life of the Goddess — the goddess most loving and generous. The *mystes* himself or herself becomes a child of Demeter. One of the Demetrioi.' I shuddered slightly; that word is used of the dead, planted in earth like seeds or vegetables.

'Yes, young man. We die and are alive again. Going in solemn procession, we come at last to the place of happy arrival and of ordeal. The hopeful initiates should stay awake all night before the final stage. After some further ritual within the Sacred Precinct, the initiates on the last night enter the Telesterion, the hall of final rites. What transpires there we are forbidden for ever to say.'

'So I understand,' said Aristotle.

Thymades resumed his seat. 'So then,' he continued, in a more prosaic tone, 'at the time of the Anthesterion festival, as winter turns into spring, we begin. If the woman undergoes the purification ritual — you should set her name down for it at once — she will be registered for the later ceremony. She must supply a piglet for sacrifice; this will first be washed in the river. It is imperative that she fast for nine days before the Lesser Mysteries at Agrai — I will also give you a list of prohibited foods. *Mystai* abstain from the marital embrace for the same period, and for three days after. The same applies to the period of the initiation itself.'

'If it must be so,' said Aristotle with resignation.

'In the midst of the month of Boedromion, after the harvests, the solemn process of the Great Initiation begins. The Truce of Demeter will have begun fifty-five days before. The first day, the fifteenth of Boedromion, is the Gathering Day. All the would-be initiates for this year will assemble in the Stoa Poikile in the Agora. There they will be greeted by the Hierophant and the Torchbearer. The Herald will proclaim that the candidates are to declare themselves, and pronounce a malediction against anyone who attempts the rite and is not worthy.'

'I suppose,' said Theophrastos, 'that if a killer did try to become an initiate, this would constitute a sacrilege.'

'Most terrible! But we hope for better candidates than persons merely free of bloodshed. The Herald says clearly that the initiate must have a soul conscious of no evil, and should have lived well and dealt justly. After this solemn address, the people register and pay the fees. My wife, as the woman's mystagogue, can do that for you, if you give her the money in advance, including also what is due to herself. I shall come with my wife on both occasions to protect her, but she will serve as the guide to Herpyllis. At the Lesser Mysteries at Agrai she will introduce her to the Priestess, who is in charge of registering the women. In preparation, my wife will come once during the winter and at least once in the summer to instruct Herpyllis in prayers and hymns.

'On the second day of the Greater Mysteries, the day of purification, the priest will shout "To the sea, O mystai!" Each mystes will go to the seashore at Phaleron – there will be carriages and carts for women and the infirm, though this costs a little. At the seashore, the candidates will wade into the water, washing off their old life. Another sacrificial pig is also offered, on this occasion washed in the sea water, cleansed and offered to the goddess. Then the whole group returns to Athens, where each mystes must sacrifice the pig to Demeter.'

'Very good pork is available in Athens at that time,' I interjected.

'Your candidate must again supply her own pig.'

'It doesn't have to be a large animal,' I commented.

'A little piglet will do. If you wish I can procure one. On the third day, Athens itself sacrifices to Demeter, and the fourth day the initiates spend in retirement and prayer. On the fifth day – the twentieth day of the month of Boedromion – the Great Procession begins, led by the Hierophant. Then comes the great Torchbearer, our Daidoukhos, and the Heralds, the Priestess and her attendants, and all the sacred servants of Demeter. The crowd leaves the Dipylon Gate and wends its way slowly towards Eleusis.'

'Everyone has seen the Great Procession leaving the centre of Athens,' I commented, hoping to make the man hurry up. 'Every year. You need not describe it. In boyhood I used to join it for several stadia.'

'It is very different when you are truly a part of it. It has to be *walked*. Lykourgos has rightly forbidden the wealthy women from coming in carts or chariots of any kind. All must go alike. Make sure, O Aristotle of the Lykeion, that the woman has clean clothes to walk in, the simplest and most inexpensive garments dyed black, as mourners' attire. It is customary to offer these garments to Demeter after initiation, so Herpyllis will need to bring some clean clothes with her for the return journey. My wife of course will join her in the procession. They will need provisions, which I can supply if you wish.'

'Very thoughtful.'

'There are some events along the way, and people to tip. When we arrive, there is the great All Night Festival, the Pannykhis, lit by torches. The woman Herpyllis should have the little compartmented dishes for ritual offerings of seeds and so on. The next day, the twenty-first of the month, is the Great Initiation itself. Your Herpyllis with other *mystai* will be invited into the Sacred Precincts. All others who are neither candidates for initiation nor already initiated will be banned from coming near. There will follow the things said, things done and things revealed.'

'And there, I think,' said Theophrastos, 'you all enact the story of Demeter, with a search for Persephone, and Pluto's cave and everything.'

Thymades flashed him a rebuking glance.

'Many know of the drama, few know what it means. The Mysteries are *secret*, their inner nature known only to those who participate. Participation entails the enlightenment of the soul. It is a different person who comes forth from the Telesterion, from the womb of the Anaktoron, a different person who returns to Athens – or wherever – and engages in daily labour. Life goes on as before, but the mind is changed. No one who has undergone the initiation can tell another who has not what it is like.'

'You must tell them *something*,' said Theophrastos, laughing.

'I accompany an individual *mystes* and explain each step insofar as I am able. My wife does the like. The essence of the great ritual is not describable – as well as not to be described.' Thymades looked straight at us, some severity threatening the serenity of his brow. 'I see you men think not much on the Mysteries, and perhaps suppose they are for simple persons – like myself, for instance.' He was shrewd enough to make us blush. 'But the very greatest have humbly gone in the procession, and made their prayers, and shared in the vision of the Telesterion. Sokrates did so, on whom some of you wise men set so much store. Your Plato, too, who is always using the language of it.'

'Quite so,' said Aristotle soothingly. 'It is good of you to tell us all this, and I will relate it faithfully to the woman. She will be prepared, both in Anthesterion and in Boedromion. She will have clean fresh clothes, mourning garments for the Great Procession, and good footwear, as well as a pig each time for the sacrifice. And I certainly wish to secure your wife's services.'

Thymades smiled. 'Yes, for you will find no better woman. But I have a strange feeling that I am meant to be – must be – the *mystagogos* of one of you.'

'No, no. You have spoken very well, however; I am sure your wife will be conscientiously instructive. The charge, as the work entails all those walks to and from Athens, cannot be small.'

'Let us consider the expense,' said Thymades. 'The fee to the priests of Demeter is fifteen drakhmai. Then there are the added costs: carriage or cart to Phaleron, piglet, provisions for the walk to Eleusis, tips, offerings of pottery and of ground meal. And some consideration for the mystagogue's own time and endeavour. So I ask thirty drakhmai,' said Thymades. 'This should cover everything. Being a Eumolpid, my wife, like myself, can sing most agreeably; she will teach the woman Herpyllis the hymns. If Herpyllis is exhausted by her experiences, as many are, we have my house here in Eleusis handy for her to rest in before she walks back to Athens – unless you propose sending a cart or something for her. There's no prohibition on conveyances for the return. If you wish me to engage a conveyance, that can be added into the bill.'

'No need for that,' said Theophrastos. 'A slavewoman can certainly walk. By Herakles, this is more expensive than I had imagined!'

'Do not fret, good Theophrastos, as it is I who will pay the bill,' said Aristotle. 'I will clap up a bargain with you,

Thymades. Send your wife to see Herpyllis and instruct her, and on the proper day in Anthesterion your wife shall expect to meet her in Agrai.'

He was ready to depart. I was not unwilling to go, though I took advantage of our farewells to invite the man to come to my father-in-law's wedding party, as Thymades appeared to be a respectable Eleusinian. Theophrastos, however, seemed pleased to be out of the Eumolpid's presence.

'It is not like you, Aristotle, to encourage this sort of thing. I beg you once again, reconsider! Now you see the cost – spending all this money uselessly on a slavewoman!'

'Never mind,' said Aristotle coolly. 'This is my affair.'

'You may well say so,' retorted Theophrastos.

I was distressed to see Aristotle attacked, as it were, by one who was usually his admiring adjutant. In order to make some kind of peace, I said, 'Come with me to Smikrenes' house and we will have a bite to eat!'

It was rash, I knew, to promise Smikrenes' hospitality when the man was so little inclined to entertain, or even to offer a wayfarer a drink of water. But the long walk and Thymades' lecture had led to hunger. It would be ungracious to part abruptly from Aristotle and Theophrastos, leaving them strangely almost quarrelling. So I offered this invitation, and they both accepted. We had turned our steps in Smikrenes' direction when we were unluckily accosted.

IX

The Speaking Corpse

'Good day! This is a pleasant surprise.'

A strongly built man with long arms and a very round head came up to us — not a pleasant surprise to me. Arkhias the spy, Antipater's man. The fellow I had been hoping to avoid when I dragged our party over to the little shop of images.

'I am glad to see you, O Aristotle of Stageira,' the newcomer announced. 'I have some matters to discuss with you.'

'Good day, O Arkhias,' said Aristotle, in a tone of imperfect delight.

'Stephanos! So you're there too. And what is your business in Eleusis?'

'Stephanos always has business in Eleusis. He is marrying the daughter of an Eleusinian farmer, and we are just on the way to this man's house for a luncheon,' announced Theophrastos. I wished he had not explained.

'Oh, really? I will be very glad to come too,' said Arkhias. 'We can talk perhaps on the way there.' And he took his place by Aristotle's side, dislodging Theophrastos. I was seriously annoyed that this man should thus invite himself. Of course, once he knew whither we were going, I should have had to invite him. But I should at least have been allowed the grace of offering, and the appearance of a choice.

There was never any way of subduing or chastising or training this man Arkhias. He came from a colony in the far West, one of a league that called themselves the Italiotes. An actor by trade, this young fellow had come to Athens, where he had enjoyed some little success. His acting at the Festival of Lenaia the past winter had brought him to the attention of Alexander's regent, Antipater, who had employed the fellow as a spy in Athens. I had perforce worked with Arkhias once, but never thought of him as a friend.

'Strange little place, Eleusis,' said Arkhias. 'Such a fuss over a maiden – and anyway, Demeter's daughter was really ravished in Sikilia, in the fields of Enna. My favourite character in the story is Ploutos. There's a role for you! An underrated god, the god of wealth. Think of all the riches that come from underground. Iron, copper, silver, gold. We compliment him when we speak of wealthy men. *Ploutokratia*, the rule of the wealthy. Persephone did not know when she was well off!'

Predictably, Smikrenes, no plutocrat, was not pleased to see four stout and healthy men descending on his household, for he saw at once we would all want feeding. The remnants of his Athenian hospitality were at war with his customary and natural meanness (he might have called it frugality). I tried to signal with my eyes that I would reimburse him later for any extra expense, but Smikrenes was not good at reading signals of that sort.

'Geta!' he yelled, and the old female slave came forth. I wondered if my bride-to-be was within doors, and listening. 'Geta, woman – bring the little table. Is there any flour left? I misdoubt me sadly we haven't much.'

'There's some barley flour,' said Geta briefly, appearing with the table, which she popped down in front of us. She came quickly back with some stools. We sat around the table outdoors, our backs to the dungheap.

'Hens don't lay eggs this windy weather we've been having,' complained Smikrenes. 'And the vegetable garden is mostly eaten up. But sit down, men of Athens, and make yourselves at home.' He sighed, but at least he wasn't cursing. 'There may be a little cheese somewhere, and some apples or something of the sort.'

'Please, do not put yourself to any trouble,' said Aristotle. 'It would be charming just to have a drink of water and to sit here enjoying your—'

'Ah, yes! Geta, water for these men – quick, now!'

We were supplied with drinking pots and fresh water, and sooner than one could have expected it food came popping through the door. It came so rapidly and well turned out that I suspected Philomela of having a hand in it. Surely the fresh barley cakes were hers.

'Is this man going to be your father-in-law?' Arkhias asked me loudly. 'Well, at least he has land, I see that.' He looked about him. 'The house could be quite agreeable if you would add on to it. Build a tower, why don't you? And a little portico and shade roof facing south.' Fortunately, the owner of the farmhouse, momentarily in the kitchen, could not hear this new design.

Smikrenes came back and sat with us, not shirking his position as host. Aristotle he knew already, but he gazed suspiciously at Theophrastos and Arkhias. The slender sunshine of a late autumn day shone upon us; it was fairly warm here out of the wind.

'This is pleasant,' said Aristotle. 'Fresh country air.' (He kindly passed over the dungheap.)

'You wouldn't think so much of fresh air if you'd been toiling since daybreak,' said Smikrenes. 'You townsfolk don't know you're born, seems to me.'

'You should get a slave or two to do all that labour,' said Arkhias, looking with distaste at Smikrenes' worn hands and dirty fingernails. Smikrenes glanced back with equal distaste at the well-shaped clean hands of Arkhias, with nails perfect enough for a statue.

'The simple life on the land has often been pronounced ideal,' said Theophrastos pacifically. 'An elusive thing, happiness.'

'It is,' I said. 'Though I sometimes think things would be solved if I had a great deal of money. I know this is not a philosophical notion,' I added, looking apologetically at Aristotle.

'I deny that anyone really wants *money*,' said Aristotle. 'Money is only a medium, or a sort of stored energy. What men really desire is something which money is a means of obtaining – pleasure, knowledge, honour—'

'Oh, everyone wants money,' said Arkhias, shrugging. He helped himself to a second cheese, heedless of Smikrenes' frown. 'But usually people want something else as well. I wanted fame very much at one time. Still do, but I've chosen a – well, let us just say that nowadays I see the advantages of power over fame. And power brings money with it.'

Certainly, I thought, Arkhias in his position as spy could hardly hope to achieve lasting *fame*. 'Spies are like women,' I observed in a low tone. 'Their greatest honour is that they are not spoken of at all.'

'*I* have wanted fame,' said Aristotle. 'Though that is rather an ignoble desire. Putting power over one's life into the mouths of other men – whether intelligent or stupid.'

'Philosophers try to be above wants,' I said sagely.

'Yes,' said Smikrenes impatiently. 'When they've got a good roof over their head and two meals a day, and fine clothes and a lot of disciples, then they can say, "Oh, I am above desire!"'

Aristotle laughed. 'I have not got above all desire,' he admitted. 'No, no. It is certainly true that desire can carry us away headlong, making us ignorant and unhappy. But I admit, I do want a few things. Time. Now I am getting older, above all I want time. Yes – I must admit to being greedy for long life.'

'But not just for its own sake!' protested Theophrastos.

'No. It's because I want to finish my work. For example, there's our great compendium on the animals – their begetting and birth, their movement and all the different parts and how they all function, and what the different kinds are. That could take several lifetimes, but with my excellent scholars to help me I have a rational hope of finishing the whole. And there are many other books I want to write, and questions to which I should like to know the answers. Oh yes, I want time. I really want immortality, but know I cannot have it.'

'Well, you have a lot of time remaining, most likely,' I said comfortingly. 'Many men go well past sixty. Look at Hypereides. He's over sixty and yet he's still a great orator, an important public figure—'

'And he keeps a lot of women,' added Smikrenes with a dry cackle. 'One of his women lives hereabouts. Phila her name is. Not to mention that he had Phryne, the most beautiful woman in the world, so they say.'

'Of course,' I remarked, 'there are some things a man cannot do after sixty. Athens does not allow certain public offices to be held by someone of those years. You cannot be sent on an embassy, for instance.'

'But to a man of ability years are nothing,' observed Theophrastos. 'Plato, now, did some of his best work at sixty – and beyond.'

'He lived to a great age, I think,' I added, seeing this as a hopeful prospect for Aristotle to dwell on. 'Plato was eighty or something.'

'Eighty-one, at least,' said Aristotle. 'And he died at the wedding feast of a former student.'

'A poor gift for the bridegroom and bride,' said Arkhias. 'That would cast a blight on the festivities, some antique fellow croaking his last!'

'Well then,' said Aristotle, 'let us say I should like to die just *after* a wedding feast – so as not to discourage the young couple. Coming back from a wedding feast, after wine and a song and a last friendly meeting. At the age of ninety.'

'Not impossible,' said Theophrastos. 'You are as active in body as a much younger man, and temperate in your habits. You always have good health and walk a great deal. It is rational to predict long life.'

'Ah, but none of you townsfolk gets the sort of exercise I do,' exclaimed Smikrenes. 'Sort of puny you all are, and pale, like the women who sit indoors weaving all the time.'

'Death comes in all sorts of shapes,' said Arkhias. 'I think it would be terrible to be old – *really* old. Though Antipater is what I consider to be old, yet he acts like a man in his prime, I must say. And he has his son Kassander to help him. They're on very good terms now.'

'So, are we to take it you've now met Kassander?' enquired Aristotle.

'Yes. Kassander is strong and efficient – he can help Antipater get done anything he needs to be done. Though this is too important a matter to bandy about before all and sundry,' with a glance at Smikrenes, which our host saw and resented. The old farmer murmured something like 'To Hades with all those Makedonians,' but so softly we were not obliged to take notice.

'Sophokles,' Theophrastos observed abruptly, 'was very long-lived – into his eighties. And Aiskhylos, Athens' first great dramatist, lived to a great age. Yet some say he did not die in his bed. You remember the story, that he died when an eagle carrying a turtle in its beak let the turtle fall. The turtle landed on the bald pate of Aiskhylos and cracked it.'

Arkhias laughed uproariously. 'There are many ways to death,' he said, 'but that is the strangest. A turtle – by Herakles! His heir could cook up turtle soup to celebrate a gala day, and make a lyre out of the shell.'

'This encouraging conversation,' said Aristotle with a smile, 'is intended to reassure me that I may live for twenty or even – almost miraculously – thirty more years. Enough time to bring all my books to fruition. I admit to that hope myself. And for my friends, including our host,' he said, rising and turning gracefully to Smikrenes, 'I wish the same: good fortune and long life. With many thanks for your kind hospitality today.'

'I can pay for it,' said Arkhias loudly. Smikrenes' face turned a beet red.

'No, no!' I almost shouted. Arkhias was fumbling about his person, his confident look changing to one of anxiety.

'My money! My purse!' he exclaimed. 'A black leather bag. Have you seen it?'

We all started looking in the usual way, but the purse patently had not dropped behind his chair on the grass, nor on the path beside the dungheap, nor on the road.

'Theft!' exclaimed Arkhias. 'Someone has stolen my money!'

This was truly horrible. For a flashing terrible instant I had a mental vision of Arkhias, naked and wrathful, going through Smikrenes' house as I had gone through the house of Halirrhothios, poking about the quarters belonging to my Philomela . . .

'Nobody here stole nothing,' said Smikrenes flatly. Fortunately Arkhias believed him.

'Did you see me with it when I met you?' We all shook our heads. 'I must have dropped it or left it in the town – I was in a marble-seller's shop, but only for an instant. I didn't take it out there, however – or I don't think I did. Or I could have dropped it in the street . . .'

'Some pickpocket took it off you,' said Smikrenes. 'Not like Eleusis to have such vermin.'

'No!' said Arkhias indignantly. 'I am sharper than other men, I have eyes in the back of my head, no common pickpocket could take advantage of me!'

'There is nothing for it,' said Aristotle, 'but to retrace our steps to the town.'

We set off in the direction of Eleusis. The day had grown cloudy and the air was cooler, but it was all the better for walking, and we had a long trudge ahead of us, first to the town and then back to Athens. 'What were you doing in the marble-seller's shop?' I asked.

'Just looking about,' Arkhias said vaguely.

'Were you, I wonder, searching for something in particular? Something to do with – oh, let's see – a murder case in Athens?' Aristotle enquired. Arkhias grinned at him, a rueful rictus as one acknowledging a score made against him in some game. It was annoying to think that Aristotle could no longer be allowed to detect things on his own, but that Arkhias would set himself up as the hunter chosen by Antipater. The spy kept peering into ditches and bushes. We had to go slowly, looking about on all sides – uselessly, it seemed – for the lost article. And we would have to pause in the town of Eleusis and at least go though the motions of assisting Arkhias and his wretched money-bag.

It was not to take us long, however, to find the missing object, though the finding did not, in the event, save us time.

'Ho! There's someone lying down in the roadway – that's odd,' said Theophrastos.

'Someone ill,' said Aristotle, quickening his pace, as befitted a doctor, a descendant of Asklepios the Healer. 'Fainted or had a stroke, possibly.'

We could see as we drew near that it was a man, lying stretched almost across the narrow road, one arm flung out. Aristotle ran, and got there first, but I made a good spurt and came in ahead of the others. The man was lying face upwards. He was pale, and blood was coming from his mouth.

'By the gods, it's that little fellow we met today – Sophilos.'

And so it was. His wispy beard was soaked, from the blood that came from his mouth – or so I thought at first. He looked, to my eyes, completely dead. I reflected that it was not the first time I had come upon a corpse on or near a roadway.

'He's still alive,' said Aristotle, kneeling beside him. He was correct. The little fellow, imperfectly dead, was even conscious. His grey eyes opened wide and his pupils fluttered from side to side, looking at each of us. He turned his eyes back to Aristotle and gazed at him imploringly.

'What happened?' I demanded of him, but there was no reply.

'His heart beats still, but he has lost blood,' said Aristotle. 'Oh – see here!' He raised the wispy beard like a flap, and we saw a neat gash in the throat.

'Done for! He's a dead man,' said Arkhias.

'Part of his throat is cut, the part that operates the voice. He still appears to breathe, but can't speak. Yet,' Aristotle added, 'he may be able to tell us – just through moving his lips – what happened. Sophilos – who did this to you?'

He gazed earnestly at the little man's lips. They formed the words 'Help! Help me!' The bubbling blood interrupted the movement of the lips. Aristotle endeavoured to staunch the flow from the throat cut, but it was too deep.

'Tell us more!' implored Aristotle. The little man seemed to be weakening rapidly. 'Lift his head a little, a very little! Gently!' Aristotle ordered Arkhias, who obeyed awkwardly. 'Now! Sophilos, tell us what you can – I can understand you.'

The lips moved again, but more slowly, in the mask-like face. It was like seeing a corpse summoned to talk, in some piece of dark witchcraft. The work of a woman of Thessaly, a witch summoning life into a corpse at some deserted battlefield, evoking Hekate with uncouth charms at midnight. We were all men, however, living sane men, and it was certainly still daylight. I could see Sophilos' lips were turning blue: in words without a voice, like two thin reddish-blue worms, they moved:

'Money. It was – the money.'

'Yes, all right. The money. But *who?*' Aristotle enquired forcefully.

Sophilos was having trouble in answering. For it now was manifest that he could not breathe successfully; he was snorting and spurting little plumes of blood and would have coughed if he could. It was painful to watch him, and almost a relief – a dreadful dirty relief – when he shuddered and relaxed, his face pale as snow and his eyes fixed in his head.

'That's a perfectly dead one,' said Arkhias knowingly. He dropped Sophilos' head back on the dusty road.

'The man has certainly expired,' said Aristotle; he sat back on his heels and gazed critically at the body for a little space. 'I believe he died in the end of breathing his own blood, like a man drowning in water.'

'Where's the weapon?' demanded Arkhias. 'A deep gash. There must be a knife.'

'Yes,' I said. 'A knife, or perhaps a sword. Not a javelin or spear. Not an arrow.' I realised I was almost too familiar with weapons, and the wounds they made. Arkhias began to search along the side of the road, and Theophrastos and I followed his example.

'Unlikely a man would throw away a good knife, especially if he were a cut-throat by trade,' suggested Theophrastos, unanswerably. But we still continued to search for form's sake. I bustled up to a bush, more to be doing something than out of practical hope – but I was strangely rewarded. A small black leather bag was lying in the centre of the bush.

'Is that yours, Arkhias?' I did not touch the thing, but let Arkhias plunge through thorns and twigs after it.

'Yes. Yes, it is mine.' He looked at the little leather bag with a puzzled expression. 'It has some coins in it, even.' He took the small black purse to the roadside, and spilled the contents out in the pale dust. We kept our backs to the unfortunate Sophilos, now taking his ease on the roadway with no further part in the dialogue.

'Here!' said Arkhias. 'That's one tetradrakhma that was mine. There should be more. I had thirty drakhmai or so in this bag! Here are a couple of drax. And—'

'I recognise *this*,' I said, picking up a battered bronze obol with King Philip's head on it. A head with the nose rubbed away. 'This is the exact coin I myself gave Sophilos this very day.'

'Well, at least we have found the thief,' said Arkhias ruefully.

'This is serious,' said Aristotle. 'We shall have to report this death to the officials in Eleusis town.'

'Leave me out of it!' said Arkhias. 'I am anxious that my name never appear—'

'It's not possible to keep you out of it,' I answered crossly for Aristotle. 'Any one of us giving evidence would have to say you were with us. If it comes to a legal hearing, Smikrenes would testify that you were at his farm when you declared the money-bag lost.'

'Here's a fine mess!' groaned Arkhias. 'If only I had not met up with you!'

'If only,' agreed Theophrastos. 'Though it would seem that you must have lost your money-bag before our encounter.'

In no very gracious spirit we returned to Eleusis town, having left a slave from one of the little farms nearby to guard the corpse of Sophilos. In the town we found the chief official of the deme, the Demarkh of Eleusis. This man promptly came with us, bringing a donkey-cart to pick up the remains. After the body had been placed in the cart, we showed the Demarkh the exact spot we were in when we first noticed the man lying down in the road. I told him how we had come upon Sophilos earlier in the day.

'At that time,' I explained, 'I gave him an obol with a very worn King Philip's head, much damaged about the nose. That very same coin turned up in the money-bag when found.'

The Demarkh was pondering this strange turn of events as we started back to the town.

'So,' he remarked eventually, in calm reflective judgement, 'this little man would seem to have stolen the money-bag himself. Now have I got this right? The four of you were *not* together when Sophilos showed you the way?'

'Only three of us,' said Aristotle. 'This man,' nodding towards Arkhias, 'whom I know, came up to us a good deal later.'

'And did you know he had money on him?'

'Not until he said it was missing.'

'How much exactly did you have?' The Demarkh looked at Arkhias, who answered readily: 'About ten drakhmai.'

'Ah! Now I begin to see it,' said the Eleusinian official. 'About *five* drakhmai are left. Thus some five drax, mostly in silver coins, have gone missing. Obviously, our little friend here,' nodding at the corpse in the cart, 'helped himself to your money-bag.' He continued to address himself to the attentive Arkhias. 'He may have seen you in the marble shop. It takes only a moment to put a purse down thoughtlessly, and these thieves can be so crafty!'

'You really think Sophilos was a thief?' Theophrastos asked.

'He's a little fellow at a loose end, pattering about the town. A bit odd in the head. It is not difficult to believe that little Sophilos might have been culpable. Had he had time to make any purchases with the stolen coins? I will set up an inquiry, to find if Sophilos bought anything today.'

'But that,' protested Aristotle, 'does not give us any idea why and how the poor fellow was killed.'

'Another criminal in the case, most probably,' decided the magistrate. 'A murderer. A stranger? A confederate? Someone came upon Sophilos on the road. Here, now we are near the city wall. Let us not sully the city with this polluting carrion, but set ourselves up here, under this oak tree near the gate. I shall have the finding of the body proclaimed, and send someone to fetch shopkeepers. Especially Melanthios, sculptor and seller of marble, since you set your purse down in his shop.'

We stood awkwardly around the cart with its unpleasant little load. The oak tree's leaves had turned brown and were fluttering, one by one, to the ground.

'Even as the generations of leaves, such are the generations of men.' One merciful brown leaf fell on Sophilos' face, as if trying to cover the wound, the beard matted with rusty red, and that reproachful white countenance.

It did not take long for a little crowd to gather outside the town gate, gazing and exclaiming. The Demarkh made his harangue, explaining our finding of the body (we looked sheepish rather than heroic) and elaborating his own exertions in the case.

The marble-seller, powdered over with white dust like a baker, complained a little about having to leave his shop in the midst of a hard day's work. Yet after some initial grumbling, he was quite polite. He agreed that his name was Melanthios, and readily complied in answering the questions posed by the Demarkh.

'I really don't know what we are all coming to!' Melanthios exclaimed. 'I remember *this* man, right enough!' looking at Arkhias. 'It is as he says. He did come into my shop – I sell stone, and gravestones made on demand, and small statuary. But he came only to price something, and bought nothing. I don't remember his taking the purse out, as he had no need for it. Yet he might have done. Sophilos was perhaps nearby. I saw him going past the shop in that kind of quick shuffle he has – had, I should say.'

Other shopkeepers of the centre of Eleusis said they had not served anyone with a large purse of silver that day. Sophilos had not bought anything, and no one recollected seeing the little man with a purse of money.

'I'd have held him for questioning had I seen such a thing as a purse about him!' said Oulias, master of the shop of images of Demeter. 'Is it likely that a workless nuisance like little Sophilos should come honestly by such a fat money-bag?'

We again gathered closely under the unleafing tree to look at the corpse of Sophilos sleeping in the cart. 'Please,' said the Demarkh's slave, 'someone's come to claim the body.'

He pointed to two dusty persons slowly advancing towards us: a young man of fifteen or sixteen, supporting a haggish-looking elderly woman who was audibly crying. Their homespun clothing was of rough cloth and coarse weave, patched in places and not over-clean.

'The dead man's nephew,' explained the Demarkh, in a condescending but not unkindly tone. 'Not a bad young fellow. He's been employed stoning the crows from the grain fields and keeping sheep. Good with a catapult to keep wolves and foxes from doing harm. Useful youngster, but no family, you see.'

'Please, sir,' the boy bravely addressed the Demarkh. 'That is my uncle Sophilos. We need to take him home and bury him.'

'What is your name?'

'Strabax. Sophilos was my mother's brother. We should take his body home.'

'Not so fast, boy. We have more questions.' The magistrate looked important. 'Did your uncle have money? Or was he a beggar?'

'Money? Oh, no.'

'Oh dear!' sobbed the woman. 'He wasn't a beggar. He used to take what people gave him sometimes, we know that, but he didn't ask for anything. We supplied him with his house and food. He had no money. He didn't work, not much. He was simple in the head, and we couldn't make him do any chores. My husband is long dead, and this here, Strabax, is my last son. The rest is all dead, 'cept one who is gone to the wars.'

'Sophilos had not brought home some money for you recently?'

'No. Oh, a couple of obols, some days ago, that some-body gave him in a tavern, he said. But that's all.'

'Hmm.' The magistrate scratched his beard. 'That sum, however trifling, might have been ill come by.'

'Please,' said the boy. 'You've got to proclaim the murderer and search him out.'

'All in good time, my lad.' The Demarkh frowned. 'Some person or persons did kill Sophilos. But you must realise that there is no indication that Sophilos himself was innocent of crime. To the contrary. Let us consider the facts. Near his body is found a stolen purse. That he had adapted it to his own use is fully attested by the fact that he put into this bag the little coin – the particular obol – this man of Athens had given him. Sophilos was thus treating this purse with silver coins in it as his *own* purse.

'Now, I think I can reconstruct the events.' By this time the Demarkh had quite a crowd to address. This leader of men swelled his breast importantly. 'As I put what happened together from various hints and signs, matters went something like this:

'Sophilos sees the purse in the marble shop, and quickly snatches it and runs off. Then he follows these men, careful-like, to see if they have more to snatch, maybe, or just to make sure he's not suspected. When he sees they are safely eating at the farmhouse, he comes back on the road to Eleusis. On the way he encounters someone.'

'Exactly,' said Melanthios. 'Some ruffian, some brigand, who seizes his purse and kills him.'

The Demarkh frowned. 'We have no brigands in Eleusis,' he reminded the marble-seller sternly. 'Our roads are always safe; Eleusis is a well-ordered town. It is likely that Sophilos met another beggar, an itinerant who began to argue with him over dividing the spoils.

Sophilos refused. We don't know that the other person came armed – Sophilos himself may have carried a short sharp knife with him. Say he threatens the other man, the fellow wrests the knife from him and in the process kills him – perhaps accidentally. Helps himself to what he considers to be his rightful share of the contents of the purse – notice he didn't take *all* – and runs off. He is probably someone from elsewhere, as Eleusis does not spawn beggars.' A grim grin adorned this conceit.

'Nor was this assailant particularly bloodthirsty – he may not have intended to kill. Sophilos was still alive when these four men come upon him. He tries to speak, but – according to these witnesses – only mouths, "The money!" Which shows that *money* was Sophilos' object of desire. Uppermost in his mind even when dying, a most inordinate love of money. The man expires shortly thereafter, without enlightening them further about who struck him, or his own culpability.'

'But you are making my uncle a thief!' exclaimed the boy.

'Yes,' said the magistrate.

'That's *wrong*! Even if you say Sophilos begged a little – sometimes – he *never* stole. And he never would carry a knife.'

'Who's going to pay us compensation?' The old widow wrung her hands. 'His killer's family ought to pay us, shouldn't they, for my lost brother? Find his killer! We are so poor – we should get something from the killer. Or from Eleusis itself. *Compensation*.'

'You don't quite understand, Mother.' Her son put his arms around her. The boy Strabax had a bright, frank face, and I felt sorry for him.

'I will give you something later,' I said. 'I recognise your loss.'

'Precious little compensation would be proper in any

case,' pronounced the Demarkh. 'This man, everyone in Eleusis knows, was a hemi-idiot, a sort of simpleton. He did no work, he was a leech upon the economy of your household, as of the town. You will be better off without him. It is inappropriate to bewail him loudly. It seems Sophilos was a thief – at least, at the end of his life. His killer will be liable to execution if caught and tried – unless he can make it out as accidental. So the mischief-maker had better keep well away from this town from henceforth. He appears to have gone in any case, taking the accursed weapon with him.'

The Demarkh glanced again at the body, and at its throat. 'The killer's weapon was almost certainly a knife. This doesn't look like a sword wound. That's all there is to say about *that*. Take him away!'

'How? How?' stammered the boy.

His mother shrieked and tore her hair. 'How can we pursue vengeance?' she cried. 'And how are we to get him home?'

'Well,' said the magistrate, softening. 'As you are really indigent, and the two of you have behaved respectably, I will let you take the corpse in my cart. No need to have this thing near our Agora. It has already polluted the area here – we must have the priests perform a cleansing ritual. For myself and the gentlemen who found the body, also. I shall send my own servant with you, to convey the corpse and bring the donkey and cart back. He is to inspect your house, too, when he gets there, to see that you are hiding no money or valuables.'

With this depressing arrangement the poor folk had to be content. They went off, trudging down the road with the magistrate's servant sitting at the front of the donkey cart and driving it, while Sophilos in the back bumped and shook, all unwitting and unconcerned.

'I am sorry,' said the Demarkh to all of us, 'that I have

detained you so long. Sophilos is a person of slight importance, next thing to an idiot, to be sure. I fear, however, I cannot hold out any hope of finding the missing five drakhmai. At least I can restore your purse.' And he gave the pouch back to Arkhias.

'Here's your obol,' said Arkhias to me, with a slight grimace fishing out the well-worn coin. I gave it to the official to compensate the slave driving the cart with its unwelcome passenger. There followed a dreary interval while proper ritual cleansing was performed. At length the four of us turned to go back to Athens, as the late afternoon shadows threatened us with evening. Nobody said anything until we were well out of the Eleusis area.

'At least,' said Arkhias, 'there won't be any further processes in Eleusis, it seems. Unless the murderer is found. But that's not likely. A man with a knife. Too general a description. And it might be only man-slaughter, after all.'

'I wonder *you* are not more interested in catching him,' I remarked. 'For this murderer – whoever he may be – has also gone off with a *lot* of your money. You told the Demarkh you'd lost five drakhmai. But you told *us* there were some *thirty* drakhmai in that bag! As only five remained, you have lost a tidy sum. Twenty-five drakhmai – or one hundred and fifty obols! Enough to cover a good workman's wages for twelve days.'

'You must be richer than I thought, Arkhias,' said Theophrastos, 'if you can lose money at that rate.'

Arkhias flushed, to his visible annoyance; the actor prided himself on having learned to show no passions he did not intend to display.

'It's my own business,' he returned roughly. 'What makes you think I told you exactly what money I had? Maybe I was just exaggerating – to impress and amuse you. You are all *so* frugal and *so* serious!'

Conversation lapsed after that exchange. As soon as we were within the walls of Athens, Arkhias disappeared into the twilight streets.

'The death of Sophilos is mysterious enough,' said Aristotle. 'But Arkhias makes mysteries on his own account.'

'You think he is pursuing the robbery at Hieron's house?' enquired Theophrastos.

'If only that were all that Arkhias does! There are more mysteries than one. What reason does he have to go hobnobbing with Antipater and Kassander? Informative, that Kassander – a strong and stubborn man in his prime – has come to join his elderly father. The Regent may well be deeply alarmed by Alexander's killing of Philotas and Parmenion. He is already at odds with King Alexander's mother, Olympias. Now he may be planning with his own son how to keep himself safe, and ride out any bad times. The paths of Antipater and Alexander could diverge completely. An unnerving thought. And Arkhias, I suppose, will keep to Antipater's side.'

'You may be right,' said Theophrastos. 'But the reason why Arkhias *lied* – not to put too fine a point on it – about the missing money is clear. Given his preference for near-invisibility, he is anxious not to get known as a rich man. Surely his first unguarded statement was the right one? He *did* lose thirty drakhmai.'

'Questions might be asked of him,' observed Aristotle, 'as to the exact *source* of his silver coins.'

'There is one thing that doesn't quite fit,' I said. 'At least not to my mind. You know the marble-seller said that Sophilos was *near* the shop, for he saw him shuffling past. But the little fellow, when he spoke to me in Eleusis, said not to go into the marble-seller's shop because the owner was in a bad temper. Or words to that effect. That sounds as if Sophilos had actually been *inside* the shop of

Melanthios the sculptor that very morning, but the shopkeeper refused to mention it. And Melanthios exhibited "bad temper" to Sophilos, but we don't know the cause.'

'Interesting,' commented Aristotle. 'I could believe bad temper in any sculptor who could carve so scowling an Apollo as the statue we saw in front of Thymades' door. We do know one thing,' he added. 'If Sophilos was a thief, he was not the only one. But – suppose he was *not* a thief? Suppose he were coming towards Smikrenes' house following us in order to *return* the purse to Arkhias? He might put his own piece of little money in the bag momentarily, for easy carriage. That's not a perfect sign that he was a thief.'

'In that case,' I said, 'he was most unfortunate. For someone seems to have murdered him for the money, of which he got no benefit, not even the repute of virtue.'

X

Preparations for a Symposium

In thinking over the events of that unfortunate day –
unfortunate at any rate for the poor man Sophilos – it
became clear to me that in a world so full of mischance I
should do well to make solid friends. Even philosophers
had to recognise that virtue might not be enough. A man
festooned about with vexatious lawsuits requires social
countenance. To give a good dinner-party before my
marriage seemed not only a pleasant scheme but a
practical defence against disasters.

I decided to give my party early in the month of
Poseidon. Maimakterion was going by rapidly; in the
event, the middle of the month was taken up with the
curious affairs of the inept bronzesmith. In Poseidon's
month there are very few public festivals. The weather is
unfriendly, the Agora less pleasant than usual, and men
are likely to respond favourably to invitations.

'As I told you,' I said firmly to Mother. 'I am going to
give a true symposium, in traditional style.' I wasn't
asking for her approval. One does not need the approbation of womenfolk for one's invitations.

'I understand,' she replied. 'You need to put the house

to rights anyway. The Holy Two may witness, I'm almost ashamed of people seeing this house during the wedding, so run-down as it is.'

'We've been well as we are. I haven't had the money to fit the house up with trifles and gewgaws,' I replied ungraciously.

'I'm not talking of trifles and gewgaws, Stephanos, but about the walls and the floors. Now that you've taken care of the roof, and some of the waterspouts, we can hope at least that the house won't be destroyed in a flood. But apart from the roof-tiling, all you've done so far is bring home a lampstand from some rank beginner of a bronzesmith!'

'That will come in useful – for the symposium, for example.'

'But the house wants painting – you must see that for yourself! Not just the outside. The indoor rooms – do you expect your bride to go into that wretched bedroom upstairs, with the walls cracking? And the bathroom floor needs replastering, otherwise you and your little bride, poor thing, will be wading in mud.'

'The bride's ritual bath takes place in her own home,' I reminded her.

'So you expect the poor little thing to ride all the way from Eleusis and go through the events here and then retire to bed with you without a wash? And you are supposed to have a ritual bath too, Stephanos, you know, before you put on your wedding garment.'

I considered the matter. 'Though it won't help the symposium, I suppose we can add plastering the bathroom floor to our list of works – and also plastering and painting the walls of the bedroom. But I was thinking rather of the *andron* – the walls show cracks. New plaster and paint are definitely required. I think this time I shall have the floor plastered too.'

'If you must,' said Mother. 'Though a floor you can scrape can be kept cleaner when food's dropped on it. But while you're at it,' she added quickly, 'you ought to see to the courtyard, and especially the columns and the part behind them. The sitting space under the projecting roof is shameful to look at. But paint the *andron*, by all means. Don't forget to take anything valuable out of it – remember the thefts. I hope you have enough money!'

'Well,' I said reluctantly, 'I had certainly planned to buy another slave with the first return on the honey of Hymettos. But I can postpone that, and Smikrenes is paying a handsome share of the cost of the wedding. And, after all, my bride herself will make an extra pair of hands – she can help you—'

Here Mother gave a loud sniff, which I pretended not to hear. 'Another hand for the olive harvest next year, at all events,' she conceded.

'And we need to use some of the money for the wedding feast itself. We have wine from our own little vineyard, but it's not quite good enough for a feast – nor for a symposium, come to that. And I'm thinking of hiring a cook.'

'Stephanos – what extravagance!'

'You only say that, Mother, because we don't give parties – not since Father got ill. We don't really have the staff for that sort of thing. I've found out that when you hire a cook you get his slaves as kitchen workers and waiters. And we shall be spared the trouble of the sacrifice; the cook's shop takes care of that.'

'Oh, have it your own way,' she said, ungracious in her turn. 'I hope it won't ruin us! I cannot say that I want to go toiling on by myself trying to prepare a giant wedding party without proper assistants. We have Tryphos, I suppose – though he's little better than an idiot. But he's strong and always with us. And we can get one of the female slaves back from the family farm, and she can bring us some oil and cheeses when she comes. Old Dametas and Tamia are pretty shaky, but they may be able to do something. But we shall be short-handed.'

'Of course the first wedding feast will take place in Eleusis, at Smikrenes' farm. And then I daresay we can bring Philomela's old nurse Geta with us in the wedding party, and she can help out here. I was hoping that Smikrenes would give us Geta permanently, but it seems he will not.'

'No great surprise there. Your bride's father is not the giving type. I hope you know what you are doing, my son. But there, young men are headstrong.'

'Did you want me to marry Kallimakhos' daughter, then?'

'No. That was your father's idea, entirely, not mine. Oh, Stephanos, there is something important! You know I told you – the day you lost the sausages and broke the *hydria* – that I would find out more about Kallimakhos and his daughter Kharmia. And I have done it.'

'How?'

'I went to the public fountain and did some washing.'

'Mother! There is no need for you to go—'

'I know. But we do send one of the slaves to the Fountain House, especially for washing clothes, when our own well isn't acting reliable. That's usually in the summer. And I have gone sometimes myself.'

I groaned inwardly. 'Mother, that is so uncomfortable for you! I know what the Fountain House is like! A crowd of people – slaves, low persons and women – pushing and shoving to get to the water. Citizens' wives mixed in with freedwomen and slaves of all kinds. Water slopping all over the place, and everyone screeching and chattering at once.'

'Exactly. It's a chance to meet everybody. People will

talk when they're doing a wash. It wasn't long before I found out that since Kallimakhos first tried to make an arrangement with you – with your father rather, when Nikiarkhos was alive – he has proposed his daughter to another man.'

'Really? Who?'

'A merchant with a large holding in Phaleron, and some interests in Peiraieus. Euthykritos, this merchant's name is. This Euthykritos invests in ships' cargoes, so they say, and the ships go all over the place and get grain and other things after selling their goods. I don't quite know how it works, but he is getting very rich. So – not long ago, Kallimakhos and he made an agreement to marry Kharmia to the merchant's second son. At least, Kallimakhos told people it was agreed – even an *engye* of some kind last summer, he claims. But then this Euthykritos got richer, one of his ships came into port with a big return. Then he grew cool to the union, either because he was so rich, or because he heard something he didn't like about Kallimakhos. Some say it was because Kharmia's father didn't really have the dowry he'd promised. So that match was broken off. *That's* why Kallimakhos has suddenly come back to you. Of course. It's a great disgrace not to have his daughter married.'

'Had Kallimakhos been straightforward,' I meditated, 'his life could have been better. He might have a grandson by now! I don't think he's an honest man. This is helpful, Mother, I have to admit. If it proves to be right—'

'It will,' said she. 'The women at the wash always know what's going on.'

'If he really has subsequently offered his daughter to another citizen, that's good! I will easily be able to fend him off. My mind is made up and my honour engaged to Smikrenes. Even if I could get out of that agreement I would not. Even if I were not betrothed I should never marry the daughter of Kallimakhos – let him hawk her about as he will.'

'Very well, then. So we must plan your wedding to Smikrenes' daughter in the middle of Gamelion. Your dinner party – when do you want it to be?'

'I must calculate the right night, with a good moon,' I said. 'Though of course in such a cloudy month as Poseidon the moon is often no help.'

'How many guests? And who are they?'

'Men that I know, Mother. A symposium is no concern of yours or of young Theodoros. Mind you keep him away.' I was lofty because I thought she was taking too much on herself. Women – the well-bred ones – are not supposed to know what male visitors come to see the man of the house.

'I can scarcely *plan* a symposium dinner without knowing how many couches, how many plates . . .'

'Six or seven people, I suppose,' I said vaguely.

I was vague even to myself, as I had not yet quite figured out who the guests ought to be. I would have to include of course my old friend Nikeratos, who had suggested the whole affair. He was well-born and very prepossessing. And I should invite his friend, whose name I did not quite remember; he seemed much of the same class. Perhaps Gorgias, who would inherit much of a silversmith's great fortune and now had the use of it. He was not as well-born as the others, but still . . . There was no denying he would be very rich when his father died. Until that time he had practical control of the family's fortune.

Should I keep entirely to men of my own age? No, for I should not be making the most of my chance of gaining influence. Nikeratos' father? No – too old. And besides, the old man was too boisterous to suit my taste. Should I fly high and ask the arkhon Lysiphon? Or the

Hierophant? Nonsense. *Too* high indeed, and too formidable. It would be important to ask some neighbours. Certainly I didn't want Halirrhothios. Nor Hieron, whom I could not see without thinking of the awful sight of Hippobatos drooling brains on the floor. Theophon the good merchant of our deme was probably a man I should try to please. Theophon, rosy and assured, who had stood up for his friend Halirrhothios and led the deputation to ask me to withdraw the charge. And Lamas with the silky brown beard. The scholar who was writing the history of Kydathenaion. These two might be heavy going in conversation, but they were men of substance, well-born citizens, and important in my deme.

I decided I should take pains to deliver the invitations to these most important guests in person. That way, if one of them could not come, I could change the day. I did not find Theophon in his massive house, only a doorkeeper who promised to deliver the message. But with Lamas I was more fortunate. The citizen was at home, and I was invited to enter. Lamas' *andron* was a pleasant place, its walls a neutral shade and embellished with a hanging showing Homer reciting or singing to a group of auditors. Rather a fine tapestry. There were a couple of figures and some wall plaques, as well as fine ancient ornamental pots and small bronzes. There were even some books – rolls in well-made leather book-buckets ranged on a shelf in the corner.

'You have some beautiful things,' I said after we had exchanged greetings. 'The bronzes and the pots. You must be careful that they don't get stolen, as matters go nowadays.'

'True, sadly true,' he replied unhappily. 'Our current troubles rather diminish the pleasure one takes in one's little things.'

'I see you have an image of Demeter,' I remarked, looking at the little statue.

'I am devoted to Demeter,' he replied. 'It is my desire to be an initiate in the Mysteries before I die.'

'Plenty of people feel that way,' I responded. 'You have also some intellectual treasures, the best kind and less likely to get stolen,' I added, looking with admiration at his collection of scrolls. 'I see you are a true scholar. I haven't seen anyone with so many books in a private room except Aristotle.'

'Ah well, I do what I can,' Lamas said modestly, 'though it is little enough. Aristotle has many more. People are kind enough to lend me what I need to write the history of this deme. Your home and mine.'

'An interesting idea,' I said. 'Some people just write about the whole of Athens.'

'Yes,' he said, pursing his lips. 'Useful – undeniably. But it is such a broad subject. I feel the greatness of Athens would be better served if first some competent historian in each deme undertook the task of telling the story of that district. We are fortunate, you and I, Stephanos. Many excellent citizens have been dwellers in our region. If the young are not taught what to admire, Athens will not be able to keep her former glory. Nor will her religious life – which sustains her excellence – be properly understood.'

'Very true,' I assented. 'It was you – and hearing of your important work – that made me dare to offer you an invitation to a symposium at my own house. I ask for this honour – hope it is not presumptuous . . .'

'Presumptuous? By no means,' he replied, stroking his long, pleasantly undulating beard. His eyes sparkled with pleasure. 'It is you who do me honour by your invitation.'

I named the day and added that I hoped Theophon would be able to come also.

'I hope so too,' Lamas said. 'If it would not be encroaching of me, I shall speak personally to Theophon and urge him to come. It would make a very pleasant party.'

As the man seemed genuinely pleased, I was sure I could count on his attendance, and felt nearly as much gratitude as I professed. Now it was clear. The persons at the dinner would be as follows: Theophon, Lamas, Nikeratos. Nikeratos' friend – Philokedes, that was the name. And Gorgias. Only five. Oh, and myself made six. Three couches full. But I ought to ask my cousin Philemon, since I was already planning to induce him to lend me a lot of kitchen equipment for the party. That made seven. Four couches.

I would have to check up on the state of the couches for our *andron*. One of them proved very rickety, having a leg that seemed about to come off. We patched it up; I intended to use it myself alone, to guard against accident. For the fourth couch we could make do with the better of the beds from upstairs, so Mother said. The walls of the *andron* were not only dusty and cracked, but the colour was a dull yellow that had by now faded to a dirty whitish nothing. I hired a painter to paint it, and decided to be bold and create a room with handsome red walls. The couches would be covered (by Mother) with white-and-black woven fabric, and they would look well, set off against the new wall. I was vaguely visited by the recollection of someone's interior wall I had seen somewhere, only partly painted and left unfinished. Now that I knew what painting could cost, the unfinished walls seemed less surprising. I was aware that I could not afford the best contractors whose work adorns luxurious houses, the craftsmen who execute elaborate patterns or even paint whole pictures on walls. The hireling – from my own deme, which would have pleased Lamas – seemed reliable, if slow.

The next step was to hire a cook for my dinner party,

a *mageiros*, who would take charge of preparing the main items of food at the dinner. Our kitchen could supply some things, pickles and olives and so on. But my *mageiros* should be able to take everything in hand. The man I settled on ran a little shop, a *mageireion*, where he butchered animals and cooked up the meat, some animals roasted whole, other carcasses cut up. People bought cooked meat from him to take home, or even to eat in his establishment. This expert could see to the sacrifice and the butchering on his own premises. Roast mutton would be pleasant. It would be much more convenient than my having to try to roast a sheep in my own courtyard while attending to guests.

Unfortunately, on a very busy day, the *mageiros* came when the painter was at work, less than half finished. I had removed all small valuables from the *andron* to the best upstairs bedroom, but everything else had to dance around the house below. Our furniture was spread about the courtyard, where anyone could stumble on it. The day threatened rain, and the furniture had that apologetic, almost terrified look that indoor things have when they are out of place and menaced by outdoor weather. Tryphos, returned from the Fountain House with water, hurried up to me (splashing as he came) to announce that he had just espied the cook on his way to my house.

I felt prepared to meet a cook at any time, anywhere, let my house be in any condition.

So when a knock came to the front door I expected to see the butcher-caterer enter. But to my surprise in walked more important company. Ye gods! Theophrastos looking proper and correct if awkward as always. And a child with him. A very well-dressed boy.

'Good day, Stephanos,' said Theophrastos, 'I apologise for coming upon you unexpectedly. I see that you are busy with household matters.'

And he glanced about the courtyard, where our couches and a lampstand and small tables suffered their exile, and along the passage to where the open door of the *andron* allowed the perspiring worker and his pots of red paint to be seen. I tried to seem easy and unconcerned. No man of good breeding should be disturbed by visitors, however untoward the circumstances. I did, however, feel inwardly and quite unreasonably as if people were invading my home. My nice house – which was becoming curiously vulnerable in its state of alteration.

'Ah! I see.' Theophrastos nodded with approbation. 'Working on your house – understandable, with a wedding in the offing.'

'Yes,' I said, gruffly. 'Time for a few changes.'

'You know who *this* is?' Theophrastos displayed the lad with something of a flourish. 'You met him before I did.'

'That's right,' said the child. 'In the country outside Eleusis. In the spring.'

'I remember now,' I exclaimed. 'You're that boy with the hoop who led us – Aristotle and me – to the house of Smikrenes.'

'And to Smikrenes' well. I'll never forget it,' the boy replied, with a smile.

'Nor will I,' I said feelingly. 'For I am about to marry Smikrenes' daughter. But you have grown since the spring.'

Indeed, the young person I looked at now, though recognisable, seemed taller; perhaps because he was nicely dressed and not rolling a hoop, he looked older. A very self-possessed, self-satisfied person this boy had always seemed, in any case.

'Menandros,' said Theophrastos, seeing I could not recall the boy's name. 'Menandros son of Diopeithes of Kephisia. His family have large holdings on the slopes of Mount Pentelikon.'

Ah, so, I thought, the family is wealthy and important enough to impress even Theophrastos, who believes one should care little for such things.

'And I want to come to the Lykeion,' said the boy, getting quickly to the main point.

'You? But you're still a little boy.'

'I am nearly eleven,' protested Menandros. He was not at all bashful and spoke beautifully. 'Aristotle told me to come – you know, I met him when I met you. My father took me to the Lykeion today, at my request. And now I know Theophrastos. I can come next year, when I am nearer twelve.'

'Age is not everything,' said Theophrastos. 'We need intelligent young pupils who may go quickly if thoroughly through the rudiments. This is an observant boy, he'd make a wonderful worker on the book of animals, or he could help me in cataloguing the plants.'

'Your painter does not get along very fast,' Menandros said. His inquisitive steps and curious eyes had taken him towards the *andron*. 'And what a lot he spills on your floor!'

'Hardly your business – but how kind of you to take an interest.'

Theophrastos flew to the defence of his new pupil. 'I must say, Stephanos, you might have chosen a better painter. And what a bright colour! It will take its time to dry at this time of year. You will be getting red paint all over your clothes, if you don't take care.'

'Then I shall have to look for a really good *fuller*,' I said, looking meaningfully at Theophrastos, who flushed; I really enjoyed his discomfiture. 'Never mind the floor – it will be scraped and repaired afterwards,' I told the boy. 'I myself wish the painter would get along faster,' I admitted, to propitiate Theophrastos.

'Such workmen often take on too many jobs at once, or

indulge in too many tavern intervals,' said Theophrastos. 'You remember the story of Alkibiades? But perhaps the boy hasn't heard it. Alkibiades was a wealthy man with good but extravagant tastes, Menandros. So wealthy was he that he could afford to have his walls painted with lovely images. He hired one of the best painters to make these pictures for him. And then – he kept the painter locked up in his house for three days, so the man would finish!'

My painter started working with furious speed at covering the wall of my *andron*. Menandros, smiling, went towards the room to watch the painter, and to question him as to his opinion of all the redness.

A knocking on the door was sounding at this point, and I had to yell to the slave to answer it. This time of course it was the *mageiros*, wearing his bloody apron in token of his office. At least he had not brought his great knives anywhere about him. Since seeing the slashed Sophilos, I was somewhat averse to sharp implements. The man paid little or no attention to my visitors, but went straight to his task, which seemed to be a brisk and impatient interrogation of myself.

'Now,' said the cook in an important voice, 'about this here dinner party. The wine's up to you, but I have to have a clear idea of the number in the party.'

'Seven,' I said in a low tone. It was a pity to have to talk before Theophrastos of a party to which he wasn't invited.

'Seven to dine. And you want a sheep roasted, as you said?'

'It needn't be a large one,' I urged. 'Well-bred gentlemen do not require a gross amount of meat.'

'That's right, it needn't be a large one. Meat's better that way. The big old ones are actually cheaper, as they don't eat as well. Stringy or fatty. Do you want me to supply plates?'

'Uh . . . yes. Probably. Yes, let us say.'

'We can throw in a few vegetable dishes,' the cook assured me. 'Though I really must insist on the whole kitchen space. Your courtyard I have already observed. We can set the sheep roasting up there. On the night, send your womenfolk upstairs, out of the kitchen, because we will have to do some reheating, and some other things. Does your kitchen have a roof on it?'

'I think so,' I said stupidly. 'Yes, certainly it does.'

'Good. Makes things easier. The washing-up we will leave to your household.'

'I see,' said Menandros, who had returned from harassing the painter. 'You're giving a dinner party!'

'Yes,' I said, 'just a small symposium. But you, Theophrastos, and Aristotle are invited to the *wedding* party of course. In Gamelion.'

'I shall be happy to come.'

'You should invite *me* too,' said the pert boy. 'Because I brought you together with old Smikrenes and his daughter.'

'Well, and that's what I'm getting to,' said the *mageiros.* 'This here wedding. The bride's father will have a party in Eleusis, I understand. That's no concern of mine. But you said you wanted something good done here. So – how many guests? How many tables?'

'I don't know,' I replied stupidly.

'How many *women* will there be? We have to allow for their eating too, you know. Brides like having a lot of females around. So – how many?'

'I don't know,' I stammered. This cook had brought no knives, but he was hacking me to pieces with his questions.

'You surely don't want to make just *one* sheep do for a wedding party? If you have any number of guests at all, you'll find they go through it much too quickly! Of course, if you're not really having many wedding guests to speak of . . .'

'By all means,' I said, resigned, 'let us have another sheep.'

'A full-grown sheep then for the party, and two for the wedding. What time will it start? When will the bridal procession get here? Oh, and do you want a waiter – or perhaps two? Or more? Do you have enough crockery? – Will you need plates and cups?'

'Perhaps. I . . . I'm not sure yet.'

'Do you have a slave who is going to manage all this for you? If you do, let me speak to him,' demanded the *mageiros*.

'Ah . . . no. I manage the household,' I asserted.

Disconcertingly, I could see the boy Menandros beginning to grin, though he tried to stop. Furthermore, I could see out of the corner of my eye that the painter was listening, suspending operations the while. He had just upset more paint on the floor – good red colouring that I would have to pay for.

'Well then, what about the victuals? Are you having fish or just meat? Do you want two sheep or just one? Shall we throw in a waiter, or perhaps two?'

'Yes . . . no . . . I don't know. Throw in as many as you like.' I tried to repress a vision of waiters being hurled like acrobats around my courtyard.

'Most unsatisfactory,' said the *mageiros*, with a frown that looked more like a scowl. He reminded me of a schoolmaster I hadn't liked when I was very young. 'I really *must* know what supplies to bring – including servants.'

'Quite so,' I said. 'I shall come to you later, with a list. Complete. Of our wants.'

'*Some* houses,' said the *mageiros*, with a yearning sigh, 'has a chief servant who can take care of all this kind of thing. Sorry to trouble you. But we need to *know*, you know. If you can give your womenfolk warning, I'll just venture a look into your kitchen.'

'Yes, just a moment . . .' and I turned back to Theophrastos and the grinning boy Menandros.

'We have come at an awkward time,' said Theophrastos. 'So we shall leave you in peace to pursue your way to the kitchen and converse further with this workman.' He and the young Menandros saw themselves out, my servant Tryphos gaping at them from the corner of the courtyard the while.

'Don't forget, you are both invited to the wedding – and Aristotle too,' I called after them.

Tryphos, out of curiosity or pride in our domestic arrangements perhaps, deigned to accompany myself and the *mageiros* to the back of the house. My mother, warned in good time, had departed upstairs, so we had the kitchen area to ourselves.

'There's a well handy, too,' I said, pointing out this facility in the little back courtyard to this workman in food. He nodded, being plainly capable of taking in this fact.

'Have you got extra braziers? Any more portable stoves?' Our portable stove, which had the merit of being fairly large, had sustained an injury, as I now saw. It was badly chipped on one side, and blackened with smoke; it certainly looked much used.

'We shall have more, at least for the wedding,' I assured him airily. I would borrow from my cousin Philemon's household, if nothing else served. Philemon owed me that much, to be sure. A few years ago, Philemon had been declared guilty of manslaughter after a tavern brawl, and sentenced to exile; he was then suddenly (and unjustly) accused of murder. Had I not saved his life? And his family's honour? Saved him by great exertions when he was in a very difficult situation, menaced with loss of property, good name and even life itself. So he could certainly let me have a portable stove.

'The kitchen's a trifle dank and there's not much room for the staff to work in. But it will do,' the *mageiros* decided. 'Some of us can work outside if the weather holds. We'll bring some pans, and plenty of our own knives,' pronounced this man of action.

'We are about to make some improvements to the floors here and in the bath,' I explained, unnecessarily. It was absurd that I, a landowner and a citizen, should make excuses for my house to a cook who plunged his knife into animals and served food at his own greasy chophouse!

'What are you going to have as entertainment?' Nikeratos asked me, two days before the party was to take place.

'Meat,' I said, taken by surprise. 'Very good.'

'What? No fish?'

'Well, then – fish too.'

'But what I meant, Stephanos, was not the food – which will be good, I'm sure. But the entertainment. Music, or something of the sort.'

'Oh. Oh, that is all taken care of,' I assured him mendaciously.

'Nothing too fine! We won't expect rope-dancers!' he laughed.

In fact, I had given no thought at all to any such matter – I had been so fixed on other preparations. But it was true, a really good dinner party demanded some entertainers; at very least, some music. Another expense! I went quietly to a brothel that I knew had good flute girls, and secured the hire of one for the evening. I also put in an order for some garlands.

The girl, carrying her flute and the garlands, arrived early, attracting comments from the *mageiros'* gang.

Under her thick cloak she was very lightly clad for such a chilly evening. Her arrival interfered a little with my progress in the necessary bustle of putting things in place, and bracing the leg of the weakest couch. Mother and Tryphos had already done much of this work before Mother retired to the women's quarters. Now I was arranging upon a shelf in the *andron* a tasteful display of objects of virtue and value, chiefly a little statue in bronze of a horse, and the small silver figure of a running man. Aristotle had said he thought it in the old Spartan style, and I had always considered this piece most attractive. The little silver man had belonged to my father personally, a gift from someone, but he had not asked that it accompany him in death, and I had managed to keep it from being sold. I was glad that we had not thrown it into the grave. It looked very well, I considered.

We had got all the couches to fit nicely, not too near the wall, which in damp weather was still inclined to shed a little of its ruddy colour on the unwary passer-by. The workman had left me provided with a little extra paint, stored in the shed beyond the back courtyard, in an office where we kept various implements next to the stable where one donkey was quartered. That was where I had to take Philemon the day before the party, when he came with his slave carrying pans, a portable stove, and a little pottery brazier. We stored the things there until we decided exactly what to use ('we' now including the cook's gang).

Philemon insisted on seeing what had been done to the house, and it was not without some pride that I showed him the 'new' *andron*, with painted walls and plastered floor. The kitchen had been replastered, as well as the bath area, but he could not be expected to take a warm interest in these regions. He was impressed by my having such a gang of kitchen workers.

'You are getting grand, Stepho,' he remarked. 'By the

way, I think I recognise your *mageiros*. He used to be an
athletic trainer's assistant, when he was a slave. Believe
he trained Theophon and his classmates, though that
would have been a good while ago. Now he's a freedman,
with a business in a different line.'

'I suppose,' I replied, 'that a physical trainer would be
strong enough to wrestle an ox to the ground, let alone a
sheep.' Philemon always knew about anyone connected
with sporting activities.

'You'd better treat the man with respect then,' he
teased.

'I have no intention of doing otherwise.'

Once Mother withdrew, the *mageiros* and his men
were not only treated with respect, they lorded it over
our house. They set up a spit in the courtyard and put the
hot roast sheep back on it, and prepared to cut, carve and
serve. They chopped vegetables and compounded sauces
in our kitchen area – certainly not quietly. They sang and
whistled, and made loud comments the while on the
worth of our crockery and pans and other utensils, as
well as the quality of vegetables provided. And the fish.
Originally I had not intended to offer fish, as that is so
expensive, especially in winter, and the meat had seemed
so nice. But after Nikeratos' pointed query I could not
deny my guests fish – though I hadn't wanted to admit
that expense to Mother. After all, I was trying to impress
and please gentlemen who were of the *kaloi k'agathoi*, the
Beautiful and Good. I had told one of the *mageiros'* men to
buy a few, and see they were cooked. They could be
presented on my favourite plate – with images of fish
swimming around it – served up in a tasty sauce. Making
up in quality for any lack of quantity. I hoped that my
guests were men of elegance and discriminating tastes,
not given to gross excesses at the table.

XI

❧❦❧

The Symposium

The first guest to arrive was Gorgias, who appeared distracted and important. He had something on his mind.

'I think my father wants to come home,' he said to me in a low voice. I stared at him. His father Lysippos the silver merchant, had gone into exile voluntarily – for a very good reason. And he had been supposed to be near death.

'His health,' said Gorgias, embarrassed, 'my father's health has improved a little. He has won Alexander's favour through his art, but he says he wants to die at home. Lysippos is vexed with Aristotle. A Makedonian trying to run his affairs, he says.'

'Makedonians are always trying to run somebody's affairs,' said Lamas, coming up behind us. His beard was rippling, well-combed and silky smooth, and I was happy to see he was wearing a very fine-woven *khiton* in honour of my party. He could not, however, have looked more serenely solemn if he had been coming to my funeral. I introduced my scholarly neighbour to the silversmith's heir. 'So this is Gorgias, son of Lysippos,' said Lamas, without indicating any warmer desire for acquaintance. I hoped that Gorgias would take no offence, but would simply recognise my neighbour's superior quality. Gorgias was only the descendant of mechanics, mere silversmiths, and not of noble blood. Fortunately, Nikeratos and his friend Philokedes bounced in next, full of high spirits at the prospect of a party, and the atmosphere improved. Lamas did not seem to object in the least to their youthful ebullience, probably because each of these young men was *kalos k'agathos*. Together they looked like an illustration of the Beautiful and Good. Philemon came next, not as well-dressed as the others, or quite as well-barbered, but with his customary energy and infectious good humour. I hoped he and the other young fellows would get along. Of course, manners required them to be polite to my cousin, in my house.

'I'm hungry – why don't we start?' said Nikeratos. 'Where would you like us to go, Stephanos – who on which couch?'

'We are just waiting for Theophon,' I explained. I should have had no qualms about beginning to eat if we had been simply waiting for Philemon, or Gorgias even, but Theophon was really the guest of honour. Like some other important men, he didn't mind keeping one waiting. But at last he came, his important knock at the street door being answered with unexpected alacrity by Tryphos. It was certainly Theophon, tall and imposing, with a smile on his rosy face – but there were two of him.

'I knew you wouldn't mind,' he said, displaying the person by his side, a well-developed man with a good complexion, like a shorter and slighter edition of himself. 'I have brought along someone else, an acquaintance whom you know likewise. Diognetos of Eleusis.'

'You will remember me,' said this person. 'On that unhappy night our friend Hieron's house was broken into.'

'Oh yes. You were there at the discovery of – oh yes, quite, I certainly remember you.' It seemed ill-omened to mention a murder and a corpse at the beginning of our festivity.

'It is kind of the noble Theophon to ask me,' said Diognetos humbly. 'For I do not forget his birth and standing. His place in life is not reliant on the merely mercantile life of exchange. I hope that you will forgive my intrusion, since it is at his bidding.'

'Since you, O Stephanos,' said Theophon beneficently, 'are about to contract a permanent relationship with a family in Eleusis, it seemed fitting to bring you yet another acquaintance in that town. Diognetos is of the same tribe as the family of the Torchbearers. Indeed, I think the present Daidoukhos is a relation of his. And on his mother's side the Hierophant also.'

'It is true I am related to both,' Diognetos confessed. 'Our family have served as *mystagogoi* for generations. Should any of you gentlemen wish for assistance in initiation, don't hesitate to turn to me. But I ought to point out,' he added with modest honesty, 'that the Hierophant, properly speaking, has no name or family. On the day he is chosen as chief priest, his name is engraved on a bronze plaque and thrown into the sea. After that, he uses no name. So in a sense the Hierophant has *no* relations.'

'The good man of Eleusis is quite correct,' Lamas observed. 'In the Daidoukhos' case the rule is not so strict. Yet, though we know the current light-bearer is named Hanias, we tend to refer to him by his title, honouring his service as the bearer of torches in the rituals of Demeter.'

'There! What could be more becoming, Stephanos, than to bring to your house one connected with two such highly placed servants of the Two Goddesses?' Theophon asked, as if the other two men had not spoken. He stretched his hands wide, sketching his generosity of mind. He seemed to be waiting for thanks, as if it were unusually commendable of him to have brought me this unexpected guest. I could only murmur my pleasure, and redesign my dining arrangements, including the garlands. As a host could not go without one, I made Philemon do without. As I led Theophon ceremoniously into the *andron*, Diognetos came on my other side, arrogating to himself a top position also. I had to intercept Nikeratos – who was thoughtlessly about to take the chief place – in order to settle Theophon ceremoniously there. Lamas looked a little put out. I hastily showed him to a place on the couch on the other side of mine. To please Theophon, I offered Diognetos the chance of sharing my own, although that was the one with the cracked leg. Gorgias had strangely assumed that he was to sit by Theophon, and as Nikeratos and his friend hopped on the next couch together, that meant that Philemon had to put up with Lamas. Certainly they were a study in contrasts.

The first part of the dinner began with some small tasty things, like pickled onions and beets, olives, seeds and a few eggs. I recommended the olives from our own ancestral estate, thus implicitly reminding my company that ours was not only an ancient family, but settled on land of great antiquity, supporting some of the sacred olive groves of Athena.

'Our own olive oil, too,' I remarked proudly. 'It supplies the fuel for our lamps on the best occasions. Like today, and in your honour.'

'I must say, Stephanos,' said Lamas formally, 'I was pleased at your invitation, when you said to me that you wished to hold a proper symposium in the traditional style. So many of the parties nowadays are merely an excuse for a vulgar drunken riot, ending with dancing and singing in the streets. Yet this civilised pleasure of dinner with conversation is a tradition of the best Athenians – quite incomprehensible to people of vulgar birth. For they may indeed guzzle food in company, but the noble pleasures of discourse are out of their reach.'

Unfortunately, just as he said that, the flute girl came in to play.

'Shall I send her away?' I said.

'As Sokrates and Agathon did at the beginning of Agathon's dinner party,' remarked Lamas approvingly.

'*Everybody* has flute girls,' said Nikeratos.

'I went to one party,' said his friend Philokedes, 'where they had a couple of lyre-players – very good-looking girls. Played beautifully. And we had a recitation, and the lyre-players played underneath the voice.'

'Well,' I said, 'we can emulate Sokrates and Agathon, certainly, and have a rational symposium. I shall send the flute girl away – she can entertain my womenfolk and the children upstairs.'

This sounded very grand, though the party upstairs consisted only of Mother, Theodoros, and Philemon's infant child, the boy Lykias, whom he had brought with him and given to Mother's care.

I looked at Theophon and Lamas, my respected guests, hoping they would provide a cue for the evening. It would be wonderful if they broke out into some interesting and weighty discourse. We might find ourselves talking philosophically about love, as they did in Plato's *Symposium*.

'She's very well developed, that flute girl,' said Nikeratos approvingly. 'A bosom like a pair of lamps. Pity she's not going to serve the bread. Bring her back after dinner.'

'Don't let her get in the way of the meat,' said Philokedes eagerly. The roast sheep, now cut into elegant collops and served in a sauce, was being brought in by the *mageiros*. It smelled delicious. The cook's youngest assistant, a perspiring little boy, took about the basket with bread in it.

'Delightful,' said Nikeratos. 'I am becoming accustomed to this repast – one seems to meet it everywhere one goes.'

'Nothing better than a good roast,' said Philemon with his mouth full. 'Stephanos is sure to have made a good bargain.'

'Dear, dear,' said Lamas. 'I hope the animal did not die of natural causes!'

'Certainly *not*,' I responded. 'One cannot sacrifice something that dies of natural causes. This sheep has been sacrificed to the gods and everything done properly.'

'Speaking of sacrifice,' said Philemon, gazing about him, 'your new red *andron* could do very well as a butcher shop, Stepho. The blood wouldn't show.'

'Oh, what a thought.' Nikeratos and Philokedes giggled. 'Stepho with a leather apron and a big sharp knife,' exclaimed Nikeratos.

'And have *you* thought of being a butcher?' Philokedes enquired with misleading courtesy of my cousin. Fortunately Philemon was never quick to see malice.

'No, no,' he said. 'I don't like killing animals. I don't dislike animals. Would love to be able to work with horses, as I did in the army.'

'Oh, you can ride, then?' said Nikeratos with more approbation.

'Ride anything on four legs,' announced Philemon.

'Oh – then we'll have to get you to ride a cow for a wager!' teased Philokedes.

'Young gentlemen will have their pleasures,' said Lamas. 'But we elders should take the lead in a real conversation.'

'Quite so,' said Theophon warmly. 'Not that Stephanos

isn't doing well by us, and I quite like his new red room. I take some interest in the decoration of houses. I have just bought the house next door to mine, which came up for sale, and am now busy in uniting the two buildings so I will have a house of good size. At last I can live as a man should! Some beautiful marble columns for the courtyard. And the interior – ah! I expect to spend a talent – maybe more – on draperies alone. One can get such wonderful fabrics now from the East, it seems foolish not to do so.'

Several of us gasped quietly. A talent! The whole of six thousand drakhmai. More than most people's houses were worth, let alone their draperies! Theophon was pleased as we gaped at this magnificence. He smiled graciously, his rosy face even rosier with goodwill and eating.

'Should we not,' Theophon benignly suggested as soon as his mouth was emptied, 'to meet Stephanos' wishes, offer a feast of intellectual reason in return for his fine olives and mutton? Let us choose a topic. I was always top of my class at school in rhetoric. The other boys just seemed to enjoy hearing me speak for some reason. I suppose it is a mere natural knack. Ah, yes, wine – I will take a little.'

Although traditionally the serious drinking is only supposed to start after the eating is done, I had bent to the newer practice of combining eating and drinking, and made sure that the wine was brought in during the meat course. I had borrowed a very beautiful *krater*, placed on a separate high little table, in which to mix wine with the cool water with which the servant (for the occasion, a waiter belonging to the *mageiros*) supplied me. We each poured out a few drops in honour of the gods, some of us hurrying this libation in order to begin drinking. In deference to the guests and the high tone of the evening, I was generous with the water. It is vulgar to drink wine too strong. I noticed, however, that Lamas the abstemious seemed a trifle disappointed. Yet he rose to the occasion.

'This,' said Lamas, 'shows respect for true Athenian traditions, which are in danger of being done away with under the pressure of foreign powers and influences. It is a time for Athenian citizens to meet together, to create bonds and pursue greatness of mind and thought.'

'Well, what shall we talk about?' asked Nikeratos.

'I've heard,' said Philokedes, 'that there is disagreement about the shape of the earth. Not about whether it's flat or not, since most philosophers say it cannot be – though that still seems odd to me. But is the earth in the shape of a ball, or a spindle with wool on it, or is it something more like a pitcher?'

'Interesting,' said Lamas. 'But awkward to make mathematical demonstrations at dinner time. Surely the higher philosophy is to do with what Man is, and what Virtue may be.'

'Exactly,' said Theophon. 'The most beautiful behaviour is the most moral. How then shall men behave well? A man, to be a true man, must be a good citizen, a member of his *politeia*, concerned for its welfare, and not only for his own. Does goodness consist in lying to gain worldly advantage? Surely not. Or in cheating and stealing? How could we say so? Can a man change from evil to good? He may pretend to do so, but the facts do not bear this out.'

'Though men in youth don't start out wise or prudent,' I interjected. 'Surely there is change.'

'Change from the thoughtlessness of youth, from rashness and impudence, yes. But the goodness in a man will show, surely, even in youth,' said Theophon, with a nod to the younger members of the party – who were, after all, in the majority: Nikeratos and his friend, Gorgias, Philemon and even myself.

'One can hardly say anything against youth in such an excellent gathering of Athenian youths,' said Lamas pacifically. 'We hope that Athens still breeds hardy young men, able to do without a cloak when the wind blows. Able to go without sandals like Lykourgos and Phokion.'

'Yes,' agreed Theophon warmly. 'Like Phokion, a great general and probably our best orator. Even Demosthenes, who certainly has the gift of the gab, said of Phokion, "Here's the man who brings the shears to my speeches." A man of action, sparing of words.'

'Well,' said Nikeratos, 'Phokion may be as excellent as you say, Theophon, but he is really *old* now – too old to lead in a military action.'

'That may be,' said Lamas, 'but he sets at least an example of how to do without luxury. Luxury! The curse of our age. Our ancestors went about simply clad, braving all weathers, eating coarse bread and drinking nothing stronger than the clear offering of the spring provided by the Nymphs. We had no money, nor did we then desire gold nor costly embroideries nor fine sauces. The young men of today let their minds run upon little but brothels and taverns. Drinking strong wine, gambling on cock-fights, spending a fortune on fish!'

Just at that moment the fish were brought in, swimming in a sauce contrived to eke out the dish and amplify their presence. I was sorry, as I did not wish to look like an example of un-Athenian conduct. I nearly apologised for my little fishes on their pretty dish, but thought it better to say nothing.

'Fish! Oh good,' said Gorgias, helping himself. And everybody else did too.

'There is a good description in Homer,' said Lamas, 'showing the conduct of a man.' And he rose gravely in order to make his point through recitation:

> 'Say, Glaukon, why we two, adored the most –
> Are given the highest place, best meat, best seat,
> With full cups honoured? Why do Lykia's sons
> Upon us gaze as gods?'

And Lamas continued his recitation of Homer's celebrated speech of Sarpedon to Glaukon, arguing that well-born warriors are honoured because of their virtuous valour. He recited this well-known passage with great earnestness, in a quavering and rather high voice, not entirely suited to stirring lines like 'Stand we then in the van of Lykian warriors /Confronting burning battle.' I was sorry we didn't have a musician playing the lyre to accompany him.

'It is true,' Lamas added at the end, when the applause (subdued, though led by Theophon) had ceased, 'that now we do not live in the age of warriors, but in the time of cities. In our Athenian democracy we win honour peaceably among our fellow citizens, vying only in excellence.'

'Have some more wine,' I said to reward Lamas for his recitation and virtuous sentiments. I took liquid from the *krater*, and poured it into his cup. 'It is from our own little vineyard – rather thin, perhaps, but not undrinkable.'

'It *is* thin, Stepho,' said Nikeratos frankly.

'Wait a bit,' I said. 'Excuse me.' I had to go out myself, rather than giving an order, because I had a secret cache of good wine in two goatskins, hanging in the out-buildings, cool and away from marauders – principally human marauders. I had saved this wine for my wedding. But obviously I couldn't let my dinner guests be dissatisfied, especially as we were nearing the point of the banquet when the food goes away and serious drinking begins.

Rather than pouring the contents into a jug, I came back with the first wineskin itself.

'Oh look, Pa, the man has killed a goat!' said Philokedes. I commanded the attendant waiter, a slave of the *mageiros*, to help me pour some of the contents from the goatskin into the wine jar. Now I could mix the new wine with water in the *krater*.

'Throw out that old stuff, Stepho,' advised Philemon. And I threw the remaining contents of the pitcher on to the floor. I had forgotten that the floor was plastered now, and not simple packed earth, and the liquid stained the plaster, and some splashed the ankles of Lamas, who looked annoyed. Then, holding the wine jar at a good height to obtain a picturesque red cascade, I poured the newly fetched wine into the krater.

'Good colour!' said Nikeratos. '*This* is something like, Stephanos.'

'It is wine of Khios,' I said proudly. Later I would have to think about how I could replace it in time for the wedding. I'd worry about that tomorrow.

'Don't drown it,' Nikeratos added in alarm.

'He's right,' said Diognetos. 'What has the good wine done to you that you should hold its head under water so?'

In response to these hints, I refrained this time from adding much water. The mixture that went around now was much stronger. To my surprise none of the older men had uttered any warning or censure, or advised me to put in more of the liquid of the Nymphs. 'We should pour out libation afresh,' said Philokedes. 'In honour of the good wine.' We all did so.

When I looked around the tables, there were signs that a fair amount of food had been consumed. Diognetos seemed to have been doing rather well, judging by the scraps of gristle and the bones that lay on the floor under his table. Lamas' plate was heaped high with tiny bones, and there was no fish left. Theophon ploughed along contentedly with his eating, scooping up great mouthfuls with his bread. Only when he was finished did I summon the slave to clean the tables and clear away the scraps that had fallen. More lamps were brought in. Our meagre garlands now adorned rather sweaty brows.

'Speaking of morals, and that sort of thing,' said Philemon in an easy tone, 'strange things have been happening out your way, haven't they?' He was addressing Diognetos. 'I mean, that little fellow who was murdered in Eleusis.'

'We don't really know what happened,' said Diognetos defensively. 'It may have been almost an accidental death – a sudden unintended manslaughter. Very probably. Two thieves falling out.'

'That's usually a bludgeoning, not getting a throat cut.'

'Accidents will happen when men play with knives.'

'We all know,' said Theophon, 'that it is not impossible for a charge of manslaughter to be mistakenly brought,' and he looked firmly at Philemon, quelling my loquacious and easy cousin.

'It would be more interesting,' said Philokedes, 'if a man of more significance had been killed.'

'Not a person of importance, certainly.' Diognetos shrugged. 'Little Sophilos. Not quite right from birth. Probably should have been exposed rather than bred. His folks live in a pitiful hovel, outside the city. He was always trotting around Eleusis.'

'One doesn't know what harm strange people like that may do,' said Lamas.

'But,' I said argumentatively, 'we can hardly imagine that Sophilos could have come to Athens and killed Hippobatos before getting accidentally killed himself in Eleusis. We still have the mystery of what happened to Hieron's brother-in-law.'

I poured out more wine for the company, who seemed ready for it. I took a full cup myself, and hoped my speech was not slurring as I talked a bit loudly to Diognetos of Eleusis, urging him to come to my Eleusinian father-in-law's wedding feast.

'Now! Bring back the flute girl!' demanded Nikeratos.

I sent Tryphos for the girl, and she soon came back and dutifully plunged into a fine dance tune. Nikeratos and Philokedes got up and pranced about the room, nearly knocking things over. My *andron* was not quite large enough to stage this kind of entertainment, and the courtyard was full of *mageiros* and skeletal sheep. So the dancers soon returned to their couches. I ordered Tryphos to clean up again, and sponge off the tables.

When a knocking came to the street door, I sent the slave off with instructions to answer it. I thought Nikeratos looked a trifle expectant, even though he was now beginning to play that game where one flicks dregs in the wine-cups from one's cup at a target. Gorgias and Philemon joined readily in the *kottabos* competition, flicking their cups at the wall, and making fine streaks of wine on the paint, light red on dark red.

'Here's this woman,' said Tryphos, trotting in. And there was a woman, indeed. She was wrapped in a plain cloak, but a crocus colour peeped from underneath. As she entered the room she cast the light embroidered veil from her face. Thratta. The prostitute who had searched the house with us on the occasion of Halirrhothios' arrest. The Thracian whore I thought Athens had got rid of.

'Good evening, gentlemen,' she said.

'Thratta!' I exclaimed. 'I didn't send for you!'

In happy humour, she walked over to Nikeratos and kissed him. 'I bring you greetings from one you know of.'

'My father!' said Nikeratos, laughing. 'I knew the old Papa was up to one of his tricks! He wanted to give us young men something to enjoy with our meal – so he said.'

'But why,' asked Theophon, talking a great gulp of wine and staring intently, 'why does the dear female not unwrap?'

'Yes – it's not cold in here!' cried Philemon.

'Thratta!' I exclaimed again, stupidly. 'There's been a mistake . . .'

'No, no, it's all right, Stepho,' assured Nikeratos. 'You won't have to pay one obol for this hetaira's company, I promise you. A treat from Papa. Dance, woman, dance! Play up, girl!'

And the flute girl played while Thratta peeled off her cloak in time to the music, and then danced before us with a fluttering of light green and crocus colour. There was not much to her attire; if she had come through the winter night in such flimsy wear the woman must have possessed the Hellenic hardihood admired by Lamas and Theophon.

'This woman's getting on in years,' Theophon judged. 'Not a young thing. But there, dear, you know I like them full-shaped.' And he reached out and pinched Thratta on a posterior cheek.

'Give the woman a drink!' commanded Nikeratos. I did so. This meant offering the others something more to drink too; it quite surprised me how fast they got through the Khian wine. And I was contributing my share to the drinking.

'Beware the assault of the grape, my sons,' one of the older men said.

'Not afraid of any 'saults,' I said. I could feel my garland slipping and my face becoming hot as I proceeded to give a general lecture on the subject of my fight with the pirates.

'Then you deserve another drink,' said Theophon. 'A hero as well as a host.'

'We'll kill your goat,' said Gorgias. The wineskin was indeed getting smaller and thinner. Gorgias seemed to wax stronger and happier.

'Like spring flowers,' said he sentimentally to Thratta, admiring the material of her scant dress.

'You want to see my flowers?' she mocked. 'Flowers of Thrake? I'll show you mine if you'll show me yours, little flower of Athens!'

Lamas drank his wine off at a gulp. So it seemed to me. His pale brown beard with its curly waves was now in disarray, and bits of fish and egg peeped through it. But his eyes shone. He stood up and steadied himself by leaning on Thratta.

'Flowers,' he said, hanging his chin on her shoulders. 'Dance like the flowers. It's a long time to spring.'

'It *is* a long time, old Papa. I can dance for you.' But Lamas hung on to her, moving back and forth without apparent volition or control, or any wish to desist.

'Get him off her – he's like an old crab crawling on a white mallow flower,' exclaimed Philokedes. 'Sir,' he said, addressing Lamas, 'we beg to inform you that despite your very long beard, and your knowledge of poetry, you are not an object of beauty. So we beg you to cease and desist from entwining yourself about this woman. Let her perform her dance without you.'

'Eh? What's that you say?' said Lamas. Philokedes reached out to remove the older man's arm from Thratta's torso, and the inevitable happened. Lamas lost his balance altogether and toppled heavily and headfirst over a couch. He lay gasping and sprawling over the couch, his legs on one side and his arms on the other; then he began not loudly but very thoroughly to regurgitate everything he had taken in at dinner. As it all came in a wash of red wine, the effect was pretty horrible.

'He's vomiting blood!' exclaimed Gorgias. 'This is serious!'

'No – just red wine,' said Philemon. 'I've seen vomited blood before. When a man was wounded in the war.'

'Well, what fun for you!'

'Good thing your walls are so very red now, Stepho. It won't show as much – not even if it were blood.'

By this time Tryphos, at my summons, had brought along sponges and a basin of water, and was setting about the unpleasant task of cleaning up.

'These old fellows!' Nikeratos was disdainful. 'Cannot hold their wine. Shouldn't have come.'

'This is very bad of you, young man.' Theophon had taken this slur personally. 'Rude and un-Athenian. Lamas was *invited* – not like that hetaira you've brought to the party, who has caused all the trouble.'

'Oh, Thratta is the cause of discord, is she? Thratta has been a bad girl then?'

'We must chastise her!' exclaimed Theophon eagerly. 'I know she won't behave unless disciplined. Here – I'll use my sandal and give her a right slippering!' Theophon and Nikeratos manoeuvred Thratta so that she was laid over the couch – my couch. They then raised her dress so that she exhibited the white globes of her posterior to the admiring assembly. Theophon slapped away at these, exclaiming as they turned pink. Had he struck harder, I should have had to intervene. Thratta wriggled, and the couch gave an alarming creak – I saw the weak leg beginning to crack. Lamas, struggling at the wall side of the next couch, crawled next door as it were to the couch where Thratta suffered, on the side opposite Nikeratos, and began to try to kiss the woman at the same time as her chastisement continued at the other end. He then reached across the couch and began to grab at her posterior, getting a slipper on the hand for his pains.

'That will do!' said Nikeratos. 'She will be a good girl, and we will free her from this old slobberer.' He pulled her dress down, and slipped some silver coins in her hands.

'Dance, Thratta, dance! You won't have to worry about any old bearded idiot grabbing your private parts.'

'Don't need the woman,' Lamas announced thickly. He was now in a semi-recumbent posture on my couch, the cracked one. It was presently at a definite tilt, which must have increased his queasy sensations. 'Don't know why I ever touch hired females. This little fellow is worth ten of her!' And he began to fondle the curly head of my slave Tryphos as he crouched with his basin, cleaning. The boy gave me a frightened look. Although Tryphos was just a slave, and not the most valuable, he was not a brothel servant, and I could see no reason to force him to endure the kisses of a visitor, especially someone who had just vomited so very freely. So I ordered the boy to the kitchen to empty his basin, and he hurried away with alacrity.

Thratta recommenced her dance. Nikeratos was not satisfied with the flute player, but kept adding in drum parts himself; then he jumped up and joined Thratta in the dance. Soon Philokedes joined on the other side of Thratta, and the trio flounced and bounced about the room. I hastily moved things out of the way, including a platter holding nuts and fruit. Then I hurried over to the niche which held our best pot, as well as the little figures I had put out earlier. The bronze horse was there, but the little silver running man – where was he?

'Help! Theft! I've been robbed!' I yelled. I repeated the dire words and the racket and whirlwind ceased.

'What's that you say?'

'Something has been stolen! The little running man in silver! I cannot see him – he was right there . . .'

'Probably got jolted off in the hubbub. You'll find it on the floor somewhere,' said Theophon.

'I'll see if the slave has seen it, or if it got into the pile of dirty dishes.' My cousin Philemon left the room like a man of action, while the rest of us were looking stupidly under couches and into cups. It was hard on my head to bend down, and I had a whirling sensation. I had drunk a good deal, and was not sure I could rely on my own perceptions or judgement. Had the silver figure really been there? And was it really gone? It then struck me that it was bad luck as well as bad manners to make such a fuss about an object and ruin my guests' dinner party.

'Let us pay no heed,' I said summoning up my self-possession. 'Come back to your couches, everyone, and nibble some olives. We can steady our stomachs and have some more wine – better watered this time.'

'Yes, my lad, you have been forgetting the water,' said Theophon. I could only think this unfair. We settled down again, not before a couple of the guests had taken advantage of this interlude to urinate copiously in one of the large common vessels provided for that necessary purpose. But now my cousin Philemon was not among us. I supposed he might have decided to piss on his own, in the freedom of the back premises. Or else, I thought, gazing into the wine-dark depths of my cup, my conscientious cousin was still looking—

'Where's my knife? I'd like to know?' An angry *mageiros* burst into the *andron*.

'What?' All I could do was stare.

'My second-best knife. Beautiful handle, such a grip on it! Corinthian, and sharpened to within an inch of your life. It could cut through a man's arm like cheese, that knife could!'

'Oh no!' Theft was one thing, the disappearance of a

murderous knife quite another. 'Everybody, quick! We must help the butcher look for his knife.'

'He'll hardly find it here,' said Gorgias, yawning.

'Certainly not,' said Theophon, yawning likewise.

'But this is dangerous,' I insisted. 'It is not the value of the knife I mind, but what such an implement can do.'

'And where do you suggest we start looking?'

'We should all go together to the kitchen,' I decided. 'Start there and work our way outward. It is quite likely to be in the kitchen after all.'

'I swear I looked – and it isn't!' The *mageiros* was not at all pacified. 'By all the gods! You think I don't know how to look around a kitchen for a knife – my *own* knife? Do you take me for an imbecile?'

Without providing an answer to this query, we all hastened into the kitchen. We troubled the work and frightened the slaves as we peered into refuse, looked into plates and pots, opened containers and little cupboards. How to go about looking was a puzzle. While I was still trying to think, there was a dire interruption. Tryphos came running in, trembling, and spoke – or rather shouted – at me:

'Oh, master,' he cried. 'There's a man in the *andron*. Lying down! And I think he has a knife in him!'

'O ye gods, it wanted but this!' I cried out distractedly. This was too terrible to contemplate. Bloodshed – in my beautiful new room? Oh, surely not! I led my drunken party across the courtyard and back into the *andron*. The lamps there had been quenched, and all one could see was the shape of a man lying between two of the now dis-arranged couches. I called for lights, and when a lamp was brought I took it towards the fallen form. The lamp wavered in my grip as I swung it back and forth, the little flame spurting up and down.

Now I could see – and so could others as more lamps

came in. I could see a man, his face shrouded, smotheringly wrapped in Thratta's embroidered veil, and turned away from us. His legs sprawled awkwardly. From his throat there ran – I gave a gasp of dismay – there *flowed*, rather, a perfect river of red. Blood trickling remorselessly and quietly along the floor, making a horrid pool or puddle. There was a significant gleam of bronze at the top of the *khiton* . . .

'Another murder!' I cried. 'Gods! Will you never have done!'

'I feel sick,' said Thratta. She wasn't the only one.

'Fetch a doctor!' said one voice.

'No – what's the use of that? Send for a magistrate,' advised another.

'I really *am* going to be sick,' Thratta insisted.

'*SURPRISE!*' yelled the corpse, springing up suddenly. It threw the cerement from its face, and removed the knife from its bosom.

'Philemon! I might have known. What a trick to play!'

'Why, you had so much red paint, Stepho, it was irresistible. And the *mageiros* here with his wonderful knives.'

'Give me the knife – here! Let there be no more tricks with it. Save that I can use it to skin alive that slave Tryphos, who played me such a trick!'

'Oh, let the boy alone, Stepho. It isn't his doing – one of the cook's servants and I arranged it between us. He filched the knife for me, and made sure all of you would go into the kitchen.'

'Thratta, feel my forehead!' Theophon sat down heavily. 'Do I have a fever?'

'No,' she announced having brusquely fulfilled this medical office.

'Most impudent,' said Lamas, sitting down as well. 'You have given us a turn! Naughty woman. I feel all of a quiver, quite trembly. Thratta should feel my forehead too.'

'I must return this knife,' I said to the *mageiros*, who had come up in time to see something of the wonderful imitation of death. 'No harm has come to it – fortunately not even any paint on it.'

'That's as well,' he said in a grumbling tone. As he stepped back, over the threshold that gave on to the short corridor leading from the courtyard, he gave a grunt of surprise.

'What am I stepping on? Here – where did this come from?' And he handed me a small silver object. The running man. He was not harmed save by the thick-soled sandal of the heavy cook. Some soup or sauce – or something I preferred not to think about – had gone over him like a film.

'Wonderful!' I said. 'So it isn't lost! It will be as good as new. Let's rearrange the couches. Sit down everybody, and have some more wine, while the *mageiros* packs up the kitchen.'

So we did, and everybody, including Thratta, enjoyed their last cup of my Khian wine.

Soon everybody was voting Philemon's prank the best joke ever, one of the funniest things they had seen. So it was in its way. I had thoughts I kept to myself. Chief among them being that I had been in that exact place in the corridor, and while holding a lamp had looked into its darker corners during my first hunt for the missing silver man. Surely the gleam would have taken my attention then? It would be best anyway to put this valuable back in my mother's treasure box, and remember that drinkers don't require elegant decorations.

Certainly, we killed my goat, and then the other one. The second wineskin was collapsed and flat as a bedspread when our party made its way into the night, accompanied by the flute girl. And the guests insisted on my joining them as we danced in a line down my street, with Thratta and the flute girl, so we could let the whole neighbourhood know that my symposium had ended in a *komos*.

XII

───────◦○◦───────

A Wedding Procession

That night of the rather vulgar symposium seems in retrospect the last night of fairly good weather that winter. The month of Poseidon became more than usually wet and disagreeable, with cutting winds carrying an almost angry rain. It didn't really rain all the time – it only felt like it. Some more work was done on the house, where everything dried slowly. Disorder in the house made it harder to go shopping and tidy the place in preparation for the wedding. I could only hope that the weather would clear by the middle of Gamelion, when Smikrenes' daughter and I would be united.

At the end of Poseidon's month there was a short and welcome interval of dry weather. But this rapidly brought on a series of colder days, when every roof was clearly cut out against the sky, and high places sparkled in a chilly veiling. Then clouds and cold came together and there was snow. Snow in Athens. Snow falling about the Akropolis, decorating the roof of the Parthenon and the frieze running round about it, obscuring even the brilliant colours of gold and red and blue. Horsemen wore cloaks of new and feathery white, ladies in procession each boasted a new white muffler.

'This snow is unusual,' Mother said. 'I fear this year's weather is disturbed. Perhaps Poseidon is angry about something! It is not good for the seeds in the ground to have too much moisture, or get too cold.'

'I worry only about how to get Philomela daughter of Smikrenes here without her freezing to death on the way,' I said. 'I shall have to send a donkey-cart to Smikrenes, I suppose, but one donkey scarcely seems enough. Dear me, it is hard to get a good procession up with such a long distance to cover! It is pleasant enough when a procession goes from one town deme to another within the walls – but how many people are going to walk all the way from Eleusis? And if they come here, we shall have to find beds for them.'

'Has that only now occurred to you? Don't think I haven't thought of all this,' Mother said loftily. 'The men will sleep on the floor of the *andron* and the courtyard. The women – there won't be many – can share my room upstairs. Slaves in the back area, or anywhere they won't be in the way.'

'I don't want a lot of chattering, giggling women next door on my wedding night!' I exclaimed in horror. 'For the love of all the gods, Mother, get them out of the way!'

'I'll see what I can do,' she said, slightly offended. 'Perhaps we won't have any guests to worry about.'

That was my worst fear, in fact – that nobody would come. I went personally to all my neighbours on my street and the one just behind to invite them warmly. Many received me kindly, but a few seemed rather cool; I could tell that the affair of Halirrhothios still rankled. On one of those days as I was walking about the district a tile fell just in front of me and shattered on a stone. It was a very large tile, the heavy end one from an important roof. Had it fallen on my head I should have been stretched out in the street. I exclaimed at the carelessness that allowed such a thing to happen. But the house whence it came was not that of anybody I knew, and it seemed an error to create hostility by taking offence or going off in fear and suspicion. Still, I did wonder. I thought about the time when I had stood on the roof myself and surveyed the ground below. How easy from that godlike height to drop something on somebody! And what a good way to kill or injure – it could always seem like an accident. Yes, I did wonder about that tile.

I implored Smikrenes to make sure that some persons from Eleusis would supply a party for the bride's house, and some walkers for the procession. I had ventured to answer the *mageiros'* questions, rather grandly, with assurances of a decently large number of guests, enough to warrant roast goat as well as two roast sheep. I allowed him to furnish such a quantity of crockery as made me turn pale whenever I thought of it.

'What about the garlands, Stephanos?' Mother thought of everything. 'And we will need a child to act as Eros.'

I thought, but did not say, that our Eros ought to be young Menandros, who had inadvertently brought myself and Philomela together.

'Eros has to be dressed up in costume, with his bow. And wings, of course,' Mother was going on enthusiastically. 'He must take the bread round on a winnowing fan. And of course he will carry the torch in the last procession on the wedding night—'

'Me!' shouted Theodoros. 'I'll have a bow and arrows.'

'Oh no, dear. The Eros-child has to be a child with both parents living – it would be fearfully bad luck else. We must ask Philemon and Melissa for little Lykias.'

'Lykias is only four years old, Mother,' said Theodoros with great scorn.

'Four years and a half now. Old enough for a pretty Eros. He will act his little part very sweetly. But we must think about garlands, for us and for the house.'

'Oh – the garlands. Of course.' I hadn't given any thought to these at all. Yet it was vital to have them, for everybody and for the doorposts also. It did seem bothersome that weddings are celebrated at a time of year guaranteed not to have any flowers. I had the happy thought of commissioning my brother to go to the country to find ivy and branches, and he toiled away during his spare time.

'I hope you're satisfied,' he said, coming in one afternoon fatigued and carrying a load of greenery.

'That's quite good,' I said. 'And we are bringing in the girl slave from the farm. She could help you string the branches and make garlands and also swags of decoration.'

'Oh, do it yourself,' retorted Theodoros. I was surprised; he was hardly ever in a bad humour.

'Never mind, child, you're tired.' I thought I spoke with a kindly air, but my little brother was not pleased with my manner.

'Oh, Stepho, you can call me "child" when you go blundering about your own wedding like this? And I want to say something to you.' He had flopped down on a stool, but now he stood up again, very straight, and looked at me. 'Something serious.'

'What, then?'

'You need to change – your life, I mean.'

'I am making a big change – getting married.'

'Yes, but – well, Stephanos, you don't think about what other people want. You're not *really* like a head of a household, you've just played at it. And it isn't good for Mother and me. Take shopping, for instance. You go out all day every day, but you often forget to buy food at the

Agora, so some days we have something and others nothing. Shopping is a man's job! The head of the household is supposed to purchase all the food, and anything needful in the marketplace. Unless he's the kind of amazingly rich man who has hordes of slave to do it, and then people sneer at that too, as it isn't democratic or Athenian.'

'I suppose I could do more shopping . . .'

'It isn't just *more*, it's doing things all the time. And not being careless, like losing sausages to a dog and a bitch. Now, if you came home for the main meal more often, you could keep an eye on the servants and the housekeeping. And you could see how little we have sometimes. But you like gobbling up funny bits of food from those stalls in the Agora—'

'I don't gobble!'

'Yes you do. You like to eat. It doesn't show on you because you are always walking, but that's another thing. You run round and about and don't bother with home—'.

'A man,' I pronounced, 'lives a public life, while women, and of course children while they are young, live in the private home.'

'I'm not talking about going to the Ekklesia, or the courts. You run away from home. You go off on any excuse, some odd law case, or those foreign philosophers you're so fond of. I know why it is,' Theodoros added. 'You couldn't stand Papa, and as soon as you were able, you just took off on your legs and roamed and rambled as much of the time as you could.'

'You can't – you don't even remember living with Papa! You're too young!' I was so angry I nearly added 'you stupid whelp' but caught myself in time.

'I remember,' Theodoros said steadily. 'You think I'm stupid, but I'm not. I remember my own papa. I was nearly six when he died. Before he got sick that last time, you and he were quarrelling a lot.'

'Well . . . that may be,' I admitted, in a less angry tone. 'I don't think you're *stupid*,' I added.

'I don't say I never understood it, the quarrelling,' Theodoros replied, in a less angry manner. 'But it's not good that you always think of Papa as a great blunderer. If you let it out, other people will think the less of the whole family. That's not good for me either. But what I *really* wanted to say is – now you are getting married you have to consider other people. You will have Philomela in your house.'

'I will,' I said smiling. 'In a few days I will have Philomela in my house. Our house. For good.'

'I hope it will be good for her,' my brother said earnestly. 'I like Philomela – you remember, I got to know her when we stayed at Smikrenes' farm last summer. She is nice. She doesn't deserve to be badly treated and ignored all the time. And not given much to eat. You don't think well of Smikrenes, and he does live rather rough, but there was always food, and the meals were at the right time.'

I could not help laughing at this.

'You want better meals, and meals on time,' I said. 'I think I can help you there – and Philomela too, who is a good cook, I have every reason to believe. Why, the very fact of my marriage means we will have better resources, both for growing and buying food. So I think I can promise better dinners, little brother. And I shall have reason to come home more often, when my wife is there.'

'Maybe you won't go to brothels so much,' he said sagely. I was shocked that he even knew about this! It seemed wrong for me to defend myself by any clarification, though actually I did not go to brothels often – not very, very often.

And I did intend to come home for meals more

regularly, and to eat less frequently at the tempting and convenient food stalls. The whores were likewise tempting and convenient, and good for the health in moderation, but I knew from experience how inconvenient they might be. Somewhat similar advice had been given me by Aristotle himself.

'You need to preserve your own strength,' he had advised. 'Do not pursue prostitutes too often, Stephanos. Be self-controlled, as befits a married man. At the same time,' he added thoughtfully, 'it is not good to distress or over-task a young bride by too much or too vigorous lovemaking. Be temperate. It would be better – you know my opinion – for women not to begin childbearing until about the age of eighteen. Your bride is much younger than that. Do not force her or wear her out. As Athenians cannot raise all the children they produce, it is better not to produce too many.'

As I thought over all this advice, it seemed rather gloomy. I was to be the man of the household, domestic, keeping things in order, eating with the family often and sleeping at home – yet I was not to be too manly, lest I father too many brats. At the same time, I should cease brothel visits. At least for a while. Even my mother had given me a hint in this direction, saying it looked bad for the bride, as if she were deformed or ugly, if her man were found in brothels again a few days or even months after their marriage. Responsibility fell on me like snow on the horsemen of the Parthenon.

I wondered how Philomela was feeling about the coming nuptials, if she was full of apprehensions. A woman changes her whole existence on marrying, not just a few things in her life but its entire setting. The time lumbered on, busy but slow. I had dreams wherein I was on a sea-journey subject to perpetual delays. Trying to reach my desired port, I kept arguing with and urging the ship's captain, who made promises, but then would put in at some other little meaningless place, taking on cargo or giving his rowers a holiday. Sometimes the ship was on the seas, but for all the oarsmen could do, we kept rowing past the same island . . . I knew things would change, yet doubted it. But the appointed time came, as times will, and my life did change.

On the day reserved for the occasion of my bridal journey to Eleusis, I took my ritual bath in our little bathtub at home, with the slave pouring over me fresh water brought all the way from Kallirrhoe spring. It is unlucky, my mother insisted, for either of the bridal partners to bathe in anything else. I dressed in a new white garment, with a white cloak, and put on my garland. My bridegroom's party was small, consisting of myself, my cousin Philemon with my brother Theodoros (riding behind him), and Nikeratos. We rode mules hired for the occasion. A group of neighbours kindly walked with me to the city gate, and even a bit beyond. The weather, however, was not encouraging for a long walk so early on a winter's morning, and they gave us their appropriate good wishes and turned back. I put a hat on over my garlanded head, as it was drizzling steadily by now, and we plashed along some very dirty roads to Eleusis.

This seemed a dull procession, and uneventful – but I was wrong in that. As we were nearing Eleusis, before we got to the bridge over the Kephisos, we encountered something more actively unpleasant than drizzle. A large clod of earth, very wet, with grass attached, came whizzing by my head and knocked my hat off.

'Hoy!' I exclaimed. 'Who did that?'

'Probably some boy,' said Theodoros.

'Or *girl*,' said Philemon loudly, 'judging by the aim.'

This was an unfortunate taunt, for my assailant

improved his aim with the next clod. It hit me on the neck and shoulder – leaving a very nasty stain on my white cloak and even my *khiton* underneath. I looked about wildly, but could see no one. The next missile was even more disagreeable. It was a stone, nicely rounded and very hard, as I can attest for it hit me in the shoulder. I now felt like a soldier on a mountain pass being fired on by enemy insurgents from the mountains. The next stone I managed to duck. But how long could this go on? My mule was frightened, not unnaturally, and began to buck and curvet with more spirit than one could have thought was in him.

'Stop!' Philemon wheeled about and charged the enemy. I gave a shout – of horror largely, for he was taking Theodoros straight into danger.

'Stop, you rascal, or I'll run a sword through your guts!' Philemon exclaimed. 'Death! *De-eath!*' he bellowed, pursuing the invisible quarry. There was a scrabbling in the bracken, and whoever it was ran away.

'Hey!' said Theodoros. 'Do it again!' But Philemon prudently turned his mount about.

'I think he's had enough,' he said. 'The coward!'

'Don't,' I begged, thinking it a poor notion to irritate my retreating enemy further. It was certainly unnerving to be attacked by an invisible opponent. Not the kind of thing one prepares for on a wedding day. I recovered my hat – or rather, Nikeratos got it for me, as I disliked getting on and off the mule, especially in my (now stained) wedding finery. He also straightened my garland, which was sliding down my face, like a dripping tree.

As we approached Smikrenes' familiar house, the drizzle ceased. At least Smikrenes' doors were appropriately garlanded. There was no sign of a wedding party yet – it was still very early in the morning, and the meat was not yet a-roasting. Yet as we arrived, a few neighbours drifted in our direction, giving us countenance.

'Here's the bridegroom, men!' announced Philemon, leaping with agility from his mount and helping Theodoros down. There were a few appropriate cheers.

'Here you are at last!' Smikrenes said ungraciously. 'We need to perform the sacrifice, the two of us – there is no time to lose!' He pulled me to the outdoor altar, where the shivering sheep was awaiting its end. We said the ritual prayers and swung the axe together in joint sacrifice. I would have been more worried about the bloodstains on my white clothes had I not already been in such a spattered state. Fortunately, Smikrenes seemed more skilled than I had expected in stripping and disembowelling the creature, and a neighbour's slave had been volunteered as a practical helper. He got a good fire going, not to be put out by mere drizzle; soon the beast was slowly becoming roast meat. I shivered, and got closer to the fire.

The master of the house went indoors to wash and change, and when he eventually reappeared he was undeniably wearing his cleanest clothes. He moved slowly over to the table, which he had caused to be placed out of doors; of course, the weather made this arrangement less agreeable than it might have been. Geta had to run quickly in and out with food, keeping it sheltered from the drips and scattered raindrops.

Dressed in his best apparel (though that was not much to boast of), and looking most peculiar in his garland, the bride's father began serving some barley cakes and cheese to his neighbours. A group of young men appeared, peasant lads of good growth. I was at last introduced to Biton, a former aspirant for Philomela's hand and the lands of Smikrenes. These hopes had been

ended when Biton's father and Smikrenes had fallen into
a disagreement one day, a quarrel which ended when the
backside of Biton's parent had made the acquaintance of
the length of Smikrenes' foot. This lad was a hulking
fellow, it struck me, not quite as negligible as I had
foreseen. I spoke jocularly to these youths, and expressed
my pleasure at the support of Smikrenes and his family
by his neighbours.

'Ah. Old Smikrenes had better watch his step,'
growled one. 'He won't dare to mess with his neighbours
any more. We're well able to deal with him now, if he
should forget himself.'

'Biton here could take him on. Biton could take
anybody on, one hand tied behind him,' the man boasted.

Biton had hands as large as pigs' hocks, and sinewy
arms. 'Biton should enter the Olympic competition,' I said
in a tone of compliment. 'Boxing, perhaps?' I thought this
farm boy looked the sort of fellow who could straighten an
iron ploughshare with his bare hands, like the celebrated
ploughboy who became an Olympic victor in boxing.

'Aye,' said one of the other young men. 'A boxer he is,
surely. But Biton's likewise a champion discus-thrower,
further than any man in Eleusis.'

While we were exchanging these pleasantries through
the light drizzle, Smikrenes continued to hand out bread.
But the hospitable activity and the joys of the day had not
wreathed his countenance in smiles.

'Well, at least *you* turned up,' he remarked. 'There's
that much to be thankful for, at least.'

'Give the poor bridegroom a cup to drink,' said one of
these Eleusinians. 'He looks like a drowned weasel.'

This remark seemed less a kindness to myself than a
broad hint to Smikrenes to bring on the drink – of which
as yet there was no sign. With a sigh he brought out a
wineskin from under the table, and offered some

potations in lumpy pottery cups. We stood about, mostly;
there were very few chairs or stools, and it was easier to
keep dry – or less wet – if one could move under a tree or
beneath the eaves.

'What happened to *you*?' the neighbour enquired,
tossing his own drink back and staring at me. 'Mule
throw you?'

'Oh – h – it's bad luck for a bridegroom to be thrown!
He must mount and ride all night!' Coarse guffaws.

'No,' I said, calmly. 'Some impudent boy – it must have
been – threw dirt. I presumed this must be an Eleusinian
custom.'

Some kind person gave me a cloth to wipe off the dirt
with.

'Keep your pecker dry and your throat wet,' advised
another neighbour, handing me a cup.

'What a day!' grumbled Smikrenes. 'All this fuss for a
party in the rain! Ah,' he shook his head mournfully, "tis
as I always prophesied. My poor girl, my one child, to go
through all this rain – and snow most probably before
we're done. Or hail or something of that sort. She'll likely
take a fatal disease and die of the cough as a result of this
wedding.'

'No, no, man,' insisted Nikeratos. 'She is going to live
in the city, which is as good as a cure for all poor young
country folk.'

'The city!' Smikrenes snorted. In honour of the day he
withheld the full blast of his contempt, moderating his
language. 'The city! Wastrels and thieves – with brothels
at every corner. Folk with more money than sense.'
There was more of this kind of thing as the day waxed,
and I was so used to it I hardly noticed. Besides, here
among his rural neighbours his sentiments met with
approbation, and it was Nikeratos, so shiny and debonair,
who was the odd man out.

I could hear female voices from within the house, which served as the women's quarters while my bride was being bathed and made ready. Not just the voices of my bride and Geta, as I had feared. It was good that a group of neighbour women would see Philomela off. I wondered if any of these Eleusinian guests would come with us to Athens on such an unpromising day. It was important that somebody should do so, for the wedding at my house ought to be attested by persons on the bride's side. We required a sufficient number of witnesses to substantiate the fact that she as well as I was the child of a citizen, a proper denizen of an Athenian deme, and that we had been wed openly and properly, starting with the feast at her father's house, attended by Eleusinians of some stature. I was determined that everyone through all generations should acknowledge our marriage as legal. I had already spoken to Smikrenes with this concern in mind. As he was not on good terms with many – I might say any – of these neighbours, my new father-in-law was not in an advantageous position to make sure of neighbourhood festivity and approbation. Biton's father, for example, after that altercation ending with the boot in the backside, would never set foot on Smikrenes' lands again. Might this Biton, equally resentful and seeking revenge, have been the source of the missiles?

Fortunately, I spied in the little crowd two Eleusinians whom I knew (and had in fact invited myself): the Eumolpid Thymades, chosen by Aristotle for Herpyllis' spiritual guidance, and Diognetos of Eleusis, recently a guest at my own dinner party. I urged both these Eleusinians, with all the warmth I could command, to join our procession back to Athens, offering lodging, and (I promised) splendid dinners both today and tomorrow. Both accepted, so there was one point gained. I urged them to bring their wives also, if at all possible, for ceremony required the female bridal party to be of sufficient size. It would be sad for Philomela if no women from her own deme accompanied her to her new home.

The bridal chariot was waiting, also garlanded. It was really a serviceable cart, rigged up with a covering so that the bride could be decorously invisible and also protected from the weather. Smikrenes had suggested an ox-cart, which is good for muddy roads. I was not very elated at the prospect of such a vehicle. Athenians would make jokes about the size and heft of my chosen bride – or they would suggest I must be bringing a houseful of valuable furniture from Eleusis, and profess themselves ever disappointed in being denied a sight of it. In fact, my father-in-law had gone one better, for the appropriate cart was drawn by two horses. However shaggy, these beasts (each with a garland about his neck) gave the apparatus of departure a certain style. The stylishness was not essentially diminished by the observation of one of the party: 'Drawn by geldings, eh? Is that good luck, now?'

It seemed a long time until the meat was ready, so that we could say there had been a proper wedding feast at the bride's home. As the scent of mutton wafted over damp Eleusis, more neighbours turned up. The slave boy who acted as chief (if unofficial) cook – for it was evident that Smikrenes had little practical experience – heeded the master's advice to speed up the roasting; he heaped the fuel on desperately, and some of the meat got charred. But at least there was roast meat, and the wine (if thin) did circulate, and this gathering was undeniably a wedding party.

It had been agreed before that we, the bridegroom and his cohort, would not spend a great deal of time at Smikrenes' home. We had a relatively long journey to be accomplished in procession before nightfall. The women were singing as they adorned Philomela. Then Geta, her old nurse, began bringing things to the cart – some good pots; some serviceable crockery; a handsome festive water-pitcher, a *loutropheros*; and a well-painted antique wedding vase. We would have time to admire these things later. Geta enlisted help from some of the guests' slaves in order to hoist aboard two large boxes. These would contain the handmade part of the bride's dowry, clothes and blankets and tapestries of her own weaving. When this bridal luggage had been placed on board, it was time to depart – especially as the weather had temporarily relented.

Now was the moment for the abduction. A bride must be forcibly taken by the bridegroom from her parental home. My bridegroom's party was sufficiently mighty to accomplish this. We lined up in a row, myself at the top, and behind me Nikeratos, the Eumolpid and Theodoros, then Diognetos, with Philemon bringing up the rear as a strong anchor. I came to the house door, pounded on it, and we were ritually resisted, her family and friends pulling against us as we tried to seize the bride. Of course I was meant to win! The tug-of-war was short and decisive. I seized the muffled shape which must be Philomela, and pulled her away from the door, then picked her up and bore her to the cart. She screamed feebly, as a bride is supposed to do, and the women made outcry and acted lamentation and tearing of hair. I deposited the girl in the cart, and sat beside her, as the King of Hades rides off with the Maiden.

A short way from the homestead, I gave the reins to the slave, who would drive the cart, and got back on my mule. It would be rude to force my attentions on Philomela, and the journey would go faster if I rode with the other men. So we proceeded along on our mules, beside the cart and its grinning driver. Men and

boys followed, cheering and hallooing. In fact, many of
the neighbours at Smikrenes' party followed us to the
boundary, so we made a goodly procession out of
Eleusis. After we left the precincts of that little city,
people dropped away, though some of the hardier sort
were good enough to keep up with us until we passed
the bridge where I had been attacked before, and a few
stout fellows, including Biton who seemed impervious
to rain, came all the way to Athens.

I could not see Philomela at all, had only the impression of her shape within the cart. I could feel still what
she had felt like, cloaked and silent, when my arms
encircled her and I grabbed her away. I had the
impression that she had been really frightened! Her old
nurse Geta was in the cart with her – Smikrenes had
allowed that much – and the veiled wives of Thymades
and Diognetos went beside her, so she was not alone.

Coming to Athens' city walls we sang loudly and
waved garlands, so those on the watch might know we
were arriving. I was gratified to see that a number of my
neighbours had kept their word, even on this chilly day,
and were awaiting us at the city gates. Thus I had a truly
respectable wedding procession into Athens, and my
deme. We wound along through the streets to my house,
which was a scene of festivity, with lights, torches and
hubbub. I need not have worried about nobody coming.
The smell of the roast meat had wafted through my
neighbourhood, and few had resisted it.

XIII

The Wedding

I put on a clean white *khiton*; this felt necessary and good. Later, my bride (freshly washed and adorned) would be secretly taken out of the house, so we could restage the abduction and procession with all our wedding guests present. The crowd became even bigger. The *mageiros* set up the second round of sacrificed meats, and plates of specially nice food, dishes of his own make, as well as a few things prepared by my mother. A good deal of food had been sent on from the ancestral farm ahead of time, along with the best of the female slaves, who had been a great help in the preparations. The old steward Dametas and his wife Tamia came in the same cart – both wrinkled and bent, but still able to supply help in the kitchen. Some neighbours living near the farm came to the wedding also, I was happy to see.

The cool day was clearing as it neared its end, and no more rain fell. Those who had journeyed were not sorry once they saw the good cheer. I was pleased at seeing carts pulled by mules and donkeys drawing up outside my door – women of the higher class were coming. Their drivers would take the carts and animals outside the city gate, and wait for their owners. One particular cart attracted my attention: I thought it smelled of honey. The two muffled female figures who descended from it seemed the right height for Philomela's grandmother and her mother. Each was carrying something. Laughing beneath their veils, they ran into the inner house. The slave hastily went away with their equipage. Sounds of mirth came from within the house, the women's quarters.

The courtyard filled with men, including some fifth cousins who had previously been so tactful as never to bother me when we were suffering from penury and harsh accusation. But I honoured myself in being polite and hospitable to all, especially my immediate neighbours in both demes.

'Why are you having the wedding here?' one of the older men from the country asked, with disapproval. 'Your marriage should take place at the farm – your ancestral home.'

'Yes,' chimed in another, also a neighbour in the country, 'you must uphold your rights to your ancient land.'

There was something in what these men said, but as the farm was rented out part of the time, it would have been awkward.

'Such a long distance!' I said pacifically. 'Unfortunately my bride is from so far away – outskirts of Eleusis, not even the town. And she will be living here most of her married life. You know it is not proper for women to keep travelling about.'

The first man nodded sagely. 'True, and I'm glad you keep it in mind. The old rule: a married woman who has not borne children should not stir from her household.'

'Quite so,' I said, as if admiring his insight. 'Please to take some more wine.'

As the afternoon advanced quickly towards evening, I

noted that the Khian wine resumed its ancient sway. I truly feared that I would not have enough to last, and had made sure that some of our own home wine took up drinking-time first. Everybody made a good meal off the new roasted goat and ewe. The *mageiros* was in his element, and he and his assistants cut up meat at a great rate with their sharp knives.

The crowd increased as the sun dropped towards the clouds that sat on the Parnes hills. I could hardly make out who was present at my home and who was not. Indeed, it scarcely felt like home any more. In some ways it felt like being in the middle of a piece of theatre, with everybody (or almost everybody) dressed up, and myself wearing garlands. Philemon's son, four-year-old Lykias, hopped about, looking distractedly pretty, an Eros who had penetrated into my domicile, a Love that had been invited in on this damp evening. His hair was curled tightly in the wet air, golden curls and inadvertent ringlets shining in the torchlight. The women had rigged up a very fine pair of wings for this Eros, and he carried over his shoulder a tiny bow and a quiver of diminutive arrows that couldn't have harmed a lamb. In his hands my baby cousin carried a winnowing fan piled with pieces of bread, for luck, as he had been bidden; the fan was almost as big as he was. Many guests stopped the child, addressing him playfully; some even stooped to rumple his hair, which he greatly disliked. Lykias did not cry, however, but went valiantly on, until he had served all the bread, and could escape to the women's quarters.

People milled about me, offering me advice and congratulations, telling jokes. I saw – to my disgust – Lykon of Hymettos in the distance. Oh, beautiful! Now he would take note of what wealth I might have or might be expected to have, so he could sharpen his demands for damages. I know I saw Hieron there, in better condition than I had seen him last. I took pleasure in urging him to eat heartily. Diognetos, very affable, had been good enough to walk with us all the way from Eleusis, and I pressed food upon him. Lamas, with his rippling brown beard and serious expression, was much in evidence, and I thanked him warmly for coming, as I did the ruddy-faced and jovial Theophon, who towered above almost everyone else. Lamas seemed none the worse for wear, considering his adventures at my symposium, while Theophon was assured as always.

'My congratulations, Stephanos. I wish you and your bride health and good luck – and may you have healthy children.'

'But not *too* many,' said Demetrios of Phaleron, coming up in time to hear this customary good wish. 'I wish you just enough children, Stephanos. And may they all be handsome.'

Nobody could be handsomer than Demetrios himself, who was looking his best. His well-cut blond hair shone in the torchlight. The distinguished youth had put on a new garment in honour of my wedding; his presence added a certain radiance. I suppose one might almost say the same of young Menandros, who was freshly attired likewise, and stood about with his father most composedly, taking in all that occurred. If he hoped to meet members of the Lykeion, he was certainly to have his way, as they were there in force – not just Theophrastos, but Aristotle himself, and others too, like Eudemos of Rhodos, the debonair, and Hipparkhos of Argos.

'I see you have let Eros into your house, Stephanos,' said Aristotle. 'Eros comes as a visitor, but never takes up residence. Ah, me . . . How well – how very well – I wish you,' he continued, heartily gripping my shoulder. 'You deserve happiness – all the right kinds of happiness.'

'You are very kind,' I said gratefully.

'It is a great moment in your life,' the philosopher said. 'A boy becomes a man at marriage, the equal of his fellow-citizens. You acquire another person, not an equal but one who takes your interests for her own – who shares your fortunes absolutely. Give the woman sway over her own sphere – her household – and encourage her to good deeds and good management.'

'Yes, of course,' I said.

'A husband's relation to his wife is not a tyranny,' Aristotle persisted. 'Nor is it even like a monarchy. No despotism anywhere. Nature gives you simply the superiority on your side that allows you command and control. You have perhaps heard me say that the love need not be equal. It is fitting that the inferior should love more, and the rational superior love less. Your bride should love you as her superior, gratefully, with more affection than is due to her from you.'

'No,' I said. 'I hadn't heard you say that before. I suppose it is right.'

'But be sure and treat your wife with all courtesy. Consult her. Let her as far as is reasonable take charge of her own household department, and you will be the better off for it – morally and materially.'

'I don't doubt it,' I replied.

'That's what Hesiod says,' remarked Theophon, with a jolly laugh: '"First a house, then a wife and a good plough-ox." That's what a man needs to set him up.'

'Hesiod only meant, get a slavewoman to follow the ox. A good plough-ox would be better than a wife,' observed another guest sourly. 'Women – the source of all life's ills! Matrimony! What an ado at a wedding feast to celebrate a man's acquiring a mouth to swallow everything he has, and to utter scolding and abuse in return.'

'Dear me,' said Theophrastos. 'Remember where you are, man! This is a wedding, not a tavern meeting.'

'It's true enough what I say, though,' persisted this citizen. 'Scolding and swallowing – that's what they're good for. Remember how even Sokrates was plagued with his dreadful Xanthippe.' He walked away, with a glance at me of commiseration and disdain. I could not think that Xanthippe and my Philomela had much in common.

'What a boor! Some men have no respect for the proprieties,' murmured Theophrastos. I was amused at his jumping to the defence not only of me but also of marriage, for Theophrastos never spoke as one favouring marriage, and did not strike me as a man likely to wed.

'There can be anger, in the daily life of wedlock,' observed Aristotle. 'But since you are the superior, it will be easy to govern without raising your voice and shouting, still less raising your hands and hitting. Be firm. Yet in all things reasonable, take account of your wife's tastes.'

'That's what I plan to do,' I said firmly. 'Would you not like to speak to Smikrenes? And to some of his guests from Eleusis? There's the young neighbour Biton whom you should meet – a champion discus-thrower.' I tried to lead him away, towards where I saw the young man glowering, his hands like ham hocks at his side. But Aristotle wasn't finished yet.

'Don't,' he lowered his voice, 'pray don't be hard on the girl sexually. Remember, tonight is an ordeal for her, not a pleasure. Treat her with the utmost respect. And do not make request of sexual congress too readily.'

'Athenian men,' I said proudly, 'are modest and temperate in relations with our wives. We are self-controlled. We treat our wives with respect – unlike so many barbarians. An Athenian man never looks at his wife's breasts, never sees her naked.'

'Maintain temperance and respect, and enlist her cooperation,' said Aristotle. 'You are sure to do well.'

'It is a happy design,' said Eudemos of Rhodes, 'that by nature man is strong and woman weak. He goes out of the home to get provender, and she is willing to stay and guard what he has. Women are also able to labour long hours at dull and sedentary jobs – weaving for instance. Tedious but necessary. Or baby-tending. Whereas men become bored with such things and demand active occupation. Put the two together and you get the perfection of household economy.'

'Unless,' said Hipparkhos of Argos, 'the woman is peremptory and commanding – then a man is driven from his own hearthstone. Or the kind of wife who keeps hinting that she wants to have sexual conjunction. And importuning him.'

'A good Athenian wife,' I said proudly, 'would never do such a thing.' I refrained from adding, 'whatever wives may do in Argos', or making an allusion to the notorious Helen of Troy. I piloted the party towards the glowering clot of Eleusinian guests, leaving both groups to make what they could of the encounter.

'Never you mind the philosophers, my lad,' a large cheery man said, coming up to me and giving me a slap on the shoulder. 'You keep a woman nailed often enough, you make her happy and obedient.'

I wondered how long I was going to have to put up with being given advice. It scarcely seemed worthwhile being a bridegroom! Instead of making a fuss over me and reciting my works and deeds, if any, people were only too happy to tell me what to do, as if I were a novice in their mystery. At least, I thought resentfully, single men should really refrain from offering me unsolicited instruction!

I could see a gang of other gentlemen coming towards me, with Gorgias behind them, and behind him – could it be? Yes it was – Halirrhothios! I modestly withdrew,

under the pretext of having to look into the wine supply
and speak to the cook.

Soon I acquired a better excuse for my evasion.
Smikrenes encountered me, and indicated that he wished
to have speech with me. He looked flushed and
important. I believed he felt the time was approaching for
the bride to be given to the groom, and the completion of
the nuptial ceremony. I was approaching him, but before
we had spoken there was a distraction. An object came
flying out of nowhere. It whizzed between my head and
shoulder, very slightly grazing the latter, and sped on to
strike the wall, where it embedded itself. I went over to
the wall and pulled it out.

'A knife!' I said. '*Who* threw that knife?' It looked like
an ordinary implement, no fancy handles, but it was
sharp, and there was blood or something on it . . .

'Here – hi!' said the *mageiros*. 'What are you doing,
messing with my knife?' And he tried to grab it from me.

'It was *thrown* at me,' I objected. I tried to calculate
where the thrower would have been standing. It seemed
to me he could have been in the entranceway – the
courtyard door was wide open – or in the courtyard itself.
But obviously nobody had seen anyone throwing a knife,
or someone would surely have said something about it.
Nor would it do to go about and make enquiries about
knife-throwing at this happy event.

'Some fool playing around with my knife!' exclaimed
the *mageiros*. 'It's the one I use mostly to start with, for
the sacrifice you understand.'

I did, and had to give it back to him. Only Smikrenes
was impressed by the incident.

'That came too close,' he said. 'I saw it. If none of the
men here saw anything – and they're all full as wineskins by now – maybe some of the women did.' He
strode off to the roofed area by the pillars, where some

of the female slaves hung about, watching and ready to serve. I trotted after my father-in-law, trying to prevent trouble.

'Here!' he cried. 'Have any of you seen some fool throw a— Great Apollo! That's my wife's slave!'

He bounced into the covered space and grabbed hold of a small personage whom I recognised from my visits to the farm in Hymettos. Mika, house-slave of my bride's grandmother, Philokleia.

'There's no reason she shouldn't be here!' I said pacifically. Indeed, in most ordinary families it would have been in no way remarkable that the bride's grandmother should be present at the wedding, and have brought her own attendant. But these were not ordinary circumstances, and Smikrenes came to the correct conclusion. He was perhaps assisted by the fact that the voices of the women within were at that moment raised in song.

'My wife!' he cried. 'My wife Philonike! She's in there – and I am going to fetch her!'

Before I could stop him, he committed the great impropriety of plunging into the women's quarters. I followed, of necessity. There was a frightened outcry, and a flutter of female garments as the women covered and veiled themselves, and tried to get away. It was not very bright within doors, even with a number of lamps lit. But Smikrenes was not deceived. With unerring instinct, surprising really after all these years, he identified his long-lost wife, Philonike. He came up to her and she veiled herself and stood perfectly still. Shrouded and quiet as if she were Orpheus' wife Eurydike already in Hades. But then – she was not like Eurydike, who would have been glad to leave the place where she was, and get out. As soon as Smikrenes laid a hand on her, Philonike resisted with all her might.

'I'm taking you away from here!' he shouted. 'I am taking you home! Woman, you belong to me, and no one else shall have you!'

The veiled Philonike turned towards me as she still fought off the grip of her unwanted husband.

'Stephanos!' she appealed. 'You promised! Oh Demeter, save me!'

'Let go of her!' I cried. The woman now seemed to me like Persephone, caught in the deadly grip of Ploutos. And I took hold of her, and pulled her away from Smikrenes. A crowd of males had come up, attracted by all the shouting. I didn't see any possibility of keeping this family scandal quiet after this. Besides, my blood was up, and my anger high against Smikrenes, who was making such a mess of my wedding.

'Help me!' I yelled, trying to fight Smikrenes off. And the young men shouted and hallooed and joined the tug-of-war. It then became an unequal contest, Smikrenes had no one to back him up and the pulling power of my team was the greater. The young men were laughing, but of course Smikrenes was not.

'Go away, old man,' I shouted. 'Leave the women's quarters! And the rest of you too!' To my surprise and relief Smikrenes, unlike Ploutos, gave up and left. The gang of young men tumbled out too, and the noise subsided.

'I'm sorry,' I said to the ageing Persephone whom I had so oddly rescued – from her own husband! 'Tell Philomela to be ready as soon as may be.' And I too left the women's quarters and went back into the courtyard.

'That was fun,' said one of the young men. 'It's not often the abduction feels so real.'

And it was suddenly apparent to me – I must have been very slow-witted that night – that he (and the other young fellows who had joined in) thought they had been playing a part in the normal ritual. There was still a chance to conceal the embarrassing split within my bride's family. I went up to Smikrenes, drawing him aside and offering him a cup of strong wine the while.

'You shouldn't try to spoil my wedding,' I said harshly, but in a low tone.

'But my wife – my own wife! I am entitled—'

'You cause a fuss and you will make us both – *and* your daughter – the laughing stock of Athens,' I said brusquely. 'Have you no sense, man? Let's get on with the ceremony. Drink this!' And I pushed the beaker of wine between his teeth, so he spluttered and choked.

'I could still keep Philomela from you,' he said angrily.

'Yes. You could do so, and much good that would do her reputation – or yours! Don't be an idiot, Father, but do what you came here to do, and I shall be a good son to you in your old age.'

Weakened by the tug-of-war, diminished by his disappointment, and convinced unwillingly by my argument against public folly, Smikrenes consented to come with me. We went to the centre of the courtyard, and stood together until there was a hush.

'Do you give your daughter to me?' I asked.

And he replied formally: 'Before these witnesses I give my girl to you, to plough and to garner a harvest of lawful children by her. And I will give a dowry as we arranged before.'

There were cheers at this, though some inquisitive souls voiced disappointment at not being told exactly what the dowry was.

A signal let me know that the bride and her attendants were at the door of the house. Now I went out and there once more was the bride in her chariot, a bride freshly washed and made trim by a horde of eagerly assisting women. I went to the cart, and lifted her out bodily. She shrieked, if feebly. As my arms tightened about her slender form, I felt that she was genuinely frightened.

'Don't fear – it's only me!' I whispered, setting her down at the front doorway.

Her attendants now made a feint of holding her back and fighting me off, and again the young men rushed forward to offer successful help. Although they were puzzled.

'Are we doing this *again*?' I heard one say.

With gentle force and really unresisted I piloted the girl over the threshold of my house portal, and moved with her where the crowd divided to let us pass. We passed among the guests in the courtyard, myself in front, leading the girl with laggard steps, while her female attendants and companions uttered ritual protests. But I was – as I was meant to be – inexorable. I drew her on and to the door of the inner house, where the women were. The door shut behind us.

And now it was just the family and some elderly women friends who pressed about us. We led the girl to the centre of the house, to the hearth. Now I cast incense upon the flame, and prayed to the gods, and to our own household gods. Instructed by me, she did the same. Now truly Philomela would forsake her own former home, and in making these prayers she joined us, her new family. The others lifted their voices together in a special prayer, and we sang. We made our own little indoor procession, with lighted torches, and the special torch carried by my cousin, little Lykias. His wings had begun to flag, but he still looked convincingly like Eros. It was he who led us, like a little Love, up the house stairs, my bride and me. Now the bedroom door gaped, half open, the last of the house's thresholds to cross; the two of us entered the treasure house of sacred marriage. I could hear the crowd of friends outside, still making merry. But here it felt very still.

Everything was beautifully arranged. The women had seen well to that. It was clean in every corner, the bed laid with new fabrics. There was a new sheet, and then another one to replace the one that would be used straight away. I noticed on a small table the cup of comforting spices and cordials that Mother had told me about.

'That poor little girl,' she said. 'It's not such an easy job for her – far from a pleasure her first time. So give her the special drink I shall make, to recover her body and her spirits.'

'Athenian women of good family,' I protested, 'don't drink wine.'

'It isn't exactly wine, Stephanos. It has a little wine in it. And herbs – various things.'

That cup told me sternly that I must perform, and soon. I turned and looked at my bride in the light of the lamp. I wondered if she knew that she should love me as her superior with more affection than was due to her from me. I wasn't at all sure she knew this. She seemed more grown-up with her hair done, and a lovely dress on, and the women had combed her and rubbed some unguents or perfumes that made her smell delicious. She suddenly did seem very desirable. I could see she was a little pale, and she trembled. I took her hand.

'O Philomela,' I said. 'Are you willing?'

'O Stephanos,' she replied. 'Yes, I am willing.' Seeing a doubt in my eyes, she sought to reassure me.

'I know what happens,' she assured me. 'I've been to weddings in our deme. Geta told me everything. I don't mind. This has been a great day in my life. Just think – I have seen my mother!'

Her eyes shone with a love that was not kindled by Eros' torch. I dropped her hand, confused at a flux of feeling that was not for me. But then – she didn't really know me. Or I her, come to that. I felt as if I hardly knew what to do. I had never held a virgin in my arms.

'Darling,' I said, 'let us go to bed.'

And we did. There was no benefit to either of us in putting off what needed to be done – I just prayed to all the gods for good success. And so I did good work in penetrating to her inner chamber, as she had penetrated to mine. And I gave the sheet with the bloody spot to the women at the door, and they exhibited it in proof that Philomela had been a virgin, and was one no more. Cradling her head on my shoulder, I fed her the spicy drink in sips, and she drifted off to sleep, even while the shouting and dancing went on below us. I lay awake for a long while, but went to sleep before dawn. And I awoke differently from ever before, as for the first time I awoke with my wife.

XIV

After the Wedding

The wedding guests kept up the celebration as long as the food held out; late the next morning some of the most valiant were ready to greet and applaud me as I came out into the courtyard. I had a confused sense of not being quite real, as if I had turned into another self overnight. Of course I had, for I was now, as so many were willing to remind me, a husband.

'And may he soon be a father!' said many. 'Of a fine lusty boy!'

That day was the day for giving of gifts, now that the marriage had been properly consummated. Neighbours and friends, particularly women, came to the house to give things to Philomela, who appeared for the first time not in a virgin state but as a married woman. Some very nice things were brought, including fine linen sheets, and a handsome ornamented *pyxis* for her to keep jewellery or trinkets in. There were useful household utensils – a good portable cookstove (was this really from her grandmother?) and a fine sturdy washing basin. That would certainly come in handy. I was more puzzled by the appropriateness of some other things: a scent bottle in the shape of a foot, for instance, which I could not like at all.

In the first part of the day the neighbours and friends were still coming, and there were snatches of song from the women's quarters. But as the sun turned westward again, the food was gone, and all the wineskins and pots had given up their lifeblood. Then the remaining guests wisely departed. Some went towards the city gates staggering and rolling in their gait, even though it was daytime. But as there were wedding celebrations all over the city and throughout the country demes, this condition would not call for unkind remark.

In the women's quarters the singing and dancing were done. The few women who now remained, like Philemon's Melissa, were working with their slaves in the kitchen, washing dishes and putting things away. Little Lykias had been overtaxed partly by his performance, but more truly by good eating. The foolish Eros had revelled in figs and dates and was now curled up with a tummy-ache, looking truly pathetic. My mother was busy tidying the store-room – as she always did after any big occasion or at times of anxiety. My bride, pale and fatigued, had joined the working women. If she had hoped to find her own mother among them, she was disappointed; Philokleia and Philonike had long ago slipped away, I suppose at first light, taking Dropides with them.

The *mageiros* then presented me with his bill of charges, a shock which would have made my head ache without any further cause. Having paid this, and wondering gloomily how I would retrieve my financial position once again, I was able to wander about in the last light of evening and note how much damage had been done. The *andron*, used by the men as an indoor gathering place, had not been filled with furniture, so no couches had been ruined. The floors were very dirty, and a great deal of wine had got thrown at the wall again. A couple of cups had been shattered. My favourite plate had been broken, the antique one with fish swimming about it, and one of the borrowed platters had also been smashed beyond repair. Little fragments of grease and bone, and date and olive stones, lay about in unexpected corners. There were various greasy marks about the wall of the courtyard. Most mysterious of all, there was a large notch in one of the supportive pillars of the roofed section of the courtyard.

I brooded on this, thinking of the thrown knife. Had somebody flung something at me when I was standing by one of these pillars – and I hadn't known about it? And then had this person tried again, with a little better success, when I was standing beside Smikrenes?

It really seemed foolish to imagine that somebody had been trying to kill me during my wedding! Or, say, just before consummation. Ridiculous! Still, there had been a number of things thrown lately: the clods and stones, the knife. There was that strange incident of the fallen tile. But objects do fall from roofs naturally, while blood-stained butcher's knives don't by nature whiz through the air. Had I any enemies? Perhaps. Was it Biton of Eleusis? He who had hoped to marry Smikrenes' daughter, and get his meaty hands on those fine lands. Or perhaps it was the abusive Lykon, my in-laws' neighbour in Hymettos who wanted to sue over land rights. But he could use the law courts. There was also my own deme's Halirrhothios – but I put that thought hastily away. His coming to the wedding was surely a sign of forgiveness, or at least toleration. He had come as a neighbour, and surely neighbours don't go around throwing knives at the host during parties. Or do they?

Then there was Theophon. I remembered that Theophon had been athletically trained – the *mageiros* had been his trainer once upon a time. Presumably that training included javelin-throwing. Theophon was a strong fellow. What could he have against me? The *mageiros*' knife was definitely lethal, and the knife-throwing seemed more serious than the other incidents.

'You're not looking too well, Stephanos,' my mother remarked. 'You should look more jovial on your bridal day. Drunk too much last night, I dare say.'

'I dare say,' I replied, not wanting an argument. This was the evening of one of the year's shortest days, and at least we could go to bed early. When I said as much, gales of laughter blew through the party, including the slaves Tamia and Dametas and the rest. But cousin Philemon wisely took his family back to their home, and my bride and I retired to rest. In consideration of her soreness I did not require sexual favours that night.

The next day things returned to normal. At least in a sense, for they would never again be normal in the old way. My days would not be an unmarried man's days. I went to the Agora and did some shopping, braving the comments and laughing heartily. Within a few days my presence in the Agora excited no comment at all on my marital state. Nobody threw anything at me either. The walls of the *andron* were washed, and all the floors cleaned, and Dametas and Tamia and the farm girl went back to the farm with their empty cart. Serenity was restored – so I thought.

'That girl of yours is moping,' Mother said tartly.

'Oh? I thought she was happy here.'

'She's a worker, I'll say that for her,' Mother conceded. 'But she's used to labouring outdoors like any peasant girl. You can see her skin isn't white; it will take a while for her to look like an Athenian lady. She must keep out of the sun and wind. She sighs a good deal. I'm sure,' said Mother, sighing herself, 'that I have looked forward to having a daughter-in-law to wait on me. But it seems as if I'm waiting on her, trying to find what will please her.'

'Give her time,' I pleaded. 'She can scarcely be pining after old Smikrenes. It's just the change of her circumstances – give her time.'

I asked my bride, in the presence of my brother, mother and the slave, to cook some barley cheesecakes. I knew she made these well – and she did, so I praised them lavishly. But this had an unintended effect.

'I don't know what's wrong with *my* cakes, that you've eaten with pleasure all these years, Stephanos!' Mother burst out. 'If you had a fault to find with them, you only had to say.'

'He didn't mean that, Mama,' said Theodoros.

'Who knows *what* he means?' retorted Mother bitterly. Philomela burst into tears.

I led her away and dried her eyes. 'I'm sorry!' she kept exclaiming.

'You did what I asked of you, and very well too,' I said. 'So there's nothing to be sorry about.'

'Oh but there is!'

Philomela started weeping again, big tears spilling out of her lovely eyes. 'I miss my home!' she said passionately. 'I'm sorry, but I do.'

'You'll get over it,' I assured her. 'After all, you must have known you'd be married sometime, and leave your father.'

'Oh yes.' She sniffed and dried her eyes. 'I was glad it was you, and not Biton. And when I thought earlier – you know when – that maybe Father wouldn't let us get married, I was – well, unhappy. I thought people would say, "Philomela must be an ugly girl, or quite stupid, as her family cannot marry her off." And I didn't want it to be anybody but you, anyway.'

I felt pleased at this. 'So,' I said. 'Nothing is really

wrong. You're here – we're married. You will soon settle down.'

She shook her head. 'It's harder than you think.' I thought that she must mean settling in with Mother was harder to bear than she'd anticipated; it would be too bitter to think she found life with me more difficult than she had envisaged. 'And,' my bride continued, 'I'm really lonely!'

'You cannot mean that! There are more people here than at your house – your father's house.'

'Yes, yes, I know. But . . .' her tears spilled over again, 'I had *always* imagined going away from home with Geta with me. Long ago, when I was quite little, Geta told me that when girls marry they take their old nurse with them. So I'd always *planned* on having Geta, you see.'

'I did too,' I admitted. 'I mean, I had imagined you would bring Geta, and we would acquire an extra pair of hands. I asked Smikrenes, but he just said no.'

Philomela shook her head sorrowfully. 'It was a great shock when Father told me it wasn't to be. I begged and coaxed, but Papa doesn't like people who beg and coax. He told me if I kept it up I'd know what it was to have a father still, for I'd be well whipped. And then I was afraid for myself and even more for Geta, who might be flogged for having entreated me, so I said no more. But – oh, I do miss her so!'

'I understand,' I replied. 'Yet I do not see what I can do to change that. Now, please, I pray you, Philomela, do not go about with a tear-stained and sorrowful face. For the neighbours will get to know about it – you'd be surprised how soon they find out such things!' I paused to smooth her hair. 'The slaves will know, and then the women. And straight away the men will hear about it, and folks here in Athens will say that I mistreat you – or that I have proved impotent and you are at your wits' end.'

She gave a shaky laugh at this, and valiantly tried to smile. 'O Stephanos – I do not wish people to say bad things about you. Or about any of us, indeed.' She caught my hand. 'I know you do a lot for us, and that my father could hardly have hoped for a better match. I am aware of that, truly. And through you I have been reunited once more with my own mother, which is so wonderful! Beyond anything I could have hoped. So I am grateful indeed!'

'Think nothing of it,' I said awkwardly.

'O Stephanos, my mother made such a wonderful suggestion. I don't know whether now is the time to talk of it or not. But Philonike my mother has been initiated into the Mysteries, and she wants me to be!'

'You – into the Mysteries of Eleusis?'

'Yes. You know I have lived in Eleusis all my life, and I have wanted since I was a little girl to be initiated into the Mysteries. People talk of it often, and say how wonderful it is.'

'You weren't old enough.'

'That's right. And even if I had been, Papa would never have allowed it. It costs money – I don't know how much. But Mother will pay for me whenever I can do it. And I would like to do it *soon*, so Mother and I could go together. Mother was initiated several years ago – a gift from her brother – but she wants to complete the second stage. She could go for the second stage as one of the *epoptai*, the Seers, while I go for the first. It brings immortal life, and freedom from the cares of the world – even for slaves.'

I could feel my brow tense into a frown. 'My dear girl, this is an odd request. You know a woman – a woman of good birth and breeding – is not supposed to go jaunting about and travelling until she is not only married but has borne a child or two.'

'But even single women go to be initiated,' she protested. 'You have to be fifteen and understand Greek and not have committed murder. I am past my fifteenth birthday – I am almost sixteen! My mother is so much older than me, one cannot be sure how long she has to live. And now I am married, I might die in childbearing, like the daughter of our neighbour. *She* married a man of the deme Phaleron by the sea, and went to live there, and died within a year of her first child. She went off so fast that nobody could get to her deathbed, which is sad, isn't it?'

'Very,' I said. 'But you are healthy, and our plans do not include your dying.'

She laughed, another shaky laugh. 'Mine neither. Though I cannot help thinking of it – it is more real now. Since the other night, you know. I would like *you*, my husband, to be an initiate too.'

'Me? Good Apollo, whatever next!'

'Yes. Because then you would have immortal life too. It would be *dreadful* if you got to Hades and couldn't find me because I was somewhere reserved for the initiates. Let's be together, Stephanos.'

'You are a wheedler and coaxer,' I said, as sternly as I could. 'You are using me in order to be able to be with your mother Philonike.'

She shook her head. 'No. Truly, I think of you too, just as much as Mama. For you will be in my life always. I believe that you want me to be happy now. But wouldn't it be wonderful if we could be happy for ever?'

'I'd settle for the rest of this month,' I said drily. But I stroked her cheek as I said it.

'I shall not be silly any more,' she said, stroking my hand in return. 'I promise not to go about looking sad or weeping. I don't want people to say bad things about us – about you! As for impotence – they wouldn't say anything so foolish! I will not cry again.'

'There's my good girl. And you do bake beautiful cakes!' I embraced her with true affection. I suddenly felt how nice it would be if we could go to bed now – but couples of good class and breeding and noble manners do not lie together in the afternoon. So I sent her back to the women's quarters with an extra kiss, and was left to ponder the situation by myself.

I was not allowed to enjoy my own company, however unsatisfactory that might be, very long, for Mother came with more complaints. She was wise enough not to begin with Philomela, but focused on the state of the house and the broken dishes, and her trouble in explaining to a neighbour how a borrowed plate got smashed. I needed to get out of the house. When I left, I found my footsteps taking me to the familiar Lykeion.

I knew very well that it is not the part of a well-bred man to speak to friends of any marital difficulties. Had I found Aristotle with company, even if only Eudemos or Theophrastos, I should have held my tongue about personal affairs. But Aristotle was alone, poring over a scroll in his own courtyard. It was kind of him to seem delighted to see me when I had interrupted his precious time of reading – the winter light is so short. After one look at me he rose and led the way into his own comfortable room with its display of handsome pots and its many rolls of books.

'So, Stephanos. You look tired and a trifle sad. Are you spent? Trials of matrimony too much for you?'

'No,' I said stoutly. 'I am glad, very glad, to be married to Philomela. But I don't think my mother is really happy about it, and that makes some little problems.'

He laughed. 'It is well known that a woman who has been the manager of her kitchen and store-room does not welcome a competitor, let alone a successor. It will certainly take your mother some while to get used to it.

But I should have thought your bride such a gentle creature.'

'She is. Oh yes, she is! But she is so very young yet, and she misses her home. Meeting her own mother was a great shock too. I don't know why I bother you with these trivial affairs of women!'

Aristotle listened with his usual courtesy. 'It is right that you turn to someone who has been married – happily married,' he answered reassuringly. 'You have no father. And your father-in-law is certainly not going to stand in that position to you.'

'Certainly not! Indeed, I blame Smikrenes for much of the trouble – I mean for the low spirits of Philomela. For I think she could become perfectly happy if she could only have her old nurse Geta with her.'

'Has she expressed a desire for this?'

'Most certainly. She begged Smikrenes to let her take Geta when she married, but he threatened her with whipping if she troubled him further about the matter. I too tried earlier to persuade him to allow Geta to come. But he says he needs someone to look after him – meals and clothes and housekeeping – as he was losing his daughter.'

'Hmm.' Aristotle fitted his fingers together. 'So all Smikrenes needs is the service – the individual person is not material?'

'Just so, that's all,' I replied firmly. 'It's not as if old Geta were his bed-companion or something like that.' (I regretted these words as soon as they left my mouth; too late I recollected Aristotle's own position. To cover this blunder, I ran hastily on.) 'I cannot afford to buy him a slave in replacement – though I wish I could. But although our prospects are now good, since Philomela and I have married, we are not well off. Indeed, Smikrenes has promised to pay for part of the wedding party at my house. After all, he couldn't have nearly as many guests at Eleusis, and it is most important for all of us that Athens accept Philomela and myself as legally and publicly married.'

'Aha!' Aristotle's face broke into a smile, and he shook his head, quite in the old manner, though the hair that once looked so fiery was now heavily tinged with grey. 'So there we are. Smikrenes owes you money?'

'One couldn't say *owe*. It is a debt of a kind, a fulfilment of a promise. I couldn't lodge a court complaint about it if he refused to pay. Yet I think he will.'

'Aha! Then go to the Eleusinian farmer, with greatest courtesy, and show him the bills for the wedding party. He will doubtless foam and fume, but will give you the money – or a portion of it. Then immediately return the money to him, as payment for a slave, *if* he gives you Geta. After all, she is only a female slave. Not only that, she is old and decrepit, not of value on the market. He could easily replace her – or by paying a little more he could get a smart lad who can do housework and some fieldwork as well.'

'I will try it!' I said, struck by his suggestion. 'It probably won't work, but it's worth the attempt. Although I shall then be very hard up. The wedding cost a purseful, I can tell you. Still, I dare say the family in Hymettos will help us out a bit. Especially if I can take a strong stand and solve the problem posed by Lykon and his complaints about the land rights.'

'There. You see, you have many remedies at your disposal. Your little bride needs time and sleep. Proper exercise too, as she is used to fresh air. Let her go with other women to some shrine or other that will give them an excuse for a walk.'

'She doesn't want to go to any local shrine,' I exclaimed. 'She has another idea. She seems to be full of them, my bride. She wants to be initiated into the Mysteries of Eleusis. And she wants me to join her!'

'What put that into her head?'

'Her mother. It turns out Philonike is an initiate, and would like to take the second or completing initiation, as one of the Seers. But I think mother and daughter would merely like to do something together. Yet – I am unfair to my bride. She has been bred in Eleusis, and heard of the Mysteries all her life. She hoped for initiation, though she knew Smikrenes wouldn't pay for the luxury.'

'Stephanos, really you should not ask *me* about this. A decision regarding religion is outside the sphere of the philosopher or the household economist. Besides, at this juncture I become an interested party.'

'You do? How?'

'As my own Herpyllis is going to be initiated into the Mysteries, I would naturally be glad of some good women whom she could join. Although your bride and her mother might think Herpyllis beneath them, yet she is a modest and well-behaved person. The Mysteries are open to all, slave or free.'

'At that rate,' I grumbled, 'I could find myself having to pay for Geta's initiation as well! I know from your engagement of Thymades how much that costs.'

Aristotle laughed. 'And you'd have to find a Eumolpid of your own.'

'You mean, for Philomela? I suppose I could easily do that,' I replied, remembering Diognetos' offer of assistance.

I took Aristotle's advice. First, I persuaded my bride and my mother to join with some neighbour women in walking to a shrine in the next deme, so my girl would have some fresh air and a little exercise. The women were well guarded and went properly veiled, so no one could

censure them. Both my bride and Mother were in better
humour after this. Theodoros had earlier offered to teach
Philomela to read, and now began his task; she already
knew some of her letters. I was not against this project.
Some folk say no woman should be able to read, for they
simply abuse the art and write love-letters, but it was
clear to me that illiterate Athenians of both sexes
managed adultery sufficiently easily without epistles.

I went again to Hymettos, and received a small
advance on the land use and the honey next summer, as
well as a money gift for myself and Philomela. The whole
family assented with emphatic agreement to the idea that
Philomela should become an initiate in the Mysteries,
and Philonike promised to pay for that as a separate gift.
She had some funds coming to her, though all expend-
itures should eventually be explained to Philomela's
uncle Philokles, who owned the land and nominally at
least was in charge of all its revenues.

I then forced myself to tackle Smikrenes, who seemed
more growly than ever. Earth and sky were grey, and the
rain came steadily down on his Eleusinian fields. We
went indoors; there was now no need to keep up an area
for the women's quarters, as the only female resident was
the old slave. We sat in the kitchen over a smoky fire,
with Geta to bring us food. I realised his house seemed a
lonely place without his daughter – and now I proposed
to detach him from his last companion. Yet I hardened
my heart, and performed as Aristotle had suggested.
Smikrenes was of course horrified when I showed him the
bills for the party, and was particularly scathing regarding the charges of the *mageiros* and the outrageous luxury
of the wine from Khios.

'Foolishness,' he grumbled. 'Why waste good wine on
a bunch of tipplers who would scarcely know what they
had in their mouths as long as it made their heads spin?'

'Because,' I replied, 'I wanted a good wedding, well attended by reputable people of Athens from within the walls as well as of external demes. A wedding that none could ever challenge. You know how many lawsuits hinge on legitimate descent, and how hard it goes on some citizens when nobody can remember their parents' wedding, or when it was! Our children and their descendants must be properly established in Athens for ever. Not too big a price to pay for that, is it?'

'Well, I'll pay something. I'm not going to pay a whole half,' he said, waiting for me to dispute. I said nothing. Muttering under his breath, he went into an inner room and quickly returned.

'Three hundred drakhmai and no more!' He counted the coins reluctantly upon the table in little piles. They were good silver, handsome owls of Athens.

'Now!' I exclaimed. 'You see all this silver you have given me?' I swept the coins into my own pouch. 'Beautiful coins, weren't they? Would you like them back?'

'What d'ye mean?'

'I shall give them back to you – if you will let me have Geta in exchange!'

'What? By Herakles, what sort of trick are you trying to play?'

'No trick at all. Your daughter misses her old nurse very much. It is unusual for a nicely bred Athenian girl of good standing not to be able to bring her old nurse along with her when she marries. I want Philomela to be happy. That's all.'

'Oh, master!' Geta overthrew a pan she was holding in her excitement. She stumbled over and clasped Smikrenes' knees. 'Oh, master, do please, please let me go to her!'

'Stop your whining, woman! Look what you just did! I don't know, the world's going mad about my ears.'

'Please, O Smikrenes of Eleusis, my father-in-law – do this one thing for your daughter. Her happiness is now my affair. I can buy the servant from you.' I pushed the heaps of coins across the table towards him. 'With these coins back in your purse you can purchase a servant who costs much more than Geta would fetch now. You could find a young man, perhaps, who can do housework and fieldwork both. Or a younger woman who is sturdy enough for planting and tilling, as well as fetching water, cooking, washing and so on.'

'*Ai!* You are all too many for me. Philomela has got round you – wives have more weapons than daughters do. And I shall have all the trouble of rearranging my household.' Smikrenes spat on the floor. 'A bad business. Still, what difference does it make what an old fellow like me has or doesn't have? Take the woman, take the coins! – and leave an old man to his misery!'

I didn't linger to console or advise him. It seemed hard-hearted, but I took him at his word, and hastened to depart before he changed his mind. I ordered Geta to fetch her things quickly and we were off. I had brought a donkey with me on the chance that I might succeed, and although it is mightily irregular I let Geta ride most of the way while I walked, simply for the sake of speed. The rainy winter day was drawing to its grey close by the time we got to the city – Geta gaping and exclaiming at the city walls, and at the size of the market.

In triumph I walked through our portal and summoned my wife to meet me. She came readily enough, my slender bride, her hair done up in becoming curls, and the soft light in her grey-green eyes. I was glad to know she rejoiced to see me before I showed her the treasure I had brought.

'Look what I have for you!' I drew aside, and showed her Geta – who did not wait like a mute in a play but sprang into action, embracing her mistress and kneeling at her feet, crying the while.

'Geta! You have brought me Geta! Oh, thanks be to the Two Goddesses! And to you my husband – thank you! Thank you!' Then Philomela threw her arms about me and kissed me, the first time she had kissed me first. I was glad there were not many hours of the day left before we would once more ascend to our nuptial couch.

XV

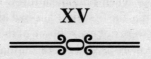

Obstruction, Instruction, and a Head

Home life settled down, though not without strain. My mother seemed more snappish than usual, which I set down in part to her fatigue after the wedding, and in part to the presence of Geta. Despite her protestations of humble gratitude, Geta was in the habit of expressing her mind very freely, and used to doing things her own way. She would take orders, to be sure, but only from Philomela. When Mother told her to do something, Geta would ask Philomela if this was indeed what she wanted. Even the sweetest nature finds such treatment galling. Of course, now Mother did have what she had formerly longed for – an extra pair of hands for various tasks. But this did not seem to give her as much pleasure as I had expected.

Philomela, on the other hand, had to get used to Mother as a constant superior. 'I know,' I said to my young bride, 'that you are used to being the mistress of your father's household, and it is odd to have a senior woman to look up to and to guide you. But this fact absolves you of many responsibilities and anxieties. You may come to find it agreeable.'

'Maybe,' she said, in tones in which doubt and duty mixed.

'Find something to do that is useful and pleasant. There are many things to do in the house!'

'Yes,' she agreed, 'that's certainly true. You need some cushions and couch covers. I'm glad I brought many coverlets with me. I was surprised, I thought the houses of the citizens in the city would be beautifully furnished and decorated. I shall make some linens for the family and then go on to an ornamental hanging, to make the place beautiful. How would that be?'

'Very good,' I agreed. 'But I wouldn't find any fault – at least not in Mother's hearing – with our current possessions. Perhaps, however, it might cheer you more to start with the ornamental hanging – why not do that first?'

'Oh, yes, if you wish it,' she said, brightening. 'I shall dye some wools in beautiful colours. I think I shall weave a basic design and then embroider upon it. A pattern of birds in flight, I think. Birds of different kinds.'

And soon I heard the thump-thump of the loom, and saw my pretty bride standing beside it, the loom weights dangling as a fringe, earnestly at work at what would undoubtedly become a large piece of fabric. Mother approved of this venture – which left her free in the kitchen to order Geta as she chose, and to find consolation in cookery.

But this was not the only difficulty that confronted me.

'You haven't said what you will do,' Philomela said to me reproachfully.

'About what?'

'Why, about Eleusis, of course! Our being initiated. You as well as me.'

'Well,' I said heavily, 'I will do it – but it is an extra expense.'

'Oh,' she said. 'Too bad! Couldn't we sell some of my bride-gifts to pay for it?'

'No indeed! The idea! People would think we were little better than beggars! No, I can manage it – though I am afraid I will accept the kind offer of your mother and grandmother to pay for you.'

'Oh!' She clasped her hands in earnest happiness. 'How beautiful! We will be initiated together – wonderful! Don't we have to do something soon – at Anthesterion?'

'Yes. Our Eleusinian guide and instructor will tell us what to do.'

I spoke as if this was all taken care of, though in fact it was not. But I intended to make use of Diognetos of Eleusis. He had shown good sense during the fateful night when we went into Hieron's house and discovered the terrible scene. Since that time, he had come to my symposium, and then to my wedding festival. So we really counted as friends. I didn't want to confront an unknown Eleusinian and entrust him with myself and Philomela. Diognetos of the clan of the Kerykes, related also to the Hierophant of the Two Goddesses and to Eleusis' ceremonial torchbearer, the Daidoukhos, was eminently suited to act as a mystagogue. A much higher personage than the commonplace Thymades whom Aristotle had selected. I decided to go to Eleusis specifically to seek Diognetos out, and make my request.

As I approached Eleusis I thought of something else hitherto undone. I had promised the poor boy who was Sophilos' nephew that I would give him something. A promise unperformed. As I was setting my life straight, ought I not to make some effort to fulfil my word, even to those wretched poor people? The boy Strabax was after all a citizen of Eleusis, and thus of Athens, though he was so very poor.

It cost more time and trouble to find where Strabax and

his mother lived than to give them the money. When I mentioned Sophilos and Strabax, some Eleusinians indicated they knew no such persons. Perhaps, I thought, only good memories and nice people were recorded in Eleusis. I did remember the road the wretched pair and the corpse-containing donkey-cart had taken, so when I got a reasonable answer I was pretty certain it was right. From that road I turned down a muddy byway, then plunged past skinny lanes and houses until I came to a very meagre home indeed. A hovel, scarcely large enough for a man to stand up in, with a roof of brush and furze that must have let in the winter rains. I stood outside and hallooed (rather rudely) for Strabax. An elderly goose came round the corner, bobbed her head curiously at me and retired, deciding evidently that she had not been sent for.

At last the poor widow came out of her house. She wore a thick head-covering like sacking, keeping her face deeply shadowed; it was almost as good as a veil. She stood before me humbly, her head bowed. Her coarse woollen homespun seemed moderately clean but full of darns and variegated with patches.

'You call my son, Strabax? My Strabax is not here.'

'He is working, then, is he? That's good. Who employs him?'

'He's going for a merchant . . .' She corrected herself. 'No, he has gone to work for a farmer hereabouts. My Strabax is a good worker. He worked for that farmer before when he was a boy, keeping off crows and foxes. Good with a slingshot. Now he has promised to be his shepherd.'

'I am sorry not to see him,' I said with false heartiness. 'A fine lad. But you will do as well. All I wish to do is to fulfil my promise to Strabax, and give him something, as I said I would do. There is no reason why you cannot be the recipient.'

I took two silver drakhmai out of my little money pouch, and held them out to her. She seized them and bit them, then visibly smiled.

'Oh, thank you, sir, thank you! What a good Athenian gentleman! Yes, for my poor Strabax, my good boy. And my poor old Sophilos. Please – you must believe, man of Athens, that Sophilos was no thief. A beggar, but no thief.'

'Nothing more has been done about the killing?'

'No. No one takes pity on us. We should have compensation for homicide, but they didn't really try to find the killer. We buried my brother, but no one – hardly anyone – came to the funeral. People say harsh things. Even though they should know better.'

'I regret your misfortunes,' I said awkwardly.

'*I* regret our misfortunes,' she said frankly, throwing her shawl suddenly back and looking me almost in the face, in a defiant manner. Her dark eyes were clear and piercing, and I had an impression of deep and even dangerous feeling. 'I am sorry that we do not know who killed him. *Revenge.* Revenge is for the poor as well as the rich. My brother was wrongfully killed, that's certain. Do *you* know more about it?'

'I know nothing,' I said. 'Nothing, at least, more than I told the Demarkh here.'

'Somebody knows,' she insisted. '*Somebody* in Eleusis knows. I wish they would question the seller of marble, that Melanthios. He makes gravestones – he'd better be careful, or the gods will send him a gravestone for himself, before he wishes it. I *know* my brother never stole a purse from a shop! They should question that marble man.'

'Probably nothing more would transpire if they did question him,' I replied. 'There are enigmas in life. I regret your loss. Please convey my best wishes to your son Strabax. I shall probably see him some time. Meanwhile, tell him I gave money.'

'Yes,' she said but with a new tone of doubt in her voice. 'Ye-es – but there is no need for *you* to talk with my boy, sir. He is not fishing for a rich lover or anything of that sort.'

I felt most affronted at my gesture of goodwill being taken in such bad part. And if she were so virtuous, why didn't she return my two drakhmai?

'I had nothing of that sort in mind, my good woman, I do assure you,' I said in my loftiest tones. 'It is no pleasure to *me* to come down miry lanes to seek out persons living as you do. Only a sense of duty drove me, because of a casual promise to your wretched child, and pity for the deep misfortune into which you all have fallen. Good day to you.'

And I flounced off through the mire and the goose droppings of the yard, while she stared after me, still clutching the coins.

After that encounter with the poorest of the poor in a back district of Eleusis, it was some comfort to me to return to the town and betake myself to a prosperous dwelling. Diognetos lived near the Sanctuary, in a fine house of two storeys; one could probably catch a view of the sea from the upstairs rooms. This friendly citizen had a comfortable *andron*, and a little fire burned in a brazier, very welcome in the winter chill. He kindly offered me a cup of wine even before he knew why I had come. Diognetos himself looked well, his beard combed and his dark hair intelligently cut, despite the receding hairline. This Eleusinian appeared to advantage in his abode, the home of a cultivated man. There were ornamental pots in niches, some plaques on the wall of the *andron*, and some books in a good book-bucket. Not that this was the time for peering into scrolls – unless one were Theophrastos, who picked up any and all books whenever he found himself in their vicinity. But Diognetos seemed the kind of person from whom one could get good and mature counsel.

'I am pleased to see you, Stephanos,' said Diognetos. 'I regret that I have not returned your kind hospitality before this time. What a delightful dinner party we had at your house! And I greatly enjoyed your wedding feast. I trust you and your bride are well?'

'Yes, indeed,' I said. 'It is, in fact, on behalf of both of us that I come to you with what may seem a bold request.'

'Dear me, Stephanos, I should be very glad to assist to the extent of my small power.'

'I hope you won't mind,' I said lamely. 'But my wife wishes to become initiated – wishes both of us to undertake initiation, in fact. And you did once offer to act in such an instance – you are an Eleusinian of the tribe of Kerykes, and I know you are an initiate yourself. I don't really know other Eleusinians very well—'

'Except your father-in-law,' Diognetos finished for me. 'A good sort of fellow, but not an initiate. I have the impression he takes little interest in our religion. Dear, this could be awkward, Stephanos. We of Eleusis are pressed with invitations to act as *mystagogoi*. People from many parts of the world desire our sponsorship. As you know, each Eleusinian can undertake to guide only one candidate each year. I had already promised myself, long ago, for this year. To another friend, a merchant.'

I am sure my face fell. 'It was too much to hope for,' I said, realising to the full my error in assuming it would be easy to find a *mystagogos* at this late date. 'I am sorry to have troubled you at all.' And I began, foolishly to struggle to my feet, thus rudely indicating that I valued my supposed friend for only one thing.

'Do not look so disconsolate, Stephanos. Pray sit down again. I was about to relate the fresh turn affairs have taken. Only two days ago I heard from this merchant – who sent me a letter saying he was soon off to Byzantion on one of his own ships and might have to stay there or in Asia for some while. This merchant wishes to postpone initiation to the following year. So – you find me unexpectedly free and at your disposal!'

'Oh, that's very good,' I said, greatly relieved.

'I should be delighted, Stephanos, to act as your *mystagogos*. And my wife can undertake the task for your wife; she is well-trained and has been many times a mystagogue. It is always a good thing when husband and wife undertake initiation at the same time – bond of unity.'

'Family concord – that sort of thing.'

'Quite right. So we in Eleusis think. Not that I would ever try to force or even urge initiation upon anyone. It must be undertaken of *free choice*. You understand? The woman concerned – your bride – is a Greek-speaker and of age?'

'Yes. She is a native of Eleusis and will be sixteen on her next birthday, which is soon.'

'Forgive me, but before I speak to my own wife I must be satisfied that your little bride has decided of her own accord to become an initiate.'

'You may indeed say so!' I exclaimed. 'Most heartily. In fact, it is *she* who has convinced me to join in – not the other way around.'

Diognetos nodded where he sat. 'It must be entirely a matter of *choice* – and on your part also,' he emphasised. 'One of my acquaintance is undertaking initiation merely because he promised his father that he would. That seems to me slightly wrong – though perhaps I take too strenuous a view.' Diognetos fitted his hands together, fingertip to fingertip, in a judicious and responsible manner. 'You are obviously of age, and we need not enquire whether you are a speaker of Greek. Before we turn to the religious matters – the essence and the cream – we ought to get the practical arrangements out of the way.'

'I know about the clean clothes and shoes,' I interjected. 'And piglets to be sacrificed for the purification at Agrai and then for the Greater Mysteries.'

'Just so. For the Greater Mysteries, you will each be dressed in new – if cheap – mourning garments. It is customary to sacrifice these to Demeter after initiation, so bring some other clothes to Eleusis with you. You have to take to Eleusis a sack of meal for offering. We should instruct you and your wife in the hymns and prayers beforehand, and be with you at Agrai, as well as on the road to Eleusis.'

'Yes please. I think that is as it should be.'

'It will cost seventy drakhmai for the two of you – pigs and priests and all included. And my services.'

'Seventy! I thought thirty drakhmai a person was the going rate!'

'Yes, but . . .' Diognetos raised a hand in a deprecating manner. 'Consider! Both my wife and I must journey from Eleusis twice – at the very least – for preparation and twice for the rituals. You are asking us to take charge of two persons – one of them a young woman of citizen rank. This is a great responsibility – it's not like seeing to a slavewoman, or even the citizen wife of someone of common condition. Your position in life, Stephanos, is not a low one.'

'Hmm,' was all I said in return.

'But there – as you are a friend, I don't mind abating the price. Say sixty-five drakhmai? You know the priests will charge fifteen drakhmai per person, with no abatement for couples. And we – my wife and I – offer personal attendance every step of the way.'

'Very kind of you. But I agree to pay the seventy drakhmai, as suggested.' Mature reflection instructed me that it would not do to seem niggardly and penurious in dealing with such an important personage.

'Now, I hope you know the story of Demeter and Persephone?'

'To be sure I do. Absolutely. I heard it most recently from Thymades.'

'Oh yes, Thymades. A good sort of fellow. The *mystagogos* of Aristotle of the Lykeion.'

I felt obliged to correct him. 'No, no. Aristotle isn't becoming a *mystes*. He just went to Thymades so his slave, who is to be initiated, could be guided by Thymades' wife.'

'I think you will find, Stephanos, that Aristotle has decided himself to be initiated. Probably the woman persuaded him. Thymades is to be the philosopher's *mystagogos*, while Thymades' wife sponsors his slave-woman. You will find,' Diognetos added with a twinkle, 'that we here in Eleusis are pretty reliable on such matters.'

My jaw had dropped slightly, I have no doubt, and I sat in silence. Imagine! A slave like Herpyllis persuading Aristotle.

'Thymades is most able,' Diognetos continued smoothly. 'Popular as a *mystagogos*, too, though one wonders what he does with the income, he lives in such a small way. And so you heard the story of Persephone from my good friend Thymades. Does your bride know the story?'

'As my bride is an Eleusinian, I don't see how she could grow up not knowing.'

'Very good. Then I need not at this moment repeat this strong and beautiful tale to you. You must be careful to tell the story to your bride, so she has a good version fresh in mind. In any case, the preliminary event, the first taste of the Mysteries, will include a great deal of instruction. At that time I shall officially tell you, as my duty directs, and my wife will tell your bride, of the story and its significance. I allude of course first to the Lesser Mysteries, a rite dedicated more particularly to the Maiden. The first rite, of purification and instruction, takes place beside the Ilissos during the time of the Flower Festival at the very first edge of spring. Be warned — you will both have to step into the flowing Ilissos, and the river is cold at that time of the year.'

'Yes, I've seen people gathering by the river for that — I suppose all my life.'

'You have certainly left your arrangements to the last moment. The Lesser Mysteries begin less than a month from now. Prepare as quickly as possible. Don't forget the nine days' fast beforehand.'

'What should we do now?'

'Start by learning the hymns. Ah! I have it. I shall give you a copy of the hymns and prayers so you can repeat them over, and teach your wife.' He hunted about among his scrolls. 'Yes — here it is. And you have no bag to keep it in? I pray, allow me to lend you this little leather sack, which will keep the writings from the weather.'

'Thank you,' I said, meekly accepting both script and bag. 'We shall come prepared to Agrai,' I assured him. Though my heart sank as I thought of the expense of pigs and sacrificial incense.

'It is a grand occasion,' Diognetos said, looking at me earnestly. 'I can see you regret at the moment the expense of time, trouble and money. But you will be glad for the rest of your life that you have done this great thing. Once you have been through the Lesser Mysteries, you will feel as if you can hardly wait until Boedromion, and the great days of pilgrimage.'

'Yes, I suppose that will be – I mean, I can imagine it working like that.'

'Do not look so anxious, Stephanos!' Diognetos smiled. 'I am very pleased to have this chance to serve you, to conduct you to Demeter and Kore and the sacred freedom which you will experience. We often have the chance to do our friends and acquaintances a good turn. But what better can there be than to help them to immortal life? I who am myself an initiate can assure you it is beyond anything that you can at present imagine.'

After my consultation with Diognetos, I left his house, blinking a little in the light of a belated sun, after the firelit interior. I had much to think about. My venture into marriage was leading me into new territory. It was not so hard, after all, to believe that Herpyllis might have induced Aristotle to do something of moment. How was it that my bride had persuaded me to do something I had never thought of doing? And here I was now, committed in effect to Diognetos – and to Demeter. The adventure would cost more money than I had calculated upon, that was pretty evident. Participation in Mysteries is an expensive business.

But as I walked through the streets of Eleusis it was not money that lay uppermost in my thoughts. Rather, I thought about my own soul, and the strange effort of leaving the normal round of life to seek a hitherto unknown existence. Initiation would bind me to my life beyond this one, something to which I had never paid any heed – save to be glad I wasn't dead. I had been twice saved from death: once when some thugs beat me almost to a pulp, and once when I was nearly killed by a gang of marauders on a small desolate island. Saved, and little the worse for wear. But every man, I realised for the first time, can say only 'I am alive now' or 'I am not dead *yet*'.

I was saved from death for the present – but could not be saved from death. In my life's course I was pressing on towards procreation, hoping for a boy-child who would complete my existence by carrying it onward through time. But marriage and procreation were symptoms of oncoming dissolution.

> Even as the generations of leaves, such are the
>   generations of men
> For the wind that blows scatters some upon the
>   ground
> While others, spring-begotten on the trees,
> Leap forth in season as the humans do.

Some of us are in the bud of springtime, like little Lykias, while at the same moment others progress towards their autumn, and even an Aristotle must fall some day. My season now was early summer, I decided, a time of thick foliage but as yet no fruit. In one sense, my worldly future would be taken care of by my having children; my family and its name would not die. Descendants of my father and my father's father would live on in Athens. But Eleusis asked other questions than these, and pointed towards another sort of future. I looked towards the Sacred Precinct, the half-obscured complex with its strong outward walls and enigmatic towers. This coming autumn I would be able to enter it for the first time, would go into the Telesterion and penetrate to the Anaktoron. I would find out what it had to tell me. But now I turned my steps away from the temples, towards the seaside.

The seaside is suited to such thoughts as I was entertaining. Eleusis has a delightful gently curving bay. There is some ship-traffic in sailing season, but it is by no means bustling like Peiraieus. This winter day out of season the place was practically deserted. Most ships were in the sheds, or drawn up high on the beach; only a couple of daring fishing vessels could be seen just offshore. It was a fitfully overcast winter day with clouds and intervals of sunshine. The sea was calmly grey, occasionally illumined with golden bands of light. Waves came rolling in with a soothing regularity. On one day during the worst of the Persian Wars, I recollected, according to Thymades, people at Salamis yonder, near despair in their resistance to the Persian invasion, had heard a heavenly procession, and seen lights shooting up from the Sacred Precinct to illuminate the dark sea and the night sky. Only the battering of wretched Thebes to dust by Alexander six years ago had been deathly powerful enough to stop the celebration of the Mysteries. And perhaps then, too, heavenly persons had celebrated, raising their own prayers for poor Thebes . . .

I strolled back and forth on the edge of the beach, gazing out over the water and remembering the bigger sea that I had encountered in my journeying, recalling the sense of limitless expanse, and the look of the night sky over the sea, with its thousand stars. I was just one little person beside this huge and ever-waking sea, one small human under that canopy of far-off lights.

I suddenly felt lonely. Not alone – I was used to being by myself during walks – but lonely, despite my family and my new marriage. Perhaps my strange feeling was the effect of being on my own after having been incessantly in the company of others. Indeed, as a married man I should never again be solitary, and yet now I was struck by this peculiar feeling of solitude, of advanced loneliness – something like being lost, something like being in grief.

So I walked by the water, pensive, and crunched along the beach looking at the random mosaic of stones and shells. Some of the stones under the water at the sea's edge were quite pretty, and the ripples sent stripes of light over them. It would be nice, I thought idly, if one could capture that effect, decorate a house with it. I peered more closely at the underwater stones, and saw one that shone particularly, a creamy white. A bigger wave than the others crashed over it and dislodged it from its temporary setting in the sand. It rolled, and to my horror it became a face – a white face under the combing wave. A child? A dead child! The waves ruthlessly pushed and pulled at the tiny face.

Disregarding the inconvenience of dipping my *khiton* in the sea, I kicked off my sandals and rushed into the waves, pulling through sand and gravel at the pallid face. It came up in my hands quite easily, but there was no body attached. No – not a child! Thankfully, not a real child. Just an image.

I looked at the little face, and it gazed at me. One ear had been badly chipped, and there was scarring on the forehead, but otherwise it was in quite good repair. The work of a competent statuary, in good marble, depicting the head of a child of two or three years. And I knew, even as I tried to keep my mind from knowing, that I might be holding in my hand a murder weapon. This head could be – could it? – the missing stone head brought to Hieron by his hapless brother-in-law. But how could it have arrived here at Eleusis' beach by the Rarian Fields? It must be something quite different. But were there many lost sculptures, so well done? We should ask the family of Hippobatos if it were theirs. And if the answer was yes – then the wet piece of marble I held in my hands had killed Hippobatos, shattered his skull, on the night of the audacious burglary of Hieron's house.

My first impulse was to cast the head into the sea again. But I could not bring myself to do it. This stone was a piece of evidence. I turned it round and about, but could see no colour of blood. But could blood soak into marble so thoroughly that even water could not remove it? I thought it might, but not unless left for a long time. It struck me that the best thing might be to take it to Aristotle, and show it to him. He could often deduce things from common objects, and might also have a good idea as to how to proceed in bringing the head to the attention of the magistrates. First of all, Hippobatos' family would have to be asked if this piece were theirs.

Luckily, I had the leather bag to carry the marble in, though I first had to wipe the head off very carefully to ensure that a wet stone bumping against the manuscript would not erase the writing of the hymns. At least nobody would know what I was carrying about with me. It was a nice point, whether I should bring this object within the walls of Athens at all, since if it were a guilty thing it deserved to be thrown out and smashed. Perhaps its sojourn in the clean sea might count as a period of ritual cleansing? I felt revolted, however, at the bare idea of bringing the object into my own house. No. I should pursue a path well outside the city walls, and take it at once to the Lykeion, to Aristotle. It could join his curious collection of objects . . .

I strode on at a good pace, soon passing the outskirts of Eleusis. The day became overcast again, and a thin drizzle started to fall, though this was only a slight nuisance to one wearing thick-soled sandals as I was. My thoughts were a jumble of the Mysteries and my uncomfortable find by the seashore. I was not thinking of any imminent dangers, nor did I even think of what had happened to me before on this road. At least, not until too late. Passing the stewponds where the priests of Demeter keep their fish, I was going up a slight incline opposite a woody place on the other side of the miry road when I heard a noise among the trees. I turned my head, but not in fear. And then – wham! A great gob of mire mixed with dung came at me. It glanced off the side of my head, and plopped into a puddle. Another one followed.

'This is foolishness!' I yelled. 'Stop it, boys, or I will see that you are well flogged!'

This threat elicited an outburst of laughter – a great belching bellow of suppressed male mirth. Was this the big Biton? Or who? Another missile followed – a stone this time. It caught me in the chest knocking some of the wind out of me.

'Rascal!' I shouted. The mist was rising, perhaps a fog from the sea, and combined with the drizzle it made it difficult to see. I caught a glimpse of a plain brown homespun cloak among the trees – but anyone might wear such a thing in the winter, from the merest slave to an army commander. Even a woman. While I tried to observe, the figure dodged, but then it took aim again. A sharp pebble struck my jaw. It was a wonder to me that it didn't knock a tooth out with it. My blood was up, my anger was great, but I had nothing to hit back with. I couldn't catch this fellow in the mist. And I had no weapon—

Bang! A very large stone just whistled past my shoulder and snapped against a tree trunk. My blood came into my head and a wrath like the wrath of Akhilleus descended upon me, so that I no longer functioned with Reason as a guide. I grabbed the one missile I had – my piece of marble – and threw it with all the dexterity and force of which I was capable. It was a lucky hit rather than anything else. I heard a crunching thud, and the unseen person cried out, most convincingly.

'That's done your business, rascal! But if not – there's more where that comes from!' I announced mend-aciously. Having thus enjoyed the privilege of the last word, I took to my heels. I was not going to try to investigate this fellow in the mist and rain, and besides, there might be more than one. Discretion appearing the better part, I hastened from this unwholesome and misty spot. It was only after going many stadia further that I realised I had let go of valuable evidence.

XVI

Purification

Wintry Gamelion had given way to the slightly gentler month of Anthesterion, the month of first flowers, whose centre is the Anthesteria festival. Last year, the Flower festival had marked the beginning of a quest that took myself and Aristotle to Delphi. Now I was preparing for a different sort of journey, closer to home. Sadly, our dedication entailed nine days of sexual abstinence before the initiation in the Lesser Mysteries. On the appointed day, chaste Philomela and chaste I set off for the little Temple of Demeter just outside the walls of Athens, by the banks of the Ilissos; Philomela carried two very tiny piglets in a basket. The container did not smell too much as the day was cool. As we neared our destination, we were joined by a number of other cleanly dressed and pig-carrying persons, all seeking the purification that begins progress towards initiation in the Mysteries of Eleusis.

Aristotle and Herpyllis lived outside the city walls, in the Lykeion, so we didn't meet them until we turned to the southern road, the last stretch of our little journey. Their little pigs followed them in a cart drawn by Aristotle's slave Phokon. Herpyllis was demurely hooded, almost as if she were a respectable citizen woman instead of a slave. I allowed her to walk with Philomela behind me; as always I was glad of the chance to talk with Aristotle. He was freshly barbered and cleanly dressed. Despite the solemnity of the ritual to which we were bound, and despite the fasting, his deep-set eyes had their wonted twinkle when he saw me.

'Well, Stephanos, this is an unusual occasion, is it not? You register no surprise, so doubtless you heard of my change of plan. You found a *mystagogos*?'

'Oh yes, Diognetos. He came to my wedding. And his wife instructs Philomela. They will be there today.'

'An unusual experience,' the Master said meditatively, 'for me to take instruction. I am so accustomed to haranguing others. It ought to be good for me. Purgative, like a dose of buckthorn. A beautiful area,' he added appreciatively, as we turned down towards the Ilissos. 'Very near where Sokrates talks with Phaidros in the dialogue of Plato, if you remember.'

There was no time for him to go off into reminiscences of Plato, for we had arrived at the Field of Agrai. Numbers of people were gathering, including foreigners, some from Africa and Asia, apparently; it was hard to move about in the crowd. *Mystai* looked for *mystagogoi*. Important *mystagogoi* rushed about looking for clients. The assembly on the banks of the cool river was so large and so mixed it reminded me of what I had read of the souls arriving at the River Styx, freshly dead from some grand massacre, and about to pass over into the Underworld: rich and poor, slave and free. There were all sorts here. A gang of slaves had come together, which puzzled me a little. And there was – oh dear, yes – Halirrhothios. Probably the person I least wanted to see. Before I could think, I grunted impatiently, 'Oh, this is too bad!'

'What is?' Philomela asked anxiously.

'Oh – just that all sorts come to be initiated,' I answered. 'But that's how it is. Look at that woman in the blue cloak – if I'm not mistaken, that's Phryne, the famous courtesan; she is called the most beautiful woman in Athens!'

'Oh, really? I would like to see her,' said Philomela, frankly craning her neck to get a look.

It was not very long before Thymades the conscientious found Aristotle and Herpyllis. 'Got your pigs?' he said. He picked up the basket containing these animals and swept them and their owners away. Diognetos came up to us a short time later, with his veiled wife, a short but broad person.

'Keep close to your *mystagogos*,' commanded Diognetos. 'You have your pig? You must keep it about you until the right moment. Some people have let the creature go and oh my, what a fuss! Squealing and yelling – the whole ceremony disturbed!'

Philomela meekly clutched the pig basket, and spoke in soothing hypocritical notes to the creatures within who were savouring – though they knew it not – their last moments.

'I should teach you,' said Diognetos. 'The Hierophant will soon give a beautiful account of the Mother's search for the Maiden. So I had better deal with the instructions as to fast days, and the foods which you cannot eat. Here – I have written a list, since Stephanos at least can read, and he should explain it to Philomela. My wife is going to tell her exactly which fish are to be avoided.'

'Is there nothing else?' I asked.

'Most of the major things will be explained during the ceremony today,' said Diognetos. 'And of course there is the purification, when you dip into the Ilissos. You must fast after today as well as before – at least three days, so

as not to lose the purity.' I sighed to think of more days
of thin soup and no marital conjunctions.

'Here comes the procession!' Philomela clutched me
excitedly.

We clung together in the damp air and watched as the
officials of the sacred rites marched into our midst. They
were led by the Hierophant, Shower of Sacred Things,
chief officiant of the Temple of Demeter and the Maiden.
The nameless Hierophant was splendid, like a king in
theatre, with long flowing locks and a purple robe. His
feet were in elegant buskins which made him appear
taller. About his neck was an embroidered stole, round
his head was tied a rolled fillet, its lappets extending to
his shoulders. Atop the fillet was the myrtle wreath.
Behind him came the Daidoukhos, the Torchbearer. His
hair, equally long (and slightly less grey), was also bound
with a fillet and a wreath. His khiton and a sleeveless
cloak over it were richly embroidered, bound about the
waist with a gold-fringed sash. About his neck there was
a purple embroidered stole with flashes of gold in it. The
Daidoukhos carried two torches, held high, one in each
hand, though these were at present unlit. Then came the
Priestess of Demeter, she whose office is most ancient,
the devoted ministrant of the Goddess, with her assistant
priestess. Some other priests, officials and temple slaves
followed. They made their way slowly through the
throngs, who parted to let them pass.

'A good turnout this year,' said Diognetos, gazing
with satisfaction at the large mixed crowd. 'Probably
because of the liberated cities in Asia. Now, the
Hierophant himself is going to address us.'

And indeed the Hierophant in his glittering stole,
looking a little like the god Dionysos in stage-play, stood
up and gave a splendid harangue.

'Men and women, of Athens and of the Greek world,

you have gathered as people seeking enlightenment. Let anyone who is not prepared in heart, who is not fasting, or whose heart tells him of any crime that sets him apart from such a holy purpose, leave at once.'

Not unexpectedly, nobody moved.

'Draw near then and hear the story of Demeter. The Goddess-Mother, supporter of corn and all fruits, had but one child, her daughter the Maiden, whom she loved. But on a day as the Maiden was gathering flowers in the fields of Demeter, a chasm opened in the earth. Rash Hades who is dark Ploutos, God of the Underworld, rushed up through it from the depths, in his dark chariot and night-black steeds. Into his chariot he thrust the hapless Maiden, torn from her friends and from the cheerful light and taken to the darkness of Hades' realm. The Mother knew not where her daughter had gone! She sought her everywhere! No other gods could help her and she wearied herself day and night with calling.

'By and by tired Demeter sat drearily at the side of the well, called to this day the Laughterless Well. The neighbouring queen, pitying the state of one whom she took for a poor forlorn woman, invited her in. The queen offered wine, but Demeter refused. She took a drink of barley and herbs and water, the *kykeion*. This is the sacred drink of which we all desire to drink – but it is a cup of sorrow. Do not join in the Mysteries unless you are willing to undergo the experience of sorrow, and drink of the cup of loss.'

There was a short silence and he resumed.

'Let us now join in the celebration and service of Kore. Form a procession, women, and make your offering.'

The Priestess carried a sacred dish towards the altar, followed by women whom she and the Herald had picked out from among the crowd, Philomela among them.

'In this special service of the Maiden who disappears

and reappears,' said the Priestess, after the altar sacrifice of bloodless offering had been accepted, 'we not only remind ourselves of her story, but relive it. Draw near and look.'

This was the signal for a flourish of music, and the Heralds' assistants made a clearing in the midst of the crowd. Into the middle of the circle there came a young actor, dressed as Persephone with a mask of girlhood. She pronounced that the first flowers of Anthesterion were blooming now, and that she would pick them, assisted by her maidens. A *khoros* of these maidens surrounded her. But as they gathered, a great noise was heard, and the King of the Underworld, all in black with grey wavy locks, burst into the midst of the throng. Amid the outcry of the girls' *khoros*, he grabbed the Maiden and disappeared. This little pageant was very popular, and even people not intending to be initiated would crowd on nearby vantage points to watch it. I knew this well because as a boy I had often gone to see it, if from an enforced distance which made the figures look tiny.

The Hierophant took up the tale again.

'In these, the Lesser Mysteries, we prepare you – and you prepare yourselves – for the loss, for the search for Persephone. No man – and no priest, no state, no king – constrains you to undergo this search, this loss, this quest. If any man or woman has been compelled to come by the force or unreasonable commands of another, and has no desire for the Mysteries, let that person freely leave us with our good will.'

I looked out of the corner of my eye at Aristotle, but he stood his ground. Nobody moved.

The Hierophant smiled.

'It is good,' he said, 'that all who are here come freely, each not only free of unusual taint of crime, but free in their will. Yet it is right that each individual be questioned as to his or her fitness for beginning initiation into the Mysteries. Stand by your own *mystagogos*, each of you, and one of the priests will deal with you individually. If adjudged fit, you will be enrolled in the list for the sacrifice of Boedromion. After this questioning, you will purify yourselves in the Ilissos and make your offering.'

This questioning took some time; priests and priestesses moved individually from one small group to another – or rather, from one pair, mystagogue and would-be *mystes*, to another. Priestesses dealt with women, priests with men. I waited my turn to be catechised, thinking privately that Halirrhothios might have some interesting things to confess, if he chose. Yet, I had to remind myself, the Goddess took no account of lying or theft as a crime that kept one from her company. If my neighbour had done nothing worse than steal jewellery, there was no reason why he should not become an initiate.

The Daidoukhos himself came up to Diognetos and me fairly early in the proceedings. At that moment I was gratified that I had chosen a *mystagogos* well known in Eleusis and capable of capturing the attention of the priesthood. This Torchbearer, carrying only one torch now, was a sufficiently impressive person to confront, even taller than the current Hierophant. Diognetos named Philomela and me both by name and father's name to the attentive Daidoukhos, and an attendant wrote the names down.

'So, O Diognetos, you have instructed the man Stephanos son of Nikiarkhos? And your wife has instructed his wife, the woman Philomela daughter of Smikrenes?'

'Yes, that is so. They know the story, which they could recite if asked. They know the first hymn, and the fasts, and the days of observance.'

'It is well,' said the assistant Priestess. 'Do you, woman named Philomela, swear that you are above fifteen years of age? That you are a Greek speaker? And that you are free of blood-guilt, having never committed any crime of bloodshed or witchcraft?' To all of these queries Philomela replied firmly, 'Yes.'

The Daidoukhos then turned to me, and asked me the same questions. Of course it was visible that I was over fifteen, and was audibly a Greek speaker, so I was proceeding nicely until we came to the last formal question.

'Do you swear also, Stephanos, that you are free of blood-guilt, having never—'

'He cannot swear that!' exclaimed Halirrhothios loudly. My neighbour was standing two places off from myself. 'This man Stephanos of Athens is a killer! He has committed homicide. He should not be here!'

The Daidoukhos took two steps back, and looked at me. He paled a little under his myrtle wreath, and his torch wobbled slightly in his hand. I am sure that I too must have gone pale from the shock. Not just at Halirrhothios' turning informer, but at my own recognition that I really had *killed*. It may seem hard to believe, but all my thoughts in relation to the initiation into the Mysteries had been of Philomela and our new marriage. Truly, it had never once struck me that I was a homicide, under the ban of the articles of Demeter. Now it rushed upon me, and I could not deny the fact.

'Really? Stephanos son of Nikiarkhos, is this *true*? You have *killed* men?'

'Yes – no – just one man,' I pleaded. 'And it was not wilful murder but self-defence. He was about to kill me and Ar— a friend. We were among pirates off the coast of Asia. I *had* to do it, to save our lives! I didn't wish to, I had not intended to kill, I was not even armed when the fight broke out . . .' I spluttered along, endeavouring to clear myself, while sweat came to my forehead. I must indeed have looked quite guilty.

'You have *killed*,' said the Daidoukhos heavily. 'Diognetos, we expected better of you! You should have caught this before. A homicide! Without even the excuse of being a soldier. Dear me, how seldom this happens.' The Torchbearer looked at me for a good while, pursing his lips. 'As I see it, young man, this is a bad business, but you are eligible for admission with extra purification. You follow in the footsteps of great Herakles, who came to be initiated and had to undergo a special cleansing for his blood-guilt. You will undergo the same. Leave your wife and the others, and stand aside.'

He continued his progress of catechism while I and two other men and one old woman stood aside, an unenviable group of our own. Others stared and pointed at us. I missed Philomela by my side – I know she would have wished to stay with me, but she was forced to move off to undergo her own preliminary ritual.

The priestly assistant came up to us. 'You have your pig?' he asked me rather inelegantly.

'My wife does,' I said miserably. 'You will find her in the crowd – with Diognetos and his wife. She has both of our pigs.'

The man came back with unexpected celerity, and delivered unto me my own runty little grunter. It was now very difficult to hold, being all wet from its ceremonial plunge in the waters of Ilissos. It whined its complaint, insofar as a pig can whine.

'Your pig has been cleansed by immersion in the river,' he announced. 'So it is ready for sacrifice. But you must also pay for the sacrifice of a ram, and upon that bloody ram's hide you must sit apart for the special cleansing.'

This was disagreeable news, but I could do nothing

but consent to the expense and the humiliation. It was the more difficult as one of the other men segregated with me was cleared of the accusation, and the third fellow decided, belatedly, not to continue. That left the old crone, who was accused of witchcraft and necromancy, and myself, considered the more interesting case. So I was led ceremonially and visibly up through the crowd to the special stone seat, by an altar where an old ram, who had been standing idly by in case of such necessity, was slaughtered. The ram's hide was at once stripped off, and placed on the bench. The priests' attendants took off my himation (a good idea, as I soon realised) and ordered me to remove my sandals. I made ready, resignedly, to sit on this reeking throne.

'Not so fast,' said the Daidoukhos sharply. 'You must be blindfolded, swaddled. An imitation of your own blindness and a preparation for rebirth free of blood.'

There followed the most horrible part of the business. Two men threw a thick and muffling cloak over my head and face, and wrapped it about my upper body, as I sat there upon the warm and reeking ram's fleece, with my feet upon the same bloody mat. It was terrible! I could hardly breathe. Veiled like a woman, meek and unseeing with head bowed, I had to sit penitently while prayers were said over me. Then the pig was sacrificed – I could tell not only from the prayers but from the squeals and the long, thin squall cut short by a gurgle. The little beast's blood was immediately poured over my head. I was glad that Philomela had brought only tiny piglets, but there was a surprising amount of blood, warm and wet, running over me, sinking into inlets in my ears and eyes, and seeking to force an entry into my muffled mouth. Blood trickled down my back and chest and fell into my private parts.

'Your sacrifice,' said the Daidoukhos, 'means your

blood-guilt is assumed by the pig. Its blood poured upon you repays you for your deed, and at the same time cleanses you from the crime. You are blessed in that your crime comes just within the boundary of Herakles, and is not wilful and premeditated shedding of human blood. Think, while you sit here, of Demeter, giver of grain and of life. Ask her to forgive and cleanse. Leave your blood-guilt behind you. Swear to kill no more!'

It was easy to promise this to the Goddess, inwardly as well as outwardly, for I had never wanted to kill in the first place, and could not imagine ever again killing a human being. The priests waved a winnowing fan above my head, sprinkling me and taking away the stain and guilt as chaff is separated from grain.

'Now,' said the Daidoukhos, 'where is Diognetos? Diognetos, you may help me to say the last prayer and to remove the veil that now obscures his vision.' The two men chanted rapidly and then – at last! – my horrid blood-sodden muffler was taken off. Unveiled, I could enjoy the light of the sun as a man should do, and look openly at the world.

'Go!' said the Daidoukhos. 'Say the prayer of purification and plunge into the cleansing river. Your blood-guilt will be entirely taken from you, and you will emerge as a new man.'

I stumbled as I rose, and Diognetos had to lead me to the river, like an old man. The flowing Ilissos, deepened by melting snows and the first of the spring rains, was cool and fast-moving. I almost lost my footing. It felt good, however, to wash off the sticky blood with its insistent metallic odour, and to see clearly the sky above me. I left the river to wrap myself in my himation – that at least had been saved from the blood-spill. No longer in a seat of shame apart, I was able at last to rejoin my bride and friends, who had made their purification and sacrifice in the ordinary manner. Aristotle and Herpyllis looked at me sympathetically. Philomela pressed my hand. I could see that she was dripping wet under her himation. She sneezed once, and I began to worry more practically about getting her home before she caught a chill.

'You're wet, child!'

'It was quite lovely,' she whispered, 'though I was worried about you. But I stayed with Herpyllis. We saw Phryne go into the water. People said she looked just like Aphrodite.'

I thought wryly to myself that at least some events and celebrities of Athens were providing her with excitement, rendering it worth her while to have come from the country. But this unworthy thought was quickly cancelled out when my bride pressed my hand again.

'I am glad,' she said, 'that you are now released from that old killing. It has given you bad dreams, I know. And we have started on our way, to live in blessedness for eternity.'

XVII

Golden Advice in the Lykeion, Jewels in Peiraieus

The next day was not a good one. I was awakened by a pounding at my door. Rather than waiting for Tryphos to respond, I went to the portal. Thrusting the gate wide, I could see only a small, neat male slave.

'What in Hades are you doing here so early? Whose are you?'

'Stephanos son of Nikiarkhos of Athens, I am bid to inform you that your trial at the suit of Lykon for infringement of right of way and water rights, also for trespass and damages, will come on in five days' time.'

'Oh, no!' I clutched my head. I had known Lykon's suit was one of my problems, but it had seemed always in the dim future. Now the menace had moved to an immediate position.

'You have – they have – the wrong person,' I protested. 'This is all a mistake. I am not the owner of the land in Hymettos about which there is dispute.'

'Tell it to the court,' said the slave indifferently. 'Meet Lykon your antagonist and the jury at the Stoa Poikile first thing in the morning, five days from today.'

The nameless servant turned his back and disappeared.

So Lykon was determined to pursue the matter! A grumbling problem, bothersome but never acute (like a mild catarrh), now threatened to take a more harmful turn. I should see Aristotle and ask his advice. And I also ought to tell him about the marble sculpture. My first impulse had been to speak to no one about what I had found on the beach at Eleusis. But by now it was clear to me that Aristotle would recognise the importance of the puzzling discovery – even if I had to confess that I had lost the object in question. I reminded myself that I had in the past tried to keep things from him and had sometimes suffered as a result.

I found Aristotle walking through the chilly groves of the Lykeion, in company with a host of his associates. As well as Theophrastos, Eudemos of Rhodos was there, a man of middle age, urbane and agreeable, and the faithful (and dull) Hipparkhos of Argos; so too was young Demetrios of Phaleron, as always so striking with his clear-cut profile and curling blond hair that one could hardly notice other people while in his presence. Impressionable men said Demetrios was just their idea of Akhilleus.

'Why, here comes the man-killer!' exclaimed Eudemos, shrinking back in mock fear. 'I hear you had a terrible time at the Lesser Mysteries, Stephanos.'

'I hope you feel better now,' said Demetrios with mock solicitude.

'Should we not run away from such a dangerous person?' suggested Hipparkhos. A notable jest by one not given to them.

'Heroic Stephanos – it was really for my sake that you were singled out,' said Aristotle. 'You are not a blood-thirsty man at all, but your one killing saved my life.'

'Now you will be known everywhere as "Killer",' observed Demetrios. 'Perhaps people will respect you more,' he added.

'And how goes my fellow seeker after initiation today? Are you in health?' Aristotle enquired.

'It is too absurd,' Theophrastos ejaculated. 'The two of you, going through all this. Mysteries and so on. It's not like you, Aristotle! It seems so ridiculous to undergo initiation this late in life.'

'Well,' said Aristotle, 'some would say that the later in life, the more urgent the need. But I don't mind telling all of you that I am willing to undertake this partly because I am sorry I did not do it when Pythias wished it. Years ago, I denied her request that I be initiated in the Mysteries. Something she wanted for my own sake. A woman I loved ten times more than any Herpyllis! Yet my docile slave woman can boast inwardly that she has had a power over me that my dear wife had not.'

'But both of them wanted really to do you good,' I said.

'True. And here, my scholars,' he added, turning to the group, 'you may see the difference between an old man and a young one. The younger one is unswerving and stubborn in what he believes to be right. Excellent qualities – but perhaps he may not always be right. Now I am an old man I see the benefit of yielding to others from time to time.'

'There is no need to stand against the Two Goddesses,' objected Demetrios. 'The Goddesses give great benefits to Athens, and our rites draw people from all parts of Greece.'

'Aristotle hardly needs convincing on that score,' said Eudemos.

'But you haven't answered my question,' said Aristotle, turning his keen deep-set eyes on me. 'Are you in good health? Is something troubling you?'

'Oh, just a little something,' I said drily. 'Like the fact that I have been summoned to attend the trial – the civil suit – for damage to property. The charge brought by

Lykon – he sends word the case will be heard in five days' time!'

'Poor Stephanos, so many troubles,' said young Demetrios, rather impertinently. 'We heard that Lykon's dog was set on you – is that true?'

'The man Lykon is an impudent boor,' I said angrily. 'He did set a dog on me for trespass – just for looking over the wall. And he then had the impudence to come to my wedding! I wish the food and the good wine had choked him, I do indeed.'

'I hope you did not tell him so at the time,' said Aristotle.

'I had other things to do on my wedding day,' I assured him. 'Besides greeting my guests and waiting to join my bride, I had to dodge an unknown assailant.'

'Really?' The others had not known of this, so I explained about the mud and stones flung at me as I rode to Eleusis in my wedding garments, and also about the knife that was thrown at me during the wedding party.

'Dear, this is very bad,' said Aristotle. 'Do you truly think Lykon is to blame?'

'I'm not sure. But he could be. *Why* did he come to my wedding party if it didn't serve his turn in some way?'

'But he has legal redress in mind. Is there anyone else who wishes you ill?'

'There was a man in Eleusis who had proposed marrying Smikrenes' daughter. He might be very annoyed that I had cut him out. Or rather his son, Biton. A big lad. Biton's a boxer and a champion discus-thrower.'

'And you a man not of Eleusis, taking its female treasure away,' said Eudemos. 'He might well make strong objection.'

'But if he's a discus-thrower, he ought to have better aim,' objected Aristotle. 'He would hardly keep missing when he threw things at you – so one would think. It might be somebody quite different. Who would throw a *knife?*'

'I don't want to think I have a long list of enemies,' I protested. 'But it is certainly puzzling. So far the attacks have been annoying rather than damaging. But Lykon's suit could be a real trouble. Though I don't see why it should be *my* trouble. The property is still really owned by Philokles, my bride's uncle. Her grandmother and mother do the work, and her grandmother's second husband just sits about and does nothing!'

'Philokles will hardly wish to abandon a good property in Hymettos,' reasoned Hipparkhos. 'He will probably return soon.'

'But he is very happy in Kos,' I objected. 'Uncle Philokles lives with a beautiful woman called Nammo. Once mistress to a general who gave her a lovely house. And she owns a sponge fishery.'

'How delightful!' exclaimed Demetrios. 'By Herakles, Stephanos, I swear it is a pity that you couldn't have found such good luck for yourself.'

'Such liaisons never last,' Eudemos assured me 'He will be back.'

'I think,' said Aristotle, 'that we must stop wishing that this man Philokles would appear suddenly in Athens and relieve Stephanos of the problem. We ought to deal with things as they are. Lykon is going to bring his suit, and he names Stephanos as one of those whom he accuses. Now, it is possible to persuade the magistrates not to give the case to a jury for a while. Stephanos can seek a postponement. After all, during the winter, with no ships sailing, it has been truly almost impossible to communicate between Kos and Athens.'

'I can swear to that,' said Eudemos, 'having most of my family in Rhodos. A few ships are starting to go out now. But the true sailing season is well ahead of us. It would not be reasonable to expect you to get information relevant to a law case for two or three months, at least.'

'I hope you do succeed in getting a postponement, Stephanos.' Aristotle looked concerned. 'It strikes me you are ill-prepared. You will probably have to argue the case with Lykon, at some time or other.'

'I meant to warn you, too, Stephanos,' said grave Theophrastos. 'I recently have heard that Kallimakhos has offered to stake Lykon in his attack on you.'

'You mean lend him money?' said Demetrios. 'But what money does he need?'

'Perhaps he needs to hire a rhetorician to help him compose a speech,' suggested Eudemos. 'But it is more likely, frankly, that Lykon would like to make little gifts to the magistrate and the jury.'

'Impossible!' I exclaimed. 'Athens has created a system that is proof against all bribery and corruption in the courts. For our juries are large, and the jurors for a particular case are chosen by lot on the morning of the trial.'

'Very true,' said Aristotle. 'But a man of wealth and influence can casually let it be known that he will not be slow to express gratitude. A confidential smile, a familiar nod might suffice. No man would pay off the whole jury – one hundred or even six hundred men! The structure of Athens' constitution is designed to keep power from falling into the hands of one man, or one family, or a few men. But a litigant may implicitly promise to grace a few leading members of the jury with benefits, and that can do the business. It's hard to prevent important people from getting their own way.'

'In any case, men don't like to lose,' said Eudemos. 'Especially not here in Athens, where each man vies with his neighbour, and everything is argued about and contested.'

'Unconscionable!' I exclaimed. 'I have no money to grease people's palms in that way. I shall protest that this is unfair!'

'It would be too late by then – the jury's vote would have been cast,' said Theophrastos. 'You know that the case is out of the magistrate's hands once it goes to a jury. There is no appeal against a jury's verdict. And if you were to attempt to bring lack of probity to light, you would not gain friends, Stephanos. It is not exactly against the law, either, to make gifts. After all, a successful litigant never has to spell out what the little donations are for!'

'You can have some hope in the weakness of Kallimakhos,' suggested Demetrios. 'His business is failing, so I hear in Phaleron.'

'I do know this much,' I explained. 'Kallimakhos had an agreement with a merchant named Euthykritos, that the son of this merchant would marry his daughter Kharmia. And the merchant has wealth through shipping goods in vessels to Byzantion and other port cities. But this rich Euthykritos fell out with Kallimakhos – perhaps hearing he had no means to give a large dowry to Kharmia – and so the match was broken off.'

'Disregard gossip and speculation, Stephanos,' advised Theophrastos. 'Prepare a writing clearly stating the terms on which you have an interest in the property in Hymettos, while making it plain that you have no ownership of that land, and no responsibility for it.'

'Sound advice,' Aristotle corroborated. 'I hope you have stirred the people in Hymettos to collect depositions from neighbours that the property has always been such as it is, and that the groves and family graves have been visible there for a long while.'

'I hadn't really thought about that!' I exclaimed, aghast. 'Oh, I hope they give me an extension of time.

This is *important* – the women at Hymettos won't know how to do it. Dropides will not have thought of it. Or if he did, he wouldn't do anything.'

'Not a dynamic person,' Theophrastos interjected drily. 'As the property is not his own, and he has no hopes of it, Dropides has less reason to fight for it.'

'I am sorry to think you have collected some new enemies, Stephanos,' said Aristotle with concern. 'I worry about the knife, in particular. Have these attacks ceased since your marriage?'

'I thought so,' I admitted. 'But recently I was attacked again – on my way from Eleusis!'

And so I told them about my walk by the beach and my finding of the marble head of a child, in the sand under the waves. And how I had meant to take good care of it, but how, when I was assailed by not just mud but heavy stones, I had used the marble stone as a weapon.

'It is too bad, I know!' I admitted. 'For I parted from what might be valuable evidence in the case of the burglary at Hieron's house and the murder of the unfortunate man who brought to the house the marble head of a child.'

'Was there *blood* on the marble?' young Demetrios asked eagerly.

'No – no blood that I could see. I don't know if blood would stain marble.'

'It could, I believe,' said Aristotle. 'I have seen such a thing. It stains the way iron clamps stain marble, unless they are sheathed in lead. But water quickly applied, fresh or salt, could wash the offensive matter away before it took effect. Submersion in salt water for a long period, however, would not benefit marble. Had the sculpture been there for a long while? Was it damaged?'

'The piece was chipped in a couple of places,' I explained, 'but that might have been from rubbing against other stones in the water. It was smooth. And it wasn't buried deep in the sand.'

'Instructive,' said Aristotle. 'Even if you have lost the object itself. Had it been long in the sea, it might have been expected to be buried deeper. If it is the sculpture we are thinking of, can it have been in the sea since Pyanepsion? Doubtful. Was this the piece missing from Hieron's house? And how did it take itself to Eleusis?'

'Once *stolen*,' said Theophrastos severely, 'it could be secretly removed to Eleusis, then thrown away in the sea. A valuable object displaced, and then thrown away, to do no one any good. It points out the futility of theft.'

'A very moral conclusion, Theophrastos,' said Aristotle laughing. Then he added, in a more serious tone, 'It *is* bad you know – all this theft. Not just because of the crimes themselves. They stimulate fear of theft, so everyone clutches his own goods the tighter. We become the more wrapped up in our possessions. Theft, an illiberal crime in itself, springing from selfishness and greed, diminishes liberality and generosity in the whole city. In the end, it is not just taking from one person – it is to take from all. We all become a little less open, a little more ungenerous.'

We were now trotting at a good pace through the Lykeion groves, as Aristotle warmed to his subject.

'A city must have a sense of its own unity, its relation of each to all. Important rituals and services to bind man to man and citizen to citizen, like Athens' great Panathenia. Communal meals are important in many states for that reason.'

'The Athenians,' said Theophrastos drily, 'go out every night to taverns and eating houses. The *kapeleia* are full, and the homes empty. Men who enrich cooks and barkeepers, going to eating houses or sending for cooks' food, do not have to undergo the sober ritual of sacrifice.

They omit to ask permission of the divine powers for the shedding of blood. Animals are killed wastefully, for mere gluttony or show.'

I felt guilty, momentarily, thinking of my *mageiros* and the cost of both the symposium and the wedding feast.

'Oh well,' said Hipparkhos, 'when you have so many rich people, they have to spend their money on something.'

'I suppose so,' said Aristotle. 'Athens has long had wealthy men. Now there are many more of them, getting rich in new ways. It is not easy for such men to be liberal. Men who have made their own fortune are very reluctant to give it away. As they made their own money, they are attached to it, as to part of themselves. You notice all men are fond of their own works – from papas to poets!'

'But could it not be,' I asked, 'that a man *thinks* he is being liberal, *thinks* he is being good, and yet deals with money foolishly – even wrongly?'

'Of course, Stephanos,' Aristotle agreed, 'that is possible. Men can think their object is good, when it is not. Or they think they are temperate when committing an action intemperate in itself: "I shall commit just a little adultery, in the right place at the right time!" Or they delude themselves into thinking that they are permitted to do things others should not do: "I shall take the bribe, but only because I am saving up to build a battleship for the state." *Very* few people say to themselves: "I am going to do a truly wrong thing and become a wrongdoer and a villain." Most people weave some sort of excuse for their actions.'

'I wish I could remain here and talk with you,' I said, sincerely. 'But I must go home and start writing out my appeal for postponement of Lykon's case.'

'Why don't you walk with me to Peiraieus tomorrow?' said Aristotle. 'I had already decided to go there myself,

to deliver personally a special packet to a particular ship.
The weather now favours us, and on the way we can talk
about your case, and anything else we please.'

On a fine morning Aristotle and I met within the city
walls and made our way to the southern gate that led to
Peiraieus. I was anxious to show Aristotle the fruit of my
labours; I had written out a statement, which I proceeded
to show him:

> I Stephanos son of Nikiarkhos of Athens deny that
> I am answerable for any damage done to the
> property of Lykon of Hymettos by the dwellers in
> the farm which borders his own. This property
> belongs to Philokles, and the operation is entrusted
> to his relatives and to Dropides his stepfather in
> Philokles' absence. Matters addressed to Dropides
> in the meanwhile should truly be referred to
> Philokles. Letters have been sent to Philokles by
> both my opponent and myself, but the corre-
> spondence is unseasonable. Delivery of letters and
> answers cannot be expected until good sailing
> weather has recommenced. I therefore plead for a
> delay until midsummer. But I wish to state,
> however, that I have no part in ownership of this
> farm, and cannot be held answerable.

'Good,' said Aristotle. 'Though I might ask them to
wait until the *end* of summer – then they are at least likely
to let you postpone the case until midsummer. It would
be a point gained to have the case put off until the New
Year – which really means until after the Panathenaia.
Pity it isn't the year of the Great Panathenaia, which
would provide an even better excuse. You may however,
later regret dissociating yourself so completely from the

family in Hymettos. What about the introduction of a sentence stating that you do not believe that they have done anything wrong?'

'I thought of that, but I don't want to get too closely tied to their case.'

'Your long-term interest demands that you sustain good relations with the family at Hymettos. It might be that Lykon is putting out a first feeler to take some of the lands of Hymettos away from them – realising the farm is run by women. You may have to stand up for the women and for the integrity of Philokles' lands. This trumped-up grievance of Lykon, however, may blow over, if you are all firm enough.'

'You think so?'

'Yes. Although a jury trial is tricky. One cannot foretell what the jury award will be.'

'I wish I was well out of this,' I said. 'And out of the suit threatened by Kallimakhos over his daughter. I wish, too, that we knew who had killed poor Hieron's brother-in-law. I am sorry that I found and then lost the stone head – or *a* stone head.'

'We have never discovered who killed poor Sophilos, either.'

'I went to see Sophilos' nephew Strabax,' I said. 'That was before I talked with Diognetos about initiation. Walked up a very filthy lane. Because I wanted to give them something, after I said I would – but all I saw was his old mother, who was quite rude, really. She took my two drakhmai, but then as good as accused me of trying to buy the boy's sexual favours!'

Aristotle only smiled at that, rather unsympathetically.

'I felt sorry for her before, but now I think she's rather a harridan,' I confided. 'She said her son was going to a merchant, and then contradicted herself and said Strabax would be a shepherd. Perhaps she's confused. She said one interesting thing, though,' I recollected. 'When she was complaining that no justice had been done about Sophilos, she said somebody ought to interview the marble-seller.'

'Did she? Then she was very right. I have just been thinking along the same lines.'

'I wish we could put a stop to the thefts.'

'You have many wishes, Stephanos. Yet, I must admit, that is true of myself also. You have discreetly not enquired why I walk all the way to Peiraieus personally to deliver a letter to a particular sea-captain. I wish to communicate directly with Alexander. He is so far away now. Some of my epistles, I fear, did not get through to him. The winter has been long! But the captain of this particular vessel braves the deep waters and at last I have a means of ensuring communication. This captain is trustworthy, and the commander who will soon travel with him on this ship will be going directly to Alexander. He will be certain to take a letter from me.'

'You worry too much,' I said. 'Because of Philotas. Too much grief. But some letters just naturally do go astray. And sometimes a ship sinks.'

'Mine is not simple grief. Had Philotas and Parmenion died in battle, shot as it might be with Parthian arrows – then I could have enjoyed simple grief! This sense of loss is mingled with a certain disgust, a certain distrust, and even fear. Fear is not a noble quality at all. Yet I have it.'

'I don't think of you as being fearful,' I said. 'You did not quail in front of the pirates. I am sure you could face death with fortitude.'

'I believe I could face death, Stephanos – an honourable death. It's harder to know how one would face an ignoble fate – a foul disease for instance, or being flogged to death like a slave. There is no nobility in such cases;

one can hardly call the endurance courage. Yet we all must die. I have by now lived longer than many men. It isn't my *own* death I fear.'

'Oh, I see. Kallisthenes.' I realised how sharply anxious Aristotle was about his nephew, who was travelling with Alexander as his commissioned historian.

'Yes. Kallisthenes is sometimes impetuous, very boyish – I think of him as a boy, which is absurd. But he tends to say what he thinks. Kings are not fond of that quality.'

'I should think they would find it valuable.'

'Oh, they all give lip service to sincerity. Every monarch will *proclaim* that he values the honest speaker. What he means is he wants a man who will offer flattery of better quality than the standard supply. Pretend to be a bluff, honest man whose admiration is wrung out of you – and you have caught your king! Alexander is getting more kingly; now he counts himself Great King of Persia. And he is far from home, full of suspicions – sometimes with good reason. I am attached to Alexander from long acquaintance, and some real affection, but now I am conscious of a need to keep on his good side. This strikes me at times as slightly contemptible. What philosopher would crawl to any man? Yet for the sake of Kallisthenes . . . And my nephew Nikanor has now joined Alexander's service also, with the same opportunities and hazards.'

We were now coming into the great port town. Talk of Alexander or of murders or the marble head was best cut off, for there were many about us to overhear, even in these wide avenues. The central city is notably beautifully designed, planned by Hippodamos of Miletus with wide boulevards and regular blocks of buildings. (Though as I knew well, on the outskirts Peiraieus like any port city peters out into the usual collection of back lanes and down-at-heel houses.) Peiraieus was waking up after winter stagnation – the Anthesteria signalled the spring season. Though the waters might be unpleasantly rough, and treacherous, some daring souls were already bound on voyages. The wide spaces imagined by the designer were taken up by street vendors with stalls, and itinerants selling everything imaginable, from tinkers repairing pots and pans to necromancers offering converse with the dead. The broad dockside space at the head of the quays was full of merchandise. The tables of the money-changers went *clack-clack* as they set down the tablets of gold and silver.

We were making our way to the ship that Aristotle had in mind, going slowly with the crowd. I nearly uttered a yelp as I was thrust forward by the press, almost into a cart carrying someone's wares.

'By Herakles! Look where you are going! These things are delicate – breakable objects!' the driver yelled furiously. I recognised him.

'Isn't that the Boiotian – Lampos, isn't it?' I asked. 'The servant of Oulias the image-maker.' I was sure I recognised the formerly shy worker of Eleusis, the man from Tanagra with the big hands and clay under the nails. I grasped the edge of his cart, so he paused in his furious driving and stared at us.

'Let go! And I am *not* a servant – not a slave neither. Assistant. Artistic assistant,' grumbled Lampos. 'And we have a shipment of our images wrapped in straw, which we must put on board ship in next to no time. So I'll thank you to stand out of my way!'

Aristotle and I meekly did so, and Lampos drove off with his trotting donkeys, shouting as he went to keep the crowd from bumping into his cart.

When we arrived at the ship that Aristotle sought, the philosopher went aboard while I waited on the quay, enjoying the smell of sea air and the exciting bustle of travel and exchange going on around me. Aristotle spent some time in civilities, before he emerged from the hold of the dark ship.

'So that is satisfactory,' he remarked. Just as he said this, there was a great outcry.

'Thief! Theft! I've been robbed!' somebody was bellowing not far away. The complainer was Lampos.

'My money! My money!' he cried. 'The money I got for the wares – all the lovely images of Demeter! My money has been stolen!'

Aristotle strode up to him.

'How much? What was it in?'

'It was in a bag – I have three bags, luckily. The rascals didn't get it all – just one bag. But oh, the lovely silver – many silver drakhmai, three or four hundred! I just got paid for the images. What will I say to Oulias?'

'Say? Why, that you have been a victim of theft. Did you see anybody?'

'Who could see anybody in this crowd? I don't think the thief even ran off – who could run here?'

'Then he is somewhere about even now,' said Aristotle, sweeping the crowd with his gaze.

'We must both keep our eyes out, Stephanos. Come, man, I'll help you. You must lay a complaint before the port officials. You can at least describe the bag.'

'Oh, what good is that?' Lampos shrugged wearily. There were tears in his eyes. 'How angry Oulias will be! All that work for nothing.' He was ready to expatiate on his misfortune when a cry was sent up from another part of the quay.

'Robbed! I have been robbed!' A grey-haired Phoinician merchant with a long robe and a very thick accent raised his hands to heaven. 'Valuable jewels! Help!'

We hastened in his direction. The barbarian's loud cries attracted more attention than had the distress of Oulias' man Lampos.

'What did you lose? When?' Aristotle demanded of the foreign merchant.

'Jewels. Jewels of great price! A buyer in Mitylene I had already. But now – nothing! Nothing to sell. Look where they were in this purse, and the purse itself has been cut – see!' The unfortunate victim held out the leather bag which had been neatly slit.

'What exactly was in it?'

'Gemstones – some set and some not. Earrings of jasper and carnelian. Blue stones uncut, the size of walnuts, the beautiful lapis of Egypt. But the most valuable thing of all was the *smaragd*, a most rare and unusual green stone of great power and virtue. It comes from far in the East. My *smaragd* – it is irreplaceable. Oh, what shall I do? What can I do?' The poor man rent his grey locks.

'Come – come at once to the magistrate and explain. Have you any list? Any proof?'

'I had showed one ship-owner, a man who brought me from Byzantion. Though most of the goods came from Damaskos before. It is hard to remember this man's name, your Greek names are so hard. The ship is the *Khelidon*. He goes back and forth – he is probably in Byzantion now, and cannot help me.'

'And you, Lampos. Can you reclaim your goods, at least?'

'Certainly not. The ship's master gave me all the money due – silver money – for the images. All accounted for.'

'But how useful this is!' Aristotle exclaimed. 'Send at once for the master of the ship, and tell him to meet us at the office of the port authority. We shall send one of the public slaves – here, boy! What is the name of the ship?' Aristotle briskly enquired, turning back to Lampos.

'The *Thalia*. And the master is Menexenos of Abydos,' Lampos mumbled, as if he were sulky, or just shy at being the centre of so much attention.

'Here then – I have written a message, just sign it . . .'
And Aristotle gave him the tablet. 'Off with you, boy, to
that ship, the *Thalia*, before she sails!'

'Now!' he said, turning triumphantly to Lampos.
'There's a good job done. For the master of the ship's cargo
can tell the magistrates how much you were paid. Thus we
can prove that you were the victim of theft, and of what
exact amount of silver money. Come with me, both of you!'

And he led the way through the crowds, myself trotting after. We both helped the tearful Boiotian Lampos,
artisan in images, to make his complaint. Menexenos of
Abydos, the *Thalia*'s master, explained the amount paid
for the images, and Lampos produced the remaining bags
with the silver coins from the *Thalia*. Once the amount
remaining was subtracted from the sum just paid out, the
missing bag proved to contain nearly three hundred
drakhmai.

'This is very bad,' the unhappy Lampos lamented to
the Epimeletes in charge, one of the ten supervisors of
the harbour market. 'Peiraieus is supposed to be the great
Emporion – one of the best markets of the world. How
can it go on if such thefts take place under our noses?'

'So – yes!' cried the foreign merchant. It was hard to
get much sense out of him, he was so disturbed, and spoke
Greek so badly. He had told us his name, which was
something weirdly barbarous like Abdelmelkart. We
were of some use in helping the distracted Phoinician
make himself understood to the supervisor. This
overseer of the harbour's great Emporion was palpably
reluctant to pay attention to the foreigner, but we at last
made him understand that the alleged theft involved
jewels of great price. Poor Abdelmelkart kept babbling
on about his precious *smaragd*, a green jewel so rare that
I had never seen one, nor had the dubious Epimeletes.

'These people,' he informed us, 'are likely to exaggerate the value of things. They get unhinged and jabber away in their barbarous tongues. Hard to know what sense there is in it. You know these Phoinicians – though they're not so cocky these days, are they, now that they've lost Tyre?'

'You are right,' said Aristotle gravely to the Epimeletes, 'in thinking it wise to ascertain the cost of what was allegedly stolen. Perhaps this man has about him some other person who can describe the gems?'

'Yes, yes,' said the merchant, eagerly. 'My slave! Old woman who looks after everything – she know. But we wasting time so. If we go back to my lodgings, time lost. Why we not pursue a thief?'

The supervisor, however, insisted on our going to the Phoinician merchant's nearby lodgings to interview this slave, and if necessary put her to the question.

'An old woman she is only,' the merchant kept explaining in his imperfect Greek. He tried to tell us the woman's name, but it was not possible to understand those barbarous syllables. 'She nothing beautiful. But this slave keeps my accounts, she know everything. Very good.'

The merchant Abdelmelkart had rented two small rooms up a pair of stairs in a modest *synoikos* near the shipping. Evidently this merchant didn't indulge himself in luxury during his travels. We walked into the first room, low-roofed and plain. Save for one bright Carthaginian cushion, it was unadorned by Oriental ornaments. Plain and cheap pottery and little enough of that, a table and a portable stove. A pallet, presumably for the slave.

'Here you see,' said the Epimeletes significantly. 'Nothing to assure us that such a fellow would have possessions of great worth. Nothing interesting here.'

We walked into the next room – and he could no longer say there was nothing interesting in these apartments. This room was bare too, as I later made out, with only one plain cushion, a chair and a couch. But it had an unusual ornament. From the ceiling there dangled a surprising and grisly tassel. Something was swinging to and fro, to and fro . . . The body of a woman, small and thin. A sharp cord was bound tightly about her neck. Below her feet was a stool, on its side. A noxious and pathetic puddle had formed just under the slender dangling body.

The Phoinician began to howl and then to speak rapidly and tearfully in his own language, raising his hands to heaven and appealing, I suppose, to his gods in his gibberish.

'Look at that!' said the Epimeletes. 'We'd best cut her down, I suppose. Get a knife from the kitchen next door! But this slave looks stone dead.'

'I believe you,' said Aristotle. He raised the fallen stool, and set it under the dead women's dangling feet, which he was able to place firmly upon it. Once I brought the required knife, Aristotle cut her down, and we laid her upon the couch. She was not a good sight. Her face was a kind of purple, and so swollen it was difficult to make out the features. Her hair was grey. I could discern at last that her face was thin and lined, or had been before the noose made it puff out.

'She's not been dead for too long,' said Aristotle. 'An elderly female. But muscular.' He moved an arm thoughtfully.

'There you are!' said the port supervisor. 'That is the answer. This woman is the thief! She knew all about the jewels this man says he carried. She stole them and gave them to a confederate. The slit purse was but a blind. *She* did it, before he left home – unless he did it himself.

There's a Phoinician ship left this very day! Going west to Karthagos, and thus not to Mitylene, where this fellow *says* he was going.'

'Thief? My good old woman is thief?' Abdelmelkart raised his hands again, incredulous. 'Not possible, not possible. She did all the accounts, she took care of the money, she was as trustworthy as I—'

'But then,' continued the Epimeletes, paying him no heed, 'after betraying her master, her conscience took hold of her – or a justified fear of the law. So – farewell, world! She has hanged herself. You know hanging is women's common method for suicide. Not just females in plays, but in real life. I've seen it before.'

'You offer a tempting possible explanation,' said Aristotle, 'but—'

'Muscular. You said so yourself. Her arms and hands are strong enough to tie the knot. If she were not strong, I might suspect this Phoinician jabberer, but after all he was the one who brought us here. There's a rope-maker two doors down – easy for her to get a piece of stout cord. And look – she was standing on the stool, and then kicked it over. You saw yourself when you put her feet on it, that stool was the right height.'

'That is so. You are very clear. All is well arranged, there is nothing that she couldn't have done herself. And yet – I am not quite satisfied,' said Aristotle. 'There are scratches on the woman's hands . . .'

'Oh, people in kitchens often get scratches. I daresay her hands weren't too steady, she is such an old thing. Well, friend,' turning to the merchant, 'you have not lost a slave of great value here. And she has helped steal your alleged jewels – whatever they were. I am afraid they are gone and she has gone to Hades to pay for them. So no more can be done. We will take a note, however, of this affair, which seems a case of foreigners committing crimes among themselves. I acquit you of any part in this old hag's death, since you're so upset about it. It's obvious to anyone of sense that she did it herself. But be warned. Best for you to leave Peiraieus soon. We will take note of this suicide. The owner of your *synoikos* is not going to be pleased.'

The merchant seemed greatly taken aback, but the Epimeletes again informed him that nothing at all could be done. This suicide made it clear that the thief was of his own party, and her confederates unknown. 'Nothing to do with Peiraieus, really,' he said, rather jauntily.

The official overseer repeated this sentiment when we returned to the supervisors' office, where Lampos, having bade goodbye to his colleague on the *Thalia*, was still dolefully waiting to find out if anything further could be done in his case. Finding that the answer was no, he departed.

Once we were together in the street, Lampos made a few choice utterances of his opinion of this port overseer. 'He does nothing for me,' he complained. 'And from what you say, the affair of the foreign merchant requires more work too. Things of great value have been stolen! That man just wants to say no Athenians had a hand in the theft. And I have lost so many silver drakhmai! How can Peiraieus our great Emporion continue to flourish if such things go on here?'

'How, indeed?' said Aristotle.

XVIII

────◦§◦────

The Lovely Girl

'I am sure,' said Arkhias, 'that this will bear investigation.' The spy was standing importantly in Aristotle's room at the Lykeion. Having heard about the latest thefts, he was giving us the benefit of his opinion. 'Thefts of valuables from Peiraieus might actually cause more disturbance than thefts from Athens. Lykourgos will not desire to lose taxes as well as commercial reputation. Antipater must wish this matter laid to rest as soon as possible.'

'As usual, Arkhias, you are perfectly right,' said Aristotle mildly.

'But *why*?' Arkhias demanded impatiently. 'Who are these people and why are they stealing? Or does Athens now breed thieves?'

'Some disaffected persons might say that Makedonia breeds thieves, since they have helped themselves to Asia,' said Theophrastos calmly.

'A very ill-conditioned remark.' Arkhias glowered at Theophrastos. 'You are confident indeed to say that kind of thing before me, when you know I have the ear of Antipater.'

'Oh, let us not quarrel about who has whose ear, I beg.' Aristotle made a slight grimace to himself. 'Theophrastos was only jesting. I have wondered myself whether the thefts are merely individual outbreaks of greed, or some more concerted scheme.'

'Antipater,' Arkhias pronounced, 'would be deeply concerned if these thefts were committed for some dangerous reason – such as to raise a mercenary army to fight Makedonian power.'

'But that would require an enormous sum!' I exclaimed.

'Such a supposition has crossed my mind, but I cannot seriously entertain it,' said Aristotle. 'Consider! The thefts have usually concerned moderate sums. Some admittedly have been more ambitious, involving large sums and objects of worth. If the villains *are* a concerted group – a difficult assumption – they would certainly have raised many thousands by now. But one would still need *much* more than that in order to bribe allies, or buy large stocks of weapons and mercenaries.'

'They could hire a spy or two,' said Arkhias. 'And some weapons – and mercenaries – are not as dear as you think.'

'I didn't know you came so cheap,' I said smartly, though I was sorry for cracking this jest when I saw Arkhias' face.

'Come,' said Aristotle. 'It is a pretty puzzle, I grant – why are there these thefts, and who commits them? The effect is to make Athens slightly miserable, and Athenians more suspicious and less charitable. The wrongdoers may not have been capable of recognising in advance the true results of their actions. Hence, we esteem prudence – an intellectual rather than a purely ethical virtue.'

'Pho! Prudence!' Arkhias snorted. '*Old* men talk about prudence when they are afraid. We need courage first.'

'You are right there,' said Aristotle. His face was re-animated as he began to engage in a philosophical discussion. 'Courage is needed by a city first of all if it is to defend itself and remain an entity, unconquered and uninjured. Courage, like all virtues, must be considered not as an emotion but as a state of being, resulting from and related to choice. The truly courageous man does not feel an emotion of courage; he *chooses* to act.'

'But,' interjected Theophrastos, 'you, Aristotle, argue for finding the mean between extremes. There can be an excess of courage.'

'Yes, but we find it easier to forgive rashness – its rare excess – rather than its common deficiency, which is cowardice. Fear is informative, fear is a counsellor, but it should never be made one's soul's commander. So we honour Leonidas and his valiant three hundred Spartans for their courageous stand against the Persian host at Thermopylai.'

'Yet all those three hundred died at Thermopylai,' Arkhias objected. 'And Leonidas had his head cut off. It would be better to think of a stratagem, like Odysseus. Oh well, you philosophers like to sit and talk. I shall make my way to Peiraieus and see if I can catch any scent of the thieves. They may well be still at work. Rich pickings!'

'Farewell,' said the philosopher, with a relief I think he always felt when the door closed on the back of the strong official spy from the West, Regent Antipater's new favourite. 'He defines himself well,' Aristotle commented in a low voice, after Arkhias had gone. 'For he does indeed value stratagem and deceit above straightforward action. A courageous Akhilleus would never have endured Odysseus' ignoble stratagem of the wooden horse.'

'Sir,' said Phokon, Aristotle's chief male slave, poking his head in at the door, 'there is a – a female to see you.'

'Really? What sort – but I need scarcely ask. Not a respectable citizen's wife.'

'No indeed, O Aristotle.' Phokon's serious face broke into a slight smile. 'This person came to see you once before. Her name is Antigone.'

'Oh, *that* one!'

'Yes, exactly. *That* one. But this time she has brought a little girl with her.'

Phokon went out and almost immediately Antigone glided into the room. I remembered the graceful sway of her walking, and the bird-like swoop of the head upon its elegant long neck! Her presence brought back a sharp recollection of her one previous appearance in this room, a long time ago so it now seemed. Before Pythias died, before Aristotle and I went on our strange journey to the East . . .

Antigone the freedwoman was taller than most women, and immensely elegant. She was well-shaped, but slender, and walked with the utmost grace. I looked involuntarily to see if she were wearing sandals with green curling tendrils, as she had done last summer. But today she came more soberly garbed. As she was not a citizen woman, she could go unveiled, but she wore a black cloth over her head. Her clothing was also black, which made the more dramatic her delicate white skin.

'O Aristotle of Athens, great philosopher, son of the honoured doctor Nikomakhos! I thank you must humbly for receiving me. My greetings also to your friend Stephanos of Athens.' Antigone bowed low, then straightened, letting the head-covering slip back. To my surprise her hair was a different colour from last year. Then it had been dressed in an odd if attractive way, with twisty points of colour, almost scarlet in places. Now it seemed to have turned quite fair, or at least in streaks of it. Perhaps, I tried to think charitably, the effect of days in the Asian sun. But no – nobody who had spent her days in the hot sun could have kept that pale skin. A delicious white.

'May I, your servant, present another unworthy servant? My daughter Glykera, who would be honoured by your slightest notice.' She took a robed and veiled figure, considerably shorter than herself, by the hand. This shrouded little personage performed a deep bow, almost as if she would petition Aristotle by embracing his knees.

'Well, Antigone,' said Aristotle, 'take a seat. And be so kind as to inform me what on earth you are doing here. I cannot see why you have sought me out – me, of all people!'

'Ah,' said Antigone, sitting down, with her daughter standing by her side, 'you are thinking of the events of last year, with that unfortunate imbroglio regarding the shop of the perfume-seller—'

'*Unfortunate*!' I burst out. 'Nonsense! You not only diddled a hapless Athenian citizen, but used your trumped-up tale to make your way to the Lykeion and spy upon Aristotle! And then you lied about him. I don't know why Aristotle has not thrown you out into the road – and set the dogs on both of you!'

'Perhaps, then,' said Antigone very coolly, 'it is as well I am calling upon the philosopher and not upon yourself, Stephanos. This is the house of the Master of the Lykeion, not yours, I seem to remember. Times alter, events change us.' She turned towards Aristotle. 'Forget our unfortunate misunderstanding. *Now*, though you may not know it, we have a grief in common.'

'You allude, I presume,' said Aristotle, without any inflection of emotion, 'to the sad death of Philotas. So then, Stephanos,' he added, turning to me, 'we guessed aright. The Antigone who joined Philotas was indeed this lady.'

'There you are! You are always right!' said Antigone with admiration. 'One can keep nothing from you, O Aristotle of Stageira. All men praise your abilities. Philotas – so intelligent himself! – always spoke of you with such admiration!'

'Did he so?' said Aristotle, softening for a moment. He wiped his eyes. 'Poor Philotas,' he said. 'A terrible fate, so I have heard. Can you tell me any more of that sad affair?'

'Oh, it is so dreadful – it is very hard to speak of it.' The woman wrung her hands nervously. 'One day everything seemed all right, just as usual, Philotas in favour and Alexander laughing with him. Then everything changed. There was suspicion of a plot. Philotas said he could make all right with Alexander if he got to speak to him alone. So he made what he thought was an appointment, and went to a room where he believed Alexander was, with some of the Makedonian officers. But he couldn't see Alexander. And then the men began to question him, and then a number of them held him down and bound and tortured him. Then King Alexander himself came out from behind a hanging – a tapestry picture of the taking of Troy – and was in a rage. He was like a furious lion, his eyes starting out of his head. And the King told the officers that they must kill Philotas. And so he was killed, in a very terrible way. I think you must know it. He ran naked between the men and everyone aimed lances and javelins at him, though some of the officers were merciful and tried to kill him outright without more pain. He yelled, "I have not deserved this!" Then he tried not to cry out again, but it was too much for him. He gave a terrible shriek just before they finished him at last.'

She wrung her hands again, and wiped her eyes with the corner of her head-covering.

'Most terrible,' said Aristotle. 'Appalling. How truly distressing – and dangerous for you.'

'Weren't you afraid,' I asked, 'that they would kill you after?'

'Oh, of course. And fearful most of all for Glykera here.' She nodded at the little figure standing by her side. 'But some of Philotas' friends must have petitioned the King for mercy towards me. They packed me off with a little of my baggage. A long, long journey, and I was ill upon the road. I wonder I did not die.'

'Very hard,' said Aristotle. 'As I knew Philotas, I will make a modest contribution—'

She flushed. 'O sir! O Aristotle of Stageira, I have not come to beg!' She pressed her fingertips together and then opened her hands palms upwards in a beseeching manner. 'How could I importune *you* for money? What a wretched beggar you would think me.' Tears, crystalline perfect globes, came down her cheeks. 'You must pay no heed,' she said, wiping them away. 'I used never to cry. Glykera and I are well enough off, for now. Yet – I confess – I do come as a petitioner.'

The amazing woman suddenly slid off her chair and prostrated her black-clad figure on the floor, reaching for Aristotle's knees. Her tear-washed profile was very clear and noble, like a goddess on some beautiful pot or old statue. Her head-covering slipped back further, and her now-fair hair tumbled picturesquely about.

'Please, please help us,' she implored, still recumbent, almost but not quite flat upon the floor. 'You think I did you wrong last year in my accusation, but circumstances were all against me. You don't know the pressure I was under – or how they extorted that accusation from me! But you are a just man. You do not cherish resentment. So I dare come to you, even though you should be my enemy, to beg your help.'

'What sort of help have you in mind?' enquired Aristotle. He made no motion to raise Antigone from the prone position she had adopted.

'I beseech you to try to restore me to the favour of Alexander. I am *so* afraid! I am frightened of what he or his men might do to me and my daughter! Even here in Athens, I fear we are not safe. Please, *please* write to the King! Explain that I was merely the plaything of Philotas, and meant no harm. I knew nothing of anything he might have been doing. Swear to the King, as you may safely do, that my child is not the daughter of Philotas, but the by-blow of quite another man.'

'What a pretty letter that would be,' said Aristotle. 'Pray rise, Antigone. You have made your point and there is no more need to roll about on the floor.'

'Don't do it!' I burst out. 'O Aristotle, *don't* deal at all with this female! Why bother mentioning her in your letters to Alexander? She is of no importance to you, nor her brat either.'

'You are so decisive, Stephanos, so commanding,' said Antigone softly. She had risen from the floor and was resuming her seat, putting back her hair as she did so. 'I admire these qualities in a man. Your forthright honesty must be greatly valued by all your friends. But yet – can we not let the philosopher in his wisdom decide what is best for himself and for us?'

'It is never easy to change a man's mind,' said Aristotle. 'Especially Alexander's. Once he casts someone off, they stay cast off. If he thinks ill of someone once, he thinks ill always. If he does now consider you, Antigone, as an enemy, any further reference to you may well throw oil on the flame. Can you bear to risk that?'

'Well then,' said Antigone, 'let me still entreat you to try. For it were best for me to risk my own life if I could save that of my daughter. I love my daughter – please believe me. If I were killed but she were safe that would be something gained.'

'No, Mamma, no!' A voice emanated from the short figure, which now moved towards us.

'Hush, child! Be still, as I have bidden you.' The covered figure stopped where it stood. Antigone continued. 'The important thing is to emphasise not only that I knew nothing of any of Philotas' concerns – beyond bed – but also that my daughter Glykera had nothing to do with Philotas. She had no carnal knowledge of him or anyone else – she is still a virgin. Most important, she is *not* Philotas' offspring. That I think ought to be said to Alexander by someone.'

'And what do you propose to do with your Glykera, presuming she is not persecuted by any Makedonians?'

'My Glykera is being bred in a very ladylike way. Do you have a harp handy? No? Pity – I could show you how well she plays. She plays and sings, she reads and writes even, and understands poetry. I am going to buy her a little maid of her very own soon, if I can find a well-reared slave-girl going cheap, so that my daughter may have more time for her accomplishments. She is fit to be the dear companion of a man of taste. *Far* above the common run. You look doubtful. You have both seen some beauty – I think you have seen Phryne – so you are fit judges. Child, unveil yourself.'

The little figure went immediately to the centre of the room. Standing evenly poised on her small and shapely unshod feet, the young girl began slowly to remove the thick cloth that covered her head. She raised the veiling slowly, as one might draw wrappings from a statue. The effect was all that Antigone knew it would be.

Glykera's hair, a golden brown and unbound as was seemly in a maiden child, fell rippling in a thousand curls beside her cheeks and down her back, a tender and luxurious profusion, sweet as new vines in spring. Her face was a perfect oval, poised on a slender neck; her straight nose was pure Greek. Her eyes were an amazing blue-green like the sea, and the kissable mouth was like the first wind-blown red anenome of spring.

'Turn about, dear,' her mother commanded, and Glykera slowly turned about.

'There! You see what a prize she will be,' said her mother. 'It would be madness to throw away such beauty! I want my daughter to have more security than I have had. A man who will keep her in a comfortable home. And no more of this going with an army, or getting mixed up in political games. So dangerous to us poor ignorant women.'

'Very proper sentiments.' Aristotle looked searchingly at the girl. 'What exactly is her age?'

'She will complete her eleventh year soon; her birthday arrives as spring shades into summer.'

'Well,' said Aristotle. 'Do you know how to spin, my child? And to weave?'

'Yes,' said Glykera, looking at him somewhat timidly. 'And I can also make fine embroidered works. I could make something for you.'

'No need for that,' said Aristotle. 'But every woman should know how to spin and weave. Also something of cookery and the care of children. Well – if you don't mind, let me look at you.' He beckoned her to stand before him where he sat, and his deep-set dark blue eyes gazed at her and roamed over her countenance.

'I beg your pardon, my dear, but I thought it best to be sure. Now that I look at you, I myself am satisfied that you are *not* the offspring of Philotas, whom I knew well. I also knew his father. You don't have the look of Parmenion's family. In fact, you don't look like a Makedonian. Do you know,' said Aristotle, looking fully at Antigone, 'old as I am, with eyesight not quite as good as it has been, I think I myself could guess the father, or at least the family.'

'Oh no!' Antigone gasped and fluttered her hands like little doves.

'Oh yes. The stamp of a father is strong, a whole family history may suddenly emerge in a nose, or the set of an eye. You need to be careful in Athens; other people are observant too. It might be wise to let the girl's hair go dark – with the help of some friendly vegetable matter if her curls will not darken on their own.'

'I understand you,' murmured Antigone.

'I think you do. And you may take it from me that, although I shall not stir up a wasps' nest by coming to your defence, I shall find some way to mention that this child is none of Philotas' getting.'

'Oh, I am so grateful. It might be helpful to say that you think that Philotas couldn't father children at all – that would please the King!'

'I am sure you know Alexander's humour best, but I would not venture so far. I have no proof that your allegation is a fact. Let matters rest there.'

Aristotle stood to signal that this interview was definitely over, and Antigone stood too.

'I am so grateful – so deeply grateful,' she murmured, adjusting her head-covering. 'Glykera too. Veil yourself, my child. My humble service, and gratitude to you for giving us of your time and wisdom. And my thanks also to you, Stephanos of Kydathenaion.'

She left, still bowing in deep humility, and the two females sought their slave, who awaited them with a donkey-cart.

'Well . . . well,' said Aristotle. He sat down again. Instead of rapping out some pithy remarks about the woman, as I expected, he stared into space for some while.

'You are thinking of Philotas?' I ventured.

'Yes – I am thinking of Philotas. Who is dead.'

'In the main, her story matched that told to you by

Antigonos the One-Eyed. I heard that narrative too, and there isn't much difference between them.'

'I dare say her story is the more authentic. Antigonos had to rely on another to tell him before he told me. But did you notice some of the details, Stephanos? That woman was there! I swear, Antigone was there – in the room where Philotas was tortured!'

'How do you mean?'

'I mean that she knows too much about it. She forgot to tell us that she was at a distance and that someone told her later, and so on. Her story is too vivid. Too clear.'

'That touch about the tapestry hanging, for instance? She said it showed the taking of Troy. Antigonos didn't tell us what its design was.'

'Exactly. That detail is almost too obvious. It leads me to wonder whether Antigone did not wish us – wish *me* – to realise that she had actually been there.'

'Why would she do that?'

'In order to let me know – with exquisite subtlety – that she is actually in the confidence of Alexander. Far from being a potential victim of his wrath, this woman may be a spy for him. In any case, it is pretty clear to me that she betrayed Philotas – as she formerly betrayed me. Though to me she owed no allegiance, to Philotas she owed friendship and loyalty. Parmenion felt uneasy about her, and he was right.'

'In your case she lied, but only by twisting a little what you had said – said to someone else too, not her.'

'She could do the same again. Suppose Antigone got nervous, realising the atmosphere around Philotas was not good. She decided to save herself by a bold pre-emptive move. Saying perhaps, "I was there when Philotas entertained this man and that man. They were plotters, I heard them whispering together." By turning against Philotas in time, she could save her own skin.'

'Disgusting!'

'There is an even worse possibility. Might she not have been set upon Philotas by Alexander from the beginning? Sent to the East by the King – or perhaps only by one of his henchmen, a rival of Philotas – on purpose to spy upon Philotas? Or at least to be so openly his bed-companion that she could be relied upon at any moment upon command to declare a plot, and to be believed. Saying whatever instructors told her to say.'

'This is very elaborate, Aristotle. You imagine conspiracies. Could anybody, man or woman, really do such a thing? Share someone's bed intending to betray the lover to death!'

'Such things have been done. Perhaps I am excessively antagonistic to this woman. Yet I cannot but think her coming to Athens is further bad news for myself.'

'Why?'

'Why? Because, Stephanos, I am surrounded by spies. I am – perhaps – being warned by this freedwoman Antigone that she is a spy upon me. And I already have Arkhias to deal with, a spy in the employ of Antipater. I do not believe that all the interests of Alexander are now channelled through Antipater. Nor do I think Arkhias and I are necessarily on the same side.' He smiled wearily.

'You, Stephanos, once came to me and I was able to help you partly because of my associations with the Makedonian power. You later risked some odium because of the connection. But now I cannot be relied on to help you in any way other than by my own wits.'

'I don't need help all the time!' I retorted. 'Anyway, your wits are more valuable than any other man's aid.'

'Kindly said. I must not regard myself any more as under the protection of Alexander. He will be concerned as to how old friends of Parmenion and Philotas are taking this turn of events, how much disaffection there

may be among allies – or former allies – in Greece. And
he will want to know how people react to his pursuing his
conquests into the wilds of Baktria, instead of resting
content with holding court in Babylon, or Susa, now that
Darius is dead and Persia conquered.'

'Never mind those strange eastern places,' I said. 'We
have to deal with Athens as it now is. And with this
woman Antigone. When all is said and done, she is only
a harlot. And her daughter will be the same.' I recollected
the look of that girl-child: the clear-cut nose, the gold and
honey-coloured hair, the full but delicate mouth . . .

'It's funny,' I added. 'Of course Glykera is much
younger and only a female, but she looks a lot like your
student Demetrios of Phaleron. He can't be the father –
he's too young. Stay – they could share a father? Is that
it?'

'Ah, you think so? Let us hope that Glykera and
Demetrios do not meet, then. Though I think Demetrios'
tastes run to boys rather than girls, but everyone is
capable of making an exception.'

'Demetrios himself is strange,' I ruminated. 'Nobody
names his father – he is always called "Demetrios of
Phaleron". Yet he was bred in the house of the
descendants of Kimon, and not at all like a slave. So the
blood of great Kimon must run in his veins.'

'Athenians are interconnected in all sorts of ways.
Noble blood is found in many who are not strictly of
noble birth.'

'That woman expects to sell her sweet little Glykera
for great sums.'

'Yes. And if any man stands in the way of her clapping
up a good bargain, let him watch out!'

XIX

—◦○◦—

The Crazy Girl

What Aristotle had said during our recent meetings gave me much food for serious thought. This was a time of uncertainty in his relationship with Alexander. However bitter his feelings over Philotas he must maintain a friendship – for the sake of his beloved Kallisthenes, and the other nephew. Then there was the welfare of his Lykeion to consider: much of the money supporting his researches for the great project on classifying animals, and even a number of curious specimens, was the donation of the young king.

After all, I needed no foreign philosophers to rely on. 'Bastards and foreigners,' I muttered ruefully to myself. Crude abuse of the marketplace, but not incorrect. Whereas I was an Athenian citizen of long descent, married to the daughter of an Athenian citizen. At the age of twenty-six, I should protect my own family. My recent efforts at making some connections with the Beautiful and Good had not been entirely ineffectual. Lamas and Theophon were visitors, and I had Diognetos as a *mystagogos*.

In regard to Lykon's suit, I presented my statement to

a magistrate as soon as possible, pleading that no action be taken regarding the law case until we could certainly hear from Philokles. The magistrate fortunately sympathised, and promised me that, although there would be a formal appearance at the end of the Old Year, when I must move again for postponement, the Hymettos case need not be brought until midsummer, at the New Year, at the time of the change of arkhons. By that time, ships would have been travelling regularly and with ease throughout the Aegean, and letters should surely have been exchanged.

Lykon was not pleased with this delay, but of course I was. Yet I was not going to allow relief at a post-ponement to tempt me to repeat my previous slackness. There was no use in expecting anything of Dropides. I would have to make an effort myself to cajole our Hymettos neighbours into giving us statements and supporting our case. Since it behoved me now to rely on myself and my own kin, I prevailed on my cousin Philemon to come with me. He was a strong, athletic young man, and might possibly make a favourable impression on the Hymettos denizens. At any rate, with him in my company I need fear no insult.

We walked towards Hymettos and then up the incline through the fields now sending their green blades into the sun. The weather was warming, the skies pleasant. Flowers bloomed by the wayside – late anemones in sheltered places, and irises on the damp banks of the Ilissos. As we went along, Philemon regaled me with accounts of athletes in training. He took particular interest in chariot-racing. He was not one of the small number of wealthy young men who could afford horses and chariots, but he knew those who did.

'Hipponax says,' he proclaimed, 'that he has a better team now than he did last year when he competed and came third.'

'Oh yes?' Few things interested me less than horses.

'Yes – now he has replaced the light gelding with a good stallion, he is sure to get on. The thing now is to train the four horses *together*. The old ones are suspicious of the new one.'

'As well they might be.'

'Hipponax did not do well in the Panathenaia last year. Next time, if things go well. He doesn't want to enter again unless he *really* thinks he can win. There's the Olympic contest to prepare for. He wants to raise a new colt. So he has asked me to help,' Philemon added, in the tone one uses when pretending to be modest about what is really an honour. 'And I said I'd think about it.'

'What is there to think about?'

'Oh Stepho, he'd want me to move out into the country for a large part of each summer. Quite a way out – in Paeonia, the flat part. His horses were bred in Argos, and they need space for running. He wants me to be on hand every day. This summer, even before the New Year begins, and each summer until the next Olympics. Three years. And of course he is offering me use of a house in Paeonia. I have a wife and children to think about.'

'Wife and child,' I corrected.

'No – no. Children. My Melissa is expecting another – didn't I tell you? I thought Mother might have suspected it. The new brat should arrive by early autumn; we intend to keep it, even if it's a girl. Anyway, Hipponax is going to pay me and give me a house so that my wife and children can be there too. It would be nice for them to have country air and space – you know our family property in town is very small. House too hot in summer.'

'Well – yes, of course. I see. So you are really going to serve as a horse trainer?'

'Not as a servant or anything like that. As an assistant, to work with the horses and train the trainers. And I can also watch Hipponax and tell him where he is doing best as charioteer, and where he is weak. And he might give me a horse to ride myself, sometimes. Maybe even let me drive the chariot! It could be most tremendous fun.'

Philemon would certainly enjoy this. But it rather crimped my new project of surrounding myself with kindred, if he were going to be available in Athens only in the winter months. He would be departing just as I needed him. Next winter was a long way away.

As we approached the Hymettos farm, I could hear the humming of bees on the sunnier slopes where the thyme was starting into flower. Philemon requested to be allowed to stay outside while I had my lawsuit conversation with Philokles' family. The house dog was tied to a stake, and the surly servant Mika, on the lookout, opened the door before I could knock. She ran to fetch Philokleia, while I sat in the main room with its jumble of furniture, in company with Dropides, who was in his usual warm chair, a sheep fleece under him and under his feet, as if undergoing a penance or purification which was never completed.

'I have come,' I said, solemnly, after Philokleia and her daughter had arrived and were standing behind the curtain, 'in order to gather depositions. I have brought with me my kinsman, a young man on whose judgement I rely.'

Mika threw open the door so that my kinsman would be visible to Dropides and even to the women. Philemon at that moment was making fearful faces at the house dog – stretching his mouth sideways with his fingers so that it looked like a Gorgon's mask. Mika shut the door and I said nothing further about my kinsman or his judgement.

'Oh, what are we to do?' Philokleia was so agitated

that she very nearly dispensed with all proprieties. The piece of fabric that usually separated us was not completely drawn, and in her agitation she addressed me directly.

'I *begged* my husband to collect statements from the neighbours. But he won't go out – says he feels too ill – and we have collected nothing. And I haven't heard – we haven't heard – from Philokles either.'

'Nor have I,' I said. 'And the court is restless. Though we have agreement for postponement, the arkhons agree with Lykon that the case should not be put off indefinitely. Indeed, the longer we wait and the longer Philokles does not reply, the worse it looks for us. The next thing you know, people will say he is dead.'

'Perhaps he is,' said Dropides gloomily.

'Not a bit of it!' I retorted. 'But Philokles is not a very active sort, that's his trouble – rather in your style.' It was the first time I had ever spoken contemptuously to Dropides.

'I?' He threw up his hands. 'What can *I* do? I cannot go out on the cold mountain. Do you know how damp it is here in the spring? I can barely stir at this time of year, with my rheumatics as well as a cough. You send me out on a cold Hymettos hillside, I won't be long for this world.'

'Your wife and her daughter seem to manage it,' I said.

'They? But they were bred to it! Hymettos is in their blood. I was born in a smooth, dry region, with nice flat places for walking, not everything aslant. You must see ...'

'Don't agitate yourself, Dropides,' said Philonike, and Philokleia said soothingly, 'There, there,' as to an infant. Had I not been present, she would likely have walked over and patted his arm. 'You must not be hard on the master, Stephanos.' She turned to me reproachfully. 'He cannot go about like a younger person in good health.

And to be fair, this is not his land, and there is little he can do. It is the responsibility of my son Philokles.'

'But *you*, Stephanos,' said my mother-in-law, 'you after all will get money from this place – you have received money already. Your wife is a direct inheritor, and your future children. So you must take an interest.'

'That is very clear to me, indeed,' I said emphatically. 'And I have come expressly to help you – and myself too, of course. We desperately need depositions from the neighbours – from citizens – about the farm and its boundaries, past and present. I realise that mere women can do nothing about collecting such statements. I have come today for that purpose. But you should tell me – who would be most likely to cooperate? To whom should I go first?'

'Well, there's a thought,' said Philokleia. 'I think Lykon will have got at some of the neighbours already – we have heard through the slaves that he has been asking people to back up his case.'

'Why wasn't I told of this? You should have sent me word.'

'You were so busy with your wedding, Stephanos, we hardly wished to trouble you. And Philonike said that she didn't see how Lykon could get too far, for all the neighbours must know the truth.'

'The truth? In a law case? You should have given them better advice, Dropides.' I forgot myself in indignation. 'We can hardly expect more from women – so innocent they think the truth comes out of a law court. They cannot speak for the estate. But you, O Dropides, you are a man and a citizen. You ought to have warned me, even if you could do nothing yourself.'

'What's the good,' said Dropides pacifically, 'of setting oneself against a parcel of women, if they want their own way?'

This man was as helpful to me as his heel to Akhilleus.

It was no use becoming exasperated. 'Please just tell me the names of the neighbours, and where they are to be found.'

'Well, there's that old man – I forget his name,' Philonike ventured. 'The one with the long white beard. His property is high up the slopes. He has taken a stout young nephew to live with him, and his rather stupid wife.'

'It's the nephew who has the stupid wife,' Philokleia clarified. 'This heir hasn't been there very long. That old fellow – his name is Pantakles – who owns the property is a widower. He keeps himself to himself, never invites anybody,' she added. 'There's probably no use in going to him – too haughty, or just too old and forgetful.'

'And there's Asimos whose place is lower down than Pantokles' place; to the left of ours as you face up the mountain,' Philonike suggested.

'Asimos is rather strange too,' Dropides interjected. 'Has a funny little daughter. Walls off his property or puts thorn bushes around it. Very prickly and suspicious.'

'I've met him before,' I said, remembering the running girl and her father. I could only suppose that Dropides had seen Asimos' daughter a long while ago, if he thought her still 'little'.

'The thorn trees keep the pigs and goats from wandering off,' said Philokleia. 'Asimos lets them out to graze under the trees. Asimos has no wife, and no son – he should really marry again. Then there's Smikythos, who lives just above Lykon's property.'

'Smikythos lost his wife just a while back,' Dropides informed me.

'You mean, he will be too sad to see anyone.'

'No – no. Likely he'll be glad to see other citizens. He's looking for another woman, well connected, with money.'

'I had best see them all,' I determined, resigning

myself to spending my day going up and down the mountain. I departed, taking Philemon with me, and whiled away our walk by filling him in with what little knowledge I had gleaned.

'Not very promising,' he said dubiously. 'You'll have to think how to turn these crabby people up sweet without spending any money. People are few and far between too. Pity Hymettos isn't a proper village, with shops, a temple and a tavern. You get plenty of news about people in a village.'

We wound our way upward, first to the dwelling of Smikythos, above the holding of Lykon, giving Lykon's house a wide berth. Smikythos' property seemed very neat and prosperous, though not as promising as our – or rather Philokles' – farm. A couple of slaves were pruning fruit trees in the background; the man tending his vegetable garden seemed likely to be the owner.

'Sir – ahem – have I the honour of addressing Smikythos of Hymettos?'

The man straightened up and looked at us. 'The same,' he said drily.

He was not a bad-looking fellow, of strong middle age. Quite a good sort for a witness in a law court.

'I hear your wife died not long ago,' I said awkwardly. 'My condolences on your loss.'

'Well – only a woman. Thank you, all the same,' he added, thawing a little. 'Who might you be?'

I gave our names, carefully including father's name and deme in each case. They seemed to make a good impression.

'Pleased, I am sure,' he said. 'Glad you have come. Always a pleasure to meet citizens from the town. I take it you have a sister or so? Too young-looking to have marriageable daughters. I won't take a widow, mind that! But a respectable virgin female of good stock, even if she's a little advanced in age – say, twenty – I might still be interested. Come in and let us talk. Would you like some garlic soup?'

'Thank you very much, Smikythos of Hymettos. I fear there is some misapprehension. We do not have marriageable female relatives; I regret that we cannot help you in that way.'

His face dropped, the smile vanished; I could tell the invitation to garlic soup was withdrawn.

'Perhaps we might help you find another man's female relative,' suggested Philemon.

'If that's not why you are here,' the man said gravely, ignoring Philemon, 'then what? What have you come for?'

'What I have really come about is the lawsuit that Lykon is threatening against Philokles and his family,' I announced.

'Oh? You an interested party in this suit, then?'

'Not exactly. But my wife belongs to this family; in fact Philokles is her uncle.'

'Oh-ho.' Light dawned. '*You* are the one that Lykon is suing. One of 'em. Now I recollect – he was named Stephanos.'

'I cannot truly be a party to the suit because I do not own the land,' I explained patiently. 'But I know that the boundary is where it has been for many years, and that you and other neighbours are aware of the fact that there are family graves in that area, from olden times to now.'

'Well . . .' Smikythos scratched his head. 'It may be that they have graves – it's long since I saw their place – but the graves may have nothing to do with it.' He put down his spade, and straightened his back. 'I should tell you, Lykon has looked for a statement from me, and he is likely to get it.'

'But that's unjust! You are giving a deposition for

Lykon, even though you must be aware of the facts of the case!'

'I don't know about that, young fellow. Lykon is a good neighbour. That other place hasn't anybody on it – only a couple of women who do all the work, far as I can make out. Just them and the slaves. The man who resides there, catch him doing anything! And I haven't seen young Philokles for a couple of years.'

'Very clearly put,' approved Philemon, who had been following this statement. 'You've defined the situation very clearly. Lykon knows how things are done, I dare say. But how can you be sure that he will give you what he promised?'

Smikythos turned rather red. 'Don't be impudent, young fellow. I hope I know my own duty, and the law. A good day to you both.' Leaving his spade in the ground, he stalked stiffly to his own door, to make sure we knew the interview was at an end.

'You are right,' I admitted to Philemon. 'Lykon has obviously promised this Smikythos something – perhaps something to do with marrying again. Maybe he promised he'd help him to a nice wife, with a good dowry. Or pay for the wedding. Something substantial. By Herakles, it maddens me! And for the first time I see clearly the disadvantage of our farm in Hymettos, with no citizen-owner visible.'

'No use staying here,' said Philemon, shrugging. 'We might as well be off, Stepho. I don't imagine the others will be any better.'

With this cool comfort we set off again in the opposite direction, and eventually arrived at the holding of Asimos. This seemed not quite as large as the farm of either Lykon or his widowed supporter, nor was it quite as tidy, though it was certainly strongly fenced by prickly bushes. A few sheep and goats were visible in the distant pasture, and a strong smell of pigs suggested their near proximity. We found the gate, double latched over a narrow gap in the giant hedge of thorns, and advanced boldly. Not far from the house a nanny goat with a swelling udder was tied to a tree; one goatish leg was neatly bound with a bandage. The length of her rope allowed her to lunch on the grass, which she was doing. Or rather, she had been doing, for as we came she turned her attention to what looked like personal garments that someone had left out to dry on a bush.

'Hi! Get out of that!' Philemon shouted and clapped his hands. The goat spun around in amazement.

One of the window shutters popped open, and a woman leaned out and shouted in turn. 'You there! Stop that! Who are you to shout at my goat?' She clapped the shutters to, but not out of excessive modesty.

Asimos' daughter came out of the door almost at once, bounding like an animal herself, like a kind of awkward red dog. Her dress was red, and her hair was a mop of auburn bound at the top of her head in a kerchief. One leg was evidently weaker than the other; I recollected noting her limp when she was running. Though ungainly, the girl moved quickly.

'Who are you? Stop teasing my goat. Are you ghosts sent by Hekate or goblins or what? Go away!'

'We have come to speak to citizen Asimos,' I explained, with distant courtesy. I didn't quite know how to address Asimos' daughter.

'Oh? Papa – papa!' She bellowed loud enough to set up the mountain echoes.

'I'm here – I'm coming, Zobia!' Within a very short time we saw her father, the sunburned man with the curly beard. A presentable fellow. He would look all right in a law court as a witness.

'Who are you?' he said when he saw us. 'And what do you want with my child?'

'Oh, sir, we had no intention of disturbing your daughter,' I said, embarrassed. 'It is to you that we wished to speak. I am Stephanos son of Nikiarkhos of Athens – we met before. This is my cousin. My bride is the niece of Philokles, owner of the holding beside yours, a little to the south on Hymettos. Lykon is suing Philokles and his people about the right of way and the water course – but Lykon's case is without foundation.'

'Oh – you're sure of that?'

'Yes, I am sure,' I said firmly. 'There is a bit of new wall, but it merely fills a gap where part of the old one fell down. The area all belongs to Philokles, it has been planted with almond trees for some years. And there are graves – a family burying-ground. It is absurd and even sacrilegious for Lykon to make any claims on it!'

'That's not what Lykon says.'

'No. But go to Dropides at the farm of Philokles and ask him for permission to view the site. You will find it is as I said.'

'I can swear it's so, Father,' said the girl.

'You?'

'Yes. I go everywhere,' she explained. 'Specially when the moon is full, and I can see my way. I have seen the almonds and the burying-ground. I like to roam about. I can climb walls and trees, and run through ditches. And I hear the owls of Athena and they cry, "Oho–ohoo! Well do you do!"'

'By Hekate!' Philemon exclaimed.

'Yes, Hekate and I are great friends. And Artemis. She brought me a baby. But it got lost. I wish she'd help me find it. I still have milk. The goat has milk now too, for the baby, when I get it back.'

'Oh, Zobia!' the man exclaimed. 'You will bring us all into great misfortune! Say nothing of your roaming, say nothing of the baby of your shame, I beg of you . . .'

'Don't look sad, Papa. I am happy.' The girl hastened in her awkward quick fashion to his side. 'Look how the sun shines today. Spring is here. Nay, summer's really beginning, with the barley growing green. The bees have come out. Soon there will be new honey again. Everything does well. Everyone gives me sweets. Demeter promises good things.'

'Bless you, poor child,' said the man, stroking her awkward bushy head. 'She is not answerable, sirs, for what she does. I have taken pains to plant thorn bushes all round the property. To no avail – for when she wants to get out, she will get out.'

'I have to look for my baby,' the girl explained.

'The child of her shame,' muttered Asimos. 'My poor lass doesn't know anything about shame. I could patch the matter up if she would lie about it, but she doesn't even know why lies are necessary. She has never been quite right. Crazed in her wits. And a bad leg from an infant.'

'I wonder you chose to rear her,' said Philemon. 'You might have exposed her when you had the chance.'

'Her mother died from giving birth to her, and begged me to keep the baby, so I didn't have the heart to expose the little thing. And when she was born we couldn't know – none of us – that she was crazy . . .'

'What a misfortune!'

Asimos glared. 'We don't want your pity. We do all right as we are. She is real handy in the kitchen and the garden, even with her bad leg. Good with animals, brings them back to life, almost. We thought the goat would die when a dog chewed its leg, but she nursed it back again.'

'Very good,' I said soothingly. 'I can see that would be useful.'

'Trouble is,' he sighed, 'now she is grown I have no control. She'll fly off in the moonlit night, roaming about, and there's young men in the area who would take advantage of her.'

'Do you know who the infant's father is?' My mind had been running on an idle fancy that Smikythos could be made to own up to rape, and pay damages . . .

'My simple girl – she never identified anybody. We cannot publish our disgrace, as there is no remedy. At least, thankfully, she doesn't want to do the things that would bring punishment on her – she doesn't try to go to the Agora, or join with polite women at great occasions. So all I can do is stay here, trying to keep people away. It's dangerous. Our water here is the source of Ilissos, sacred to Aphrodite. It's strong enough to give children to the barren; I fear it encourages begetting.'

'Well,' said Philemon, 'all women are unreasonable, it's just a matter of degree. You still might marry her off to some man who'd keep her with a strong hand.'

'No, I think not, thank you,' Asimos said coolly.

'Well, Asimos,' I said, 'we did not come to intrude upon your misfortunes. I simply wish to ask if you would be willing to write out a deposition, or sign one written out for you, saying that you know the situation of Philokles' farm, and that the portion Lykon claims as a water-course and part of his right of way is really part of Philokles' property.'

'Oh, I don't want to draw attention to myself where Lykon is concerned,' he said, pushing out his under-lip dubiously. 'It's best for me not to get into trouble – not to do that.'

'Look, man,' said Philemon briskly. 'The demon is out now. We know about your crazy daughter, and her ramblings and the baby. If this were published you would be a laughing-stock—'

'Stop that!' I said to Philemon, as sharply as he had spoken to the goat. 'I beg you, pay no heed to him,' I assured the poor father. 'Of course we should do nothing so base.'

'I'm sure, I'm sure,' said Asimos, passing his hand over his brow. 'I will say what is right – of course. And if you could keep me in mind when you want a pig, I should be glad.'

I had some statements with me, already written out, and he read one and signed it, standing on that spot. I warned him that he would probably have to write it again in the presence of a magistrate, if the case came on. Document in hand, we made our way out through the small gate in the thorn-beset wall.

'Well, there's one good piece of work,' said Philemon. 'You ought to be grateful to me!'

'It was not ethical to threaten the poor man.'

'Use what comes to hand, Stepho, that's what I say. You wouldn't have done so well on your own. Lucky you had me along, to apply pressure. I wonder if we should visit the white-haired old fellow who lives further up?'

'Probably not,' I said. It wasn't the climb up but the difficulty of tackling another household that put me off. We stood in the roadway, slightly indecisive. The air smelled good, of pine needles and fresh grass, not yet abashed by the fierce heat of summer.

'It's funny,' I said. 'If you kill a baby by exposure, that is not homicide. But if you, Philemon, tried to become a *mystes*, you would have to undergo purification because of that old manslaughter.'

'Yes,' he said laughing. 'We're a pair of killers.'

'Gentlemen, I'm sorry to interrupt you.' A white-haired man stood almost at my elbow. He was coming up the narrow road, and needed to pass between us; but courtesy forbade that he should push us aside.

'Isn't your name Stephanos of Athens?' the man continued, looking at me. He had the longest white beard

I could ever remember seeing; his years and stately dignity commanded respect. I murmured assent as the old man continued. 'Why then, I know why you have come to these parts. You are seeking witnesses – people who can swear as to how Philokles' land has always been.'

'Yes, exactly so – Pantakles, is it? Because of the lawsuit that Lykon is irrationally bringing against us.'

The old man nodded. 'Pantakles it is, you've got that right. I won't ask you to my house,' he added. 'My house far away up the mountain. But let's meet tomorrow. In the Agora – or just outside it, say. In the tavern nearest the Hephaistion.'

'Well, yes, I'm agreeable to that.'

'Tomorrow then, when the sun is in mid-heaven.' And the white-haired fellow set off on his steep homeward path, going fairly briskly for a man of his years.

'Well done,' said Philemon. 'Your witnesses come to you. I like that – no more climbing uphill. You can talk to that ancient person tomorrow. Come on, Killer. Let's return to Athens.'

We did so, and by the time we came to the flat area near the city walls, the dusk was looming, and Hymettos was already in purple shadow. After we entered the city gates, Philemon went off to his home, and I continued through the streets of familiar Athens, wrapped in my own thoughts. I almost stumbled into a small person trotting between me and a wall. A child, a female child, who ran her hand along the wall. This person was muttering, or rather saying something in quite a loud voice: 'Sixteen – Seventeen – Eighteen . . .' Each number was uttered slowly and followed by a whimpering sound, a cry or moan deep in her throat.

'What? Were you speaking to me, child?'

The person turned and looked at me and her eyes widened. It was the child Eurynome. She had changed greatly since I had first seen her with her doll and her earrings, happy in Halirrhothios' house. Now her tunic was torn and dirty, her hands grubby. These are normal phenomena in children, especially the children of slaves. But she looked very unlike a child, her face thin, pale and drawn. She walked like someone moving in sleep – in a nightmare – muttering to herself like an old woman. She looked at me with such horror that I expected her either to strike out at me or take to her heels. But she did nothing swift and lively. She stood still and put her face against the wall, and covered it with her arm and hand. Like a limpet, she had nothing to do but to cling to her rock.

It would have been normal for me to take her by the hand, to insist on returning her to her home, as people are wont to do with stray children whom they know. But the horror in her eyes as she looked at me forbade this. She seemed surrounded by an atmosphere that made one feel dread, like one of the gods it is better not to meet. By Artemis and Apollo – the child Eurynome had gone quite mad!

XX

❦

An Old Man's Request

Halirrhothios had reason for hatred of me! This thought flashed through my mind on the instant, and came back to me next morning when I awakened. I had never thought such a thing before. It had always seemed to me that others who disliked me or tried to do me harm did so most unjustly. But now I seemed to be outside myself, looking at Stephanos as someone might who had good cause to hate him. Someone who might well want to throw a knife at him. The damage done to the little girl Eurynome . . . The child walking in the infernal nightmare, repeating the counting of the strokes of the whip in never-ending succession. I argued to myself that it was all Halirrhothios' fault. Had my neighbour not been a thief, his house would never have been searched, the things would not have been found, and he would not have had to choose between his own life and the well-being of his poor bastard child.

Yet I could not deny that I had been eager in undertaking the search, and I had first accused Halirrhothios. Had I not accused him, what followed would not have followed. Had I not thought about theft, we could have gone on with our supper of beans in happy Pyanepsia celebration. Perhaps I need never have known of Thratta's bracelet contaminating our happy *eiresione*; this unwonted gold fruit could have been plucked off by somebody – probably the very person who was meant to find it. And I could have gone innocently on, stupid, a victim of theft, yet free of wreaking a catastrophe. But then – could I say that no citizen should seek redress for theft? Unendurable, monstrous! Certainly I had right on my side. Yet, if only for a while, I saw myself as Halirrhothios saw me – as the child saw me. I was an instrument of torture and object of dread. There was no redress, no way to make it right. What could I do? Give the crazy little girl a trinket? Offer her a poppied drink to take memory away?

These thoughts put me in a sombre mood. With a sigh I betook myself to the appointment made with the white-haired man. I found him, as he had said, at midday in the tavern nearest the Hephaistion. There was quite a crush this warm day, a crowd of workers from the bronze shops.

'Too many people here,' said the white-bearded elder, glancing about with disfavour. 'Mere artisans and such-like. Let's go somewhere quieter.'

And he led the way to another *kapeleion*, on the western edge of the Agora in a quieter section. Pantakles offered me a drink and we sat outside; he found a warm stone half shaded by a pine tree, out of earshot of drinking companions. Only one other person graced the area: an old clodhopper with a farmer's boots on, a man who had come early to market and was snatching a nap in the sun – and even he was, fortunately, at a distance.

'I should be glad, O Pantakles, to learn what you have to say on the subject of Philokles' land.'

'Boundaries.' The old man nodded, very wisely.

'Boundaries offer a lot to talk about – is it not so, Stephanos son of Nikiarkhos of Athens? I too am a citizen. I live on my farm in Hymettos with my brother's son. My oldest nephew and heir. I have lived on my little property up the mountain there' – he glanced eastwards, towards Hymettos – 'for a long, a *very* long time.'

'Quite so,' I said. 'That makes you a neighbour of Philokles and his family and also of Lykon. You must know something of the history of the estates,' I urged. 'Such knowledge is valuable. If you have lived there for a long—'

'All my life. And I'm seventy-two, young fellow, although I don't look it.'

'You don't say so – amazing! By Herakles, seventy-two, who would think it?' I replied with polite promptitude. Though I should not have been in the least surprised if the old fellow had informed me that he was eighty-odd.

'My health is good, from walking up and down the mountain. Good for another ten, maybe twenty years. Still, I need to take thought for the future – serious thought. About who will come after me, I mean.'

'Yes, of course. Prudent. Good for you and your heirs to have matters properly settled and to live in accord with your neighbours. For Philokles has the right claim and he is certain to win the case in the end.'

'Not so fast.' The old man raised a knobby and bony forefinger. 'You want a rush to judgement, my lad. My knowledge is valuable, like you said. You want me to promise, straight off, that I'll swear to the boundaries of Philokles' property, and his father's and grandfather's. That I'll swear the family graves are where they have always been. And no right of way for Lykon. Always intruding where he's not wanted!'

'Exactly. You are right.'

'Could be. Could be done. But I need to know the value
to you.'

'What do you mean – the value? Our Athenian law
proscribes bribery—'

'What a harsh word, my boy! Who said anything
about bribes? I just require to know if you're serious
about your claim. After all, *you're* no blood kin to
Philokles. When you ask a poor old man, old enough to
be your grandpa to do you a favour, you ought to be
willing to do a favour in return.'

I said nothing to this, but puffed my cheeks and blew
out the air, as a way of expressing my surprise. What the
old man was asking was unexpected, yet perhaps not
unusual.

'I *might* be able to do something for you, Pantakles,
certainly, some time – in the way of friendship.'

'Right. That's all I ask. In the way of friendship, of
course. And no word would ever pass my lips. I wouldn't
even need to be there. In fact, I wouldn't want to be.'

'Wouldn't want to be where?'

'It's about my heir, see.'

'You want to give your heir something?'

He burst out into a cackle of laughter at this.

'Exactly. I want as *you* should give him something.
And maybe you can guess what it is, and maybe you can't.
But it's – think what you two was talking about on the
path yesterday when I happened to come by.'

'Talking about?' I had a hazy recollection that
Philemon and I had exchanged some pleasantries – still a
trifle dazed by our meeting with that uncontrollable
Zobia . . .

'Yes. *Killer*, eh?' The man nudged me knowingly in the
ribs. 'Oh, he said – the other one – you were "a pair of
killers". But I know that you really *are* one. It was quite
the talk, you sitting on the ram's fleece. Like Herakles.

That's what I want, a Herakles.'

'To perform what sort of labour?'

'I want you . . .' The white-haired Pantakles leaned close to my face, so I could take in his wrinkles, the dirt seamed in with them, and the gaps in his row of teeth, where more soldiers had fallen than remained. '*Killer*,' he whispered. 'I want you to take him away. Get rid of him.'

'Get rid of your heir?'

'Yes. My stupid nephew. My other nephew, my sister's son, is really sharp, and much nicer to me. So then I could make my sister's son my heir. Which I cannot do as long as this great fat idiot of a brother's son is alive. I'm *tired* of him. Day in, day out, he orders me: "Do this, do that." Sometimes treats me like a labouring slave, other times as if I were losing my wits. Now, if you could just take a hand – I don't need to be there at all. Just trip him by the heels as he goes up the mountain, with some drink taken – that would be the easiest way, to my thinking. But you know best. Could be you have your own methods. Or you'd like to study the situation for a bit.'

I didn't know whether to burst out laughing or to punch the old fellow in the face, knocking him off his perch on the warm flat stone. Or maybe I ought to throttle the old horror then and there.

'How dare you?' I said with unfeigned indignation. 'What an insult! You must be senile, indeed, or crazy! Losing your wits indeed to imagine such a thing.'

His face fell. 'I should ha' known,' he said meekly, 'that it wasn't enough just to do you a favour about Lykon. I'm not saying at all there wouldn't be money in it. The nephew I want you to make away with has a wife, but she's main useless and luckily childless. She'd go back to her father and wouldn't take much off the land save a small dowry she came with. So I'm not asking you to finish off the two of 'em – just the one.'

'Get rid of the abominable notion, once and for all,' I said through clenched teeth, 'that I have anything to do with making away with folks. I have never done anybody harm in my life.' My heart suddenly smote me as I said those words. 'Save in self-defence at the utmost extremity – and I don't hire myself out to "finish off" people! Take a course of hellebore to clear your brain of vain fancies. I pity the poor nephew who lives with you. Someone ought to speak to him.'

'Don't say nothing!' The old man rose hastily, knocking over his wine-cup (half full) as he did so. 'Don't say nothing to nobody. It was just a joke, see! Just a jest. To see how you'd act when somebody called you "Killer".'

'Oh, that's the way of it, is it?'

'Yes. A prank, a piece of harmless fun. No need to fire up. And as for making a statement about Lykon and the property, of course I will do it. For nothing. Civic duty, that's all.'

This horrible old fellow was departing. I breathed easier when he had actually gone. I arose, in what I hoped was an easy manner, and left the tavern. I then sauntered to the Agora, but the strange conversation had undeniably shaken me. I felt I needed a drink, of plain water, and went towards the eastern Fountain House. Predictably, there was the usual throng of slaves and women getting water, each with a large *hydria* or two. As ever, the floor was fearfully sloppy, and there was a babble of voices . . . But no, all was not as usual. Matters were at a stand. No water was issuing from the main pipe.

'It's gone wrong,' one middle-aged slave was saying. 'There must be a blockage somewhere.'

'How long do we have to wait? A public fountain, they ought to keep it in good repair.' So complained a thin, shrewish woman who had come prepared with an enormous jar. As her walk home would be probably long and certainly difficult lugging a water-jar that size, I could understand why she was anxious to be on her way.

'Never mind,' said one of the others. 'There's a public slave gone up to look at the pipe – they can replace it.'

'Something got into the conduit,' said this slave, now entering on the scene himself, and brandishing an iron bar with a hook on the end. 'We can't budge it. We're going to have to break it open and replace a length of pipe.'

'Earthen pipe at that point,' one of the older men was telling a companion. 'Likely tree roots or something got in. Let's try the western Fountain House.' A few left, but a lot of the folk stayed, interested in the progress of repair and in discovering the cause of the trouble.

'I wager it's a dead dog has got stuck in there.'

'Drowned weasel?'

'No – it will turn out to be some child's toy.'

'Nonsense – just a collection of leaves and dirt.'

'Found it! We have got it!' The workmen set up a shout. One of them came out and held aloft the cause of the blockage. Delighted applause broke out, as the sight was unexpected. Not a child's ball or a dead dog or a bundle of leaves. A piece of statuary. A white piece of marble, a child's head in stone.

'Well, there's a public-spirited benefactor. Giving the city a statue.'

'It's only a piece of one.'

'Ho – anybody lost a baby?'

Jokes and high spirits reigned, as people enjoyed an unusual event, the workmen were more concerned with replacing the length of broken pipe. I registered my own dismay. There it was – the missing head! The piece of statuary that should have been in Hieron's *andron*, the property and means of death of the brother-in-law from Thorikos. Removed from Athens, and discovered by me

on the beach at Eleusis. I had thrown it away upon an
unknown assailant in the mist. And that unknown
assailant – had he tried to hide it deliberately? Tried to
get rid of it, rather, by throwing it into the aqueduct, or
perhaps just down a hole in the earth above a broken
water-pipe. Imprudence. Not imagining that the thing
could cause a stoppage in the water supply. Did my
unknown assailant himself know the true significance of
this head? Or had it passed from my assailant to someone
who knew that it was a guilty object, a thing to be
hidden?

A guilty object. It struck me that I ought to speak up.
That object was *not* an innocent obstruction, like a child's
ball. It was under a ban, it was accursed as the instrument
of murder. But – should I tell them?

Yes, I decided. However reluctant, I had to speak out.
The Agora is a holy place and must not be polluted by
dreadful objects.

'Stop!' I cried. 'This piece of marble may be – it *is* – an
accursed thing. It is in all likelihood the murder weapon
that killed Hieron's brother-in-law! Cause of the death of
Hippobatos of Thorikos. Take it from the Agora, and
expel it from the city!'

My cries brought everybody about me. The man
holding the head hastily set it down on a stone coping.
Reactions were loud and numerous, for the crowd had
multiplied since the discovery with the addition of all
kinds of hangers-on and idle seekers for amusement.
Among those in the throng I recognised, though at a
distance, was the old farmer who had been sleeping in the
open area behind the tavern, where Pantakles and I had
had our ridiculous conversation. The peasant was not one
of the loud talkers, but there were many to exclaim, and
not only the slaves and women. At last an arkhon arrived
to see what the fuss was about.

'What is all this uproar?' he enquired. 'A little thing like the stoppage of a pipe should not bring chaos. I told the workmen to mend the fountain.'

'Yes, the fountain is being mended,' said one citizen. 'But that is not the problem any more. The trouble is, the stoppage was caused by a piece of marble, and now *he* says' – pointing at me – 'that the thing is accursed.'

'Yes,' chimed in another. 'He says it is the weapon that killed Hippobatos of Thorikos.'

'By Zeus and all the gods!' The arkhon recognised me, but not with pleasure. 'Stephanos, what possesses you to say such things! You are causing a disturbance. So tell me whether this is serious or a joke.' This magistrate looked at me most severely.

'It is no jest,' I affirmed. 'Summon Hieron and Diognetos of Eleusis. And Halirrhothios, too, from my own deme. For we know – the murdered man's wife confirmed it – that Hieron's brother-in-law Hippobatos was bringing to Hieron's house the image of a child's head in marble. That image was not found in the house where Hippobatos' body lay. Hieron, Diognetos and Halirrhothios all saw the corpse, with its head crushed by a hard round object. So it was deduced at the time that the missing object, the child's head in marble, was the instrument that had done such damage to the head of the man from Thorikos.'

Even the arkhon turned a trifle pale. The crowd had stopped laughing and jesting, and stood back from the marble object in a respectful manner, as if they expected the child's head to explode and emit a troop of armed men like those that once came from a dragon's teeth.

'Oh,' groaned the arkhon. 'That would mean the pollution of the fountain and the whole Agora. Certainly, if it is a murder weapon it must be carried away and tried. But fetch Hieron and question him about this thing, before we proceed further.'

There was a tense wait. Nobody could leave, because if this were the murder weapon we might all be polluted and require purification – as would the sacred Agora itself – before we went about further business or returned home. Even the hardiest would not want to bring murder-stained water to their own homes, so the few who had collected water before the trouble started began to empty out their pots.

By the time Hieron arrived, breathless and hurried, the ground had become sloppier than ever. Above the watery mess the child's head smiled serenely, as if confident of its own earthly immortality. Hieron had a good look at it.

'I believe – yes, I do believe this is the piece,' he said finally. 'I never actually saw it, of course, but my sister-in-law described it to me after. Hippobatos was bringing it to me. This is an image of my wife's little brother. It is damaged, isn't it? The ears – and there is a gash in the marble . . .'

'We don't know when those injuries were acquired,' said the arkhon. 'Stay – here is a sculptor and marble-merchant who can tell us more. Are you not a marble-seller in Eleusis?'

'I am.' It was Melanthios.

'Take a look at this thing.'

The Eleusinian sculptor and marble-merchant walked about and looked at the marble head from a respectful distance.

'One of the gashes is new,' he observed. 'Probably made with the crowbar just now. But the other marks of damage were made some while ago. Yet the skin of the piece, as it were, shines in the undamaged parts. Not a bad piece of work when new.'

'So,' said the arkhon, 'it may have been that the piece was stolen, but got damaged. Then the thieves decided to get rid of it. It may not be a murder weapon at all! No blood on it, is there?'

'That's so,' said one of the workmen. 'But then it has been washing about in a lot of water.' I could have mentioned that it had been washed before that, in salt water, but I held my peace.

'No blood that I can see, certainly,' said the marble-seller cautiously. 'I would prefer not to examine it more closely, under the circumstances, if it is the dreadful thing you speak of.'

'Oh, quite. But my point is,' said the arkhon hopefully, 'it is probably not a murder weapon, just booty from a theft. And stolen property does not pollute the Agora.'

'Oh, but – yes!' Hieron clasped his hands earnestly. 'If you had seen how the poor man's head was bashed in! It would take a very heavy solid object to do that, and there was no other such object in the room, nor were there any signs that anything else had been used for the purpose. Aristotle of Stageira pointed all this out and it is true—'

'Aristotle of Stageira!' the arkhon sniffed. 'I might have known that this busybody philosopher would be involved in such a troublesome affair.'

'We shouldn't lose time,' said a citizen in the crowd. 'Stephanos and Hieron both believe this was used to kill Hippobatos during a robbery. That's enough. I vote we take it away forthwith, put it to its trial and destroy it.'

The arkhon ordered that the two public slaves pick up the head and place it on a flat wicker basket, turned upside down and used as a sort of tray. We underwent a first purification as the priests came to cleanse the fountain area. The water that had been drawn and then pronounced impure lay in pools; the women and slaves who had been washing clothes were in a peculiarly distressing condition, as their wet fabrics were now considered unclean. With no laundry to consider, I went off with the first of the crowd, walking behind the arkhon. The arkhon himself walked behind his two slaves, who carried the almost-smiling marble head on top of the wicker basket. The two men appeared like the slaves of some eastern potentate delivering to him a severed head on a charger.

'Strange,' the arkhon addressed me suspiciously as we walked along, 'strange – is it not? – that you know so much about this murder, and how it was done and with what instrument.'

'We were summoned,' I insisted, 'by Hieron in deepest night, after his house had been broken into. Halirrhothios and Diognetos were with him. They can testify also about the appearance of the body and our deductions. Send for Diognetos of Eleusis, a highly respected man, and he too will tell you exactly what led us to such a conclusion.'

We stopped and the arkhon bade the two slaves to display the offending marble head. The priest who had been summoned came to attend also. It was a solemn occasion. The ritual went very quickly. 'Whose is this marble object in the shape of a head?' asked the Basileus.

Hieron answered, 'It belonged to Hippobatos, my brother-in-law. He intended it as a gift, but was murdered before he could give it.'

'What has this head of marble done?'

'We believe . . .' Hieron paused, searching for a suitable form of words. 'A number of us who saw the corpse believe that this stone was used to kill the unfortunate Hippobatos. His head had been crushed by some round and heavy object, and no other such was in the room at the time. This stone was not found at the scene, but the gods have brought it back now.'

'Where is the slayer?'

This time the arkhon replied. 'He is being sought for. He is at present unknown.'

'You all hear.' The priest turned to us. 'Is this the stone that struck the fatal blow?'

And the congregation of us replied, 'Yes.'

'Then, acting under the eyes of the gods, by the power of this court and by the law of the city of Athens and the right of the murdered man, I condemn this piece of marble. This stone head has no more business in Athens and no right to abide here. It must depart from Athens for ever. I condemn it to be thrown into the chasm and no more to be seen. Let the executioner remove it and fulfil this sentence.'

The executioner, our 'public man', came importantly up to the front, took the accursed thing, still smiling on its tray, and went off with it. The head of a bright little boy would be cast off a cliff into a deep pit, the Barathron. Living criminals in olden days had been flung into the Barathron. Nowadays we did not execute men that way, but wicked objects still were served so.

'You may go,' said the Basileus to us. 'Be sure to cleanse yourselves of all pollution,' he added.

So the spectacle was done, and we turned about and went our separate ways, to cleansing and then back to our business – save for a few youths and idlers who went off to see the execution of the offensive thing. I had thought, near the end of the proceedings, that I had spotted Diognetos in the crowd, which had grown in bulk at the prospect of attending an entertaining trial of an object. Had I known earlier that he was there, I should have summoned him to corroborate my account of the house-breaking.

After a further purification I walked off to the Diokhares Gate, thinking to warn Aristotle, who might possibly be questioned by the arkhon about the marble head. Wrapped in my own thoughts, I scarcely noticed that someone had drawn up beside me. Out of the corner of my eye I glanced at this person. It was the peasant who had been snoring in the sun behind the tavern earlier that morning.

'So, O Killer,' said this person, in a vulgar accent. 'You need to be circumspect in conversation. Especially if you know too much about murder weapons.'

I threw back the man's hood, but I scarcely needed to do so, as I had begun to recognise the voice, however changed.

'Oh. Arkhias!' I was disgusted at my own obtuseness. 'This is the first time that you have ever really taken me in with one of your disguises.'

XXI

The Marble-Seller

Arkhias laughed. 'Indiscreet and trusting soul! Sleep is so easily shammed. Lucky the napping peasant was poor old I, and not your enemy – nor the unfortunate nephew of the old white-haired rascal!'

'Why were you eavesdropping like that?' I demanded.

'I was waiting for somebody else. I am often lucky, however; a good spirit prompts me. I didn't go to that tavern in the first place for any reason to do with you or your affairs, I do assure you.'

It was not easy to be satisfied with this assurance. It occurred to me that perhaps Arkhias had been set to spy upon me (if for friendly reasons) by Aristotle, but I quickly dismissed the notion. Aristotle was himself suspicious of Arkhias, a rival for the confidence of Antipater, and would never make him privy to any matters concerning himself or his friends.

When we got to the Lykeion, I feared that nothing of importance could be communicated to Aristotle at present; I did not wish to discuss important affairs in front of the spy. Aristotle already knew of the event, but Arkhias gave him the benefit of his own commentary.

'Apparently they found that marble head that was stolen from Hieron – or perhaps we should say Hippobatos – on that infamous night,' he remarked. 'I suppose it was the right head? I thought the arkhon and the Basileus somewhat slack in being content with Hieron's word. They might have sent to Thorikos to find the man who made it, in order to make identification secure.'

'A careful magistrate would have done so,' Aristotle agreed. 'But on the other hand, it makes the populace very uneasy to hold such a contaminated object within the walls. An object of such note, found with such public ado! I can comprehend why the authorities would not wish to wait an extra day before getting rid of it.'

'Very true,' I agreed heartily. 'Anyone would be glad to get rid of the impious thing.'

Aristotle shot an amused glance at me. 'I daresay someone thought he *had* got rid of it,' he remarked. 'Strictly, it is not *the thing* that is impious, but the hands that employed it to kill.'

'Well,' said Arkhias, pursing his lips, 'if the head is the murder weapon, nobody seems any nearer finding a solution to that crime. Silly! It's no solution to throw away a good piece of marble. Why doesn't this city catch the criminal? I think we of the Italiotes are more rigorous in catching and executing criminals. The question remains: *Who* killed Hieron's brother-in-law? Also, nobody has really done anything about the robberies and thefts.'

He stood up and stretched. Even in his plain and abbreviated costume as a poor peasant, Arkhias was an imposing figure. 'This is not satisfactory. My own daimon – for like Sokrates I have one – urges me on. I feel that I have been remiss in this case.'

'Surely not,' said Aristotle. 'If you have been remiss, that reflects even more badly on myself.'

'You people in Athens,' said Arkhias, 'are too talkative. Just sit about and gossip and complain, waiting for something to happen. You imagine that your lives are always going to continue in the same way. Now, things don't act like that. You may not have heard, but Alexander has lost a battle. And he has been ill.'

'Yes, I have heard that,' said Aristotle calmly. 'I have very good intelligence. The battle was one of many fights with the Skythians. The Makedonian commanders whom he sent to oversee the work of the native Persian leader were hesitant, and did not perform well.'

'Didn't like working with Persians, I guess. A lot of Makedonians killed,' said Arkhias. 'Many were shaved, so they say.'

'Many shaved?' I echoed. 'I suppose the Makedonians then are like the Spartans who do their hair before they go into battle, especially in a desperate fight.'

Both Arkhias and Aristotle laughed, but not merrily.

'"Shaved",' explained Arkhias, 'is a nice word for something else. The savage Skythians take off the tops of the heads of those they slay – when they have the time. Ah, well. Men say Alexander is like Akhilleus – and you know Akhilleus did not live long.'

'His army is fighting in the wilds of mountainous Sogdania, and has been surprised in one ambush,' said Aristotle. 'Important – there were real losses – but not fatal to Alexander's purpose. I should not bid Antipater's son Kassander fear – or hope – too much. Alexander is, or has been, ill, true, but with diarrhoea. That's not necessarily fatal, you know. Bad drinking water makes it a hazard of armies on the march. It is curable, and Alexander has the best physicians.'

'He will be sending for you as his doctor perhaps?' said Arkhias. 'You might like to travel East again some day. Farewell for the present.' And he went off, to my relief.

'There he goes,' said Aristotle, 'to make his court to the Regent Antipater – or to Kassander, or any person he thinks of as a rising sun. He would make more court to me if he thought I were able to rise in power.'

'You proved to him,' I observed, 'that you have the latest intelligence, too, and need not rely on him for news.'

'He must have suspected as much. Yes, I had a letter from Antigonos the One-Eyed. Reading between the lines, I can see Antigonos is concerned that morale is failing among the Makedonians. Those generals who lost the fight made some elementary errors. Either the Makedonian leaders are now too frightened of Alexander himself to think effectively, or they are angry at working with the Persians. It is a difficult thing to get Greeks to work with barbarians. I don't understand Alexander myself, but presumably he put a Persian in charge as the Persian commanders know the terrain and the peoples. Or perhaps these Makedonian officers have become careless, or are disoriented by the wilderness.'

'Perhaps those men were merely unfortunate.'

'What men call "misfortune" is often brought on by mistakes. Any incompetence in his picked companions will make Alexander feel more lonely. His trust in his own Makedonians may be dwindling, feeding new suspicions of plots, and renewing his antipathy to any opposition.'

'Alexander will get well, and win another victory against the Skythians,' I encouraged. 'He will be victorious over all barbarians in Baktria and Sogdania – where is that, by the way? – while Persia becomes peaceful and prosperous. You borrow trouble, Aristotle.'

'Trouble charges highly for the privilege, to be sure,' said Aristotle. 'To calm my spirits, I think I shall take a long walk tomorrow. As far as Eleusis. I should be delighted if you would accompany me. We may be allowed to hope that Arkhias' helpful daimon will not lead him there. I ought to see my *mystagogos* again, to bring back a manuscript he lent us.'

This plan seemed good to me, the more because I had been trying to nerve myself to see Diognetos again and win his favour after his natural chagrin at my hidden case of homicide – kept hidden from him only because I hadn't thought of it. I too had the excuse of an Eleusinian manuscript to return to my *mystagogos*.

'I fear I am not very good company,' Aristotle apologised, as we set off. His man Phokon was sent on ahead of us, with a donkey so his master could ride back again. 'I cannot get the contents of Antigonos' latest letter out of my mind.'

'You are anxious for your friends, that's natural,' I responded. 'And for Alexander's friends, too.'

'I am not sure they are close friends any more. Alexander used to have a band of loyal brothers in adversity. But now? We all use the word "friend" loosely. Perhaps we don't have enough words for connections between people. Many men have people whom they see often and even work with who are not truly beloved. The good man is capable of conducting rightly this kind of relationship – for which we have no real name. The success of enterprises depends on the ability to associate in an ethical and responsible manner. A good man maintains his own judgement, will not acquiesce in his associates' desire to do anything dishonourable or foolish. A weak man wants only to please those about him, whether real friends or not.'

'Naturally,' I said, 'a good man would not acquiesce in his companion's bad action – for instance, if a close associate said, "Let us murder so-and-so." Or, "Let us commit a theft."'

'Not only that, Stephanos, but the good man will refuse to join with a familiar associate in doing something that will injure that other person himself. Even if refusal gives displeasure. A man ought to refuse, for instance, to obey his acquaintance's demand to furnish him with food or drink that the good man knows would be harmful, even if the associate craves it.'

'Thus being a better friend to the acquaintance than that weaker person is to himself.'

'Yes. A true friend, even when not constrained by bonds of affection. Yet to refuse to fall in with a bad plan demands prudence also – if only to see it *is* a bad plan. The challenge is to refuse at the right time and in the right manner.'

'It is hard to deal with other people,' I remarked. 'Our real ties are at home,' I added, 'and only at home can one be sure of being a good person.' I thought happily of my own place in dear Athens. Among the families I had united in familial bonds we had olives (mine), fields of grain and vegetables, and some livestock (Smikrenes); some grain, and a deal of honey (Hymettos). I would make a good provision for my son, but Theodoros should have something too . . .

Aristotle interrupted these reveries.

'Might it not be a good idea,' he was saying, 'to visit Oulias' shop and find out if he heard any more of the theft in Peiraieus? We might at least commiserate with his loss.'

I assented. 'But I doubt if he will have traced what was stolen, so he's unlikely to have anything to report. Money in coins is so easy to spirit away.'

'Not like a bronze figure, or even a gold wreath. Or a marble head.'

'Money is such a funny thing,' I said. 'Coins never stop. I mean – other things are supposed to stop. I buy a cabbage – I take it home and eat it. I buy a little statue of Persephone – I take it home and put it on a shelf or hang it on the wall. Those things are not supposed to move. But the money I paid for them will already have moved away.'

'A good observation,' Aristotle affirmed. 'Objects, however, do move – they can be traded in faraway places. Even gifts given to the dead as grave-offerings can be dug up by unscrupulous persons. Herein perhaps lies the attraction of large important objects like statues, which are hard for thieves to move. Perhaps,' Aristotle added, 'we ought to use this opportunity to talk with Melanthios the marble-seller who lives near the shop of Oulias.'

'Aristotle!' I exclaimed, laughing. 'Did you intend that all the while as your chief errand, rather than an exchange of hymns? You are like Odysseus, man of many wiles, who did nothing without a stratagem.'

'If it is so obvious, I am not wily,' he retorted. 'You distress me in comparing me with a liar like Odysseus. The older I get, the more I come to see the value of Truth. No matter what the purpose, a lie is a wretched thing.' I wondered privately about the exact truthfulness of renaming somebody 'Theophrastos', but decided against introducing this point.

'Truth alone is noble,' Aristotle continued. 'The good man loves truth and speaks it. He therefore could not break his word, or cheat for the sake of advantage – not such a man as I am thinking of.'

'Most people are somewhat truthful,' I said cautiously. 'But they don't tell the whole truth, very often. Is telling less than the truth a lie?'

'Depends what you mean. A good man, far from exaggerating his worth, will underestimate it or speak lightly of it in preference to boasting.'

'Some people boast a good deal,' I said, 'even well-born

educated men. Theophon boasted to me that he was going to make his house bigger. He is going to spend a talent on tapestries and bedspreads!'

'He seeks honour – of a sort. A man like Theophon claims to possess things valuable to *himself,* and his reward is to be envied. Theophon may not be lying, but the liar for the sake of reputation gives himself credit for qualities that others admire, even envy: for instance, he says he is very hardy, or extremely wise, or enormously rich. But I cannot help thinking that the man who lies for the sake of gain is more reprehensible – and his lies are different.'

'How do you make that out?'

'Look at such a man and see how he goes about his business. The man who lies for sheer practical gain claims to possess qualities that are valuable to *others.* So, a man may claim to be a good physician, even if he knows nothing of the matter. He will help another out of a trouble, make good a deficiency. He is more than tactful – a good quality; he is over-respectful, finding virtues invisible to others in quite an ordinary person – when he hopes to get something out of him. Acting like the crafty itinerant fortune-tellers who pretend to tell their gulled customers what the future holds.'

I could not help smiling.

'What is it? What is funny in what I have said?'

'Well – but . . . Aristotle, these could be said to be the qualities of a *teacher*!'

He had the grace to laugh.

Once we arrived in Eleusis, we did not first visit our *mystagogoi,* but turned by common consent towards the little Agora and to one familiar street, where I had formerly led us to the little shop of images in order to avoid meeting Arkhias. Oulias, maker of images, was working under a window, his back bent over a high table at the side of his shop. There were fewer ceramic figures than I had seen the last time I was there.

'Good day, friend Oulias,' said Aristotle. 'I hope you are well. A bad business, that theft in Peiraieus!'

'I am sorry we could not get the bag of coins back for you,' I added.

Oulias frowned. I wasn't sure if he was squinting at his work, or felt displeased, or was simply trying to remember us.

'Yes,' he said, coming slowly to the front of the shop, wiping his hands on a damp rag as he did so. Fragments of yellowish clay clung to his fingers. 'All that money vanished – a bad business, truly. A very bad business! I have had a great loss.'

'You had sold the images to a sea-captain. It still seems strange to me,' I said, 'that a sea-captain should buy quantities of religious statues. After all, a ship only needs one or two religious figures for prayers.'

'It's not for his ship and he isn't just a sea-captain,' Oulias explained. 'He's a trader, owns the ship he commands.'

'You mean,' I said brightly, 'Menexenos of Abydos. And his ship is the *Thalia*.' I was proud of recalling these names.

'Yes. Menexenos does a variety of business – all legal. He buys our images and takes some to a shop in Byzantion, others to the area around Sardis, and further south.'

'You must be proud,' I ventured, 'to think that the works of your hands are known throughout the nations. People you will never meet say prayers before your images.'

'It *is* good.' Oulias smiled for the first time. 'Yes, Demeter has been good to me – until this last trouble. It will take a long time to make up the money lost. To Hades with all these thieves! Peiraieus must be full of them. I understand there was another theft the same day, and a Phoinician merchant's slave was found hanged. Lampos said you seemed to think that crime was the work of the same local thieves. A killing too – quite frightening!'

'Lampos was correct in saying I thought it a homicide,' acknowledged Aristotle. 'But complete proof is lacking. The Epimeletes thought the Phoinician slave's death a suicide.'

'Those supervisors think only of their good name, not of the victims. *They're* no help!' Oulias was emphatic. 'I keep wishing I had done differently. Lampos and I were both at fault for allowing such a large shipment to go out at one time, with only one of us to take care of the money. Next time we shall have sharper eyes – and won't send just one man.'

'Peiraieus is generally well supervised and tended,' said Aristotle. 'Athens has an interest in keeping our great Emporion at Peiraieus free of crime. Astonishing that there should have been two sizeable thefts in the Emporion on one morning. The Phoinician alleges that he had a large quantity of jewels, including some rare gems, which he was to sell to customers in Mitylene.'

'All these foreigners! They add to our problems,' grumbled Oulias. He picked up a hollow piece that was one half of a Persephone, and attached it skilfully to the other, so that Persephone became a full figure with a front and a back.

Aristotle laughed. 'But without "all these foreigners" who come as *mystai* to Eleusis, you would lose much of your custom,' he pointed out. He had wandered into the main shop where Oulias stood, and gazed at a table covered with figures of the Two Goddesses.

'Now this is quite fine,' he said, peering. 'May I

examine it?' He picked up a statue of Demeter and held it close to his face.

'Careful!' said Oulias, turning and going to him. 'Be careful! These are very breakable. Don't drop it!'

'Oh, quite so,' said Aristotle serenely. He wandered over to the fresh Persephone, and picked it up.

'Don't touch it!' said Oulias. 'It could be damaged by thumb prints, it's still soft.'

'I see,' said Aristotle, setting it down carefully. 'You make each of the larger images out of half pieces made in separate moulds. Is that right?'

'Yes,' said Oulias. 'We have to wait for moulds to be vacated before introducing new clay.'

'And it demands skill of hand,' said Aristotle. 'This material is delicate – it is very like working in pastry! And then, as with pastry, you have to cook it for a suitable length of time.'

Oulias snorted, perhaps not flattered by the comparison. It was true, however; the unfinished Kore did look like a piece of pastry, in colour and texture. I understood the shopman's annoyance – I found it irritating myself, the way Aristotle was flitting around touching things in this meddlesome fashion.

'I hope you were not too hard upon your poor man Lampos,' I said to Oulias, to change the subject. 'I don't see him here today.'

'Lampos is off buying some more colours to mix paint with.' Reluctantly, Oulias turned about to face me, while Aristotle continued his inspection of the little statues. 'I cannot berate or punish Lampos. He's *not* my slave, he's my assistant. And a very fine painter. I have no quarrel with the fellow – Lampos suffered in the theft too, losing his share.'

'Oh, so Lampos himself has a share in the business,' Aristotle observed. 'He isn't just doing labour for hire. A sort of partner.'

'I wonder how the bankers manage,' I pondered. 'To guard against theft, I mean. They have to carry not only silver and coins but bricks of gold about with them.'

'Not my concern, the banks.' We don't borrow—' Oulias turned to look at Aristotle, who had gone off to another table of shapes lying down. 'Ho! Stop, please. Those are still in the moulds.'

'Who makes the moulds themselves?' Aristotle enquired.

'We bought some with us from Boiotia. But now I make them myself – a pretty business it would be if I had to send to Boiotia every time! They are breakable too, the moulds. Yes, it is a deal of trouble to make a new one, but if we take care the mother-mould can give us a multitude of figures. Please – don't *touch* them!' Oulias reiterated sharply. 'Damage one before it is baked, and we'd have to throw it away.'

'Merely admiring your craft,' Aristotle responded mildly. He came meekly around to my side of the front table, to admire the finished little statues.

Oulias tossed his cleansing rag to Aristotle. 'Do you need this?'

'No – no. I haven't got into your clay.' Aristotle displayed his hands meekly to Oulias, showing that his palms and fingers were clean. The master of the miniature statues took up the rag and scrubbed again at his own fingers.

'Now, may I sell you a Demeter? Or what about a pretty little Persephone?'

'No thank you,' said Aristotle. 'Though they are attractive – even unpainted.' He looked back into the shop. 'You use truly excellent paint on the finished ones. They shine like jewels. Now, that big one over there, the one I was looking at – is Lampos going to paint it with carmine and real gold?'

'Yes. He is getting more gold and also some lapis lazuli for the blue – though we use lapis only on the very best pieces. We create good effects with the soft rose shade, as well as deep red. Only the largest or most regal ones have the touch of gold in the crown or garland, and the bracelet or necklace.'

'We may be interested in making a purchase later in the year – for Stephanos and I will be here in Boedromion, as *mystai* ourselves.'

'Excellent!' Oulias now broadened into a real smile. 'Our best display is to be seen at that time. Though what about taking a small statue for the mean time? To aid devotions. Or one for your women? Women are always partial to these statues.'

'Well, as to that – I shall think about it,' Aristotle promised.

'I will take one – a small Demeter,' I said resignedly. It would be a pretty present for Philomela, and appropriate in view of our coming initiation.

I paid, took the figure, and we smiled ourselves off the premises.

'I hope we were sufficiently sympathetic,' Aristotle said as we walked up the street towards the corner.

'*I* was,' I said. 'I even bought an image. *You* were rather meddling, I thought, too curious and not sympathetic at all.'

'Wrong in me, then. It is a dreadful blow to lose one third of an expected income. Yet Oulias' business is obviously doing very well indeed, if Lampos can buy the most expensive materials – lapis and gold! – so soon after such a loss.'

The marble-seller's shop displayed few painted images. Rows of objects all in white marble blankly met our gaze, still awaiting colour in hair, eyes, clothing. They were strongly chiselled with large blank eyes. And white with a surpassing whiteness. It was like being confronted by ghosts.

'Who are you?' The man Melanthios came abruptly from behind the row of ghosts. 'Ah. Sorry – the light was in my eyes.' He looked appraisingly at the two of us. 'I should remember faces – it is my trade. If I mistake not, the senior of the party must be Aristotle of the Lykeion – am I right? And you, young gentleman, I well remember seeing you under the oak tree. But I regret I don't recollect your name. Set it down to the infirmity of advancing years.'

'Stephanos of Kydathenaion,' I said briefly.

'Right – Stephanos, of Kydathenaion, of course!'

This man Melanthios was not bad-looking when one beheld him close to. My chief impression before was that he was a dusty-looking fellow, like someone from a mill. He was still whitely dusted, but under this marble snow his hair was dark, and hair and beard well-trimmed. Melanthios had a very fine nose; I wondered if that had led him to his profession. Certainly, statues require beautiful noses. His teeth, white and even, showed to advantage when he smiled. He smiled now.

'What can I do for you? Alas, that such a question from me should often elicit such distressing answers. I hope it is not a funeral monument?' His smile disappeared and he looked sad.

'No, no,' I said hastily. 'Nothing of that sort. But I am interested in these figures that you carve – I take it you have more in the back courtyard where the light is better? May I look?'

'Come along,' the proprietor said, and Aristotle swept ahead of me through the back room into a courtyard almost paved with marble chips. There were many blocks of marble, some square, others oblong, some thick and others very thin.

'You have a good deal of space here,' Aristotle observed.

'Yes. The premises once belonged to a bronzesmith, quite a while ago. A bronzesmith has to have space for a large casting-pit and so on. Lucky for me I could find such a good place to work in. A marble-worker requires a deal of space.'

'All for grave monuments?' I enquired.

'Some of them. Look, I am even carving a dog able to sit by himself! As part of the tomb of a young man who hunted with a favourite dog. The young Athenian is being carved by a greater artist than I.'

'And you carve gods as well as dogs, I see,' said Aristotle. 'I am amazed that you can do so much!'

'I wonder,' I said, looking about me, 'that you, Melanthios, are not better known. Why, you deserve to be famous if you produce figures at this rate.'

Melanthios laughed. 'You give me too much credit,' he said. 'You must not think you have discovered a Praxitiles. My figures are largely made to order, according to a pattern. At the quarry someone cuts the marble into a block, and then another man gives the block a rough shape of a man or woman, and then I am sent the shape to finish off.'

'Your honesty does you credit.'

'Not that I don't sometimes take a hand of my own in the matter,' Melanthios added. 'Occasionally I create an entire figure. Of course, tastes are simpler here; people seem content with my humble efforts. I produce most of the grave monuments for our deme. I am glad you need no grave markers – but you would perhaps like a statue? A herm for the doorway, or a pretty image for the courtyard?'

'You wrought the herm of Thymades,' I exclaimed. 'And his little Apollo!'

'That's right.' The man nodded and smiled.

'The faces you create,' said Aristotle, 'are rather severe, don't you think?'

'Well,' said Melanthios, 'I agree with the painter Melanthios, after whom I myself was named. He says in his treatise on painting that a certain self-will and even harshness should mark works of art, and the same for one's character.'

'Well then,' I said, 'you ought to have a good time doing the dog then, especially if he's big and fierce.'

'Melanthios the painter was certainly an admirer of resolution and independence,' Aristotle commented. 'You are obviously a strong and independent individual, Melanthios. Your work makes you a good observer of people. Our worthy Demarkh did not allot much time for that inquest over the body of poor Sophilos. But you are a noticing sort. Do you remember seeing Sophilos earlier on that day?'

I was surprised to hear Aristotle ask the question that had already been asked – and answered – at the brief inquest, but I certainly wasn't going to intervene. The man of marble hesitated.

'Perhaps,' Aristotle suggested, 'we ought to go back into the shop. To refresh your memory, you could stand where you were that day, when you had that large-sized customer.' We two stood at the front, just inside the entrance, with Melanthios behind the front table.

'Well – yes, perhaps. Memory is a bit hazy at this distance. But I was here – then that big foreigner was leaning over to look into the shop. I asked him in, and followed him to the centre of the room.' Aristotle and I followed these motions, and stood in the inner part of the front shop. 'He was interested in the marble heads on display. I remember that.'

We looked at the white marble heads. One of them was

small, I noticed with some excitement, a rather well-modelled head . . .

'Is that of a child, Melanthios?'

'That – yes. I made it, however, later than the one that was made in Thorikos for poor Hippobatos – which wasn't made by me. You know, the one that was found just now in the Fountain House. The family that ordered this one moved away, and left me with their little one on my hands.'

'And the foreign man appeared interested in buying it. When did Sophilos come in?'

'Sophilos never came in. He was shuffling along outside at one point, I think. The little beggar went round and round the town regularly.'

'Are you sure that you did not, from the liberality of your heart, give him some alms?'

'Now I remember – yes, when I caught sight of him, it passed through my mind that I would give him a trifle if he came into the shop. But he didn't. I was attending, as you suggest, to that big man. He was interested in the small marble head. We were both staring at it, I remember, me and that foreigner who later claimed his purse was lost.'

'The purse *had* been lost – stolen. It was found,' I reminded him.

'Oh, yes. Strange how details soon begin to pass from memory. But I cannot believe that Sophilos could come into the shop unnoticed. I suppose he *could* have committed the theft. But I find it difficult to believe that the purse was stolen here. Despite the Demarkh, I am not at all certain that Sophilos had anything to do with its loss.'

'Your doubt does you credit,' said Aristotle. 'Most people are willing to jump to conclusions.'

'I was taught in school always to be reasonable,' responded the smiling marble-cutter.

'Quite right,' said Aristotle. 'Well, good day—' He was cut short by a terrific bang outside the back shop as of something heavy falling against the door.

'Ye gods!' The marble-cutter's countenance changed in an instant. 'That's the *second* time he's dropped a statue!' Melanthios bellowed towards the back of the shop, addressing someone invisible. 'Take care, you idiot! Or you'll find yourself back in your goose manure looking for weeds to live on! Or sent to handle statues at the side of the Styx.'

The door to the marble yard opened, and someone cautiously entered the back shop. A young male figure in a tunic. But long-haired, not a slave.

'I'm so sorry!' the youth exclaimed. 'Please, please don't be angry! I couldn't help it.'

'Couldn't help it?' the owner cried, turning and walking towards the newcomer. Melanthios seemed to have forgotten we were present – perhaps he believed that we had already gone. His figure now blocked out of our direct sight the youth on the further side of the shop. Melanthios, arms akimbo, proceeded to address the young man. He spoke in a loud voice, though his tone was flavoured with the wine vinegar of the best sarcasm.

'Couldn't help it!' Melanthios mimicked. 'Couldn't help being born, that's where *you* went wrong.' 'Bad temper' Sophilos had said of the seller of marble, and now I could see what he meant.

'If only you were a slave, my boy,' the marble-seller continued, 'I'd have the satisfaction of taking it out of your hide – and I'd do it sooner than eat breakfast. My fingers itch to be at the rod or the strap. As I cannot do that, I'll have to take satisfaction some other way. I thought I'd taught you well the other day! You want some more of the same?'

'No, please, Melanthios,' said the youth plaintively. He came towards the shop owner, arms outstretched beseechingly, lifted as in entreaty or prayer.

'You prefer to be black and blue over your whole body, is that it? If you've broken anything, I swear by Dionysos I'll break you! I can discharge you with plentiful kicks in the breech. And I don't care if I break a bone or two – and to Hades with the magistrates!'

'Oh, please, Melanthios, do not discharge me! Let me serve as your apprentice.'

'Serve as my peeler of onions! You're scarce fit to do that, I reckon. You used to be more pretty than useful. Now you're neither. Prepare your limbs for a thrashing!'

The object of these terrific threats moved forward until he was no longer blotted from our view by the menacing figure of the master of the shop.

'By Herakles!' I exclaimed. 'It's Strabax! Sophilos' nephew. What do you here?'

'I thought,' Aristotle said to me, 'that you said this young person was going to be a shepherd.'

'I was – I found a place – but then Melanthios offered me a position as his assistant,' explained Strabax. He moved forward to speak to us, and became a pathetic sight as the light caught him. One side of his face was a multicoloured bruise, well aged. His lip was seamed with a cut, and a couple of teeth seemed to be missing. One eye, which must have been closed until recently, was squinty, and the bone over that eye bore a long scab. I could not help staring at all this damage.

'You see how it is,' said Melanthios. 'It's partly his own carelessness, that hideousness, but partly my doing. If a boy won't obey, he must be taught – even at the cost of his teeth.' He raised his large hand slowly.

'Oh, please, no!' Strabax averted his head, protecting it with his hands. 'Please, I entreat you, Melanthios!'

'Not in front of visitors, then.' Melanthios dropped his paw. 'But don't say you aren't warned.'

Strabax, his eyes darting nervously, seemed anxious to sustain contact with us. 'I am Melanthios' assistant,' he repeated. 'I have only just started. I don't get paid yet, but I get board and some extra food to send to my mother. And I hope soon to be able to earn something.'

'A likely story!' said Melanthios. 'You could have made money from older men, maybe, if your pretty looks hadn't got spoiled. Just do your work and hope for a dinner out of it.'

'I am glad,' said Aristotle, 'to find that a young man who is the sole prop of his widowed mother has acquired a position. We would be willing to offer a small gift of money to Strabax, and hope you forgive him any damage he may have done. I am sure he will try to please you.'

'Oh, thank you!' cried the boy, looking vastly relieved.

'Thank you indeed.' Melanthios was suddenly wreathed in smiles like a summer's day. It was odd to watch a man change with such celerity as he took three drakhmai.

'What a fuss and hullabaloo!' I exclaimed to Aristotle, after we had been bowed out of the marble shop by the now-smiling owner. 'Melanthios didn't show much stubborn independence when you offered him the money, did he? I suppose that scene with the boy, shouting and all, was put on precisely to make us feel sorry for the lad and offer something – as you actually did!'

'Yes,' said Aristotle. 'I think your word "scene" very apt.'

XXII

A Mixed Basket

'There's something else I noticed,' I said. 'I am sure you did too. Arkhias was searching for the missing marble image of the child. So that was why he was in Eleusis, and in Melanthios' shop. I wonder if Sophilos not only saw them both together, but found out what they were looking at. Melanthios might be upset that anyone could think he had the missing image in his shop. He might have got angry at Sophilos.'

'But that doesn't answer the question of who stole Arkhias' purse,' Aristotle observed. 'Unless you have an answer.'

'No, I don't. But I am surprised to find young Strabax working for Melanthios – such a bad-tempered man, who insulted his poor old uncle too!'

'But Melanthios may have given small pieces of money to Sophilos from time to time. There is no reason why Strabax should turn down a good job. Suppose,' Aristotle continued, 'Sophilos had already been doing some work for Melanthios? The little man may have known more about the dealings of these shops than we imagine. What exactly did Sophilos say to you?'

I repeated his words again, as exactly as I could remember, not forgetting 'bad temper'. 'There's something else,' I said. 'Sophilos was chatting away, while you and Theophrastos walked on ahead on the day we met your *mystagogos*. And Sophilos said, "Do you have business in Byzantion?" And indicated that *he* would like business in Byzantion. Of course, he had just heard people in the shops talking about shipping things to Byzantion, and picked up the notion. Fancy poor little Sophilos in business!'

'But this is of some interest, Stephanos. Melanthios' crude statues would scarcely be in demand in Byzantion or anywhere other than Eleusis. It is Oulias – and his partner – who have business in Byzantion.'

'I scarcely know where that place is,' I confessed. 'But now apparently many go there.'

'Byzantion is on a promontory in the Bosporos, at the top of the Propontos Sea. It is a good site for trade with Thrake, as well as Mysia and Bithynia on the Asian coast – all of which Byzantion once owned. And it is a gateway to the great inland sea, the broad grain fields and other riches.'

'People mention it more,' I said, 'since the wars with Philip, when it was on our side. But I suppose the city will now get rich from the liberated cities in Asia. We've heard of it a lot recently – Sophilos wanted business in Byzantion, Oulias trades there and is connected with a sea-captain of Abydos who apparently owns a shop there. Theophon said something about a connection with Byzantion. And then, I was able to get Diognetos as my *mystagogos* late in the year only because a merchant with business in Byzantion cancelled. He couldn't be in Athens at the right time.'

'It is the right time to think religious thoughts; we approach our venerable *mystagogoi*!'

We were indeed nearing the apartment house of

Thymades; Phokon had parked the donkey outside the open gate, with a good view of the short and scowling Apollo. Thymades, delighted to see Aristotle, welcomed him in and plied him with bits of writings on tablets and on papyrus.

'The great Hymn to Demeter!' he said. 'I have a copy of that complete – very valuable. But I will let you have it, as you are a man who knows how to appreciate such things.'

'We have a copy in the Lykeion,' Aristotle assured him. 'At least, I believe we do.'

Diognetos, like Thymades, was well content to see his *mystes* – to my relief he had got over his righteous annoyance at finding out about my inconvenient homicide. Now he was insistent that he and I should do more work in going over materials before the great celebration of the Mysteries.

'For it approaches rapidly,' he reminded me, 'the time when we must gather together in Athens, and after sacrifices make our way in procession all together to the great Temple at Eleusis. By the way, as you both have women coming, please be clear on the new rule of Lykourgos that forbids travel in carts or chariots to women – even high-born women.'

'Isn't it true,' I asked, 'that Lykourgos' own wife was the first to break the rule?'

'It is hard to control wives, as you will find. But the rule is this: nobody save the Priestess and her attendant associates may have the privilege of going in the procession in any kind of carriage, or on any animal. All are equal, walking humbly on their own feet.'

We assured him that we had never thought of putting our females into chariots. They were both healthy, and good walkers. They would stand up to the journey, even if the weather were hot.

'I myself sometimes use a small cart, or a donkey, for travel to Athens,' Diognetos admitted. 'But not for the Mysteries, naturally.'

'I thought I saw you in Athens, in the Agora, the other day.'

'It might have been I. There was unfortunately an unusual delay, the trial of an object that stopped up the fountain. Occasionally I must go to town on business; if possible I take in a meeting of the Ekklesia. I prefer our quieter Eleusis, where I have enough to occupy me.'

'I see that your home takes your attention,' remarked Aristotle, 'for you are having your courtyard painted, and you have had this room painted too. You see, Stephanos – you are not the only householder who repairs and re-adorns his house.'

'I noticed also,' I said, looking about me, and walking over to the new wall to admire it. 'You have chosen the new style, I see, Diognetos, which I think is very handsome. Different colours laid on in bars. An artificial brick wall of many colours. I saw one like that some-where else, but there the painting was unfinished. I suppose the owner couldn't afford to go on. *Who* was it? Now I remember. Halirrhothios. Your room is rather in the style of Halirrhothios' house.'

'I do not see that at all,' said Diognetos stiffly. 'My house is finer – at least, I think it would be held so by any competent judge. Though Halirrhothios' room is *not* unfinished.'

'There is so much work of the sort going on now,' said Aristotle, 'that those of us who don't undertake it will be quite eclipsed. Which reminds me, my own home awaits. Thank you for your kind hospitality.'

'I cannot allow that!' exclaimed Diognetos. 'Stay, both of you, I beg, and go back in the morning. Two such long walks in one day are not a good idea.' I could see he nearly added, 'for a man of your age', but refrained. Aristotle mentioned his donkey, but he was looking a little tired; I knew he had sciatic twinges occasionally. Diognetos was so pressing, in the upshot we both had to consent; as for Phokon, he could stay too, and take care of the animal. It was very kind of Diognetos to put us up. I thought it showed the superiority of my *mystagogos* to Aristotle's chosen Thymades.

'And now for dinner,' said our kind host. A pang – not of hunger – shot through me.

'I had forgotten!' I exclaimed. 'The shopping! I forgot to fetch my family anything to eat.'

Diognetos burst out laughing, and even Aristotle smiled.

'The day is already well advanced,' observed Diognetos. 'You could hardly get back to Athens in time to give them a really good dinner. Surely they will provide for themselves for one night? I have some neighbours coming, and some other visitors – one whom I think you know. So we can have a merry meal. Stay! I have a good thought. Stay two nights, and you will meet some of the best men in Eleusis.'

'Oh no!' I burst out with more honesty than grace. 'I am sorry but I cannot – one night is enough.'

'You must not worry so much about shopping,' said Diognetos, with a faint smile. 'We can send some provisions with you when you depart.'

'Oh no, thank you. It is kind of you to offer, but I must be home tomorrow. I have pressing business in Athens on the day after tomorrow. Urgent law business.'

'It is better that we both go back tomorrow,' said Aristotle, mildly but firmly. It was kind of him to back me up. He knew that on the day after tomorrow I was to file a formal renewal of an appeal for postponement of the case of Lykon. Once approved, this would carry us into the New Year. This little hearing seemed a mere formality, but if I didn't appear for it – why, then Lykon could take the game into his hands.

Diognetos kindly forbore to press me to stay, or even to enquire further as to the business that required this urgent hearing. The dinner was indeed very good – we had fish, I remember. The guest whom we already knew proved to be Theophon, rosy-cheeked and talkative as ever. He was accompanied by another familiar figure. A full and buxom figure running to flesh. Thratta.

'My apologies for bringing this female along,' said Theophon. 'You know how I am pestered by the attentions of women – they cannot seem to leave me alone! But it would be ungracious to try to get rid of this one, since I promised to take her back to Athens tomorrow, very modestly in a closed cart. I hope you don't mind her slipping off to your women's quarters? She will be quiet as a mouse.'

'Mice are best known for squeaking and spoiling grain,' said Diognetos. 'But you are certainly welcome to send her to eat with my own slaves,' he added. The Thracian whore disappeared into the back regions.

'I had hoped to have Eurymedon, the distinguished exegete, to dine with me,' Diognetos said. 'But he has been compelled to send his excuses. A busy man, and much in demand.'

'People say he will be the next Hierophant,' said Theophon. 'Admirable, quite admirable. Not every Hierophant is so tall or looks as good as Eurymedon.'

Aristotle and I said nothing to counteract this praise of one whom Aristotle counted his enemy. I gazed speculatively at ruddy and handsome Theophon. He picked up a knife to hack off some bread. Could he have used a knife quite differently? After all, Theophon, a man with interests in Byzantion, had been at my symposium when the silver man had briefly disappeared. And at my wedding party when the knife was thrown at me. He had had some athletic training when young; although he was getting stouter, he might retain his ability to throw a missile. Or could Thratta . . . at his instance, perhaps . . .? But no, it was nonsense to think a woman could throw with vigour or accuracy. My drifting thoughts might have betrayed suspicion too plainly on my face. Fortunately, there was another guest, Diognetos' neighbour, and this Eleusinian was courteous and agreeably talkative. Diognetos was an attentive host, with a nice taste in wine, so our time passed pleasantly.

In the early morning we set off, restored and cheerful. 'We shall have a pleasant journey between harvested fields of gracious Demeter,' Aristotle remarked, getting astride of his donkey. 'The air is pleasantly scented with grain and hay. "Fragrant Eleusis", as the poem says.'

'Now is the good time,' said Diognetos, 'for us in Eleusis. The harvest comes, and people give us their first fruits of the wheat and barley. We need to build another tower and more granaries to house the goddesses' store. The whole Sanctuary needs enlargement. Alas, the harvest is not all it should be this year. The snow and damp made some seed rot in the ground. Farewell!'

It was a happy time, the harvest season, though a hard-working one. At my farm my servants and my tenants' servants would be fully employed. I knew Smikrenes had hired a labourer to help him bring his crops in. As we went by the Eleusinian fields, Aristotle riding his beast and Phokon and myself walking beside him, there seemed nothing the matter with Demeter's corn. The fields in the sunlight were white with grain. Birds called loudly about the grain-rich fields and the tempting threshing floors. Pigs were allowed to hunt among the stubble of the corn. I found a cut stalk of wheat in my path, and amused myself as in childhood by chewing on the sweet-flavoured grains and spitting out the husks.

'I didn't know,' I remarked, 'that Theophon was on such good terms with Thratta. I suppose they may have begun their affair at my party.'

'Don't you think it more likely that Theophon knew Thratta before then?' asked Aristotle.

'I suppose – yes. He did know that she could be "disciplined". Perhaps he was accustomed to the spanking game of the slipper.'

'Thratta disappeared from Athens, you will recall, Stephanos, after that – well, let's term it "difficulty" about Halirrhothios' house. Somebody had to see to taking her away. Presumably she was not imprisoned, but well-treated, and merely working in her vocation.'

'Diognetos spoke of her as of a slave,' I remarked. 'But she really is a freedwoman.'

'That is sometimes hard to prove,' Aristotle pointed out. 'Especially if someone remembers one of your parents as a slave.'

Aristotle rode his calm donkey and Phokon and I walked on in leisurely manner, all of us (even the little ass) enjoying the sunshine. Even the heat was agreeable, as we found some shady spots to rest in. It was like the old days, I thought, going roaming with the philosopher. Save that as a married man I ought not to be so happily footloose, enjoying the walk through a landscape smelling of midsummer.

'I wish I had clever servants at every corner as you do,' I said to Aristotle. 'The man of the house is supposed to do the providing. I really thought I had been getting on better about that.'

'I am sure you have been attending to all the duties of a husband. As for my servants, perhaps I am spoiled for they are very good. Yet the responsibility of servants can add to one's cares.'

'It *is* quite a care, maintaining a family,' I commented. 'And expense. I wish now I had not spent quite so much on the wedding – or, at least, on adorning my house. The *andron* could have waited. Now I understand how people can run out of money and leave work unfinished.'

'As you believe Halirrhothios did.'

'I am sure – no matter what Diognetos says – that Halirrhothios' *andron* was unfinished,' I maintained. 'At least at the time when I saw it – and you too. The man must have been too poor – at least then – to afford to have the work completed. It is a skilled sort of decoration, those imitation coloured bricks. Not the sort people can do for themselves.'

'Therefore,' said Aristotle, 'since Halirrhothios – according to his friend Diognetos – has been able to complete the job after all, he must have come into some more money. Or found a way out of his financial difficulties.'

'Halirrhothios is not the friend of Diognetos,' I corrected him. 'At least, when they first came to us, on the night of the burglary, Diognetos was *Hieron*'s friend. Hieron brought Halirrhothios to help him, as his near neighbour.'

'Then they have become friends since, perhaps. Since Diognetos appears currently informed about the interior of Halirrhothios' house.'

'The real puzzle is how Halirrhothios came into money. Since he had to return what he stole. I wonder if he had his roof retiled? But that would have been earlier, before the troubles.'

'And what would be odd about that?'

'Nothing. And I don't think he can have done, for the *kalameia* lining of his roof was musty, not new. You remember – when we went through his house, and into the women's quarters on the upper storey. But here's the odd thing. One of the workmen doing my own roof seemed almost to faint when he caught sight of Halirrhothios looking up at him. The man – one of the workers for the tile-master – dropped one of his tools. So I think he knew Halirrhothios, and knew something bad about him, though he would say nothing.'

'You never mentioned this incident before, Stephanos. A slight matter – a workman drops his hammer. Yet . . . Where were you and the tile-master's slave when the worker saw your neighbour Halirrhothios?'

'I and the tile-master's two men were all three of us up on the roof.'

'Very good. *On the roof* a man can have a fine unobstructed view. Now – what might a poor drudge working on a roof see? He could see passers-by below. He could see into people's courtyards and even some windows. A roofer could see a man steal from another man's house. When the thief – or robber – didn't realise the watcher was there.'

'But then the roofer could tell everybody!'

'No – no, Stephanos. Not if he were a slave. He would be terrified of giving evidence, for he would have to be tortured. He would certainly keep quiet about it. But I wonder what upset your worker so much? Did he fear that he was known to the criminal? Had someone threatened him? Or had he seen a crime worse than robbery? No – that's nonsense, for the one killing we know of in Athens connected with the thefts took place at night. Roofers work only in the daytime.'

'I don't suppose I can get anything out of the tile-master's slave. I don't want him tortured – and think how angry the tile-master would be! I dare say I could never have my roof repaired again.'

'True. Anyway, the slave would deny having seen anything. We need not trouble ourselves with the roofer's man. You know, with all this theft and robbery going on in Athens, it is impossible to think of Halirrhothios as the sole criminal! Nor can I see him as the chief, the one who commands the others.'

'I don't want to think of him at all,' I said with a transient impatience.

When we came to Athens, and entered the Agora, I sought the food stalls, to find something edible to take home. I ought to make up to Mother and Philomela – and Theodoros too – for yesterday's dereliction. As I walked towards the area of the market that offered offal, sausages and fish, I was surprised to be accosted. By a woman.

Although she was properly and even heavily veiled, this woman somehow managed to be enticing, too. For one thing, as she came close I could not but notice that she smelled lovely. Not the smell of ripe corn and sunshine, but the scent of subtle flowers. Her veiling was of the finest weave. And beside her was a diminutive elegant veiled figure.

'Antigone!' I said. 'What do you and Glykera do here?'

'Hush,' she bade. 'Let us turn to a corner where we are less public.' She moved towards an angle between two stalls, and I followed.

'I have dared to speak to you,' she said, 'because I wish to offer my thanks. For your encouraging – or at least not discouraging – the Master of the Lykeion in graciousness unto us. I should not draw attention to you and your family by venturing to come to your home – that would not be proper. But I have a – I have something, I can scarcely call it a gift, it is so cheap and modest, but I beg you to accept it. Glykera, the basket!'

Glykera held up a well-woven basket of willow, and Antigone with her slender white fingers took off the lid.

'A nothing — barely worthy of acceptance,' she pleaded. 'But we so wish you to take it. For the favour you have done us in hearing our pleas, and in token that you will keep us in mind.'

The basket was certainly interesting. The contents included a plain ceramic stewpot, with the most enticing odour; the lid of this ceramic pot yielded to my curiosity, and allowed me to see inside a warm fish stew. Another smaller ceramic pot contained vegetables. A beautiful loaf of risen bread completed the offering.

'I had fish yesterday,' I said, stupidly.

'But not *my* fish stew. We use onions, I hope you like them.'

'Well — yes, but . . .'

'I would not offer you olive oil, as I know you have your own oil, of superior quality. But I will take the liberty of having a skin of wine sent round — a very light wine, but fragrant and thirst-quenching.'

'Really woman, I cannot allow you to bribe me like this!' This woman whom Aristotle privately suspected as a liar and a spy, should not think she could wheedle me.

'It is not a bribe!' she exclaimed. She seemed thunderstruck. Pushing aside her veil, she faced me, looking me earnestly in the face. 'Oh please, don't say you won't take it, when Glykera and I have gone to such pains to make it nice for you! Oh, we entreat you, look pleased. Be pleased!'

'It doesn't seem right . . .'

I stopped as her lip seemed to quiver and her beautiful eyes filled.

'What could be wrong about taking a fish stew?' she demanded. 'Bribes are when rich men give each other many talents, not a dish of food. But we hope there is enough here to feed your household, and enough wine to put you in good heart. I racked my wits to think what I might give you, and at last hit on this simple offering. But it is too small, too lowly – I see that! Yet I might kneel and plead—'

'Stay,' I said, resigned. I did not want some sort of scene to develop. Certainly not a public drama featuring myself and a woman of colourful reputation. 'If you put it that way, of course I shall take it. But I should not be taking gifts from strange women . . .'

'But I am no stranger – you know me,' she protested. 'You know how I have asked Aristotle's help. And you too. You both help to keep us safe – to keep my little Glykera alive.' At this point Glykera twitched off her veil a little, and I found myself looking at that well-cut nose, those eyes of such unusual colour, and hastily jerked my gaze away again.

'I will not feel right unless I pay something of the debt of gratitude,' implored Antigone. 'Do, I entreat you, have pity on the feelings of a mother, and take the basket.'

I accepted the handsome basket, with mixed feelings.

'My Glykera has prepared much of it,' she promised. 'Her sweet fingers make everything taste good. You will find that to be true. Now do not forget this dear child, she needs your protection too. Aristotle is amazing, but he is not a citizen, and you are. Your voice carries weight. We know that.'

I couldn't be at all certain of this, or how she could know if it did. I knew I should be putting a distance between myself and this female, and yet I would have to take the basket of dinner with me, and a debt to her in the bargain. I stalked off, now laden with the wicker basket. I should certainly be richly supplied with dinner, and my family would all be delighted. As long as I did not truly explain where it came from. The stew certainly smelled delicious. I could feel my mouth watering, ignobly savouring in advance the tasty bits of white fish-flesh in the rich (but not over-rich) broth. I wondered what was in it; certainly there was more than a hint of onion and also of bay leaves, mingling with but not overpowering the essential savoury scent . . .

Enjoying these physical musings, I had not gone very far in the direction of home when I experienced another unwanted encounter. This was with a person who did not offer me good things. The man Kallimakhos of tedious recollection, he who had once begun negotiations with my father regarding a marriage between me and his daughter Kharmia, this man stood before me, rather as he had done before when I was encumbered with a *hydria* and sausages. The basket at least was more manageable.

'Well, Stephanos,' said Kallimakhos heavily. He was as good-looking as ever, though his handsome beard seemed just a trifle more streaked with grey. I gave him a brief but not uncivil word of greeting, hoping to proceed on my way. But he stood directly in front of me, blocking my advance.

'It is *time*,' he said in a loud voice. 'Time we had a settling of scores! I repudiate your paltry sum of money!'

'What?' I said stupidly. But this didn't really make any sense. I had not paid or offered Kallimakhos any sum of money, grand or paltry.

'Take your dirty money!' Kallimakhos bellowed so loud that he attracted the curious. Men who had been shopping or conversing in the Agora now began to gather about us, as if we were two boxers in a contest.

'There!' And Kallimakhos threw down a number of coins in the dust at my feet. One or two spun further than he perhaps intended, and I saw him following their progress out of the corner of his eye.

'It isn't mine,' I said loudly. 'I have given you no money. Nor do I owe you anything.'

'Nonsense – you tried to buy your way out of an

obligation. Look at this money! A hundred drakhmai!' He waved a hand at the coins, very dramatically. I could tell he had set some fingers itching among the crowd. Though looking at the coins I could not imagine that they added up to one hundred drax.

'See here, all of you! This man, this Stephanos, tried to buy me off with a trifle – a man who has broken his contract with me, a sacred promise to marry my daughter. He insults me, and then suggests patching up the injury with base coin in a ridiculous petty sum. And Stephanos sends me this little sum, suggesting it be under the pretext of his buying a dog from me – so Athens would not get wind of his perfidy.'

He turned rhetorically, his arm outstretched, and faced the audience. 'Disgraceful,' one of the spectators murmured. 'A weasel,' said another.

'I had thought,' Kallimakhos exclaimed. 'I had thought – for the sake of my poor daughter, I *wished* to think . . .' Here he stopped and swallowed, as one overcome by emotion (a very effective trick). 'I had expected that Stephanos son of Nikiarkhos would be reasonable. I asked him to come to negotiations with me and some mutual friends as mediators. He indicated he would, and then refused.'

'Not true,' I said, speaking as loud as I could.

'And then he slyly *marries* without telling me! Hitches himself to the daughter of some peasant from far away. And he still will not meet with me to acknowledge his fault and make reparation. I have been patient – very patient—'

'No you haven't,' I said. 'You are unreasonable. There was no such agreement, no *engye . . .*'

'You hear him, how brazenly he denies the facts! I was still trying to negotiate a settlement for this grievance when he sends me money by a slave, with a message. The message is that I am to take this money in recompense, but to pretend it is for the sale of a dog. Well, young fellow, that dog is dead. Do you hear me? I take no dirty coins for a dead dog – or rather to support the mongrel of your deceit!'

'I don't know how you made up all this story,' I said. 'It is a false tale.' It was very awkward having so many eyes upon me. I couldn't speak as effectively as I wished, having to keep holding the basket and shifting the weight of it about.

'And you, with all your crimes on your head, are about to be a *mystes* of the Mysteries,' said Kallimakhos, in the tone of one in deep sorrow and perplexity. He shook his head. 'Yes, all men say that you are, despite your former misdeeds. I don't know how you can go about the matter so calmly with another crime on your conscience – a crime of fraud.'

'There's no fraud – you're being ridiculous!'

'And this Stephanos now has a father-in-law in Eleusis – a dirty-legged farmer who trudges along with his plough – when he could have had me as his father-in-law! But no doubt there are riches buried in the farmer's fields. Tell us – you have come from Eleusis just now?'

'Well, yes, but what—'

'Trying to get your dirty father-in-law's money? What for? Stephanos doesn't need money, my friends, to keep the wife that he has got. Men of Athens, his wife – the little earthenware wife is a peasant girl used to standing up to her ankles in mud at planting time. You, Stephanos, will never make her into a proper Athenian lady. Pop her back to the place whence she came.'

'Why, you – you scoundrel! Dirty-tongued bastard!' Anger took over the whole of me. I suddenly burned to strike the man, and strike him hard. I set down the basket and moved towards him. 'Take back your vile insults!' I said. Some in the crowd sympathised with me, for Kallimakhos had really gone too far in mentioning my wife. 'Hit him, Stephanos!' somebody yelled. I scarcely needed the encouragement. My hand was ready. I raised it intending to slap the man on the side of the face and then punch his jaw. I was so carried away by rage that this seemed the proper proceeding.

'The Agora, Stephanos, the Agora – a sacred place!' A voice rang out, and a slab-sided, awkward figure with square shoulders pushed himself to the front of the crowd. Theophrastos. I paused on hearing his warning. At the same instant one of Kallimakhos' friends hustled my opponent a few paces back, despite his wild flailings and expostulations.

'Let me go, Euthykritos!' Kallimakhos passionately entreated. 'Let me punish this dirty capering goat who dares insult me!'

'Be calm, be quiet,' his friend insisted. 'Be reasonable, Kallimakhos.'

So this was Euthykritos. Even in my flustered and angry state, I took a good look at this merchant. He was well set-up enough, only a little above the middle height, yet sufficiently strong to hold Kallimakhos. He seemed a person capable of decision, and used to managing others. It occurred to me that this merchant was certainly not inimical to Kallimakhos – at least not now, if they went about together. But he was undoubtedly the superior of the two men. Kallimakhos, tamed by his friend, stood breathing hard and glaring at me.

'A timely warning,' Euthykritos acknowledged, addressing Theophrastos with condescending approbation.

The warning had indeed been timely. Brawling in the Agora is not only a crime, like brawling anywhere, but a special crime against the gods, as it is a holy space. If I thought I was badly off for lawsuits now, they would be nothing to what might ensue after striking a man in the Agora. Yet even while realising this, I felt sadly frustrated. It was hard to hold back, especially as the disappointed bystanders indulged in critical comments.

'The coward!' sneered one of the onlookers, looking straight at me. 'Big words but not enough guts.'

'He's anxious to guard the money in his basket,' jeered another.

'That's it,' said Kallimakhos. 'He probably has some of this new father-in-law's riches with him. Cheese? Or just a tidy sum of Pa-in-law's dung-spattered coins?'

'Let's see,' said one of the idlers, a sun-scorched tattered ruffian. 'Here! Kallimakhos! Catch!' And he picked up the basket and sent it off – not sailing high in the air, but scudding along at a good speed a little distance above the ground. It bumbled over and landed with a crash at Kallimakhos' feet.

'Give me that! You have no right to it! Give me that back!' I strained to reach my abused basket, but to no avail. Kallimakhos' friend had cautiously let go of him, and my antagonist was too quick for me. He bent down and opened the basket. The ceramic dish holding the fish stew had broken, and out it poured upon the basket and upon the dust and even a little upon Kallimakhos' feet.

'Well! Fish from Eleusis – who'd have thought it! His daddy has given him a nourishing stew. Poor little boy! Is that all you get out of this wonderful marriage!' Laughing, Kallimakhos was ready to crow, and his two friends, Euthykritos and the sunburnt ruffian, joined with him, both wearing such extensive grins that they looked like masks of Comedy.

'Well, the poor little basket – did it lose its dinner then?'

'All is not lost,' said one of the practical onlookers.

'This nice plate is broken, but there are vegetables here in a dish, both intact. And the bread is only a little dusty.' With officious care he set it to rights, first removing the hopelessly fragmented dish and its smelly contents.

Some dogs came up and sniffed, but the stew upon the ground didn't seem to their taste.

'Well, you haven't lost much of a meal, then, Stephanos; even the dogs won't eat it,' said one spectator in mock-consolation.

'Let him go with his basket – the fellow has suffered enough in losing his dinner,' said another.

'Very well,' said Kallimakhos. 'But you, Stephanos, will hear from me again. You have not settled our account with these few dirty coins.' By this time Kallimakhos was picking up his coins, which were genuinely dirty now, not only from the dust but also in some cases from the stew. He tucked the money into my basket. I took it out and tossed it again on the ground.

'These dirty coins are not mine,' I proclaimed loudly. 'Unlike some people, *I* don't meddle with what does not belong to me.'

With this parting shot I had to be content. I went home with my dishonoured basket, and had to explain to my wife and my mother that I had obtained a nice dinner of fish stew for them – they could smell it – but that the basket had met with a mishap, and all that remained were the vegetables and a loaf of bread which, brushed off and heated up, would do quite well.

'Strange,' said my mother. 'This looks too fine to come from a fish-stall. Where did you get this basket, Stephanos – and the stew?'

'Diognetos gave it to me,' I lied. 'I was visiting him in Eleusis, about our initiation, and he offered the meal to me, as a parting present.'

'Well, that wasn't very nice – you had to walk all the

way carrying it,' exclaimed Philomela. And Mother said frankly, 'That's the stupidest thing, Stephanos! It is not healthy to carry fish stew about for long periods in the heat – you know it can go bad, and cause gripings and sad sickness in the stomach and bowels.'

'I know that stew can go off,' I said, remembering all too clearly. But in the instance I was thinking of, somebody – as I knew full well – had put things into the stew that would ensure its violent disagreement with anyone who ate it.

'Just as well it's gone,' said Mother. 'Next time, buy some fish in the market, if you must, and I will make a fish stew or whatever you wish. Meanwhile, we may dine on the bread and vegetables. At least we have some fresh cabbage in the house, and greens for a salad.'

So that was what they served me, and I tried to eat but little of the made dish of vegetables sweetened by Glykera, so that the women of my household would have something sufficient when they ate after me. Although it was a frugal meal, it did well enough.

XXIII

Facing a Jury

Next morning, I went in good time to put in my formal appeal for a postponement until after the New Year. I had hoped to be first, but found awaiting me both Lykon and his supportive neighbour Smikythos, the man who was looking for another wife. I supposed they hoped they would be able to say I was too late, and rush matters through to their liking. In fact, I was early. Lykon's face fell when he saw me, I noted with satisfaction.

'Greetings, Stephanos. Here you are at last. I trust you are well?'

'Extremely well, I thank you.'

'But then, some people are never ill,' Lykon observed, looking at me narrowly. 'You have the constitution of a horse, I'll give you that.'

'Always trotting round and neighing,' said the neighbour Smikythos, laughing. A perfect toady I thought him.

'I hope you are using your opportunity to find a wife,' I said. 'There are some nice young women in that establishment' – pointing towards a well-known brothel. 'One of them would be glad of a permanent appointment.'

Despite these pleasantries, we went through our formal procedures with decorum. Lykon was not happy about accepting the postponement, but he had already known that the agreement to wait for Philokles would stand, as long as I was there to defend the cause.

Once this was over with, I was at leisure to ponder the unreasonableness of Kallimakhos. He seemed determined to pretend that I had broken an agreement of marriage made between us. I could not think what the man could intend by this behaviour. When I encountered Eudemos of Rhodos in the Agora, I found myself telling him about this problem.

'And I still cannot see it,' I explained. '*Why* is Kallimakhos so earnest now to protest against my marriage with the daughter of Smikrenes? Had he hoped to stop my marrying, that might be slightly rational. But why should he suppose, now my marriage has actually taken place, that I would be willing at all to bring it to a quick end?'

'Well,' said Eudemos, 'I should imagine that he hopes to push you into giving him some money, in order to pacify him.'

'Exactly my thought,' said Aristotle, who had come up behind us. 'I take it you speak of Kallimakhos? He must know as well as yourself that your best prospects of having money to pay him off arise from the union you have just formed. There is one way to test whether he is serious – or not. Has he approached Smikrenes on the subject? Has he tried now or formerly to induce Smikrenes to take his daughter back from you? Or – has anyone sent word of such a thing to your wife?'

'Certainly not! Not as far as I know,' I amended. 'And by law, a divorce cannot be granted on the petition of a woman's father or any other relative. The law requires that a woman appear herself to petition for it.'

'And that was the undoing of Kallias' sister,' said Eudemos, laughing very heartily. 'You remember, Aristotle, how she wished to leave her husband, the notorious Alkibiades. For he disobliged her and spent his time with a variety of harlots and hetairai, even bringing some of these light women to his own house where his wife lived. So, on a certain day the poor female leaves her matrimonial home and ventures forth to put in her petition. But Alkibiades, getting wind of it, follows her up the street. And before she can get to any of the officials, he seizes her. Then he throws her over his shoulder, like a sack of grain, and carries her back home, the helpless woman shrieking and half of Athens watching and laughing. And that was the end of her divorce proceeding.'

'If Kallias had been seriously concerned at his sister's unhappiness,' I suggested, 'he would have gone with her, with an armed guard. So perhaps he didn't want to break off the match with someone as important as Alkibiades.'

'I don't know,' said Aristotle. 'Kallias became Daidoukhos, and was instrumental in prosecuting Alkibiades for impiety in mimicking the Mysteries. Kallias got the priests to curse him. So perhaps he bore a grudge for the way his sister was treated.'

'But about Kallimakhos,' I said. 'You think that if he was serious about trying to break off my marriage, he would also approach my wife's side? In that case, his pursuing me in the streets and yelling abuse and throwing baskets and so on would be just for show. Your logic implies that the man does not really intend breaking off my marriage, or inducing me to marry his daughter.'

'Exactly,' said Eudemos. 'Money is in his mind, never fear.'

'The man's behaviour is irrational, however,' Aristotle observed. 'The danger is that he might become so unreasonably fond of making you miserable as to forget the rational – if vile and mean – purpose of simply extracting money.'

'I don't have any money to extract,' I grumbled. 'And if I did, I think Lykon would like to get it first.'

This was indeed a serious concern. As the summer bloomed and then parched around me, and the waves of heat came over Athens, I was perpetually reminded that the time was flying towards the crisis of the case of the property in Hymettos. The last hearing had given us a respite until after the middle of the summer, the New Year at the beginning of the month of Hekatombaion, when there are many changes among the officials. Now we were advancing into the New Year. Vegetables ripened and began to droop. The first harvest was over, and the second harvest could be expected. Our new Chief Arkhon, after whom the year would be called in all the records, took up his post. On the twenty-eighth day of the month came the great festival of the Panathenaia. The birthday of Athena was marked as always by a great procession and much festivity. It was not, unfortunately for people like Philemon, a year of the Great Panathenaia, which is celebrated not only by musical contests but also by games and chariot-races. Philemon in fact had already departed for his horsy summer in Paeonia.

The Panathenaia festival marks summer at its height. Fruit ripened everywhere, and we enjoyed new figs on hot summer nights. The month of Boedromion would bring some cessation of the heat, and of course the great event – the initiation into the Mysteries. Meanwhile I was not at all sure how the people on the Hymettos farm could escape the attack of Lykon. We had managed to put the civic case off once, under the plea that we had to hear from Philokles, but the end of the Panathenaia spelled the ending of all postponements.

It was only a few days after my discussion with
Eudemos and Aristotle that I received a message,
delivered by sturdy Mika, that the family in Hymettos
needed to see me without delay. I went at once in
response to this urgent summons, which I was sure
concerned Lykon's dreadful lawsuit. I walked as I had
walked to their farm for the very first time a little over a
year ago, through the hot land and up the slopes. The
cool Ilissos and the plane trees that grow along it
provided welcome relief as I made my way, sweating, up
the narrow winding road that rises along the flank of
Hymettos. Wild thyme and oregano perfumed these
heights, and the bees in field and grove kept up a loud
steady humming as I approached the farm door.

All was just as it usually was, Dropides lapped up in
robes and blankets, with a drink in his hand, and the
women busy about the place. They were on the look-out
for me, however (modestly veiled, and hidden behind the
old hanging), and patently eager to talk with me.

'What is it? What has happened?'

Dropides waved his hand. 'Let them tell you. It
exhausts me too much. I don't understand any of this.'

'Indeed,' said Philokleia, 'it has little enough to do with
Dropides. But a man called Kallimakhos sent a message
and then came himself. He told Dropides – but he knew
that we were listening—'

'Told him what?'

'That if we – all of us and Dropides here – could
persuade Smikrenes to get his daughter to divorce you,
Stephanos, and come back to her home, we would all
benefit. Smikrenes to get four sheep, and ourselves to be
free of Lykon's lawsuit.'

'It *would* be very nice not to have to think about any
lawsuit,' said Dropides wistfully.

Well, I thought bitterly, here was the answer to

Aristotle's test. After all, Kallimakhos must be in earnest! Pressure was being cleverly applied to the people of the household of Hymettos, rather than Smikrenes directly. Smikrenes was a hard man to approach, let alone persuade.

I sat down heavily. 'This is new,' I remarked. 'I had thought Kallimakhos might try to press Smikrenes to end my marriage. But instead, he presses you. What is the connection? *Where* is the link between Lykon and Kallimakhos?'

'I wonder,' said Philonike, 'if anyone has tried any form of persuasion upon my daughter?'

'No one is permitted to approach her – she is a well-guarded Athenian matron,' I protested stoutly. 'And any attempt would be of no use, I am sure. For she is a modest as well as affectionate girl. Both of us believe ourselves truly married and have no wish to change.'

'She is lucky so far,' said Philonike. 'But someone could threaten her that something terrible would be done to *you* if she did not avail herself of the opportunity to divorce.'

'Nonsense!' I said. 'They have already tried, with silly attacks – but that is ridiculous. Philomela would tell me about any alarming messages, like a good wife.'

'Maybe so,' said Philonike. I was not happy with this reply.

'What should we do?' said Dropides. 'For my part, I am willing to give this troublesome neighbour whatever he wants, if he will only leave us in peace. That's *all* I ask, a little peace. And you, Stephanos – so young! So well acquainted with brothels too. You could divorce the girl. Take on another wife as a duty, a piece of business – Kallimakhos' daughter, what's the harm? Go elsewhere for your pleasure. Many men do so.'

'Scandalous!' said Philokleia roundly. 'We are not to be bought and sold! And why should we rely on the word of a couple of scoundrels?'

'Asking our young people to sacrifice their lives so we can sit around wrapped in fleeces,' said Philonike with a passion that overran politeness.

'We are getting worked up for nothing,' I pleaded. 'Let us treat Lykon's suit simply as an ordinary legal case. We can and will fight his false claims. If there is a connection between him and Kallimakhos, then they are both doing something not only illegal but also irrational. There is – or should be – no connection between the two cases. One is about property in Hymettos, the other about an alleged breach of promise on my part.'

'You mean,' said Philokleia, 'that if we begin to believe that there is a connection, they will confuse us.'

'Exactly. Accept the fact that there will be a civil suit. We must prepare! We need to be ready to bring witnesses. We were told the case would come to court in the new arkhon's term of office, and the new arkhon is already arrived. Now the Panathenaia is past, it will not be difficult to collect jurors. I take it there is still no word from Philokles?'

'No,' said Philokleia, flatly. 'He might have dropped off the end of the earth. We cannot be sure he is even alive. And if my son *is* alive, he is treating *us* as if we had dropped off the edge of the world.' She spoke with unaccustomed bitterness.

'Do not lose heart,' I advised. 'But if any of us' – here I deliberately glared at Dropides – 'if *any* of us tries to treat in a sneaking way with them, promising things not in our power to give, matters will go much worse for all. *No one* has the power to bring my marriage to an end. Even Smikrenes. My wife would have to petition for it. Surely, any such thing is as far from her heart as from mine.'

'You would be married to a much richer man's daughter,' urged Dropides. 'Consider the many benefits—'

'Stepfather!' Philonike cried indignantly. 'That you should say such a thing and injure my poor Philomela!'

'Speaking my mind,' said Dropides doggedly. 'You women won't face facts. The lad may not have realised his position. You could get more of what you want, Stephanos, allied with a rich and strong citizen. Smikrenes can't do you much good, and the land here belongs to Philokles. Your children cannot really inherit it.'

'I see you would be willing to wash your hands of me,' I said bitterly. 'But if you are trying to make me mercenary, you have chosen a weak case. Kallimakhos may not be at all as rich as he pretends – not now. One hears rumours. He may just want to marry his daughter off respectably before the crash comes – think of that!'

'And who knows,' said Philokleia, 'whether this girl is worth marrying? She may have something seriously wrong with her. You notice Kallimakhos hasn't been able to get her off his hands so far. Maybe—'

'I know nothing of her,' I stated. 'Let us try to get by without speaking scandal of the poor female. It would be unjust to put an end to her chances of marriage just because her father's acting like a crazy person. But it *is* puzzling. Kallimakhos knows that I will have very little money indeed if I estrange myself from Smikrenes – and from yourselves and Philokles. How could he truly desire an impoverished son-in-law? So – does he want something else, like damages? Probably needs immediate cash to tide him over.'

'I hope you are right,' Philokleia said. 'Then we might unhook him from Lykon, and deal with just one antagonist, not two.'

That was my thought too. But I left the farm at Hymettos feeling low, even the promise of new honey soon to come did not cheer my heart.

*

Some men assert that the things we dread are largely imaginary; thus, we should not get worked up about the future, for what we fear may never happen. Experience denies this. My experience at least. Unpleasant things rationally anticipated usually do happen. It was evident that I was not going to be allowed to forget the mad threats of Kallimakhos, nor the hostile designs of Lykon on the property at Hymettos. And we had proof that these two men were – strangely – working in conjunction. Their plans reached far into my own life, for they proposed to knock a hole in my house and create a divorce between myself and Philomela! I gritted my teeth at the thought. *Nothing* was going to take my wife from me. Fortunately, our participation in the sacred Mysteries coming so soon would draw us closer together. Surely Philomela of her own volition would never petition for a divorce.

One thing that I dreaded did come to pass, almost at once, for I received another summons to appear in five days' time to answer Lykon's suit.

'I am glad to hear your court case is ripe. Time your suit came on and was resolved,' said the arkhon from Kholargos, when I met him accidentally in the Agora.

'But,' I protested, 'this is a special case, with the real landowner away—'

The arkhon did not wait to be impressed. 'You know, Stephanos, everyone has been very generous in allowing the postponement, but such stalling cannot continue.'

I was to appear along with Dropides and Philokles, and any other chosen representative of the women and of Philokles (if the latter were absent). The family from Hymettos, thus warned, descended from their heights the day before the trial – Dropides came carried on a sort of litter. The party stayed at the house of a friend of Dropides. I met Dropides there. I could hardly speak freely, since the host was Dropides' friend – it seemed odd to me to think of his having any friends at all.

'Wearisome,' said Dropides, speaking in a faint and weary tone. 'Tedious and *so* unnecessary. I was badly jumbled about on the road. You know, Stephanos, you could bring all this pain and strife to an end, if you chose.'

'I do not for a moment believe that,' I said stoutly. 'The only way to ward off Lykon and his coveting the land is to get a good "no" from the courts. That will put him in his place.'

Dropides could only sigh. Expressively. The women were shut up in the women's quarters and I was not able to converse with them, but I could imagine their apprehension.

'Have you acquired someone to represent Philokles?' I asked.

'If it isn't you, it will have to be myself. Dear me, it's a long while since I studied rhetoric. I am sure the sight of the jury will put me off completely. It will be lucky if I don't faint.'

Plainly, Dropides was not at all the right person to represent Philokles. But if I put myself forward as Philokles' representative, then all the weight of the charges would fall upon me. If this case dragged on, I would never get free of it. Hitherto, my defence had rested on the argument that I was in no way responsible for anything at the Hymettos farm. If Lykon and Kallimakhos could transform me into a deputy land-owner, then they might almost do as they wished. Any failure on my part to keep the land together and evade any damages would be attributed to my inefficiency. And we would all be even more vulnerable.

Such thoughts as these were sufficient to give me a sleepless night. Philomela would know if I tossed and turned, so I had to lie quietly open-eyed in the dark, waiting for the dawn light, and the beginning of an uncomfortable day. I dressed myself in a clean *khiton* and tried to look presentable; my beard and hair had been trimmed the day before. I set out swiftly, with no desire to eat nor even to drink, though I probably should have taken a cup of water. The day was hot and sultry, even early in the morning; people moved slowly and warily, anticipating the wall of heat that would enclose them by midday.

One might have thought that the prospect of an oppressive day would have kept the elderly in their homes. But no. As we neared the area of the courts, the number of old men became noticeable. Grey locks and white hair, men stumbling or shuffling along, men fulfilling Oidipous' riddle by walking with three legs (two legs and a stick) at the ending of life. These were the jurors. There is always a shortage of younger or middle-aged jurors. After all, men at the height of maturity and health, men engaged in their work or tending distant farms or seeing to business outside of Athens' walls, cannot be expected to waste valuable time in civil lawsuits. But there is always a great pool of jurors among the old men. Particularly old citizens of the poorer sort, who truly value the jurors' pay of three obols a day each, an income which makes them more considerable at home.

Paying for jury duty upholds the equality of the democracy; the principle is to ensure that poverty or the need to work for a living cannot prevent a man from serving on a jury. A good idea it seems, yet as long ago as Aristophanes' time certain drawbacks to this system were apparent. The pay attracts old fellows with nothing else to do with their time, like the irritating old father in *Wasps*. Like Aristophanes' character, these idle old boys enjoy the rhetorical performances of the courts, hoping to be entertained by speakers who might tell stories, or fables from Aisopos, or relate juicy gossip about well-known families. Jury duty also gives a superannuated person of small means the opportunity to enjoy being flattered by important men.

My previous experiences with law courts, frightening as they had been both for myself and for others, had been with the venerable court of the Areopagos, whose members, all former arkhons, are among the most respected men in the city. The members of the sort of jury one customarily has for a civil suit are citizens of a different sort, less wealthy and less educated. They love finding fault. Looking at these old fellows toddling into the court, I was reminded of the *khoros* of Aristophanes' waspish jurors:

> You will have to weave a good tale
> And be wily and witty, don't fail.
> For your youth can't assuage
> The force of my rage;
> If I don't like your tone, you I'll nail.

Truly, the jurors can nail a litigator. The Chief Arkhon and the Basileus have nothing to say in the business. Once a case is heard before an Athenian jury, there is no judge but these jurors, and their vote is final and without appeal.

These expectant greybeards – *white*beards in many instances – were nodding and chattering, appreciating the prospect not only of a few bronze coins but also of some (brief) golden power. Not that everyone who turned up offering himself for duty on a particular day would be chosen. It is a strict rule, a preventive against corruption, that juries are to be chosen on the day of the trial, and by lot. Since it would take for ever to draw lots for each individual of these hundreds, the men who present themselves assemble according to the letter of their name. The lottery (for a relatively unimportant case like Lykon's) consists of allocating a particular case to a letter of the alphabet. Our case drew the letter 'Delta', and all the men to whom this applied separated themselves out, and trooped off to the common court. We were then allotted a small jury of one hundred men.

The space allocated to the hearing, little better than a large shed enclosed on three sides, was becoming packed with people. The heat of the day made even partial enclosure disagreeable. It would have been nicer, I reflected, to meet in the open air, as the court of the Areopagos always did. But our case had no shadow of offence to the gods about it, like murder cases, so there was no reason to do without a roof. The old fellows made haste slowly to take their places – they did everything pretty slowly. The smell of old men's bodies, some palpably not washed that day or the day before, began to rise, along with the smell of garlic (from breakfast) and bad breath (from rotting teeth) and farts (from the gift of nature, and poor digestion). Heads poking out at the end of wrinkled necks, the old jurors glanced curiously at us, with about as much friendship in their expressions as could be found in a confabulation of turtles. Looking at their little beady eyes, I was not encouraged.

Dropides was brought in by two men, and deposited carefully on a bench, but I could not see any flicker of sympathy for his ailments in the countenances of these men who were (for the most part) his seniors. Most of them had to put up with the pains of rheumatism or something, I reflected; the role of invalid adopted by Dropides was unlikely to elicit their sympathy. At another time this might have pleased me. Not now.

Lykon was looking very spruce and businesslike. He too had been carefully shaved and had had a haircut for the occasion. With him was his neighbour Smikythos, who had agreed to make a deposition in Lykon's favour. Dropides told me that Asimos (father of the strange girl) had said he would come, and would make a statement in our favour, but Asimos was not yet here. Dropides seemed more and more pathetic and ridiculous. I had no confidence at all in his putting on a good show for these wasps.

In fact, Dropides' appearance might weaken us still further. His elaborate parade of debility could encourage men to think that the farm in Hymettos was in shaky hands, and might be better off if taken over by its energetic neighbour. Laws regarding the inalienable quality of family land would play in Philokles' favour – but there are ways of picking holes in this principle, in particular instances. If Lykon won this cause today, the next phase would probably be a new lawsuit, on the plea that a great patch of Philokles' land was acquired and not inherited from time immemorial. It might be claimed that in the past this parcel went with the lands of Lykon himself, or had been unjustly sold off and should be sold back to him for a low set price. Such iniquitous things have happened! Not only jurors but magistrates too are somewhat disposed to let land go to those who can make it yield the most produce. A farm run by women and an invalid – tempting. Would Lykon *really* drop the suit and such prospects of aggrandising his lands simply to oblige Kallimakhos? Would he truly give up this and any other lawsuit if I were willing to dissolve my marriage to Smikrenes' daughter and wed Kharmia? Why should he?

As I was thinking thus cheerlessly, Kallimakhos himself entered the court. His dark beard with its touches of grey looked quite youthful against the grey-white banks of aged jurors. Holding himself erect and walking with a light, confident step, Kallimakhos marched over to

Lykon, and offered greetings without dropping his voice. The two looked impressive, standing together, with neighbour Smikythos trying to join in their conversation and live up to the importance of his companions. Our man Asimos sidled in at this inopportune moment; his bashful appearance and plain clothes did nothing to render our case more imposing. Oh well, at least we had one deponent on our side.

I kept rehearsing inwardly the statement I had gone over with Aristotle during our walk to Peiraieus, on the day of the thefts from Lampos and the Phoinician: 'I Stephanos son of Nikiarkhos of Athens deny that I am answerable for any damage . . . This property belongs to Philokles . . . Matters should truly be referred to Philokles . . .' It sounded very lame, and rather timid.

The man who kept the records was telling the slave to look to the water-clock. Then he was looking about the room, counting heads. He cleared his throat, and called for silence. As he was clearing his throat again, in preparation for the formal request to Lykon to state his case, there was a disturbance. Someone was erupting into the room, and shouting, bellowing even, 'Wait! Stop!'

A man wearing strong thick-soled boots, although it was in the heat of summer. A sturdy homespun *khiton* that seemed rather the worse for wear. A familiar face. Smikrenes. My father-in-law. He shouted again, 'Wait! Stop!' Then he came rushing up to me, waving something in his hand.

'What are *you* doing here?' I exclaimed, dismayed. 'It would be better to keep away – you don't want to get sucked into this—'

'But I am!' he exclaimed. He was breathing so hard from running and shouting, he could scarcely get words out. 'Explain – later. But read – take these!' And he handed me what I could now see were a pair of travel-

worn tablets, tied together with string. My direction was
written on the exterior: 'Stephanos son of Nikiarkhos of
Kydathenaion'. I fumbled at the string but it was straitly
tied and I couldn't undo the great knot.

'Give 'em here!' said Smikrenes. Bringing his still-
strong teeth to the tablets, he bit through the string, like
a dog or a wolf. 'There!'

'Stephanos of Kydathenaion, perhaps you may best
enjoy your private correspondence at another time,' said
Lykon.

I paid no heed, for I was taking in the message on the
tablet:

> *Stephanos son of Nikiarkhos, Greeting*
>   *I hope you are well. We are well and busy too, have
> been travelling roundabout. Winter will be busy because
> of sponges. Kalymnos very fine. Hymettos business bad
> but I shall come to Athens in Boedromion just before
> sailing season ends to set matters right. Nanno says this
> is best. More news when we meet in a little while, greet
> your bride from her fond uncle,*
>   *Philokles*

Not an elegant epistle, but certainly a welcome one.

'Hah! Stop!' I cried. 'We must stop proceedings before
we go any further!' The clerk, though but a slave, looked
pained as I interrupted his exercise of power.

'I fail to see,' Lykon said icily, 'what gives Stephanos of
Kydathenaion the impression that *he* can call off a trial
whenever he chooses.'

'But Lykon,' I protested, 'your case is not primarily
against *me*. Not at all, really. It makes little sense to
prosecute me for things that happen on the Hymettos
farm, which is not mine. And it doesn't belong to
Dropides either. This is a message from the *real* owner.

Philokles. Look!' I waved the tablets in the air. 'Anyone who likes may read this message – I beg someone else will read it to everyone, before any trial gets started. You see, Philokles himself is coming to Athens – all the way from Kos! He will attend to the matter personally. This law case can be properly held in Boedromion, when he is here.'

I kept waving the tablets above my head, joyfully, as men wave ribbons and banners. One of the jurymen got off his bench and came over to me. He was a little younger than most of his fellow jurors (say between fifty-five and sixty), and better dressed and groomed. From the respect the other jurors paid him I gathered this man Damasippos was well-born, not one of the lower ranks. He picked up the missive, and read it aloud.

'Well,' he said after it had been recited twice, 'that does seem to settle it. If the legal case is truly a charge against Philokles – and it is on the register that it is, and that he is the legal owner of that farm in Hymettos – then it is only right for Lykon to wait until Philokles has made the long journey from Kos and returned to Athens.'

There was a groan of disappointment from the other jurors.

'What – no trial!' screamed one. Another shouted, 'Damasippos, you cannot mean it! What about our three obols?'

'Yes, yes, give us our three obols! Trial! Trial!' A cacophony.

'We are fortunate,' said Damasippos, addressing each Damon and Dio and Drakontides of his Delta company. 'Luckily the trial has not started, in which case there would have been a legal question as to how to proceed. But if you are quick enough now, you may be a jury for another cause.'

At this hint they started hopping over benches and hobbling to the door, and left us in their quest for the three obols.

I now had time to thank Smikrenes. 'I am so glad to
see you, so astonished,' I said, amazed that he had
brought me such good news. 'How come you to be here?'

'Wanted to hear how this nonsense went,' he replied
gruffly. 'Came within the city walls at dawn. Went first
to your place. Wanted to see my girl. You were gone. But
a messenger was just coming with a letter for you. Said
'twas from Kos. So I thought it must be that idiot
Philokles, and came on to the court with it. That's all.'

'I am so thankful—' There was an unexpected
interruption. Kallimakhos was beside us, towering over
Smikrenes.

'It is to your esteemed father-in-law, not to yourself,
that I would speak, Stephanos,' Kallimakhos said
smoothly. Evidently he felt this a sufficient explanation
for half turning his back on me, and taking Smikrenes
confidentially by the forearm. Smikrenes drew back, and
shook his arm free.

'Please understand, O Smikrenes of Eleusis,' said the
suave father of Kharmia, 'that my respect for your good
self is very great. I want to assure you personally that it
would be in my power to make you ample recompense for
any inconvenience incurred by the divorce of your
daughter from Stephanos. I believe the original offer
which was conveyed to you was four sheep. But if you
think five more suitable . . .? Or something else. What
about a strong young ox? Always useful on a farm,
especially in good flat country like yours.'

Smikrenes folded his arms and stood glowering until
Kallimakhos had finished this little speech. Then he gave
his opinion.

'Rubbish!' He spat on the floor, not far from
Kallimakhos' feet. 'Never heard such rubbish. I am to
break my word, and take back my poor girl – no longer a
virgin – and you'll give me sheep, or an ox? You might as

well offer me lice and fleas. I'm not having any.'

'Consider, my good sir,' said Kallimakhos. 'I know this is an awkward time. Maybe I have chosen the wrong moment. But every advantage will accrue to you—'

'If,' said Smikrenes, 'you think my son-in-law Stephanos here is such a great purchase, why shouldn't I value him likewise?' He creaked out a harsh laugh which cut off abruptly. 'I've had enough. No more of this foolishness. Play your games somewhere else.'

'Ah! Somewhere else? I understand you.' Kallimakhos tapped his nose. 'Too public here. Quite right. We will meet again, my friend, at a fitter opportunity.' And he turned to depart, joining the halt and lame at the end of the disappearing crowd of jurors. When we ourselves got outside, I followed Kallimakhos, letting Smikrenes go in the opposite direction.

'One moment of your time, good Kallimakhos,' I said with intentional irony. 'I do not comprehend your conduct,' I continued, having the man's attention, and the pleasure of taking him by surprise this time. 'I cannot see why you think it is to your advantage to pursue me as a son-in-law.'

'No great treasure, Stephanos, indeed,' Kallimakhos replied caustically. 'But you should know that I am accustomed always to getting my own way. I count disappointment as but temporary. You have had warnings. Your hopes could be cut off. Do I not make myself clear? My girl is known to have been engaged to you – our honour is at stake. Now, if you are coming to see reason, we can make that peasant girl's transition as pleasant as possible.'

'Please understand,' I said. 'Insults to my wife are not allowed. And I want you and your associates to know just one thing. You have probably heard of my reputation at the Lesser Mysteries. People call me "Killer" – which I *don't* appreciate. Yet it is only fair to inform you of my determination. If any man should meddle with or harm my bride in any way, I shall kill that man. I mean it. Be he seven times an Athenian citizen.'

I had the satisfaction of seeing Kharmia's father turn pale and take a step back before I turned on my heel and walked away without giving him time to answer. I soon rejoined Smikrenes.

'I don't know why they keep to their nonsense,' Smikrenes complained. 'If Philokles comes back Lykon's case is done for. It *is* nonsense, isn't it?'

'So – you heard this proposition before,' I said. 'About the divorce, and four sheep. Who came to you with this suggestion? When? *Who* made you the offer?'

Smikrenes shrugged. 'A man I never met before. Fellow was next to me in the tavern, and began this kind of chat. He said he had something to say to me if I was Smikrenes, and I said I was. "Something to convey to you" – those were his exact words. He told me someone had taught him the message and paid him to tell me. Then he repeated this yarn about how if I took my daughter back I would get four sheep. I didn't take it serious. Someone's idea of a joke, thought I.'

'It isn't a joke, apparently,' I said. 'The proposition has been made to me by that man who was here just now. Kallimakhos. He wants me to marry his daughter Kharmia. He claims it's out of pride – he has some ridiculous story that we were engaged before. But I really cannot understand why. If I were to sunder myself from you and Philokles, and had to give back my bride's dowry to boot, I would have little enough money or property to offer a man of his station.'

'Athenians! They're all addled, living in the city,' complained Smikrenes.

XXIV

❧❧

Processions and Jests

Although I applauded Smikrenes' stout resistance to the
enticements offered by Kallimakhos, it sickened me to
realise that this insistent man had indeed approached
both sides of Philomela's family. Evidently, according to
Aristotle's test, Kallimakhos was quite in earnest. Of
course, if Lykon had won his suit against them – against
us – Dropides would have been more abjectly ready to
capitulate. Now, with the real owner threatening to come
home soon, it seemed less likely that Lykon would have
his own way.

'You must see *that*,' I argued with Dropides. 'Once
Philomela comes, your troubles are over. Lykon won't have
a leg to stand on. It's absurd to ask me to treat with
Kallimakhos now for the chance of having Lykon withdraw
– when he will withdraw soon anyway. Gold for bronze!'

'Well, my young friend, I don't know if Philokles is
going to be such a wonder-worker as you say,' retorted
Dropides. 'I don't remember that he was any orator.'

'His mere presence should suffice. Philokles' claim to
the property will be remembered and recognised. Once he
is back, and people have a real citizen to deal with about

his own land, they will be more careful. Smikrenes of Eleusis is standing firm – he will never accept any offer to take back his daughter! Kallimakhos and Lykon in alliance cannot offer anything truly desirable to me or to my bride's kindred.'

'*Why* are they in alliance – Lykon and Kallimakhos? That's what I'd like to know,' exclaimed Philokleia, listening behind the curtain.

Why indeed? I could give no satisfactory explanation to myself. Who was using whom? Which of these two men first asked for the other's assistance in this campaign against us? Were they behind the strange series of attacks against me? At least those personal assaults appeared to have ceased. Perhaps, I thought uneasily, because Kallimakhos had devised another plan of campaign. But Kallimakhos had used an odd phrase: 'Your hopes could be cut off.' 'Cut off' – what exactly did he mean? Was that a reference to the bloody knife thrown at me during the wedding?

I praised Smikrenes' firmness, and asked him not to mention the strange proposition to anyone else. I begged him especially not to mention it to his daughter.

'You needn't vex yourself,' said Smikrenes. 'It's best not to tell womenfolk anything of importance anyway. You know how they love chatter – any piece of news they seize like a chicken with a barley corn! And the men inside the city walls are about as bad, talking away in taverns. My girl would only grieve. Or else her mind would go gadding after a new big match.'

With this I had to be content. I also implored Philomela's grandmother and mother never to let my young bride know that any such idea had been mooted.

'I cannot bear,' I said, 'to have *divorce* even mentioned or thought of in my house. It would torture both of us – to no purpose.'

The two of them agreed, but what Smikrenes had said about women chatting struck me as quite true; hard to believe they would remain entirely silent. I couldn't keep Philomela separate from her mother, since they would be going to Eleusis together, Philomela as *mystes*, Philonike as an advanced pilgrim of the second year, one of the *epoptai*, the Seers.

Philokles had not said when precisely he would arrive. I was in a state of expectancy at the beginning of Boedromion, but days went by without a sign. It seemed no time before Philomela and I had to begin the fasting period in preparation for the Mysteries. We both felt well instructed by Diognetos and his wife, who had generously visited us twice; Diognetos had given me the manuscripts to read aloud to Philomela.

On the sixteenth day of Boedromion the cry went up at dawn: 'To the sea, O *mystai*!' Immediately there was a great bustle and pattering of feet, the sound of carts being harnessed, an outcry of donkeys. Philomela and I, in appropriate attire, made haste to join the hurrying crowd as it moved, everyone going at his own pace, down to Phaleron. As wheeled transport was not forbidden on this day (unlike the day of procession to Eleusis), many women of good birth chose to proceed in a cart. Others among the *mystai* rode asses or mules. This was not altogether agreeable for those of us who were going on foot.

'It seems likely,' said Aristotle, who had been hurrying to catch up with us, in a very gratifying manner, 'that the original ceremony of purification by water was held at Eleusis, where the salt stream flows into the sea. Demeter sprinkled salt water on Triptolemos there, so the story goes. But now there are so many of us that they take care of the business in the broad bay of Phaleron.'

'As long as it is true salt water of the sea,' explained

Thymades, 'it does not matter. Most of the scenes show Triptolemos naked, a sign that he went into the sea itself, as well as being sprinkled with water. You must be careful to do both – step into the sea, and then wait for one of the priesthood to cleanse you with sprinkling from the sacred sieve. Wash your pig first.'

The little pigs that Philomela carried in her basket were more resigned than the previous couple – at least, they made very little disturbance. We had brought ropes to tie them securely before immersion. The road to Phaleron seemed long because we had to go so slowly. I was surprised and impressed at how large a crowd we were; I kept bumping into people whom I did not know. It was a relief to be able to catch sight of a few whom I did know – Phryne, tall and elegant; and there was Antigone, very modestly veiled, but quite recognisable. She walked for a little way with Aristotle and myself (our women being respectfully in the rear and not contaminated by this improper female).

'Do you get any news – you know – of Alexander?' she asked in a low voice.

'Just what everyone knows,' said Aristotle, 'that he is leading his forces against the wild tribes and slowly gaining victory. His mind and time must be much taken up with military affairs.' The Master of the Lykeion smiled, but not with his eyes, and changed the subject. 'How does young Glykera's education go on?' he enquired.

'And have you succeeded in purchasing a slave for her?' I added.

'Very well. Oh yes,' Antigone replied to both questions. 'Glykera has learned to play some new music. And we have found a child slave for her – cheap. I think the little wench has been in trouble once for stealing, but that lowers the price. We shall complete the purchase, if the omens are favourable, after the Mysteries are done. The little one is only eight years old or so – young enough to be teachable. Quite a bargain. Glykera spent a morning with her and thinks she will do. The child isn't talkative – a good thing – but my chatty Glykera says she induced her to speak.'

I could think of a child answering this description. It was a relief to imagine that Halirrhothios' slave-daughter, the beaten Eurynome, might be able to get away from his house and make a fresh start. And if Eurynome were speaking to Glykera, perhaps she was coming out of her dazed state.

I dropped behind to make sure Philomela was all right, and Antigone with her Glykera soon melted away into the crowd when we got to the beach. An immense crowd and worth seeing. Scores and scores of persons, male and female, black and white, young (though above childhood) and mature and old – all stripping off their clothes. Removing outer garments, we stood baring ourselves almost entirely to the kindly sun of summer's later end. Each man wore a modest but skimpy loincloth, and each women one meagre plain tunic. The plainness of our attire did not conceal the enormous differences in charm.

'Take your pigs. Hold them firmly!' the Herald and his henchmen kept saying. This is not a liturgical injunction but a piece of advice. Each of us grappled with his own pig, and took it to the margin of the sea. There we plunged it, squealing mightily, in the water at the sea's edge, and dipping into the salt water with a small pot, shook the contents on to the indignant porker. Subsequently we had to put our astonished purified pigs back in their cleansed container. By this time, after the long walk and then struggling with the piglet, I felt ready for a wash anyway, and so, as I could see, did Philomela. Our *mystagogoi* did not disrobe, but encouraged us from the shore.

'Walk into the water!' Thymades cried with gentle encouragement. Aristotle and I stepped boldly in. With more hesitation Herpyllis and Philomela soon followed. The water was cooler than I had expected. I could see that Philomela felt the shock – she let out a little squeak as the refreshing but chilly element took hold of her. Herpyllis bit her lip rather than make any fuss. All the women were naturally quite unused to entering the sea; for most, this would be the first time in their lives that they had done so, while many of us men had been used to swimming since boyhood. But today one wasn't at Phaleron to swim, but to receive the purification – as last time from fresh water, so this time from salt. I stood, at leisure for a little space, inhaling the scent of the sea, that mysterious combination of unknown things, along with the smell of seaweed in sunshine. The crowd of washed bodies swayed back and forth. Beside me, Philomela let out a gasp.

'Look! Oh do look at Phryne!'

I looked in the direction in which her eyes strayed, and saw what was certainly a majestic sight. Phryne, naked in all but name once the water took her and pasted her tunic to her beautiful body, was advancing through the wavelets. Nowise abashed, she welcomed the water, and her water-blessed body gleamed in the sunshine, as did her hair, her beautiful golden hair, which unbound tumbled in its own waves towards the sea.

'Aphrodite!' said Herpyllis.

She was not the only one to gaze in awe at Phryne. Herpyllis the slave herself looked unusually handsome, her rounded limbs displayed, and I looked modestly away, so as not to gaze on Aristotle's woman.

'Aphrodite arising from the sea,' said a man near me. 'Now I know what it means. We have been blessed with a vision.'

At this moment one of the priests came to me and gave me a generous shower on the head with the sieve-like vessel he carried. Now mundified, I could wade back to shore and dry clothes. When we got back to our *mystagogoi*, people were still exclaiming about the sight of Phryne.

'Aphrodite, truly,' insisted Herpyllis.

'Not so,' said Diognetos. 'We are here today to worship Demeter. That was not Aphrodite but a *hetaira*, a common woman of Athens, in the water.'

I thought this over and decided it was true and not true at the same time. Philomela said nothing, but by now I could tell from a certain set of her chin when she was disagreeing inwardly with something said.

Packing up ourselves and our piglets, we walked home again. On the next day the pigs were offered up as sacrifices to Demeter and Persephone, and that was the end of our well-washed animals. The poor of Athens enjoyed feasts at this time, as the sacrificial meat (all but the Goddesses' share and that of the priests) went to the people. The following day was the day for staying home and just thinking, while those who were not *mystai* could participate in a procession in honour of Asklepios, and in a vintage offering to Dionysos – from which we were barred. Diognetos had already explained: 'For, just as Demeter abstained from drinking wine during her affliction and loss, the *mystai*, Seers and *mystagogoi* also abstain from wine on this day of Dionysos. Rather, it is on this day that the simple drink of Demeter is prepared – the *kykeion*. Barley, water and herbs. But we do not partake of that on this day – nor of any grain foods. This day is the opposite of the Pyanepsia.'

The twentieth day of Boedromion dawned, fifth day of the festival, day of the important journey towards the heart of the Mysteries. Dawn began with the Gathering, the meeting together of all the fasting *mystai* dressed for their pilgrimage. Running along with a sense of joyful expectation was an unshakeable uneasiness in my soul. Was it true that Kallimakhos would leave us alone? Was there any danger of seduction or a more brutal attempt being made on Philomela? I was anxious that she should stay close to me or to her mother Philonike the whole time we were part of the monstrous crowd. Naturally, I said nothing about this to my wife, but cheerfully donned my crown of myrtle leaves as she did hers, taking up a good bunch of green leaves bound with white wool. I had been careful to obtain a large supply of good myrtle; the quality of our crowns meant we could easily be identified by each other, and not get lost in the crowd.

The great crowd of us *mystai* assembled within the city walls behind the gate, talkative, excited people wearing clean black garments, like those of the poorest of travellers. Each of us was carrying a modest offering of meal and incense, and some food and clothing for later in a bag slung over the shoulder. Philomela carried ceramic vessels for the *kykeion*. Nobody carried wine. Many pilgrims held a staff to aid their walk to the holy shrine.

It was strange in such an oddly dressed crowd to see so many familiar persons. Of course Aristotle and Herpyllis were with us, and likewise our *mystagogoi*, faithful Diognetos and Thymades with their wives. Phryne would be there somewhere, but I didn't see her on this day of modest dress. I saw Halirrhothios, looking pale but expectant; I was determined to give him a wide berth. To my surprise I also saw Lamas, my neighbour the historian, with the long rippling brown beard. I didn't remember seeing him at Agrai. It was difficult to spot the women, even Philonike, but I did recognise one of the females as the woman who was sister to Sophilos and mother of Strabax. I had not seen her earlier at Agrai either. But then, my own penitential condition during the ceremonies in Agrai was not conducive to taking account of other people.

I pointed the humble woman out to Aristotle. 'There's Sophilos' sister – I am surprised she could afford to be here! They are so very poor.'

'A gift, most likely,' said Aristotle. 'Possibly your good Strabax has pleased his master the marble-seller, despite his self-professed temper. For Melanthios the marble-seller of Eleusis is among us as well.'

It was true. Melanthios of Eleusis *was* there. I had not seen the marble-seller at the earlier rites either. I wasn't certain whether as an Eleusinian he was perhaps allowed to undergo initial purification in Eleusis itself. There was another Eleusinian, and this one I did not wish to meet. The big discus-thrower Biton, son of Smikrenes' disgruntled neighbour. Biton's pilgrim attire could not disguise his physique, or those great hands like the hindquarters of a pig.

Although in imitation of the mourning of the Goddess we were all wearing the garb of mourners, happy voices arose on the morning air. We didn't sound like a funeral. The statue of the young god Iakkhos was brought out of the Eleusinion and held aloft near the front of the procession. Iakkhos, whose name means the shout of rejoicing, is greatly loved, a light-bringer in his own right.

We sang, in full voice, very impressive from such a mass of persons:

> 'Iakkhos most honoured, creator of song
> Creator of festive song,
> Come march with us to the Goddess,
> March with us,
> Accompany us to Eleusis!'

Heralds and our own *mystagogoi* were trying to bring us all to order, and make sure that we got off on time. We were also disciplined and organised by the military contingent: young Athenian men doing their military service were annually ordered to give the procession an escort. I was pleased to see there was some real military protection, and recalled how Alkibiades, making up for his previous alleged impiety against the Mysteries, had formed an armed guard to protect the *mystai* in procession during the war against the Spartans. *Epheboi*, pleasant youths of some seventeen or eighteen summers, many with the down of youth upon their cheeks, did not promise too much protection. Yet their officers were armed, some with spears as well as swords, and most of the young men had light javelins, at least. Athens thus proclaimed its sway over the worship at the Mysteries even as these troops protected Demeter's people from insult and highway robbery.

The pressure of the crowd – of at least a couple of thousand – was almost overwhelming before we began to move. Then we started to wind our way through the Dipylon Gate and the Kerameikos to the Sacred Road to Eleusis. At first the going was painfully slow. Some worshippers were still arriving; others were searching for friends or guides. Innumerable spectators crowded along the way, some perching upon the very gravestones of Kerameikos to watch us. The van of our procession was well worth watching. There was the Hierophant in his ceremonial purple garments, followed by the Daidoukhos in his embroidered *khiton* and purple stole, holding high in each hand above his filleted and wreathed head the sacred torches, still unlit. The High Priestess of Demeter and her subordinates proceeded in their decorated waggon, carrying upon their heads the sacred objects in baskets bound round with purple ribbon. The mystic chest perched on top of her head gave each of these female celebrants a kind of crown.

I looked fondly at Philomela, dressed in her simple black garment, the colour and sheen of her hair brought out by the dark twining myrtle, the plant of love and marriage, of abduction and death. Behind the great black crowd of *mystai* moved the much smaller group of the Seers, those who had already passed the first stage of the initiation. Philomela's mother Philonike would be among these. Evidently my girl would be separated from her mother during the first most formal part of the procession, and during the initiation itself; I should have to watch over her.

The first ritual event took place when we crossed the narrow bridge at the little river or stream of Rhetoi, a salt stream that runs into the sea and marks the boundary of original Eleusis. The king of the country hereabout was once called Krokos, and the men of that area now came out as representatives of King Krokos and bound each *mystes'* right hand and left foot with a yellow thread of wool. This took some time, as there were so many of us.

'I wonder,' said Aristotle, 'is this crocus-coloured piece of yarn supposed to act as magical protection for us – or does it simply serve as a reminder that Eleusis has not given up all rights to the area? Does this yellow strand constitute a kind of permission to proceed?'

'Whatever it may be,' said Thymades, 'and it may be many things, do not let go of your yellow thread, but keep it on your left foot and on your right hand. It is a token that you are a true seeker after initiation.'

We walked on through the pleasant day, warm enough to enervate some of our number. We had to go slowly, in keeping with the pace of the weak-bladdered, the short-winded, and the rheumatic among us. It was very different from walking to Eleusis at a brisk pace, as

I had done so often. The *mystagogoi* and the priests helped us with hymns and prayers at ritual points, and there was time for desultory conversation.

'Diognetos is such an excellent *mystagogos*, he has taught me the hymns so well. I am lucky to have him,' I exclaimed to Aristotle when the 'excellent *mystagogos*' was out of hearing.

'Did you not once tell me,' Aristotle enquired, 'that Diognetos could take you on, even if late, because a merchant of Byzantion who planned to be initiated had dropped out?'

'Yes. I wonder who that could be? I thought later it might be Theophon. *He* is a merchant with interests in Byzantion. Diognetos knows him, he was at dinner with us in Eleusis. And he isn't one of the initiates.'

'We seem to be running into merchants of Byzantion,' said Aristotle. 'The Phoinician who was robbed has connections with Byzantion too. And the merchant who is assisting Kallimakhos has likewise interests there. This man Euthykritos would not marry Kallimakhos' daughter, but has apparently compensated Kallimakhos in some fashion. Do you know, I quite like thinking of that man,whom neither of us has met—'

'I have met him,' I said. 'He dragged Kallimakhos off me. Euthykritos behaved like a well-born citizen on that occasion at least. Not like Kallimakhos – so rude, and indeed unhinged!'

'Ah well. Is Euthykritos a candidate for the role of what I like to call *the* merchant of Byzantion? Someone of importance. This individual tempts me with the only link we have – possibly – between your troubles with Kallimakhos and other things that are going wrong in Athens.'

'You are making great jumps,' I objected. 'Why should there be any connection? Kallimakhos' friend has nothing to do with initiation – or with Diognetos.'

'Whereas Theophon is undoubtedly connected with Diognetos and with Eleusis. I see that, too.' Aristotle began to walk faster in his impatience. 'Go back to an earlier time. That deputation of three men – Hieron, Lamas, Diognetos – who came to see you to beg for mercy for Halirrhothios. Did you clearly give them to understand that you would still pursue the matter of the thefts?'

'I certainly did.'

'And it was shortly after that time that you were harassed with Lykon's lawsuit, and then threatened with Kallimakhos' suit for breach of promise. You are certainly being kept busy! We tend to think of Kallimakhos as the prime mover in the attempt to break off your marriage. But might it not be a useful exercise for the mind to think of it the other way around?'

'I'm not sure I know what you mean.'

'If we imagine for a moment that Kallimakhos is the instrument of another? Rather than the chief agent in his pursuit of a husband for his daughter. The object is to keep you busy and anxious, rather than to find a spouse for Kallimakhos' daughter. Interesting. Some possible solutions begin to suggest themselves, but they are cloudy and contradictory.'

'Best to forget all of it for now,' I advised. 'Just think of the Mysteries.'

The second ritual event happened when we reached the bridge that crosses the river Kephisos. (The old bridge, not the great new one built recently.) I knew about this event, because as a boy I had a couple of times followed the procession thus far and watched the peculiar show – educative, in its way, to a growing boy. At the other end of the bridge, blocking the passage of the foot-passengers, was a clumsy waggon, flamboyantly decorated. It carried figures elaborately and grotesquely attired, enlarged by stuffing and padding, and wearing colours outrageously in contrast to our black and sombre garb. One of these personages stood up in the cart and addressed us. We were confronted by the figure of a woman, an exaggerated padded shape wearing a wildly ugly if feminine mask.

'Now, Iambe!' men shouted. 'Say something really funny for us!'

Foreigners have a hard time understanding this part of the ritual, which is also part of the holy story. Demeter in her wanderings, constantly searching for her daughter, was so low in her spirit that she had not smiled or laughed in a long time. At length a low-born but witty woman, a biting satirist and jokester named Iambe, took it upon herself to make the goddess laugh. Here we encountered the Iambe who makes jokes.

'Oho! So now,' crowed the joking female, 'you think you're so good, so smart, but let me tell you the story of Androkles and the ram.

'There was a peasant called Androkles who had very dirty feet, a very broad bottom, and a very fine big black ram. One day he said to himself, "Oh, today I shall go to market and sell this ram!"

'"Don't!" said the ram. "But I will," said the man. So off they go, the man pulling the big ram with his great big horns along the road to the marketplace of the holy city of Eleusis.

'"They can use your fleece religiously – that's what they're famous for in these parts!" said the man.

'"Don't!" said the ram.

'Androkles kept pulling his big male sheep along, and soon they could see the towers of Eleusis. "Nearly there," said the man. "They will use your flesh for food for the poor. They are very pious in these parts."

'"Your feet," said the ram, "are too dirty to enter a nice fragrant city like Eleusis. They stink. Look, you have a ball of dung between your toes. Or is it just a pebble?"

'"Where?" said the man. And he bent over to look – and WHAM, the ram let him have it just where the wind he sucked in was going to have to come out. And the ram's big right horn found the best spot. And when he'd had quite enough, the ram capered off, saying, "When you find the pebble, put it where you found the ram." And away he went.'

The jokester had a series of bawdy jokes after that, each of which ended with the line 'And put it where the peasant found the ram.' At each jest, the huge joking woman stuck out her padded bosom, and wagging her head displayed her headgear, a ridiculously ill-tied cockade of myrtle, like a bush full of coloured ribands. The High Priestess and the Hierophant and the other religious officials remained solemn, though the crowd of *mystai* and our outlying cloud of spectators were increasingly giving way to laughter. Then, myrtle wagging and ribands waving, Iambe climbed out of the waggon and on to the bridge itself.

'They won't laugh,' she said, addressing one of her costumed confederates on the waggon. 'Athenians – like a lot of old dried fish on a slab. You'd never dream they were alive! They look at me so stern, like as if I was a corpse – it's *not* kind!' Iambe unfurled a large cloth and mopped her eyes. 'No it ain't! But there, I have had a sad life, I surely have.'

'Sad? You? You look fat enough to be merry.'

'Oh – oh! *Ieu! Ieu!* Such a sad life. All ins and outs, ups and downs. I never get enough sleep.' The big jokesmith rubbed her eyes. 'I have a man friend, you know. A lover.'

'Really?' said her confederate on the waggon, another hideous female. 'At your age? A lover?'

'Why not?' Iambe bridled. 'My own lov-yer.' (She drawled the word out.) 'He's *very* handsome. Oh, I've been so banged about, I can't tell you.' She clutched at her central point. 'Didn't know if I was coming or going!'

'If you were going, he put it where the ram put his horn!'

'Don't be rude!' Iambe flicked a gigantic kerchief at her interlocutor. 'He's *very* polite, a very polite boy. Said he to me, "Let's exchange favours." And he didn't half favour me!' (Clutching her skirt again, and knocking knees together.)

'Lucky you!' said the other creature sardonically. 'And what did *he* want from *you*?'

'Want from me? Why, to get into my bed to be sure.'

Laughter and ribald noises from the other persons on the cart.

'Into *your* bed? He'd rather think about getting out again,' retorted the unsympathetic friend. 'Come now, old girl, what favours did you give him?'

'A warm himation, and clothes for his sister.'

'He was cheap at the price. Was that all?'

'Just twenty silver coins and a bushel of wheat.'

'Good favours, good favours! A modest man to be sure. And faithful to his profits. Will he favour you today?'

'No – no!' Iambe whimpered into her large kerchief. 'I am so in love – just *so* in love. But that beast has changed. I sent him a pie, a *beautiful* pie, and a note saying I'd visit him tonight. And he sent me the pie back, and a cheesecake to boot. Here's his letter!' (Producing it from her bobbing bosom.) 'It begins well enough – "*To Iambe, Greetings.*" That's nice, isn't it?'

We were all laughing by this time, and standing on tiptoe to see Iambe haul the letter (a long scroll) from her capacious bosom. The 'Bridge Jests' were a break in the fasting, mourning, prayers and solemnity. I was so absorbed I had nearly forgotten to watch Philomela. The crowd, and the natural division between men and women, had propelled her some distance from me. Now I glanced up and saw where she was, about ten persons away to the right, and nearer the front.

'Nice enough,' Iambe's friend was saying. And things did seem all right. But Iambe burst into tears.

'No-o-oo! For here's what he says! *Not* "You are my life and my soul!" *Not* "My deary, my lambkin, I'll see you tonight!" Not at all! This is what he says (sigh, sniff!): "Have your pie – and take this cheesecake too, in payment for letting me off!"'

I was in mid-laugh when I saw a figure, tall but curiously indeterminate, move towards Philomela. I watched in disbelief as this person, black-draped as we all were, myrtle-crowned, with a black veil over the lower half of its face, crept up behind Philomela and snatched at her shoulder. I tried to push my way sideways, to get to my wife, but the struggle was slow and nightmarish. People were pressed together, laughing too hard to notice me – and the few who did tried to silence me and make me stand still.

'I have to get to my wife!' I was saying.

'*She'll* keep till after the fast,' said one of the men. 'Iambe got you going, eh?'

'Oh, deary me! What a *trouble* men are!' Iambe mopped her eyes, blew her nose, farted, and hiccupped. By this time most of the audience were doubled up with laughter. The High Priestess and the Hierophant and the others continued decorously to imitate Demeter, for Demeter did not laugh at anything Iambe said. But the rest of her audience had broken up by this time. All except Philomela, turning slowly about and trying to resist the grip on her shoulder, and myself, striving – but slowly, far too slowly – to get to her.

'Well, you're too unkind!' cried Iambe to the audience. 'Nasty folks, laughing your heads off.' She climbed awkwardly to the topmost part of the cart, holding the cheese pie in her hand. 'And I won't give the pie back to my bad lover – *no!* See how you like it!' Suddenly Iambe threw the pie with all her force. Whether by design or happy accident, it flew straight into the face of my wife's assailant! People crowded round this unfortunate person – surely it was a man – laughing, and snatching bits of pie, though they were not supposed to eat any. The victim was spluttering through the veil, trying, I suppose, not to let the foodstuff pass the lips. Philomela ducked away from this scene and made her escape. I yelled at her, and she came to me, winding her sinuous way between the spectators.

I grasped her firmly as Iambe went into the last part of her performance.

'Who was that who tried to take hold of you?' I asked Philomela.

'I don't know,' she said. 'The person was behind me – I didn't get a good look. Like a woman with a veiled face. But I'm not sure if it was man or woman. It was tall like a man and strong, but maybe padded out to seem bigger. Anyway, that person grasped my shoulder, and whispered, "Come away. I must speak to you." But I didn't understand what about.'

There was nothing else to do but to hold Philomela surreptitiously and continue watching the show. Iambe had to act upset and angry that Demeter didn't laugh at her jokes. And so she did, in a rapid series of pouts and reproaches and rapid bawdy remarks. At last she ended her show with the one joke that really *did* make Demeter laugh. With a quick gesture she pulled up her clothing and tunic together and displayed her naked belly and her privates. Even I got a shock, because I had been thinking this was a male actor dressed as a woman. I expected that what we would see would be a false replica of the female body made of cloth with hair and markings stitched on. But this performer of Iambe turned out to be a real female. Padded she may have been, but underneath this was the genuine thing itself. Truly old at that, all her hair, unshaven, turning grey. I couldn't help thinking of the grey-haired old slavewoman we had found dangling from the end of a rope. Would her private parts have been likewise grey? Surely that distressing creature could not have been anybody's bedmate? I laughed with the others.

'That's the only thing Demeter found funny,' I explained to Philomela. 'An aged woman's coney is funny.'

'I don't think it's very funny,' said Philomela. I was not sure myself how to explain why pot bellies and greying pubic hair were amusing, but they are, though their comedy points to the end of reproduction and the end of life.

'It is not just a joke,' said Thymades. 'Women's parts exposed to the fields nourish the crops; that is well known. Not of the old women, of course. But we are reminded. Out of that hole we each came, and came mortal, so that we will all grow old like Iambe and disappear.'

'You will see,' said Diognetos. 'This is the end of one part of the ritual, as it is the end of one way of living. After we cross this bridge, we look upon quite other things – things seen in a different way.'

'I begin to discern,' said Aristotle, 'an inward sense and structure. For the episode of Iambe reminds us of carnal life and mortality, and our birth and death. With Iambe we are born and die. I imagine things are so arranged that we are to experience rebirth.'

'You could almost be a *mystagogos* yourself,' said Diognetos.

'We drink the *kykeion* now,' Thymades said. 'Let us remember that we share in the experience and the drink of the Great Goddess, and drink first in silence and thanksgiving.'

As we were hot and thirsty, and all of us fasting, the barley water flavoured with herbs was welcome. We were sharing in the experience of the bountiful goddess Demeter herself, as she consented to be restored with this simple drink. The crowd's laughter had died out as our *mystagogoi* reminded us of the importance of this moment. But with the drinking of the *kykeion* to soothe our parching throats joy resumed its sway and there were cries of '*Iakkhos!*'

The crowd of pilgrims trooped onward along the road. We still had our tail of onlookers and hangers-on, who followed behind us, or crept up roadside banks or knolls to observe the procession. I could not see clearly who they were. I realised I knew very few even among our black-clad marchers. A woman was walking beside us, a black-clad *mystes*, a woman with very black hair and very pale skin. She seemed thinner than the person I had seen clutching Philomela before, but I immediately moved in to check her as this person turned to address my wife. Hers was not the usual casual greeting or kind of question.

'Philomela daughter of Smikrenes, you may have great prospects. A wonderful rich marriage. Your father will be richer too. Take your divorce, and it will not be long before you remarry. You will bring your father piles of silver in chests of cedar. You will have a happy life.'

This woman spoke in the tone of a mantic visionary. Before I could seize her she vanished into the crowd, leaving Philomela with her mouth open.

'Who was that, my husband? What was she talking about? *Divorce?*'

So much for my attempt to keep this unkind pressure from Philomela. A joke on me ...

'Nonsense,' I assured her. 'Your father and I know about it – we didn't want to worry you. A man named Kallimakhos wanted me to marry his daughter long ago. Kallimakhos has offered benefits to Smikrenes if he will take you back, and let me marry his daughter. And I suppose they would offer some particular gifts to you – if you would.'

'If I would do what?'

'Divorce. Divorce – me.' It cost an effort for me to say this.

'And they offered *you* good things too?'

'Yes, in a way. Kallimakhos' daughter, and a dowry. But I swear to you I would never marry Kallimakhos' daughter, no matter what.'

'What did they offer my father?'

'Four sheep, even five – or an ox. But Smikrenes was splendid, just growled "no".'

'My father is not to be bought,' she said proudly. 'But – I barely know what divorce is. I know the word. Usually – isn't the woman disgraced in some way? Because she has been bad?'

'Not always,' I said. 'Usually the woman has been adulterous. But sometimes a man and his wife just decide to part. Or, if she is unhappy, she tells her male relatives and they make the husband give the dowry back with her, and so on. That has been done in Athens, certainly.'

She looked directly into my eyes – a rare thing in a woman's gaze, at least a modest and well-bred woman.

'And *you*, Stephanos? Do you want this?'

'*No!* I almost shouted, so people about us stared. 'No,' I whispered. 'Not on my life. I don't know why they are playing with me in this way. Playing silly games, like the Bridge Jests.'

I reached for her hand, to try to reassure her, but was unsuccessful in the crowd and the pushing. Frustrated that Philomela eluded me, I quickened my pace and almost bumped into Halirrhothios, walking doggedly on just a little in front of me, his head and face shielded with a thin black mantle from the sun. He plodded along with the help of a tall, stout stick to which his bag of provisions was tied. Just as I noticed him, there was a commotion. Someone had burst through the thinning wall of spectators, pushing through the *mystai*. A person not in the garb of the pilgrim, a man wearing an old *khiton* dulled with the dust of travel. He was yelling, 'Halirrhothios! Pray, sir! Halirrhothios!'

The *epheboi*, chagrined, gathered sternly round the sweating intruder. Lucky for him he had not been brought down by a swift-flying javelin. The fellow in the dirty white *khiton* was obviously one of the lowest class of citizens, and ought to have been frightened. But the man was too concerned with his errand to take fear. He only cried the name again, and Halirrhothios turned.

'She is lost, Halirrhothios – lost!' The man waved his hands in an agitated manner. 'Your little daughter. I couldn't do anything. They came and took her!'

'What do you mean?' Halirrhothios glared at this man. 'My Eurynome – gone? Who came? How could you let her go? You and your wife were supposed to attend on her, to keep her safe.'

'We did what we could, but I could do nothing. The crazy child had rambled – you know how she is. She was outside the house door, and two men with hoods over their faces seized her and carried her away. She did not run – or walk – they carried her like a little bundle. She is gone.'

'*No!*' Halirrhothios had turned white. He clutched both sides of his face. 'No! Not my little one! How dare they! She is afflicted! Where has she gone?'

'As to that, sir, I know nothing. I looked about and asked questions of passers-by, but could get no clear news. One person, a young slave, thought he'd heard one of the men say that they'd "caged the other bird". But they all disappeared. No trace. All I could think of was to find you, O Halirrhothios. For you would know what to do, better than I.'

'Oh!' The man groaned. 'By all the gods, I do not know what to do!'

'Well, you cannot just stand here holding up the procession,' said one of the young soldiers. 'Move on, old papa, and don't block the way.'

'Come along,' said another man, obviously Halirrhothios' *mystagogos*. 'You will feel better when you have observed the Mysteries.'

'No!' said Halirrhothios. 'I must go home! I must go back to Athens and search for my poor child!'

He threw down his stick and the bundle tied to it, and turned about to go back. 'You will lose your place,' said his *mystagogos*, almost weeping. 'So far advanced as you are – you cannot think you will get your money back at this point!'

Halirrhothios paid no attention, but continued to move very fast in the direction from which we had all come. The little man in the dust-stained *khiton* went padding after him.

XXV

All Night Long

The rest of the crowd of worshippers, including ourselves, continued to walk towards Eleusis. Those of us who had seen this by-play were puzzled.

'Strange fellow, to be so perturbed about a slave child,' one man remarked. 'Ought to have more fortitude.'

'It's the fasting in the heat,' said another. 'Does funny things to people. Look at that woman! Why, she has fainted!'

It was true, a female figure ahead of us had swooned and crumpled up in the roadway. 'Don't be alarmed, this sometimes happens,' said one of the *mystagogoi* efficiently, brushing by us. He bade two other women to assist in raising the female off the road.

'She'll be all right,' said one of the hopeful initiates. 'Give her a sip of water. Heat and long fast takes some like that. But it's main peculiar, the man acting so.'

'No point in going off when he did,' another agreed. 'He's lost his Mystery fees. By the time he gets to Athens those raptors who stole his slave will be long gone.'

'It is perhaps best,' said Diognetos mildly, 'not to discuss the doings of another person while we have set our faces towards the holy place.' We walked on for some distance in silence, and then were happy to join again in one of the great hymns:

'Demeter we sing, bright-haired goddess, most holy, most feared,
And her daughter, the lovely girl, slender-ankled, the Maiden whom Hades
Ravished . . .'

At the end of the song, Antigone slipped in behind our little group. Her headscarf was slipping, and she was sweating. 'Oh, *when*?' she asked. 'When do we get to Eleusis?'

'It's not far from here,' I said, puzzled. '"Fragrant Eleusis", as it says in the hymn. You can see the towers for yourself. Look! We shall soon be there, and then you'll be able to sit down.'

'You look ill,' said Aristotle. 'Is anything the matter?'

'No – I mean, yes.' Antigone laughed uncertainly. 'My feet are tired, and as Stephanos indicates I wish to sit down and rest. Somebody fainted and that upset me. It is hard to go fasting so long and in the heat.'

The heat of the day, however, was now beginning to abate. A cool breeze stole in from the sea, and the shades of evening drew slowly in upon us. There seemed nothing in our general situation to warrant the pallor and agitation of Antigone. Of course, women are weak by nature. Still, Herpyllis and my Philomela were bearing up well.

'Do not fear,' said Diognetos to Antigone. 'Be calm, my child. Soon you will be able to break your fast. Here, we gather in front of the Sanctuary. We shall drink of the *kykeion* and then take supper together.'

And so it was. We gathered, a huge crowd, before the great edifice which we should penetrate on the morrow.

'Keep together,' the *mystagogoi* advised, trying to keep away from us members of the curious crowd of onlookers, now augmented by some local people of Eleusis.

'Let us make camp,' said Aristotle cheerfully. And we found a good place where we could sit and open our bundles, preparing to share our bits of provisions. First there was the last sacrifice of the day to be made. A straggly stream of people, we stood in rows to make the presentation of food to Demeter, holding the miniature plates, the *kernoi*, with their little ceramic divisions, so that corn or vetch could be put in one part, and, say, chickpeas in another and barley in a third. After this small sacrifice to Demeter of food in the *kernoi*, and *kykeion* in tiny cups, we sang another hymn.

At last we could eat. Building separate little fires, we sat about under the stars, munching things brought from home. Houseless and wandering, we were at leisure to appreciate the rest and the serenity. The waxing moon rose and shed a lustre over the towers and the sea. Ritual dances and hymns were performed by the women; once, long ago, some say, the celebration of Demeter was performed entirely by women. Men and women were supposed to be segregated, but it was very tempting for family groups like ours to coalesce, particularly as the women were carrying our food. Although there was no wine at this festivity, the faces became less those of mourners and more like those of true celebrants. The singing began, and went from group to group. Some of the older or weaker people rolled themselves up in cloaks and went to sleep, but it is not considered quite right to sleep on the Pannykhis, the all-night festival before the great initiation. So we kept vigil too, talking quietly and singing occasionally. Some strolled about from one group to another. Men sought men friends, and women, women, for chat and laughter in the fire-dotted night.

At the hail of some friends I went briefly over to utter some greetings, though I was anxious not to leave Philomela unattended. As I was coming back I almost bumped into a woman sitting on the ground, not the thinnest and youngest of women. Her head-covering was slipping off. And I could see crumbs on top of her head.

'Good evening, Thratta,' I said, casually if caustically. 'You have got cheesecake in your hair. I daresay you could eat it now – a present from Iambe.' In a moment I was certain that the person who had tried to intercept Philomela during Iambe's show had been Thratta. She made no attempt to deny it, but looked up at me, and gave a half-rueful shrug.

'Quite a joking afternoon. A lot of Bridge Jests. All in fun.'

'Indeed. I suppose Theophon has paid for your initiation?' She nodded. She was evidently ill at ease – but that might be because solemn occasions didn't suit her. 'Did *he* pay for you to speak to my wife?' I pursued.

She blushed. 'No,' she muttered. 'It wasn't him.'

I had a sudden bright thought. 'The last time I saw you – were you paid to take fish from Diognetos' house to Antigone, with orders for her to make a fish stew? For me?'

'Well, yes – but that was just kindness, I'm sure.'

'I'm not so sure of anything,' I said. 'Be well,' I added curtly, 'and don't get into any trouble. By the way, my wife has absolutely *no* wish to converse with you.'

And I left her. At least I had identified the person who had accosted Philomela, and I could tell Philomela about the person, and what to watch out for. But what, I wondered, as I sat beside my wife under the stars and munched barley cakes, was Theophon's part in it all?

'Stephanos of Athens?' A big figure loomed over me.

'Biton!' I exclaimed, scrambling to my feet, while Philomela veiled herself and shrank against Herpyllis.

'I wanted to say,' the big man said, blushing awkwardly, 'that we may as well let bygones be bygones. And I'm sorry I threw things at you.'

'So it *was* you!'

'Yes – on your wedding day and all. When you was in a procession from Athens.' He laughed reminiscently. 'Mud on your fine white clothes.'

'And you threw the knife at me – at my wedding feast, in my own house?'

He looked puzzled. 'No. Never threw no knives.' He drew himself up. 'I have an excellent aim, though I do say so myself, and I'd be feared to try it with a *knife*. I might naturally not try to miss, I am so used to hitting targets. And then, you see – well, I wouldn't miss.'

'But you missed when you threw the stones at me later, when I was coming back from Eleusis,' I protested. 'And then I hit *you* with a big stone, didn't I?'

'No.' He shook his head decidedly. 'You never hit me with nothing. I gave up them games soon after you was married. Didn't seem worthwhile any more.'

I believed him, which was unsatisfactory, because it meant I still had an enemy or two unaccounted for. 'You're a good sort of fellow to tell me this,' I said.

'Right,' said Biton. 'Before the initiation. I mean – no good harbouring old grudges. I wish you and your wife the best. I expect to get married to somebody else soon.'

'Excellent,' I approved. And to cement our friendship, or at least the relaxation of enmity, Biton and I went together to join in the line of men dancing in honour of Demeter and Persephone. As the dance changed and the line changed, I found myself next to a man with a long brown beard rippling over his black clothes. Lamas, of course. My neighbour Lamas the historian.

'That big man you were talking to,' he said to me after the dance, when he could get his decorous breath back.

'Untamed, I hear. Violent, especially in his cups. A dangerous fellow, a real bear. I wouldn't believe everything he says to you. There are much better people in Eleusis.'

Lamas looked so disapproving, I laughed inwardly. He was so stiff and pious, he would consider most young men too wild. Yet he was not always so stiff. I recalled how he had made part of our *komos* at the end of my party, and how much he had drunk. The dancing of Pannykhis picked up again, and we were swept off by the urgency of stamping feet. Dances were to be kept seemly and reverent, in honour of the occasion. The all-night vigil, however, is not without its wilder side. Dancing continued, the rhythms faster, and the musicians more adventurous, more raucous. There were sputters of mirth, breakings-out of stories and gossip. As the night grew later we heard some very common songs mixed in with the hymns. Harvest and threshing songs, songs about love for a beautiful boy, a song about a barmaid in a *kapeleion* . . .

'It is getting noisy, isn't it?' said Herpyllis, putting a protesting hand over her ears.

'Yes,' said Aristotle. 'Yet not too rowdy, considering the great crowd. This is a temperate party, a mean between the extremes of austerity and unfettered *komos*.'

'That is so,' I said, remembering regretfully my own symposium. Despite some loud singing, most people were truly behaving very well, including even the less reputable pilgrims among our crowd. Antigone, for instance, who was sitting with her female mystagogue in a little group next to ours, was very quiet and sedate, not even joining in the singing. She was clutching something, I could not see quite what it was. Then she held it over the fire and a liquid seemed to run out of it. The fire sputtered, but certainly did not go out.

'*Io! Io! Iakkhos!*' A loud and sudden shout – a whirling figure was in our midst. A most intemperate person tumbled out of the shadows and bounded among us, interrupting the hemi-sanctified mirth. The apparition was decidedly female. Dressed in sober black, like ourselves, she had an uncovered great bush of red hair that streamed about her shoulders. Under her mourning garment could be seen by the lamplight and firelight a glimpse of red-coloured cloth. This woman began dancing. Or, if not exactly dancing, she was jumping up and down and turning rapidly about. I thought of Iambe at the bridge. Was this another planned exhibition, a jest performed by an actor?

The woman – or was it truly a female impersonator this time? She was distant from me, and I could not see her clearly – held something aloft. Something small in a long skirt or covering that gleamed a little in the firelight.

'Demeter, Demeter, lost a child!' she chanted. 'Demeter looked for it in the wild. Mother Goddess, I have found a child. Who has lost it? Did the child *die?*'

'Ahh!' A light gasp from Antigone, whose sitting figure slumped over sidelong on the ground, disarranging bundles and a wooden dish.

'She's not well!' said Aristotle, moving towards the apparently insensible *hetaira*.

'*Who* has lost it?' repeated the whirling woman, holding up again the object that formed her topic. 'Is this *your* baby? Or yours?' She moved with a lurch from group to group. There was something familiar about her. 'I found it,' she insisted. 'A baby. I thought it was mine, but it isn't mine. It had no clothes.'

The strange woman exhibited the object held tenderly in her arms, as a woman holds an infant child.

'It isn't mine,' she repeated. 'My baby is safe

somewhere else. But this baby – this baby was thrown into the pit! Bad, very bad. Look how the poor thing is hurt!' She stopped by a large campfire to display the object she held, and uncovered a face that gleamed in the firelight more ruddily than it had under the pale moon. 'See how it is hurt!' she repeated. The 'baby' face looked up at us. It was the face of a marble child, a head that had been somewhat damaged.

'I want to complain,' said the woman – a real woman. Not an apparition, nor an actor. Of course, Asimos' daughter. 'I must complain to the Daidoukhos, to the Priestess and everybody.' She moved towards us, not far from Antigone, who seemed to be recovering. 'They threw the baby into a deep pit, and I had to scramble down and get it.'

The crazy woman, Zobia of Hymettos, was slowing down in her movements now, out of breath. Spinning slowly and holding the baby aloft, she came near me. I felt for a moment an unnatural fear of being touched by her or by the object she held. Yet it was but the marble image of a little boy, which I myself had once held in my own hands, not far from here.

'Put down that baby nonsense,' a voice commanded sharply. Diognetos. He stood up, approaching the young woman, who was revolving about like a slow Maenad.

'You are not supposed to be here among us,' he remarked sternly. 'You are not wearing the yellow yarn of King Krokos. You did not come with us as a *mystes*.'

'And she is polluting the area with that – that thing!' somebody else remarked heatedly. 'That marble head – I know what it is! The accursed instrument of murder, that was tried and cast away!'

'Come, give it here!' Diognetos approached her but with some reluctance. 'Guard, come here!' he called to the captain of the *epheboi*.

'I need to feed it first, I think,' said the girl uncertainly. 'My milk has come, and my own little baby is still far away. I should put something in this little thing's belly.'

'Come, my dear, give it to me.' Antigone stepped up. She was still very pale, and seemed to be trembling slightly, yet she spoke in a calm manner. Gently she put her arm about the girl's shoulder.

'It is not your real baby – not exactly a baby at all, you see. Only the image of one. Just a carved head.' She took it gently from the girl. 'See? It doesn't have a body. You made up a body for it, but it is cloth.'

'Oh. Yes. Yes, so I did. But it wanted me to! My papa loves me and the baby. He needs me to care for it.'

'Let go of it, my dear. It is only a toy, and you don't need it any more.' Antigone unwrapped the bundle of rags and baby clothes with which Zobia had contrived to embody her 'infant'. Zobia sat down, soothed by the woman's caresses and tone. 'Here – you may take this away,' and Antigone handed the battered marble head to the captain of the *epheboi*. The military man did not look at all happy with his charge.

'I? *I* should take a cursed thing? Where?

'Throw it into the salt sea,' Aristotle advised. 'All things are believed to be cleansed in the sea. You as well as these two women may undergo a cleansing ritual here. There are sacred places and many priests in these parts.'

'We must be grateful,' Diognetos observed, 'that the weird young woman, who appears demented, did not come into the holy Sanctuary itself and foul it with this noxious unclean object.'

'True,' said Thymades. 'And it is almost the day of initiation, for I see the first streaks promising dawn.'

He was right. I decided that it would be hard to go through this new exciting day without any sleep at all, and bade Philomela also lie down wrapped in a light cloak and try to sleep for a few moments. The campfires dimmed as the grey light in the east grew stronger. I went to sleep but almost instantly, or so it seemed, the bright mid-morning light awakened me. Campfires were all dead or being doused, and people were packing their possessions (there was not much food left) into their scrip again. The mad Zobia had awakened also out of an apparently sound sleep, and was being cared for by Antigone, who accompanied her to the fountain. The odd bushy-haired girl looked more rational, though most unkempt. After such a night, we were all somewhat dishevelled.

As I was stumbling off to get some water to throw on my face, I passed by the campfire where Antigone had been during the all-night festival. I noticed a piece of unburnt board by the side of the ashes, a small piece like a writing tablet. I picked it up. It was indeed a tablet, though cut down to about half the normal size. The wax was gone, the epistle erased. Yet the writer had pressed hard enough to leave traces on the wood itself. I read the fragmentary statement:

> *Maiden . . . Treasury of Hades.*
> *2000 Dx.*

'What's that?' said Aristotle, looking over my shoulder.

'I think this charred letter belonged to Antigone,' I replied. 'For I saw her melting off the wax last night. But the poplar wood hasn't entirely burned. I suppose this is part of a hymn or religious play. Something written out for her by her mystagogue. It is like what we have been singing. "The Maiden is in the Treasury of Hades, goodness gone underground." But two thousand drakhmai? That has nothing to do with a hymn, surely?'

'Assuredly not,' he said, and put the little piece of poplar into his own scrip.

It took a good long while before everyone of our large crowd got himself or herself fully dressed, washed, packed up and ready, even though there was no question of taking food this morning. The Herald and the Daidoukhos kept reminding us to be expeditious. Eurymedon was very noticeable among the pious officials, his clear-cut face with its remarkable profile looking noble and serene as he towered above the rest. He would, I reflected, make a truly fine-looking Hierophant, when the time came. I wished I thought I could ever like him. At last we were all arranged. Then it was time for the sacrifice to the Goddess of the meal ground from wheat and barley. As each individual has to sacrifice, that proceeding took up most of the middle of the day. When we had finished, the sun was advancing down the western sky. Then the Herald of Eleusis addressed us.

'O *mystai*! Today is the day of days – the day of increasing knowledge, followed by the night of illumination. Prepare your inward mind for the greatness of what is to follow. Let us sing a hymn to Demeter, and dance the first of the sacred dances. We shall see the Sacred Well where the Great Mother sat in her weariness, but it is forbidden to us to sit there. Let us dance. Then we shall enter the Sacred Precinct.'

In the area in front of the beautiful Propylaea that led to the wonderful place, we approached the holy well. The virgins in our company were first invited to approach and entreated to dance about this Well of the Beautiful Dances. This the maidens did, very gracefully, white arms in the air, slender-ankled feet stepping nimbly.

Then everybody danced. Not all together, but in groups, of men and women alternately. This of course took a goodly while, as there were so many of us, and some were clumsy and slow with the day's fast. In any case, the priests wished to take up most of the day, as the proper initiation could begin only with sunset. At length, we each had danced about the holy fountain while Demeter's musicians played. Purified by a sprinkling, we then passed through the adorned outer gate and proceeded to the inner gate.

'Now,' said the Daidoukhos, carrying his still unlighted torches before him, 'the Hierophant and the Priestess lead us to Demeter. Be prepared, all who come. Come for the right reason and in truth. Come to seek the Goddess and for nothing else.' His purple stole had gold thread upon it; the intricate embroideries gleamed in the first of the sunset light. There was a moment of silence. Then the Herald spoke in a voice that seemed to thunder over the little rocky hill and echo among the columns.

'Keep far away, all those who are not *mystai*! On pain of death, anyone not purified and not mindful of the quest for initiation is to leave herewith. For we are about to tread on holy ground!'

Nobody moved, nobody departed. Indeed, our numbers had swelled slightly, since Antigone, who had dropped behind, had rejoined us. In a troop organised by the priests and our mystagogues, we walked in a decorous manner under the archway, through the second and smaller of the two gates. Now at last we were in the Inner Precinct, within a sacred space that was entirely the domain of the Two Goddesses.

There is a processional road through the centre of the precinct, with shrines and temples to left and right. We were led at length to the right, and told to pause here. There we beheld a very new, very bright temple of clearest marble. Or rather, we saw the skeleton or sketch of such a temple, with upright marble columns, but not complete as yet.

'Behold!' said the Herald. 'The Ploutonion!'

'It is a new work,' explained Thymades. 'It is still going on, will probably take a year or nearly to finish. But you can see what it is to be.'

The Daidoukhos stood in front of this elegant unfinished temple, his unlit torches held high.

'Here is that holy and terrible place,' said the Daidoukhos. 'At that time, the God of the Underworld took Persephone against her will into the dark Underworld. Within this temple is the cave whence he came. This temple marks the entrance to Ploutos' domain.'

There was only one door, a sort of half-curtain of hide, not the beautiful door that would be put in when the temple was finished next year. The leather curtain was drawn aside, and we peered in to dark depths. We could see that there was a cave in the background, a shadowy cave.

'Turn. Assemble.' So our Daidoukhos commanded. 'And be prepared to watch.'

We moved away from Ploutos' temple with its cave and turned from it, facing westwards, a multitude standing expectant as the evening began slowly to drop round us. There was music from somewhere at the side – a lyre, then two, some pipes and one clear flute. Dancing towards us came a beautiful girl – or someone made up to look like a beautiful girl. She was accompanied by a group of dancing maidens who circled about her, while she danced in the midst of them and plucked imaginary flowers. She seemed to sparkle with silver in the uncertain light, the first hint of the coming moon. The maidens sang, a sweet *khoros*:

> She played with the deep-breasted daughters of
> Ocean,
> Plucking the flowers: rose, crocus and lovely violets
> In the meadow so sweet with iris, hyacinth,
> Narcissus set as a trap for the maiden . . .

Then suddenly there was a rumble as of thunder from deep within the Ploutonion. We swung about again. Out of the temple emerged a majestic and solemn figure, tall, wide, and completely dark. A godlike being, yet of the earth. He advanced upon the maiden – who did not see him. The music continued and she went on with her happy dance, until suddenly – with another crash of a gong – the tall, dark form seized the dancing maiden. Sounds of lyre and harp stopped abruptly. He grasped her and tore her away, into the depths of the Ploutonion. The pair vanished.

'Come,' said the Herald. 'Those who truly cannot see, now they cannot see.' And the attendants and *mystagogoi* bound our eyes, each with a strip of black material. We were alone then, each alone, and groping. The friendly hands of the mystagogues faded away from us. We knew the *epoptai* were watching, their eyes unbound, but these Seers could not approach and help us.

'Search!' the Herald ordered. 'Search!' repeated the Daidoukhos. 'Search for the Kore. Go back, go forward. She is here somewhere. Search, all ye true seekers! Find the Maiden, O ye who would be enlightened!'

We were on a sort of earthen plateau, a platform supplying space for us to wander in, but it was to no avail. We stumbled and made false starts. A few fell down, and not only the feeble, for the ground, though flattened, was uneven and scattered with stones and fragments of cut marble. If you dash your foot when blinded, it is easy to go crashing down. Some among us giggled, but the situation became too tense and frustrating to allow for much of that. We also knew we were being watched by those others. The already enlightened stood on the periphery, like statues, as I imagined them, staring at us as we reeled about. The space seemed terribly wide, and yet much too small as one bumped into people. With groping hands outspread we moved. Back and forth, around and about, like drunkards. We were blind, each man, each woman, going blindly to and fro. Voices came to us, and snatches of music, mocking (so it felt), emanating from different directions. I heard a voice near to me whisper, 'My dear, do not fall into the ditch!'

'Of yourselves you know nothing,' proclaimed the Hierophant. 'Yet you seek for what you do not know. Who is able to find that which is away from us? Who is able to rescue the Maiden?'

'I am!' came the unexpected cry.

After this liturgical question, the celebrant, who had not expected any answer but was proceeding with the next part of his ritual speech, paused and spluttered. I had recognised the voice. Now I lifted up a corner of my bandage. Aristotle, next to me, had already cast off his own blindfold.

'Come!' he cried. 'I know where she must be!' He was already off, and I ran after him. The light was fading very fast, and the torches had already been lit. The crowd hesitated. A few followed us, including Antigone and the Daidoukhos, and our own women, Philomela and Herpyllis. '*Who* is that madman?' I heard the Hierophant ask as we sped off in the direction whence we had come.

When we arrived at the Ploutonion, it was quite dark, and I hesitated at the thought of breaking through the boundary and plunging into that dark interior. Aristotle, however, went ahead without slackening his pace. Had there been doors, well-made, locked and guarded, it would have been no easy matter for him to force his way into the temple of the God of the Underworld. But as there was only the leather curtain marking the entrance of the as yet unfinished temple, he was able to plunge in. Not without some reluctance, I followed him.

Had the whole cella been completed and all the walls

filled in, we should have been blocked by darkness. But enough light penetrated from the watery moon and a few stars to enable us to see the mouth of the cave. The passageway to Hades, to Ploutos' realm of the Underworld.

Aristotle went boldly on. At one side of the mouth of the cave another curtain trembled. Twitching that aside, he discovered an alcove which held the the two actors – one dressed as Persephone and the other as Plouton. They were startled and uttered indignant exclamations.

'You have no business here!' they cried. 'Get out! Go away!'

'I am seeking the Maiden,' Aristotle said calmly – or as calmly as a slight shortness of breath brought on by running would allow.

'This is not your part – the *mystai* are supposed to wait and watch. Oh – you are ruining everything!' the actor who played the Maiden expostulated, raising his voice. (This time I felt sure that the female role was being acted by a man.)

'It's not you I have come for,' said Aristotle. He moved aside, into the cave itself, and then advanced further into the dark hole. There was a scuffling behind us as the crowd – or, rather, the fragment of the crowd of *mystai* who had chosen to follow us – arrived in a lump.

'Let me – allow me!' said the Daidoukhos firmly. He advanced, carrying his two torches, now lit, into the gloom. Aristotle gave a shout of triumph.

'Look here!' The light played upon a white form in a deeper part of the cave. Aristotle I could see was grabbing at it, picking it up, forcing it – a person now – to stand upright. There was a faint moan.

'You will be all right,' said Aristotle encouragingly, supporting the unidentified being, who seemed to be dressed in white or light-coloured clothes. These clothes fluttered as the two persons, man and maiden, came to the mouth of the cave and crossed the threshold into the night breeze. The Daidoukhos' torches shone full on the pair: an elderly man with a grey beard, though with some remaining twinkles of golden-red still in his hair, a man dressed in black mourning clothes, supporting a young and very pale female. This delicate person was pulled into the light like someone being drawn up from the grave.

'Here – give her back to her mother!' said Aristotle, looking outward at us, as if he could see Demeter standing in our midst. The onlookers were startled and awed.

'Who is this? What do you mean?' asked the Daidoukhos.

'This, I believe, is young Glykera, daughter of Antigone who has recently returned to Athens. She – Antigone – is one of us. One of the *mystai*.'

While Aristotle was saying this, the woman Antigone had rushed into view.

'O my daughter! I thought I had lost you – what did they do to you?'

The daughter began to speak. Her voice was faint and her eyes blinked as if the new light dazzled and pained her.

'I don't know. I feel that somebody hit me on the head, and I fell down and everything was dark. Then I was waking up, but it was very dark where I was. There was something bound about my eyes. Somebody gave me barley water and herbs to drink, and I fell asleep somewhere that smelled like earth. And then this old man came and said, "You will be all right," and took the bandage from my eyes and picked me up.'

'There – no more of that! It will only distress you, my pet. A bad time, but it is in the past – let us try to forget.' Antigone grasped Glykera about the waist, and Aristotle dropped his hold.

'Antigone, tell us,' he said in a low voice, but urgently. 'You suspected when you heard that the child Eurynome was taken that Glykera was in danger. The abductor was quoted as saying that they had "caged the other bird". Glykera was "the other bird", was she not? The two girls had spent time together, and Glykera might now know whatever dangerous things little Eurynome knows.'

'It must have been Antigone who fainted on the road,' I commented. 'Realising the danger to her own child, she passed out when Halirrhothios got the news. Clever of you, Aristotle, to work out that lovely Glykera would have been taken.'

'Taken and hidden in the one place where nobody would go to search for her,' said Aristotle. 'The letter with the wax melted away told us some greedy person was asking for a ransom of two thousand drakhmai. I should have *known* once I saw that. I realised something was amiss with Antigone, but my mind was following the other case, of Halirrhothios' daughter. I believed that it would be Eurynome whom I found in the "Treasury of Hades". So I am not so clever after all.'

'This is all very bad,' said the Daidoukhos. 'You have been carried away – an appalling lack of self-control. Look how you have disrupted the service of the Goddess!'

'But to save lives!' Aristotle argued.

'Save her life? Nonsense. This silly girl has been playing at being Persephone. Most reprehensible and impious of her to enter the Sacred Precinct, but she is obviously quite well—'

Aristotle interrupted. 'I'm sorry but we cannot wait. I said "save lives". *Two* girls, not one, were abducted and made captive. I think the two cases may well be related. And I believe I know now where the other one must be! It would be best to lose no time!'

Aristotle, surprisingly quick for a man of his age,

began to run towards the Lesser Gate and the Greater Gate.

'Mad! He is a madman!' exclaimed the Daidoukhos. 'Who knows what harm he may do in Eleusis? I fear I must follow him.'

And the Daidoukhos with his bright torches hastened after the flying philosopher. Two of his little attendants caught up with him, carrying a supply of fresh unlit sticks of pine to renew his light. Despite a pang of regret at losing the initiation, I determined to follow Aristotle. My wife came flying with me, followed by Herpyllis. Then came almost all of the rest of the group we had attracted in the first place, save Antigone, who stayed with Glykera and urged her gently along.

Aristotle could not keep up the running pace, and was slowing down by the time we got to the Great Propylaea.

'What is it? Where – where are you going?' I asked.

'Melanthios. Marble-seller,' he replied briefly.

The two of us, oddly dressed in our mourning garments, pounded along as fast as we could – or at least as fast as Aristotle could. I grasped Philomela's hand, and pulled her with me. The others didn't know where we were going, so we had the advantage, though we had to be glad of the light afforded by the Daidoukhos' torches behind us. Even in the hand of a running man, his were such excellently bright torches they cast a very strong, if erratically mobile, light. A few houses offered lamplight, and that helped too.

When we arrived at the marble-seller's shop, Aristotle knocked once and then pushed the door open. Somebody had been trying to bar the door as he heard the sudden commotion of our arrival.

'Good evening, Melanthios,' said Aristotle, as the door pushed against the retreating shop-owner. 'You decided not to complete the celebration of the Mysteries after all? I wonder why.'

'Good evening. Personal reasons. If you must know, I had toothache so bad I had to leave and get the tooth extracted. Nothing to trouble you.'

The sculptor and marble-seller was dressed partly in the black mourning clothes of a *mystes*, but had, oddly, put his leather apron over them, as if in workaday attire. He smiled with his lips closed, and leaned against the table that separated us from his main shop and working area. 'You have come to look at some marble figures again? Very good, very—'

'Let us look indeed,' said Aristotle, 'with what light we have.' He grasped the little lamp that the shopkeeper had placed on the table that stood between himself and us.

'You want a figure of Demeter?'

'Of a Kore, rather – but one who breathes.'

The marble-seller laughed. 'I am afraid our art cannot cheat nature so far,' he replied. 'Not yet. We make objects that are life*like*. Human, divine or animal, we imitate these.'

Aristotle was already moving restlessly through the shop. His lamp raced up and down, looking at the images in their niches. Marble faces, unpainted, gazed at us with rebuking white eyes. As the Daidoukhos coming up behind us brought in the torches, the whole place suddenly flared with light. Stone figures, flickering and gesturing as if freshly animated, seemed to crowd about us.

Aristotle did not pause, but moved on, behind the shop, into the yard of larger figures in various stages of completion. White slabs of unworked stone appeared to leer at us, as if figures not yet visible in the marble were trying to emerge. Monuments to the dead crowded about us. The painted dog of stone seemed to growl in the shadows. A few gods looked on, as if asking what the trouble was. Most of them had the rather surly

expression we had come to associate with Melanthios'
work. Aristotle went about the yard in the strangest
fashion, stamping his feet. Marble chips crunched
underfoot and gleamed in the lamplight.

'There!' said Aristotle, pointing to a spot towards the
rear of the yard, but about equidistant from the side
walls. 'I believe that will be right!'

'What do you mean?' I asked.

'I don't think much real digging will be necessary,'
said Aristotle. 'Melanthios told us this place was once a
bronzesmith's yard. Therefore, it had formerly a large
casting-pit in it. A pit carefully cut in the earth could
serve very well to store or hide things in.' He addressed
the owner's slave. 'Sweep the chips and sand and so on
away from this area,' he commanded. 'And perhaps we
shall be fortunate enough to find an entry.'

'I protest – this is my property!' objected Melanthios.

'Quick, quick,' said Aristotle impatiently. He grabbed
a broom himself and went to work. I was ashamed to see
the philosopher engaged in such undignified and low
activity.

'You do what he says, or it will be the worse for you,'
I said to the slave. 'This is a criminal matter.' (I didn't
know then whether it was or not.) 'By the law of Athens,
dig!' I even took up a spade to start digging myself.

'Most irregular!' protested some members of the
crowd. 'We must send for the Demarkh of Eleusis.'

'Excellent suggestion. The Demarkh, by all means,'
said Aristotle. Melanthios, looking thunderstruck, did
not interrupt the Master's work, though he did exclaim,
'This is robbery!' and 'I protest!' at regular intervals.

The marble chips and sand and some earth and other
debris were scraped aside and a rough wooden planking
appeared.

'So – an entry to the chasm,' said Aristotle. 'A door in

the ground. I think I see the handle – that bronze ring. Pull!'

The slave did as he was asked. Slowly one end of the simple construction of wooden planks, a floor that had become a door, rose into the air. Aristotle took a lamp and peered over the edge of this pit. I knelt also and looked down through the gloom into the little chasm. There was the animal smell of humanity, of urine, of fear. The flickering light fell into the pit of darkness and there was a faint glimmer of white. A movement. A thin cry that was really little better than a whisper: 'Help! Help!'

'Herpyllis – where is Herpyllis?' Aristotle demanded urgently.

'I'm here.' The gentle-voiced young woman stood at his side.

'Help me to lift her. You'd better do it – she's frightened of men, I think.' And Herpyllis reached down into the pit with her strong young arms and grasped what we could not see.

'Give me a cloak, please,' she said as she brought the pitiful object to the surface, its clothes sodden and muddy, its head not held upright. Someone supplied a cloak and Herpyllis quickly covered the child, so she should no longer be shamed by the inevitable incontinence of nearly two days in the dark and terrible pit.

'Poor child!' Herpyllis exclaimed, gently rocking her. Bright light fell on her from the torches of the Daidoukhos. The captive's little head lifted. It was indeed the unfortunate Eurynome.

XXVI

Illumination

'Oh child, your father has been searching for you!' I said.

'What a pity Halirrhothios is not here!' exclaimed another of the *mystai*. It was Lamas, Halirrhothios' friend. The man with the curling brown beard and patient white face, which in the lamplight looked longer and more solemn than ever, set off by the black garments he wore for Persephone's sake. It seemed hard to believe that a short while ago in the Pannykhis vigil Lamas had been dancing.

'It must have been this slave-child Halirrhothios went off to look for. In quite the wrong direction, it seems. But why is *she* a prisoner?'

'Oh. Only his slave,' said another man, disappointed, shrugging his shoulders. 'Presumably this slave has done something wrong and got punished for it.'

'Wasn't she a thief? I seem to remember that she was flogged as a thief, in Athens,' another citizen supplied.

Aristotle stood up and addressed the group.

'No,' he said slowly. 'I believe this child Eurynome is not a thief. This child's trouble was that she knew about theft. And her trouble did not end after she was flogged for a theft she did not commit. No, her condition rather grew worse. Not only was her mind disordered from the ordeal, but her eyes were opened to the evidence of continuing thefts. And perhaps she overheard talk of something even worse than theft. In any case, somebody needed to get her out of the way.'

'Mere assertion. Not to say fantasy,' pronounced the Daidoukhos.

'It is as well for you to say so,' said Aristotle, not perturbed by this rebuke. 'It is certainly imprudent to rush to judgement. Hear me then, all of you. Then judge. But first come to a place nearby – where, I think, I can make all things much clearer.'

And he led the way. On the way out, he picked up an object from the marble-merchant's tools where they lay on the table, and whispered to Herpyllis. Aristotle left swiftly, the object in his sleeve, but surmising where he was going, I soon caught up with him. Rapidly we walked together to the next street, and the shop of the image-maker. Oulias, master of this business shop, was at home. He had not retired to food and rest, but was working in his shop, which was – for a wonder – still lighted. Paintbrush in hand, he was bending over an object on a table before him at the side of the shop, where two lamps cast the best light. Pots of paint and a pitcher of water stood on a side table close to his hand. When Aristotle and I entered, he looked enquiringly at us, as at unexpected customers; when the Daidoukhos and the rest began to enter too, he looked quite startled. But anyone would be startled at such a multitude.

'Good evening, Oulias,' said Aristotle. 'Keep back, everybody. There's no need for all this noise and trampling. We just want to look at some of your images of Demeter and Persephone.'

'By the Two Goddesses,' Oulias ejaculated, 'have I lost

count of the days, then? I thought surely this was the night – the great Night of the Mysteries.'

'It is,' said the Daidoukhos grimly. And Eurymedon, glancing disdainfully at Aristotle, added, 'This meddling fellow has interrupted our holy rites.'

'We reverence Demeter,' said Aristotle firmly, 'and wish to purchase figures. I told you I would come back to buy some at the time of the Mysteries. I trust Lampos is here – ah, yes, there he is. Stephanos, would you mind detaining Lampos so we may get his assistance.'

I needed no further hint, but laid firm hold of Lampos. Aristotle was now looking over the ceramic figures, in a considering manner, like a customer who is eager to buy but difficult to please.

'You have more and better images, Oulias, than you had when we were here before,' he commented. 'Working your pastry well. What a handsome row of Persephones! Almost alike, yet each with some difference in the painting. Lovely! I see you succeeded in obtaining the colours you wanted. Rose and blue. With the touches of gold. This Demeter, for instance.' He held up a figure of the Goddess and looked at it admiringly in the light of the Daidoukhos' torches.

'Lampos has done his painting extremely well,' he praised.

'Do take care,' Oulias implored.

'Yes, yes. Most certainly,' said Aristotle. 'I do take care. I believe I am most attracted to those taller images of Demeter, the ones wearing the crown of gold. They seem a touch heavier too, more substantial – better weighted, and more likely to stand up well. Your price?'

'Fifty drakhmai!' Oulias spat out this outrageous price and there was a gasp from our collective throat at the request for such an immense sum for a mere figure of clay. 'Best Boiotian style. Take it or leave it.'

'Ah well, I dare say I shall get the worth of my còins. So – I shall buy this one for fifty drax. I have it about me somewhere, or Herpyllis does. This is—'

'No, no! I can't sell that one!' Oulias cried. 'It's already sold,' he explained, trying to take the piece back. Lampos wriggled, but I did not let him go; I heard a sort of gasp deep in his throat. I wasn't sure what was going to happen next. And while I was being unsure, Aristotle plucked from his sleeve a small but sturdy mallet, wooden with an iron edge.

'Thief yourself! You stole that implement from Melanthios!' the Daidoukhos exclaimed.

'Borrowed,' said Aristotle amiably. 'I told Herpyllis to put some obols on the counter for it.'

Herpyllis nodded, watching her master and Oulias intently, while she held and half carried the swathed Eurynome.

'Now!' said Aristotle. He laid the lovely image of Demeter down upon the table.

'*No!*' cried Oulias – just as Aristotle's hammer fell upon the beautiful clay statue. It sprang into fragments, and ceased to be.

'The man's mad! Where is the Demarkh? He must be restrained!' moaned some voices from the assembled crowd, who were craning their necks to see. The Daidoukhos had withdrawn his torches suddenly, so it was next to impossible to see the fragmented image.

'Difficult without light,' said Aristotle suavely. 'Herpyllis, will you take one of the new torches from the little boy there and light it? Thank you. One of the men here can hold it aloft.'

'Outrageous! Like an animal, destroying! You are committing outrage on citizens of Eleusis!' cried the Daidoukhos.

'This is not legal – it is not even decent behaviour. It

is blasphemous.' It was Lamas who spoke, my neighbour with the long brown beard; he was now pushing himself to the front of the crowd. 'Stephanos of Kydathenaion, I beg you to make this man behave. The Makedonian from the Lykeion seems to have taken leave of his senses. He is disturbing the holy Mysteries, and now robbing shopkeepers and insulting the Goddess!'

'The Makedonian philosopher is undoubtedly insane,' pronounced Eurymedon. 'At least the Demarkh has come. He can arrest him.' Our old acquaintance the Demarkh of Eleusis, who had been in charge when we discovered the corpse of Sophilos, had indeed arrived. He looked bewildered, as well he might. He came with a slave to light him and he came armed, for he had a serviceable dagger in his belt that glistened in the lamplight.

'Arrest this man and put manacles on him,' Lamas commanded the official. 'He has broken out in a mad fit. Either that or a malicious attempt at damage and robbery!'

Aristotle, paying no heed to these criticisms, was picking among the pieces of ceramic ware. Triumphantly, he held up a fragment of the statue's round base.

'There!' he said. 'This is one of the jewels, I fancy, that the merchant going to Mitylene was bewailing the loss of, not long ago.'

He held up the piece. In the renewed lamplight we could see, like a nut in pastry, the bulbous rough jewel in its protective coating of baked clay. Aristotle peeled away the dry clay, and our eyes were blessed with a gleam of strange green. I knew what it was, though I had never seen such a thing before.

'The *smaragd* stone that the Phoinician lost – it must be.'

'That is worth much more than fifty drakhmai,' said Aristotle judiciously, looking at it. 'And I dare wager that these other pretty pieces of ware will be found to house similar gems and valuables. Indeed, the best of Oulias' statues seem to be pregnant with riches. I would take as a sign the heavy gilding on the crown of a figure. Look into each of those first.' And he laid another figure down on the table, and took up the hammer again. There were groans and cries.

'What does this mean?' asked the Demarkh, scratching his head.

'Mean? Why, that you have a ring of thieves here. They have robbed in Athens and in Peiraieus, but their headquarters is here in quiet Eleusis.'

'This is all nonsense,' protested Oulias. 'Why, I was robbed myself! You know that!'

'Yes. Most interesting. It was ingenious and timely, to arrange a theft from Lampos and draw suspicion away. I began to feel some doubt of Lampos on that very day. By the way, what a cruel thing it was to string up the old woman who did the accounts of the Phoinician! We assume that was Lampos' handiwork? He has such strong hands.' He darted a sharp glance at Lampos, who looked down.

'As I thought over the case,' Aristotle continued, 'my doubts spread to include yourself, Oulias. For you are highly skilled and intelligent, and you export so many figures away from Athens! What could be a better means to get the more costly or identifiable of the stolen goods out of Attika – away from all suspicion? One particular merchant must have been an important member of your confederacy. A man enjoying connections with Byzantion.'

'Foolishness,' said Oulias. 'A number of merchants and sailors have business in Byzantion – and many in other places, too.'

'Yes. It is useful to have such a merchant as a member of the band,' Aristotle retorted. 'I do not know who are your confederates abroad. Undoubtedly you have several: men of sufficient honesty to remit the cash value of the jewels and other identifiable objects you send them. But the cash and small things that could be disposed of without notice being taken – old cloaks, housewares – these I suppose you sold in Attika.'

'Slander! Most deplorable,' complained the Daidoukhos. 'All this man says is supposition, a structure of straw. Wrought of a fevered imagination hostile to the rites of Demeter.'

'No,' said Aristotle. 'Look at the dark clothes I wear and the myrtle I carry. Surely you know I am one of the *mystai*. I seek enlightenment through Demeter and her daughter. Rather, you ought to term those hostile to the Two Goddesses who profane their images out of a vile lust for riches.' And he gestured with his hammer at the painted figure, prone and awaiting sacrifice, and then at Oulias.

'That's *not* true!' Oulias cried. 'We didn't do anything just for ourselves. It was our agreement that we would not profit by it, but give all the money to the Sanctuary. That was the whole idea! We – I – I – wanted to praise and assist Demeter.'

'Aha,' said Aristotle in a deeply satisfied tone. '*Now* we come to it. It did not make any sense to believe that such an efficient scheme could be carried on in Eleusis without some cognisance on the part of some person or persons of note. The most important people here are connected with the Sacred Precinct. Now I know. Glykera could not have been hidden in the Ploutonion without active connivance. I have long asked myself, *why* do people steal? What for? You will answer, "To enrich themselves." But great theft is seldom if ever committed out of mere abject need. Does a tyrant become what he is because he has no warm cloak for the winter? No. Oh – by the way, you had better take this for safe keeping.' And Aristotle handed to the surprised Demarkh the clay-encrusted green stone.

'Almost like a little pebble, yet the object of desire,' he commented. 'Theft is a product of ardent desire, serving an end which the thief sincerely believes to be right. An ordinary thief believes his personal survival or prosperity is a good cause. But let us suppose there is an important thief, a king or chief among thieves. Suppose this King of Thieves is intelligent and conscientious. Suppose he believes that he is serving the highest cause. That he is gaining money – and everything that can be converted into money – in order to serve the highest Good. What a fascinating thief would he be!'

'You are talking gibberish,' sneered the Daidoukhos.

'He always does,' said Eurymedon with disgust. 'This man is always getting above himself, he is only a *metoikos*—'

'But this King of Thieves in sacred Eleusis, devoted to the service of the Eleusinian religion, cannot do everything by himself. He must take on a coadjutor, an organiser within Athens, who shares his sense of what makes for the power of Athens. Perhaps this second person is slightly less devout. Perhaps he serves himself a little more. But then this organiser has to recruit several trustworthy persons in Athens to act as thieves. And not get caught. Difficult it must be, to please the Chief of Thieves and at the same time not attract any attention within Athens or roundabout.'

'There is no such person,' said the Daidoukhos in a decided tone. 'You are making up stories.'

'A Makedonian habit,' said Eurymedon, scowling. 'A plot of this cheap sophist to slur the reputation of Athens and of Eleusis.'

'Well,' said Aristotle, moving around the table, towards me, 'perhaps we can find somebody to help us enquire into this mystery of the ring of thieves. Now that we have discovered the stolen goods, the hidden truth cannot be far away from us.' Aristotle kept moving towards me, but I thought he was looking just behind me. 'Stephanos, you had the wisdom – and rashness – to accuse Halirrhothios—'

'Ah, Halirrhothios!' exclaimed a member of the crowd. 'So it was he, and not his little slave daughter?'

'Fetch this Halirrhothios,' ordered the Demarkh, fingering his dagger.

Nobody moved except Aristotle, who suddenly lunged and grabbed one of the dark crowd of *mystai* at the edge of the lamplight.

'This is one of those we seek,' he proclaimed. 'This person can be of great help to our enquiry. For he is – look, all of you – dressed as a *mystes*. You note his black mourning garments. And he has the crocus-coloured wool tied about his ankle and his wrist. But –' Aristotle whirled this person about to display him – 'you see that he has inadvertently put the yellow threads on the wrong wrist and the wrong leg. He is a *mystes* in reverse, as it were! This is what he has become in order to spy on us.' He flipped back the dark hood of the young man whom he held.

'Strabax!' I exclaimed. 'Sophilos' nephew. The youth who was going to be a shepherd and then took a job with the marble-seller.'

'Yes. Strabax. I think you will find that his employment, arranged between Oulias and Melanthios, was not of such recent standing. Likely he was employed to get rid of the marble head, after it had come to rest for a while in Melanthios' shop. One day when we were here, he and Melanthios put on a great scene before us, regarding this novice's ineptitude and Melanthios' harshness. Melanthios not only uttered blood-curdling threats, but seemed to have beaten the boy severely already. But of course they had to explain how Strabax came to be so battered and bruised.'

'The marble head – when I threw it!' I said. 'It hit him. Not Biton the discus-thrower but this stone-flinging lad. Strabax was throwing things at me, trying to make me drop the image of the infant. He must have seen me recover the little statue from the seaside, after he had cast it into the water. And then I hurled the marble stone at him and injured his face, even knocking out some teeth.'

'I don't understand a word of this!' complained the Demarkh.

'There's no need to understand it,' said Eurymedon, looking tall and disdainful. 'Lies! All sophistry—'

'The interesting thing about Strabax, however,' pronounced Aristotle, 'is that he is a murderer! And murderer of his own kin. He killed Sophilos!'

'How can you say such a thing? No – no, I wouldn't do a thing like that!' The boy was turning his head this way and that, looking for help, or more probably for a pathway to flight. But the crowd pressed in upon him and blocked his way.

'Look me in the face, Strabax, and deny it if you can. You *did* kill Sophilos.' Aristotle thrust the lamp close to his face and stared at him sternly. The boy blenched.

'Yes – oh yes.' Strabax broke suddenly into sobs. 'I didn't think it would be so bad. He was such a nuisance, so embarrassing. He didn't seem much loss to our family. But I wouldn't never have done it if I hadn't been ordered to. Sophilos saw something – he was in the marble shop that day. You are right about the marble head. He had seen that before – and some other things. I had already cast the head into the sea, but Sophilos knew enough to make trouble. And he would go on and on about Byzantion! *They* were afraid he would tell.'

'"They" being Melanthios and Oulias, I take it?' interjected Aristotle.

'Yes – yes. Melanthios swore at Sophilos, and Sophilos was offended and shuffled off. I had just taken the pouch of money from the rich foreign man who was in the marble shop, and I was told to kill Sophilos and make it look as if he was the thief. I kept back a lot of the silver money in the pouch for them. So they'd be pleased with me. To add to the special fund, they said, for the Treasury of Demeter. They took things for the Two Goddesses.'

'Well,' said the Demarkh. 'Here's a surprise. A boy to kill his own uncle! What wickedness. At least it does solve the case of Sophilos.'

'Behold – here is your thief and murderer,' pronounced the Daidoukhos. 'This ill-educated and graceless lad. Shocking! A blasphemer against the Goddesses too! We need not believe his tales attempting to blame others, but he has certainly confessed to many witnesses – and in the presence of a magistrate – his guilt in theft and a shocking murder. I recommend he be punished outright and at once. Let him be put to death, and the land be cleansed of him.'

'That's not quite right,' said Aristotle. 'This poor boy – truly poor, and scarcely more than a boy – has been the agent of others.'

'You daren't kill me!' cried Sophilos' nephew. 'You daren't have me executed! I can tell what I know—'

'You will tell what you know *now*,' said the Demarkh. 'If you want any mercy at all shown to you in the manner of your punishment.'

'You don't understand! It was always the—'

As Strabax began to speak, Lamas seized the dagger from the magistrate's belt, and before the boy could finish, the quiet man had thrust the blade deep into the lad's chest. Strabax made an astonishing noise, which was also astonished, vomited a little blood, and began to crumple before our eyes.

'Impious and wretched youth!' cried Lamas.

One of the men nearby bent over the huddled Strabax, and with one movement pulled out the dagger. The boy did not cry out.

'He no longer breathes,' said this helpful *mystes*, laying the red-smeared dagger upon the table by the broken image. 'You have killed him!'

'I was carried away by a noble anger!' Lamas flung his hands up in a gesture of prayer and entreaty. The crocus-coloured thread about his wrist was now reddened here and there with blood. 'Inspired by a divine rage, I could not bear to hear the lad speak ill of the Goddess and belie her servants.'

'You are justified,' said Diognetos. 'What good can come of such impiety?'

'What good?' A man burst in among the crowd, and stood there in the flickering lamplight. 'What *good*? You are a pack of thieves and liars! Sorry the day I became connected with you. "Steal for us," you said. "Do good to the Goddess and enrich yourself. We'll give you part of the proceeds." And I did as you said. It brought my little daughter into grievous trouble, to save my life. But even then I couldn't stop. And then you took her! Why? *Why?* How could you do this to me?'

Trembling with rage and grief, Halirrhothios stalked over to Lamas and actually shook him so his long brown beard waved like a banner.

'Let go of me! I had *nothing* to do with the little girl,' said Lamas. Halirrhothios let go.

'Don't believe him,' said Lampos sullenly. 'One of them wanted to *kill* the child.'

'Who?' said Halirrhothios. 'Tell me at once.'

'There were, I believe, two men who particularly

wanted your daughter out of the way,' said Aristotle. 'One was possibly the merchant of Byzantion, the man who postponed or cancelled his initiation into the Mysteries. The other, I believe, was unwilling to kill precisely because he was a *mystes*, and could not go through the rites as a murderer.' He turned to address my neighbour, who was smoothing his crinkled beard with a trembling hand.

'You, Lamas, were most interested in being respectable, even while you concocted such magnificent plans. You yourself – so I believe – seriously willed to draw the line at murder, for you earnestly wish to become an initiate before you die. Therefore, though committing theft was in your mind no bar to happiness, you have baulked at murder – at least up until the last few moments. Therefore you had the two girls kidnapped and imprisoned during the Mysteries rather than put out of the way permanently.'

'That's right. That one was talking about how he would sell the children – the girls,' said Lampos. 'He said once they were sold to hard service far, far away they would pose no danger.'

'It might not be difficult to sell them,' said Aristotle. 'If you could find a compliant sea-captain – by the way, I think that Menexenos of Abydos might be worth investigating. Certainly not hard to sell such a little beauty as Glykera. But hard to guarantee that they would never speak of what they knew. One man wanted simply to hold Glykera to ransom. But somebody else had harsher plans for both girls after the end of the Mysteries.'

'I *didn't*!' protested Lamas. 'We planned no homicide. In fact, *not* killing was always part of the plan.'

'You are talking about *your* plan, Lamas,' said Halirrhothios. 'Nice thefts and pretty robberies, but no

killing. All for the greater riches and glory of the Two
Goddesses. That was my plan too, really. But it wasn't
the plan of the man who organised it all. *He* was willing
to kill if necessary. Willing for other men to kill, at any
rate. Not that he cared to set his own hand to the plough
– he wasn't interested in doing any of the hard work
himself.' Halirrhothios sighed heavily, and then
straightened his shoulders.

'Willing to kill,' he murmured. 'Willing to *kill*. So am
I too, now,' he announced. 'I want to finish it all, to put an
end—' He grabbed the dagger, still wet from the blood of
Strabax, and turned upon the Daidoukhos.

'You!' cried Halirrhothios in anguish. 'You – the
torchbearer to the Divine! The light-bringer! You have
betrayed your Goddesses and plunged us all into deceit
and darkness!'

Halirrhothios lurched unsteadily towards Hanias the
Daidoukhos. Not without resource, the light-bearer
thrust his right-hand torch into Halirrhothios' face, and
the man stepped back.

'Watch out, you parcel of brutes!' said the angry
Daidoukhos. He drew himself up to his full height, raised
both torches on high, his bright ceremonial garments
gleaming in the light he shed. 'I have a sacred calling! I
have served great Demeter by giving her gifts. Gifts
diverted from those who are not worthy!'

He waved his torches in emphasis, but with such
agitation that pieces of pine broke off and fell in burning
lumps about his shoulders. He dropped one of the
torches, which hit his thigh on its way to the floor. The
short skirts of his tunic and embroidered cloak began to
smoulder and burn.

'He's on fire!' someone screamed. 'The judgement of
the Goddess!'

'This shop will burn!' others cried. 'Come away!' The

second torch had dropped and was rolling across the floor, adding to the erratic streaks of light. The tunic and cloak of the Daidoukhos began to glow and send out little tongues of flame.

'Put it out! Put it out!' Aristotle yelled. While some stamped on the burning torches, many hands holding cloaks or outer garments beat upon the Daidoukhos. Philomela, who had spied the pitcher of water on the side table, hurled the contents upon the flames. The fire was soon out, or just smouldering a little on the edges of the cloth. You could still see the bright embroidery; the clothes were damaged but not totally ruined. The man wearing them can have been only mildly singed. But a change had come over him. His face turned blue, he caught at his breath and then leaned forward, gasping. His hand sought his chest.

'I can't – I cannot!' he whispered. 'I did not – I did not know – only for the greatness of the Goddess, for the Treasury. For Eleusis . . .' Our Daidoukhos coughed and seemed to sway. Then it was as if he tried to cough again, but could not. He fell down in our midst. He groped about a bit with his right hand, yawned a couple of times, and then made a convulsion that jerked his limbs in their bright embroidered garments. Then he lay terribly still. We looked with awe upon his fallen figure.

'The man is certainly dead,' said Aristotle, examining him. 'Dead of too much light, as it were. The fire did not destroy him, but the idea of the fire.'

'It is the will of the Goddess,' said Eurymedon, resigned. 'Who would have thought of such wickedness? Put a cloak over him, so that profane eyes may not see the wreck of one who was once favoured for his service to the Two Goddesses.'

There was a moment of pure silence as the Daidoukhos' servants did as they were requested. 'So much of evil, so much of violence,' said Lamas, in a low tone. 'I bewail what I have done this night. In the midst of my rage for justice, I too have killed! Alas, I have blood on my hands. I must seek to purify—'

'Purify nothing!' said Halirrhothios. He waved on high the bloody dagger with which he had menaced the Daidoukhos. 'How can *you* be cleansed? Liar! You killed the lad, true enough. Your hands are red with blood. But not because you were moved to execute a wrongdoer. You were just trying to cover up your own part in the business. And who caused me to be sent a message to take me back into Athens, when I should have been looking here for the little girl?'

Lamas threw out his hands entreatingly. 'That was a kindness to *you*, Halirrhothios. I knew you were about to commit the most terrible impiety. Taking part in the initiation when you had blood guilt upon you! Remember the murder of Hieron's brother-in-law? You killed him with your own hands – holding that stone! Thus it would have been eternally bad for you to have been a *mystes*. I saved you at almost the last moment from great offence. It might have had everlasting consequences.'

'*You* saved me!' said Halirrhothios with immense scorn. 'You who wanted Hippobatos dead as much as any of us.'

'Yes – *I* saved you. I have been looking out for your good all along. I don't know why you want to shove all the blame upon me for these terrible thefts! Didn't I save you from the law in Athens, when you were in danger of death? Even when you had been so very foolish as to confess? Well – didn't I?'

'It might appear so,' said Halirrhothios, with a sullen grimace. But at least he was listening. Heartened, Lamas went eagerly on.

'Was it not I who got the Thracian bitch of a witness

out of the way by persuading that good-natured idiot
Theophon to take her and keep her out of the market for
a while? Moreover, who persuaded even a stubborn
enemy like Stephanos here – a quite unreasonable young
man – to come round and withdraw his charge?'

'Yes.' Halirrhothios looked at the floor. 'I saved my
own donkey hide very well then. At the price of all
honour and all happiness.' He turned to me and scowled.
'It is *your* doing that my child had to suffer.'

'Well, but Halirrhothios, did I not promise you
revenge?' said Lamas.

'Revenge?' I asked. 'Against *me*? So it was through
you, Lamas, that Kallimakhos and Lykon started to
persecute me?' I could feel my anger rising, even at that
solemn moment as we stood about the body of the dead
Daidoukhos.

'You could say so, Stephanos,' replied Lamas sourly. 'I
did it all for *you*, Halirrhothios. You may as well know,
Stephanos, as you're not bright enough to figure it out.
Euthykritos, merchant of Byzantion who helped our trade,
was an associate of that dolt Kallimakhos – to whom I lent
a little money. At my suggestion the good merchant
induced Kallimakhos to insist that you, Stephanos, had
broken an agreement to marry his daughter.'

'What does all that matter?' said sullen Halirrhothios.

'It does matter,' urged Lamas. He seemed very
anxious to placate this angry partner; his eye never
wandered far from the dagger that Halirrhothios held,
that bloody implement with which he himself had killed
Strabax.

'It was all for you, O Halirrhothios. You know that
Stephanos said he intended to pursue the matter of the
thefts. For *your* sake – for all our sakes – we had to head
him off. What would keep Stephanos too busy to inter-
fere? Withhold him from meddling? Why, threatening to

break off his wedding, or arranging a divorce. And Kallimakhos first made sure Lykon included Stephanos in his lawsuit. We have had *some* revenge – though not yet enough. He has not had such a delightful wedding after all.'

'Oh!' Philomela gasped.

'All this is no help. It did no good to my Eurynome,' said Halirrhothios.

'If only you hadn't been such a dolt as to confess!' expostulated Lamas. 'Confessions are very troublesome things. Suspicion remained, even after we got you off. After all, nobody had *seen* you committing the thefts, which is a great point.'

'Nobody as far as I know,' Halirrhothios admitted. 'Nobody but a tile-maker's man.'

'Who? How was that?'

'A fellow who works on roofs. Unfortunately this man was on a neighbouring roof at one point when I, thinking no harm, crawled out of a back window of a house with a gold cup in my hand. Who expects watchers from the sky!'

'Well, but that witness said nothing.'

'I made sure he would not,' retorted Halirrhothios. 'Luckily the wretch is a slave. I told him about the torture that awaited any slave witness in a law case. More than that, I told him if he said a word to anyone at any time, he would be seized at night, castrated, then killed and his body cast into the sea. Never buried, never able to cross the Styx.'

'Enough to frighten the poor wretch,' remarked Lamas, trying to laugh reassuringly. 'Very clever.'

'That accident taught me more caution. But I was imprudent.' Halirrhothios sighed. 'Lost my chance through carelessness. Too much robbery.'

'There, good people and men of Athens – you see?'

Lamas spread his hands wide. 'A hardened criminal, by his own account. I had believed Halirrhothios innocent at first, I tried to act the part of a good neighbour – but now he displays his brutal lying. What a stout rascal! This Halirrhothios terrifies people with threats of horrific death – and then he kills. The murders are to be laid at his door.' He faced Halirrhothios. '*You* are the guilty one – don't try to bring me into it, man of blood!'

'You have blood on your own hands at this moment.' Halirrhothios seemed to rouse himself from a kind of stupor in which he had heard Lamas' speech.

'Indeed, that is the fact,' said Aristotle. 'And how, O Lamas, could you wish to save Halirrhothios from the impiety of being a *mystes* and yet a killer, if you yourself did not know the truth of that killing? By your own admission, you were there at the time! *You* were one of the thieves who unexpectedly encountered Hippobatos in Hieron's house, and your confederate, if not with your active encouragement certainly with your complicity, battered Hippobatos' head in.'

'*I* did no murder!' insisted Lamas, stroking his brown beard. 'I always said that killing was wrong, and would complicate our lives terribly.'

'You knew all about it!' said Halirrhothios. 'You and that infernal Diognetos, who kept bringing us the messages from the Daidoukhos or somebody at the Goddesses' temple, and from that busy sea-merchant. It was you who planned the robbery at Hieron's house, and Diognetos took part in it with us. Afterwards we met, as you had designed, with poor Hieron, who had been drinking quite a lot—'

'I had *nothing* to do with killing Hippobatos,' protested Lamas. 'Your fault – you couldn't manage better—'

'No other way for it.' Halirrhothios shrugged. 'We had packed up too many things. The man from Thorikos got

a good look at us. You were frightened too that he could
have testified against us. We managed well to get out of
the house with some of the stuff.'

'Although you forgot the gold crown,' Aristotle
reminded him.

'We forgot the crown, and left it in an old lamp where
we had packed it. But we went on and met good old
Hieron at the *kapeleion*, just as you and Diognetos had
planned.'

'A false accusation! Too bad Hieron got the bright idea
of going to see the philosopher about the break-in,' said
Lamas. 'Well, Halirrhothios, you used to be a friend of
mine and a good neighbour, but I can no longer shield
you from the power of the law. I must ask the Demarkh
of Eleusis to take this man into custody.'

'Step back!' Halirrhothios now seemed to call up
renewed strength, on the instant, like a flame leaping up.
He repelled the Demarkh with a violent movement of his
fist, which the Demarkh did not choose to encounter.
Halirrhothios' angry glaring face was enough in itself to
give pause to a timid man. I did not want to let Lampos
out of custody, so I nodded to Aristotle that he was to
take hold of the image-maker's assistant while I edged
closer to my enraged neighbour. But I was too slow.
Herpyllis, coming under the angry man's arm, took the
dagger from his grasp; the move was deft, though she
must have been agitated, for she let the instrument of
death drop on the floor. Halirrhothios did not stoop to
look for it. Instead, he suddenly seized from the table the
hammer that Aristotle had brought from Melanthios'
shop and used to crack open the bright image.

'Do not do anything rash and absurd, Halirrhothios, I
implore!' Lamas, his face the colour of ashes, was backing
away. He thrust his arms out in front of him as
Halirrhothios the long-armed came on. Paying no heed

at all to the older man's feeble efforts at self-protection, Halirrhothios brought his strong hammer down on the man's head. It made a really odd sound – a bang, a crack, and a crunch combined. Lamas fell in a heap beside the table, blood trickling out of his nose. His face already seemed awry, as if his head were in pieces, like that of Hippobatos.

'One villain the less!' announced Halirrhothios grimly. Waving his horrid hammer and without uttering any further words, he easily persuaded the spectators to make way for him. He moved slowly, pausing to pick up the unclean dagger. He stuck the hammer in his belt, and holding the Demarkh's stained weapon in a businesslike manner found his way to the door, no man obstructing or objecting. His flying footsteps could then be heard through the night.

'Great Goddesses! Such crimes to be committed here – here in Eleusis!' said Eurymedon. 'And what a polluted place we stand in,' he added. 'Three corpses in one room.'

There came a new sound, a high voice singing, sweet and unfamiliar to the ears of our desolate and dirty crowd. A child was approaching the doorway. Its clean and bright apparel announced that this was a temple child, a servant of the Two Goddesses.

'An assistant to the Priestess,' said Eurymedon dully.

'The Priestess sends for you, the celebrants who left. She bids you come back and recommence the work of the Mysteries.'

'We are too unclean,' protested Eurymedon. 'There are corpses here. Criminals have been unmasked and have slain each other. And our Daidoukhos has died to see such terrible things! A natural death, but most sudden. We have no torchbearer.'

'The Priestess says come,' insisted the temple child. 'For repurification is available to all at the Great Gate.

With water from the Well of the Beautiful Dances you may completely cleanse yourselves of all impurity. Come all of you – save for anyone who has killed this night. Come. For the night is spending fast, and this is the night of the Mysteries which shall bring joy to all!'

At this blessed and welcome summons, we trooped back the short distance to the temple. An assistant priestess took charge of Eurynome, so Herpyllis could join the celebration. The Priestess herself met us wandering *mystai* at the Great Gate, and offered the sacrifice and the prayers of purification, sprinkling us with water from the Well of Beautiful Dances by the Laughterless Stone.

'We have no Daidoukhos,' lamented Eurymedon.

'Then yourself shall be Daidoukhos on this occasion,' said the Priestess. She had already had brought to the gate another set of vestments, and the child attendants handed them fresh supplies of torches.

We errant and erratic *mystai*, once cleansed and sprinkled with water from the holy well, were allowed to rejoin our fellow seekers on the platform. And our *mystagogoi* – all save Diognetos and his wife, who had disappeared. The rest of the great company were not best pleased, as they had been compelled to watch the performance of the search for Persephone twice in our absence. Now we were come they were resigned to undergoing it a third time. But the deep stillness of the night, the wonder of the search for the girl in the shadows, and the beauty of the music calmed our spirits and brought us all to peace.

Then we were allowed, reverently and silently, to move within the deep place of celebration, the Telesterion, where the final rites were enacted. Of these I am forbidden to speak. Indeed, I have said more than enough already. But I carry within me the recollection of the going into darkness and fear, and of what it means to come out of darkness and into the full splendour of light. And I *know* – know within and for ever – that this life is not the end, but that our destiny is to be reborn. Rebirth is the nature of the dance of the world. Just as the grain of wheat or barley is scattered into the ground and appears again in a more glorious form, so shall all who have been initiated into these heavenly Mysteries.

Therefore I am more confident in life, as fearing death the less, and knowing what a slight veil hides us for a time from the splendour. And despite all the trouble that entering into these Mysteries cost me, I am glad that my wife Philomela and I undertook initiation, and together. I think Philomela was right. It is a great thing to know that neither of us will be destined to miserable solitary wandering by the banks of fiery Phlegethon or the dew-drenched lotuses of pale Akheron. Both of us will be partakers of delight and fulfilment. And I love my wife better after this strange ordeal of the Mysteries, which had such a happy outcome.

Epilogue

I speak of the 'happy outcome' as it was for myself, really, but it was not happy for all. Three persons had paid for their offences, that dark night of the Mysteries: Strabax, the Daidoukhos and Lamas had all descended into Hades' realm. Halirrhothios had managed to escape. Oulias was arrested, and subsequently tried and executed. Lampos, whom I had hoped the Demarkh would keep in charge, contrived to get away in a general mêlée and milling about once we *mystai* returned to our ritual. Herpyllis told us that Melanthios had rushed out of the marble shop immediately, not waiting to pick up the few obols she had left for the hammer. Diognetos had been deeply implicated in all that had been said in Oulias' shop. It occurred to me even then that it might have been he who had tried to steal the silver man at my symposium, and then had second thoughts. I would never be able to ask him. Diognetos and his pale wife had assuredly seen their danger, and simply melted away from the Mysteries and from Eleusis, leaving behind all who were convinced of their guilt. But there was much recrimination and suspicion left over.

The statue-maker's shop was soon closed down. Shop and contents were sold, and the money was used to recompense some of those who had suffered from the thefts. Some jewels and valuables were recovered from images in Oulias' shop, but most of the goods that had been stolen in the past were vanished and irrecoverable. Abdelmelkart was not in Athens, but I insisted that he be sent for and the green *smaragd* stone kept for him, for the honour of the Emporion. And this was done. The Phoinician was also due some compensation for the wrongful death of his slave, but as she was valued at but a trifle he ultimately refused to take the low sum as a kind of dishonour to her. Strabax's unfortunate mother was scorned and repudiated, even though she had been an initiate in the Mysteries – until her son had borrowed her cloak and the crocus-coloured yarn. An outcast, she wandered off to beg through the world. Euthykritos, the singular merchant of Byzantion associations, wisely went on a long journey.

Kallimakhos came to see me. 'I wanted to assure you personally,' he said anxiously, 'that no further measures will be taken regarding breach of promise. As you say, it was not a real treaty of marriage. There was nothing like an *engye*, so there can be no lawsuit.'

'Exactly so,' I replied, bowing coldly. Something drove me to add, 'And I hope there will be no further attacks on myself or on my wife.'

'It was only to make your wife listen to reason, Stephanos! It was to her own interest. The two women in the crowd were only asked to *talk* with her.'

'And one of those women was Thratta,' I said. 'Paid to do it. I suppose *she* wasn't a knife-thrower as well? Females don't have such good aim.'

Kallimakhos had the grace to look a little ashamed. 'That was just to – to scare you Stephanos. And to make your wedding night less comfortable. But *I* didn't throw anything. It was the *mageiros* who actually did it. He'd been my athletic trainer once, and I knew he could – on a bit of a dare, a wager. You know what cooks are like when they've taken a drink or two. But it was only a kind of joke, you must see that.'

'Let there be no more of such jokes,' I said firmly. 'Do not engage drunken cooks to throw knives, even in athletic contests. Such jokes are not as good as Bridge Jests. Next time someone will certainly get hurt.'

Lykon became decidedly amenable likewise, and our lawsuit no longer appeared a dreadful threat to the Hymettos property. Most of the other neighbours in Hymettos went on as before. The girl Zobia was no less crazy, and her father kept planting thorn bushes. Smikythos the widower was still looking for a wife. One neighbour changed. The nephew of Pantakles, the old man who had wanted him out of the way, actually died.

'Just imagine – he must have been walking drunkenly along the mountain path, and slipped over the edge,' said Arkhias to me. He looked at me very directly and remarked, 'It is as if the old white-haired man had a spirit of prophecy, is it not?'

'Well, at least he doesn't need me,' I retorted.

'No, he doesn't need you,' said Arkhias.

I was not really terribly surprised a month or so later to find that the old man Pantakles had met exactly the same fate as his nephew. 'Must have been pining for him,' some people speculated, pityingly. I myself speculated about the amount of money in Arkhias' purse. There was nothing I could say or do, but I did remark to him once, 'It is a good thing that you have no interest in becoming an initiate in the Mysteries.'

'So it is,' said Arkhias.

*

'It seems to me,' said Aristotle, 'that the Mysteries offer what true philosophers ought most to seek and value. Contemplation. Contemplation of the things that do not fade away. Things in the world fade fast and change always. We see that even a marble to commemorate the dead may itself be subject to rapid alteration.'

'The story of the marble head,' I commented, 'is quite complicated. As I make it out, it came with Hippobatos to Hieron's house, was used to murder him, was hidden by Halirrhothios about his own house – probably – and then taken to Eleusis by the third thief in that party, Diognetos, who put it in Melanthios' shop for a while.'

'Yes, quite so. Melanthios told Strabax to get rid of it; either following orders or on his own initiative, Strabax threw it into the sea. Strabax must have been watching you anyway, Stephanos, on the day that you went to see Diognetos and afterward strolled down to the seashore. He saw you pick the stone up, and followed you, assaulting you in his attempt to get it back.'

'And he did get it back,' I said laughing a little, not too much. 'It hit him. Melanthios and Diognetos planned to dispose of it again. I suppose it was Diognetos who threw the object away so that it got into the Fountain House. He was in Athens' Agora that day. I suppose he just wanted to get it well away from Eleusis. The object was tried and cast into the pit where Zobia found it. She brought it back to Eleusis.'

'The story of the circulating head. At each point it suffers some damage. The Eleusinians are right to wish for something more lasting than monuments. Things that pass away.'

'But you, Aristotle,' I objected, 'are always studying things that pass away. Like the animals – flies and octopodes included. And even constitutions of states are things that pass away, as do not only kings but also cities.'

'True,' he said. 'I love the things of this world, the phenomena. But there must be something greater and more stable to contemplate, above the shiftingness of things. After all, if we consider the great deity, the Divine Mind, it must be above even the ethical life. For who thinks of the Divine Mind as signing contracts and keeping oaths, or being courageous, or giving alms? If the gods have no bad appetites, there is no need for temperance. So all our virtues are imperfections in a way. Human imperfections, and necessary. At best a means to an end, like money itself, which cannot be an end.'

'I suppose I see what you're getting at,' I said. 'But it is very hard to imagine the life of the gods.'

'The divine life – the Divine Mind. To know that would be the great adventure. Now, the Mysteries tell the man or woman of ordinary life about what it is to contemplate. But they do so in a strange way – at least, not at all the way a philosopher would do it. For the Mysteries offer an experience, not an instruction. The initiate undertakes certain actions, undergoes certain ordeals, and thus acquires certain feelings, and is made to *know* – or rather to do something like knowing, in a way that is not strictly rational. Yet I value that experience. Now I comprehend why the Mysteries are so important to the thought of Sokrates and Plato, and also to Aiskhylos, who was born in Eleusis.'

'And Herpyllis?' I added. 'I hope she was satisfied?'

He smiled. 'More than satisfied. But she is a dear creature. I think I see her still with poor Eurynome in her arms!'

'What will happen to that child?'

'Antigone tells me,' Aristotle said, 'that she will go through with her plan to take Eurynome as a servant to her daughter Glykera.'

'Oho – so Antigone comes to see you? I wouldn't trust

that woman still, you know. I thought at one time she might be in league with my enemies; it even occurred to me to wonder if she tried to poison me. I think she has been in the pay of the Daidoukhos or some of that gang – probably induced by Diognetos to try poisoning.'

I told him about the affair of the fish stew. 'It is true, isn't it, that Antigone is not trustworthy?'

'Yes. She herself trusts nobody. Probably a real desire to find safety from Alexander – even if she were still working for him – encouraged her to turn to those of Eleusis who said they could befriend and shelter her. Oh well, neither Strabax nor Lamas – and certainly not Oulias – said anything to incriminate her. The woman's distress over the loss of her daughter was, I am convinced, quite real.'

'Why were the two girls taken? You have talked to these women – I have not.'

'Glykera knew what Eurynome told her, but that could be passed off as child's babble. But Glykera tells me that she saw two gold bracelets of foreign work in Halirrhothios' house, and Eurynome told her where they came from. Glykera says Eurynome urged her to help give the things back, so she wouldn't be whipped again. The thieves realised that Glykera would learn too much from Eurynome. The pretty girl could be a witness. As she isn't a slave, she wouldn't be tortured, and as she is so composed and clever, her testimony might be believed.'

'Well, I shall worry no more about Antigone. Nor about Kallimakhos. For he has got into great financial trouble. Yesterday I saw the mortgage sign at his door. Just think, how shameful!'

'Nor need Halirrhothios trouble you. One wonders where he can have gone.'

'It's the talk of our deme,' I told him with some satisfaction, 'how Halirrhothios' household has been taken over by the city council. His slaves will all be sold, and his poor wife has to return to her father. It is doubtful that her dowry can be recovered.'

'So Halirrhothios makes more noise in your neighbourhood than Lamas?'

'Well, I don't think people are very clear about what Lamas was doing or how he died. They know he was killed in a fracas in Eleusis, and that somebody claimed he was one of the thieves. But I think his nephew can save his credit and the property. And Lamas, though a historian of our deme, isn't – wasn't – a man people miss too much – they didn't drink with him every night at the *kapeleion*, or anything like that.'

'Diognetos has managed matters very neatly – disappearing absolutely, with some temple money to which he had access. Dear me, Stephanos, you chose the wrong *mystagogos*. I am satisfied with little Thymades, a true enthusiast and I believe an honest soul.'

'Never was I more taken in!' I admitted. 'Diognetos is a good actor. I was mistaken also in thinking Theophon was involved, and he was perfectly innocent. Yet, how shaming it is that such a number of rascals got away! Including that Boiotian image-maker Lampos. I wish I had held on to him.'

'Doubtless Lampos will set up his image trade and paint his deities in some other part of the world. One must hope he will not go on stealing, and hanging people.'

'We could not prove the hanging. It may be my own fantasy,' I said very carefully, 'that there were more persons in Eleusis – I mean in the priesthood – involved in this plan to enrich the temple than just the Daidoukhos.'

'We shall never know, Stephanos. I privately suspect the exegete Eurymedon, but he is highly placed, intelligent and very guarded. These events will not lead to any greater love of me among the powers at Eleusis. Yet the discoveries have given the felons a serious check.

Dear me, such self-delusion! Let nobody say, "I will engage in just a little adultery, in a temperate way," or, "I shall be a truly moderate and self-respecting thief." Moderation does not apply. There is no middle way in a vice or crime! The love of grandeur, too – and of honour. What strange forms it takes.'

'Perhaps it might have been better,' I suggested, 'if the religion of the Two Goddesses had been left up to Eleusis, and not made so important to Athens. With just the Priestesses and not the Hierophant and the Daidoukhos and so on. These are powerful men who live in Athens at least part of the time and have great connections.'

'We shall never know,' Aristotle said. 'Things are as they are. You once asked me, Stephanos, "What is the best way for a man to live?" And I do not entirely know. But we must start with Ethics, individually, before our life can be right. We are but mortals. To be ethical is a humble duty. We should suspect anything that presents itself as a good for which we must depart from the ethical. Contemplation urges, "Go beyond the ethical." But it never says, "Deny the ethical." Never say, "It is good for my country or my family that I lie, steal, and murder."'

'Men will go on arguing, however, about Ethics,' I said, rising to take my leave. 'I really ought to go to take my dinner at home. Then everybody will be well fed, and my family at least will be pleased with me.'

And I left, feeling that I understood a lot more this autumn about the way a man should live than I had last year. For had I not my wife to go to bed with at night? And to wake up with in the morning. And a life beyond the grave as well, when we would waken together too.

Aristotle and Poetic Justice

Margaret Doody

330BC: Stephanos, son of Nikiarkhos and his teacher, the philosopher Aristotle, are drawn into solving the perplexing abduction case of Anthia, the heiress of a prominent silver merchant. Someone has snatched her from her home, but what is the motive: rape, a forced marriage or murder? All that is known is that the abductor and the heiress are on the road to Delphi and its ancient oracle.

Stephanos and Aristotle pursue them but along the way there are plenty of distractions: it's spring time and the country is full of reborn life, the thought of romance and marriage is never far from young Stephanos' mind, and rumours of mysterious strangers passing in the night abound, of disguises and swapping of identity. Then the actuality of murder shatters the idyll. It seems that there is a psychopath on the road pursuing abductor and heiress. But who the abductor is and who the murderer is are mysteries that only Aristotle with the aid of the Delphian oracle will be able to solve.

arrow books

Aristotle Detective

Margaret Doody

Athens, 332BC – an unhappy city under the rule of the Macedonian 'barbarian' Alexander the Great. In the midst of this unrest, Boutades, an eminent citizen, is found brutally murdered. Suspicion falls heavily on young Philemon, and, by Athenian law, his cousin Stephanos is elected to defend his name in court.

In desperation, Stephanos seeks assistance from Aristotle, his former mentor – and Aristotle turns Detective. The young, inexperienced boy and the great philosopher form a classically uneven partnership. Their efforts culminate in the gripping trial scene when Stephanos uses all the powers of rhetoric and oratory instilled in him by Aristotle to clear his family's name of this bloody murder.

'Why did no one think of this before?'
The Times

'Wit in a first novel is rare enough, and when allied to the skillful unraveling of a murder story set in Ancient Athens it makes us doubly grateful for Aristotle Detective'
Daily Telegraph

'Eminently enjoyable'
Colin Dexter

arrow books